The Conspiracy Clash

Marc B. DeGeorge

MUSEMARC STUDIO

MuseMarc Studio, LLC.

Cover Design by: Lance Buckley

Author Photo by: MuseMarc Studio

ISBN: 978-1-956487-06-0 (digital), 978-1-956487-07-7 (paperback)

First Edition: **July 2022**

9 8 7 6 5 4 3 2 1

Acknowledgments

A story may be written by one person, but it takes many to turn it into a novel. To that end, I'd like to thank the following for their contribution to turning my typing into reality.

First, my dedicated and awesome reading group, Ben Pick, Salone More, Tracey Canole, E. Marie Robertson, Michelle Darnell and J. Logan Rice. Thank you for your critical commentary, positive support, and friendship.

My amazing editors, Joanne Machin and Ariel Anderson. You have been a huge help in making this book a reality. Thank you.

Also to my wife and family, for giving me the time to forge this first work... and all the ones that come after.

Chapter One

NOTHING HAS BEEN BETTER for achieving my big dream than doing absolutely zilch. As single-minded as I've been lately, I suppose I was way past my maximum level of effort months ago. The wound I received, courtesy of Ms. Nilsson-Lim's gun, was a definite sign that I needed to slow down.

In our mission to protect the people of Angelcanis from rogue government agents, we haven't had it all that easy. Friends of ours have died, my mom was kidnapped, and my buddy Grady's parents are in jail. We've been shot at, arrested, chased, beat up, and labeled as traitors. We've survived all of it, but it's left us more than a little raw. A few months of recovery was exactly what we needed. I'm glad we all agreed on a sabbatical.

"So, you really liked it that much?" Afton asks as we walk towards our local mainstay of nourishment, Wylde Thyme. "I mean, it was just a big space battle. Haven't you had enough real-life experience with exploding objects already?"

"You're not getting it," I reply. "Didn't you see how well the director and the editor worked together to make that last battle sequence really hit?"

I love the cine. It doesn't really matter what I watch, I know I'll enjoy it. Stories for children might not be for me, but I can appreciate the work that's gone into them. I have seen an animated cine or two, and I thought the writing was better than a few with live actors.

"Yeah, I *saw* it," Afton replies. "I just didn't like it. But thanks for coming out with me today anyway. I know you could have been...elsewhere."

"Come on. Why would I miss celebrating a bud's birthday?"

"It's not actually my birthday. Not yet." Afton shrugs. "Besides, haven't you enjoyed your alone time with Kayley? I don't want to get in the way of that."

I want to tell her the truth, but I don't want to make Afton feel left out. I've submerged myself deeply in every second that I've spent with my girlfriend. Nothing has been more healing for me than that. As much as my shoulder still aches from the plasma blast that fried it, all the extra-special attention I got from her made it worthwhile. Not that I'm going to get shot again just so Kayley can coddle me more, although I did consider it for a short time.

Besides the cuddle time, we've also spent a lot of time talking—about us and our future. No decisions yet, but I get a big grin on my face every time I think about our conversations. Let's just say things are looking bright.

"You are never an obstacle, Afton. You're Kayley's best friend, and if you want to spend some time with her, I'm totally fine with that."

"Yeah, you say that now that you've monopolized her for two months." She's totally right. I have. But I'll never admit it.

"Say whatever you want, but it's not like you've been knocking down her door asking to hang out with her."

"And how would you know that?"

"Come on, you don't think she talks about you?"

"No." Afton grabs the door, but stops and stares at me, her eyes opening wide. "What did she say? Anything specific?"

"Just that she misses you and that she's looking forward to our big party on Saturday."

"Big party?"

Oops. I let that one slip. We were going to surprise Afton for her actual birthday, since everyone else couldn't be here today. Grady's in design hell, Parrish has rehabilitation for his wounded knee, and Kayley's...well.

Giving a speech before Parliament. Not our planet of Angelcanis' rustic government house, but the actual lawmaking institution of the Empire. I wasn't invited, or at least Kayley told me they wouldn't allow any of our gang to go. "Too divisive," they said. Not sure what about my presence there would have caused an issue.

"Um, yeah, well...don't tell anyone I told you, okay?" I ask, following Afton in. "We really wanted to make it a secret, so it would be, um, you know. Special. Turning twenty is a big deal, right? And after all we've been through—no, forget us, after all *you've* been through—we wanted to show you how much you mean to us, you know?"

"You want to show me how much I mean to you?" Afton grins. "Then go grab our seats and order me two plates of tempura fries. I'll be right back."

I blink as Afton walks away, presumably to go use the restroom. That isn't weird, but two orders of fries are a bit excessive. I wonder what she's been up to that's got her so hungry. Afton's always been a big eater, but the staff here knows that, and they always overload the plate to where at least a handful of sweet potato slides off when the cook drops the dish on the counter.

No matter. It's nearly her birthday, and I don't mind splurging a little on my bud. I bought the cine tickets, so what's a handful of jorins more? I wave to the cook and make my way to our usual seats at the counter.

And stop.

There's a goddess in my seat. It could be the Goddess Sophia herself. A woman about our age, perhaps a little older, watches the vid screen up on the wall, a finger moving lazily around her throat. She wears a flowing robe of ivory, gilded with gold trim about the sleeves and skirt. Her champagne hair cascades down her back in such perfect form I can't believe it is anything other than magic keeping it in place. She is breathtaking, an apparition of beauty that rivals even Kayley.

And she's in my seat.

The cook shrugs as I catch his eye to silently ask the question. Everyone here knows those five seats at the end of the counter belong to my buds and me. Nobody sits there or asks to be seated there. No one would really want to, honestly, as they're not all that comfortable, and the location is less than desirable. Yet this deity of a woman chose my seat to sit in. I can already guess she's not from around here. I hope she's at least considerate enough to move.

"Excuse me," I say, stepping up next to her, and then I freeze up. Goddesses, she even smells amazing! I take a moment to remember what I was about to say. "Sorry to bother you, but would you mind moving to another seat?"

"Why would I do that?" she replies in a sultry voice.

Okay...not what I hoped for. Let me see if she responds to reason.

"Well, you see, they've reserved that particular seat for me," I say.

She turns her head to examine my face. Then the diner goddess' eyes narrow in suspicion. I step back, wondering what I did to provoke that response.

"Your aura is troubled," she says—spoken like a true goddess. "I cannot give you this seat."

"You can't give me that seat because of my aura?"

"No, I cannot give it to you because I am waiting for someone." She returns to watching the vid.

I chew on my lower lip. This is not only one of the oddest conversations I've ever had, but to have it here, at Wylde Thyme, with this woman, just makes it that much more bizarre. I don't want to be rude to her, so I'll try to be nice for the moment.

"Oh, you mean you're just meeting someone here and then you're going to sit elsewhere?"

"No, I do not mean that."

I press my lips together. Her vague responses are making my arms itch. I'm going to keep trying the friendly approach, though.

"Listen, I'm pretty well known here. If I asked, the staff would give you the best table in the place. It's not that large a place, anyway, so whoever you're meeting could find you without trouble."

The would-be goddess' eyes slide over to glance at me again. Even just at side-eye, her penetrating gaze gives me the shivers. There is something about her that is beyond beauty. She has authority, or at least thinks she does.

"If you are that popular," Ms. Goddess says, "then the staff would have no difficulty giving you the best table as well."

This is getting more surreal by the moment. Here I am, having an argument over a seat at the local serve-all diner with a woman who is dressed like she should be the high priestess at some sacred site.

Still, if she were acting as benevolent as a goddess should, then my level of irritation wouldn't be shooting up as fast as it is. She should just take the hint and move already. I may be acting selfish, but it's my seat, and I want to sit there and eat fries.

Okay, one last time, I'll try to be nice.

"I don't usually do this, but if you'd be willing to allow me to sit in my seat, your meal is on me, okay? Whatever you want, I'll pay."

"Do I appear to you as someone who is in need of charity?" she asks. "Or rather, a bribe disguised as charity? Do not darken your aura more than you already have today, it is unbecoming."

I sigh.

"Listen." I raise a hand. "My friend is coming any moment, and she gets cranky when she's hungry. So either you do as I ask, or you'll have to deal with her bad mood. And trust me, you don't want to do that."

The woman spins the chair towards me, putting her hands on her legs. I catch my breath at the intensity of her direct gaze.

"Violence is not a means to achieve your goal," she says. "It only begets more violence as the desire grows with every forceful motion. It is a hard lesson to learn, but learn it you should. Let go of your desire for aggression, as you should this seat."

I blink. Did she just try to teach me a precept of the Three Goddesses and then use it to tell me to buzz off? Who is this lady? It doesn't matter. I've had enough. No robe-wearing bohemian is going to tell me what to do

.

"Now you listen here—"

As I raise my hand to point a finger at her, someone grabs my wrist and spins my arm around. A fist slams into my stomach, and I get kicked on the back of my knee. A second later, my head impacts the floor with a hard thud. There's a gasp and a cry from the surrounding table. The cook shouts out my name, and several pairs of feet scuffle around me.

Sparks fly across my vision as I attempt to make sense of what just happened. When five guns fly out from jackets and take aim at my head, I realize that I should have been more careful. Ms. Goddess *is* someone with authority. Most definitely.

She waves her hand, and the guns disappear, but the five tough guys who were brandishing them remain looming over me. A voice comes from behind them, and they open up to let someone through.

"Rance, what did you do?" Afton asks, leaning through the pair of bodyguards on my right.

"Nothing," I reply and point a finger at the goddess-woman. "I was just trying to get my seat back from her when these guys jumped me."

"Her? You mean Nayla?" Afton reaches out and offers me a hand to help me up. At least my bud is here to help me away from—

"Wait, what? You know her?"

"Of course. Nayla's my girlfriend." Afton shakes her head and wrinkles her forehead. "Didn't Kayley tell you? You said she had been talking about me, so I figured she told you already."

This moment calls for a severe eye roll, and I don't waste a microsecond before performing said action. I think I just had the wind knocked out of me three times in a row. Once, when the bodyguards took me down, another when Afton admitted she knew this woman, and the third when—

"Hold on! You're dating her? Afton, how long have you been together? Why didn't you tell anyone?"

"I told Kayley."

"And why does your girlfriend have bodyguards?"

"That is the Princess Nayla Isabella Amenty de Avila," one bodyguard says. "You should be more careful about raising a hand around her."

"P...Princess? Afton, when did you meet a princess?"

Afton shrugs.

"We met in the park," Princess Nayla responds, sliding over to Afton with a smile. "It was a day written in the stars. I had foreseen it when I divined my horoscope for the year. Fate has spoken, and I have found my true love."

I feel my jaw go slack. Fate? True love? This is too much to take in, and my spinning head isn't helping. I should be jumping up and down in excitement for Afton right now, but I'm feeling a bit overwhelmed at the moment.

There's no doubt she deserves someone. But...a princess? I don't even know where to start with that. Opposites attract, I suppose. I want to learn all about her, but that sudden drop onto the floor has taken the curiosity, and the hunger, out of me. Maybe they want some alone time, anyway. If you call being surrounded by five bodyguards alone.

"Hey, you okay?" Afton asks.

"I think I'm going to go," I say as I put a hand to my head.

"What about the fries?"

"Maybe another time," I say. "I need to go lie down."

"Well, come meet us at the park later," Afton says with hope in her voice. "Maybe the fresh air will help."

"Uh, sure."

"Hey, no hard feelings, right?" One bodyguard claps me on the shoulder so hard my legs nearly buckle. I can only give him a wan smile and try to stop myself from collapsing.

Afton is dating a princess. It's going to take a while for that to sink in.

Chapter Two

"Ransom Quigley He'?"

A woman's voice, and not one I know. I pause and turn with a sigh. I was almost home, and someone had to stop me. It's likely just a fan of mine, looking for an autograph or a picture or something like that. I don't have many fans left, but there are a few holdouts from when we saved Angelcanis from attack who remain steadfast in worshipping our little gang.

Except that our fans aren't usually this dressed up.

The woman and the pair of men who flank her wear some serious military garb, toned in the royal blue and purple of the Emperor and topped off with shiny gold epaulets on their shoulders that are so tall they could double as protective gear. I've never seen anything so fancy in my life. They've all got a museum's worth of medals and decorations emblazoned over the left side of their jackets, and caps on their heads so wide, I could see them taking off in a light breeze. But despite her showy outfit, the woman doesn't look all that impressive. If she wasn't wearing all that fruit salad, she might fit right into our little town's community hall as one of its clerks.

"Yeah? Who are you?"

"Yvonne Daughtry, Chamberlin Tyrwhitt Sitwell Egerton's bailiff and senior aide."

I blink as I connect the title and the uniform together.

"Chamberlin...as in the chief of the Imperial household?"

"The very same."

Yuck. I'm mentally allergic to all things Imperial. There has never been a situation in my life where I had a run-in with the Empire and it turned out well for me. That this woman is seeking me out is not a good sign at all.

"Well, whatever it is, I didn't do it. My friends didn't do it. Nobody I know did it. We've been doing nothing for the last two months but hanging around town and watching bad cine."

"Oh? I thought the last scene was rather well done."

I cough. Twice. So, this isn't some random meeting. She's been following me since before Afton and I went to see the cine. That's even worse.

"And I am not here to arrest you, Mr. He'. You are not under any suspicion from His Majesty nor the Chamberlin. It's quite the opposite, in fact."

I cock my head at her. Not under arrest is good, but what does the rest of that mean?

"Let me explain," she says. "I am on Angelcanis with a specific directive from the Chamberlin—to seek you out and retrieve you. His Lordship requests you attend a meeting with him on Albion."

"Well, that's nice, but I'm kind of busy."

"You just got done telling me how you've been doing nothing for the last two months."

Shoot. I did, didn't I? That's because I've had my mind on Afton and her new paramour. I should excuse myself from this pomp and annoying circumstance and go be cordial to the two of them. Then again, I wish she was here. She's had a lifetime of military nonsense growing up as the daughter of a space cruiser's executive officer. If there was some offhand regulation that would get me out of this, she'd know it.

"The Chamberlin has authorized me to let you know there is significant compensation for you, if you agree."

"Agree to take a ride to Albion?"

"Not just that, of course. There would be other stipulations."

This sounds like either a bribe or a job, and while Imperial money could be significant, I have a feeling that whatever I'd have to do to get it might be more trouble than it's worth. Of course, we could always use some funding. Grady turned down any pay that his parents' lawyer offered us. It was coming from his parents, anyway, so he didn't think it was right to accept it, given that they're stuck in jail for three years.

Still, I'm curious enough to play along.

"Such as?"

"I do not have that information. The Chamberlin will inform you of all the necessary details."

"So, why me?"

"Again, I only am aware of what the Lord Chamberlin directed me to do."

"Take a guess, then?"

"He also instructed me not to speculate for you."

I run my tongue across my teeth and cross my arms. This was interesting for about ten seconds, but it sounds way too sketchy for me to just say yes. I'd want Kayley to be there so we could face the Chamberlin together, and I know she'd want to come. Kayley's already on Albion, so I'd just have to get a message to her to hang out until I arrive. Then we could spend a few days touring around the capital planet before we came back.

But I'm not going, so I won't be doing that.

"Okay, well. Nice meeting you, Ms. Daughtry, but I have to go meet my girlfriend."

"Your girlfriend is not on Angelcanis," she replies flatly.

"No, sorry, I meant my female friend. You must have seen her come out of the cine with me."

"I did, and Surela Afton Jee is now otherwise occupied. I suspect she would take an interruption of her current conversation as unwelcome."

I drop my arms and step back. How much does she know about us? Names and the like are no big deal to find, since we've been all over the news for much of the last six months. But how long has she, and however many people she commands, been watching us? Months? Longer? I'm almost tempted to go so I can find out.

"Also, before you attempt to make another excuse, your friend Parrish Beltrami is home with his mother, your other friend Mutsumaji O'Grady-Sugiyama is at home watching some questionable entertainment, and your mother is gardening out back." Ms. Daughtry folds her arms with a small sigh, and then she says, "Fifty thousand."

"Fifty thousand what?"

"Jorin."

That's at least a number, but that's like pocket change that fell into the cracks of an Imperial sofa for the Chamberlin. His breakfast probably costs double that. Not that I couldn't use fifty thousand jorin. That'd be enough to open an office and make our saving-the-world business more official than it currently is. Our only computer is a spare one that Grady gave to Afton. But then she gave it to Kayley, who never used it, and now I share it with her because she didn't want to give it up.

"Sorry, but I have to get going."

"Fine. A hundred thousand."

"Thanks, but no thanks." I turn to go, but the click of her tongue halts me in place. It's one thing to bribe me to go bow and scrape before some bloated jerk who doesn't deserve my respect in the slightest. But it's another thing entirely to look down on me.

"Two hundred and fifty thousand, Mr. He'," Ms. Daughtry says to my back. I glance around, wondering if anyone around us heard that. I could almost pay off my mom's house *and* rent an office for that much. My mom could retire early and spend her days watering lilies rather than rubber-stamping forms. But no—if I give in now, I'll just be another Imperial lackey, like Crowley, or Brownrigg, or even my father.

"No." I look back at her. "Thank you, but no."

"Five hundred thousand."

I sigh. I should have known it was going to happen like this.

"Ms. Daughtry, I'm sure we could stand here all day with you raising the number until I give in and agree to go with you." I shake my head. "But that's not going to happen, even if you made it ten million jorin. The Chamberlin can't buy me because it's not about the money. It's about His Royal Majesty and his minions understanding the people of Angelcanis. We're not for sale. We came to this planet on our own, we built a society here without help from anyone, and that's how we do business—on *our* terms. Not yours."

The Chamberlin's senior aide chews her cheek and regards me with a face unmoved by my little speech. I'd expect it would take more to ruffle her than a few sharp words from me. I wonder what her next move will be or if she's even got one.

"So, what you are saying is that you are asking for something of more significant value. Do I understand that correctly?"

I'm just curious enough to know what she's getting at, so I nod.

"I suspect, Mr. Ransom Quigley He', that your friends and family are quite important to you, yes?"

"Of course they are." I point a finger at her. "And if you think threatening them will get me to go along—"

She stops me with an upheld hand.

"I'm not here to threaten, Rance," she says with a small shake of her head. "That would hardly be necessary, given the authority...and the generosity of the man who employs me."

"Then what are you getting at?"

"You and your friends have found some...let's call them *unique* ways to infiltrate and investigate some deplorable people, as well as to liberate some not so bad, but slightly bothersome others. As you may suspect, the Anti-Sedition Ministry, as well as local and regional authorities, are maintaining a file on your activities."

"Now wait a second! We haven't broken any laws! Sure, we were on some list, but we got cleared from that."

Ms. Daughtry raises her hand again with a small curl of her lips.

"As you must understand by now, I am well aware of your standing with the authorities. The Chamberlin is offering to clear your and your friends' records. A...removal of that file, and a fresh start to your relationship with His Imperial Majesty. But only if you agree to come along. Surely that must be worth more to you, yes?"

I rub my chin and feel the two-day-old stubble that's there. Kayley hates it, but since she's been away, I've been lazy. She's there, right now, on Albion, fighting for better representation of our little colony planet. No—not better. Any. As a colony, we have few official rights and no say in what happens in the Empire. If there is something still in a file somewhere, we'd have absolutely no chance of removing it because we're not citizens. Non-citizens can't petition the government for things like that. We can't petition the government for anything.

Part of that is our own fault for so fiercely demanding independence, but even as much as I hate it, there are a few good things about being a full-fledged citizen of the Empire. If we've still got a file, then we're even less than non-citizens. Which means a hard future for all of us. I'm sure Afton couldn't care less, and I might not be that bothered, either. But what about Grady? Will he get blocked from becoming a brilliant engineer and ship designer because of some little file? And his parents? Will they never design anything again? Parrish? His military dream is gone, but lately he's been thinking of coaching. Will top-flight university gigs be closed to him because he's on vid trying to break into a prison?

And Kayley? The love of my life banned from politics or medical school because someone somewhere didn't like a few words in her speeches? If I could wipe away all their problems with a simple "yes," then I think I can sacrifice my time to take a ride and talk to some windbag who's got way too much money at his disposal for his own good.

"It is worth more," I reply, "but add that ten million on top, and you got yourself a deal."

"Well." Ms. Daughtry smiles. "Finally, the negotiator has come out. Ten million is out of the question, though I will do something for you since you are at least working with me now—the removal of the records and the file, plus one million jorin. That is the best I can do."

I feel a little twinge of excitement in my heart. Just wait until I tell the others about this.

"Okay, deal."

Goddesses, please let this be the right decision.

Chapter Three

I FOREGO GETTING REST for my spinning head and make my way towards the park, hoping that Afton and her lady might already be there. I really want to tell someone about this right away, and though I have my Sergo handy, I think this would be better told in person.

The gang is really going to be excited about this. Freedom for the entire team to follow their dreams, as long as their dreams don't take them too far away from mine. All of them figure in it big time, so it wouldn't work if everyone disappeared. Saving the world by yourself is a lonely job.

I'll still have to go home and pack, but Ms. Daughtry gave me time, so I'll go tell Afton the good news and then go home. My mom deserves to know I'll be off-planet for a while, though she's been so busy lately that I'm sure she won't mind. She even has weekly correspondence with Danny Lecker about the hand-hunter's travels. I still don't think my mom realizes Danny abducted her.

While I'm at it, I'll upload a note to Teddynet in case I need a ride home later. I wish I could take a Teddy taxi to Albion, but Bailiff Daughtry insisted I accompany her on their Imperial cruiser.

It'll be the first time I'll have actual authorization to be on one.

I take the street that runs by Kayley's and my favorite park—the one with the hidden grotto that's surrounded by weeping willows and a nice tall hedge of flowering quince. We have a lot of memories there, not all of them happy, but it's our spot away from home on Angelcanis and—

Wait, there's someone there. No. There are lots of someones there. In our special spot! What's going on? I cross the street and make my way over to the steps that lead to the grotto, but before I can get there, they exit.

I crane my neck to see as buff security men lead a gaggle of girls in white robes tossing flower petals across the path. Those are the bodyguards from before! Does that mean Afton and her girlfriend are with them?

Yes, there they are! But hold on, my bud has a strange vibe about her. Well, strange for Afton. Is she actually...beaming? And are her cheeks rosy? I'm dying to know why.

Wait...I need to tell Afton the good news first!

"Hey, Afton!" I call and dash towards the group. She doesn't hear me, so I call louder. That gets the attention of the security dudes. They turn towards me as I run at them.

Now, just having had a negative experience with these guards and their standard procedure to shoot first and ask questions later, I should have realized that they were going to continue to do their job and stop me from getting to the person they were hired to protect. But my mind is on Afton, so I completely miss the security dude's foot coming around to connect with my face—knocking me flat on my back.

"Rance, hey." My eyes open to Afton patting my cheek. "Hey, you okay?"

She's crouching over me. We're surrounded by the security dudes, who still hold an aggressive stance, but there's some confusion in their eyes. A few of the flower girls poke their heads in between, their mouths and eyes wide. I guess none of them expected me to know Afton, or vice versa.

"Yeah." I rub the side of my face and sit up with some effort. "That was my mistake. I shouldn't have rushed towards you like that."

"You're lucky I didn't shoot you, buddy." The security dude with the impeccable roundhouse kick offers his hand and helps me up. My head is flying in loops, so I take a moment to get my balance. Afton holds me steady as she shakes her head at me. "We figured you knew better already, but we can't take any risks, you know? Anyway, no hard feelings, right?"

Before I can respond, the guards and girls suddenly part, and in floats the woman of the hour, Princess Nayla Isabella Amenty de Avila. I get a better look at her this time. She's tall and thin, with graceful hands and perfectly poised posture. Her face is oval shaped, but it's still stunning in a unique way. Soft, full lips, a nose that is aquiline but short and slightly upturned, and eyes that engulf you into her gaze. Her hair is pulled back into some kind of ponytail, and this only accentuates her features.

Maybe a princess could be good for Afton.

"You," she says in a soft voice as she comes to a stop before me. Her hands come up to glide in front of my face and down to my torso. They stop at my heart, and one hand turns on its edge and aims for the center of my chest. "I am concerned about your aura. Do you partake in the flesh of animals?"

Afton nearly retches, but she tries to hide it. I'm just confused. I would have expected an apology, or at least...an introduction?

"Nobody on Angelcanis does," I reply. "Didn't you know that?"

"It is my first time here." She presses her hand to my chest and inhales, her breath slipping between her teeth like the hiss of a snake. "Yes...I knew it."

"Knew what?"

"You are married."

Afton bites her lower lip and covers her mouth with her hand. She's struggling not to comment and, amazingly, succeeding.

"Well, no. Not married. I'm—"

"Engaged."

"Uh. No, sorry."

"Yes, you are. I see that within you. You have made the commitment of a lifetime."

"Well, *that* might be true."

"What is his name?"

"Er, *her* name is Kayley."

"Are you sure? Who were you in your last life?"

"Kayley is the friend I was telling you about." Afton nods to me. "This is her boyfriend, Rance."

The princess runs her index finger under her chin as she watches me. Her eyes narrow just slightly, and then the index finger points towards me. She holds it steady, then folds her hand back, pressing against her collarbone.

That's when I remember I need to tell Afton about the Chamberlin and the good news! But before I can open my mouth, Afton turns me towards the princess and casually motions to her.

"Yeah, so Rance, um, sorry I didn't introduce you before. This is Nayla," she says, her voice meeker than I've ever heard it before. If I'm reading her right, she's nervous about this introduction. Afton doesn't get nervous.

"Yeah, um, nice to meet you...but hey, Afton—"

The princess grabs my hand and yanks it towards her. I have to grab the arm of one of the security dudes so I don't fall on her. Then she bows, pressing my hand to her forehead.

"I am honored to meet a comrade of Surela's," she says.

"Surela's?" My gaze immediately shoots to Afton for an explanation. She avoids my look, her cheeks getting that rosy tint again. Nobody calls Afton by her first name except for her father. She's threatened a slow and painful death if anyone is caught using it. I think I'm a little jealous that this princess lady gets to use it when I might lose a few fingers if I do.

"Nayla is princess of Canis Ludis," Afton says.

Ah. Maybe that's part of the reason for Afton's sheepish attitude. Canis Ludis is not a planet that any of us have warm thoughts about. Danny Lecker, troublemaker extraordinaire, is from there, and even though we're now friendly with her, it didn't start out that way. Also, I got zapped pretty hard the last time I was there, and I'd made a conscious decision never to go back.

Supposedly, the royal family of Canis Ludis is a bit wacky. We've all heard stories about the queen, but those were just rumors. I've got her daughter standing right in front of me, and while I don't think Princess Nayla Isabella Amenty de Avila is psychotic, she's not exactly a normal, either.

Semi-nuts is a good fit for Afton. I might approve of this couple sooner than I would have expected to. I want to know more about her before I make that decision, though, so I'll ask a few harmless questions...oh, and then I'll tell Afton about the bailiff.

"So, what were you doing down in the grotto?" I ask.

"We communed with the trees," Nayla responds.

"Oh? Do tell." Afton just smiles as I watch her for a response. I wonder if she realizes I just received an entire night's worth of material to tease her with.

"Yes, of course. There was one willow, just near the intersection of a power line, that had quite the interesting story to tell."

I frown, trying to understand her statement. All the power conduits in our town are underground to protect them, and to maintain the aesthetic qualities of the environment. As for talking willows...I've got no idea about that.

"Nayla wanted to get more in touch with the natural planet, so I thought I'd take her here," Afton explains.

"To *our* grotto? Kayley's and mine?" So this princess steals not only my seat but my grotto as well?

"Well, yeah. You guys are always talking about how beautiful it is there."

"Well, it certainly is." I smile as the vision of Kayley and me enjoying a quiet moment there pops into my head.

No! Enough of that! I'm here for a reason!

"By the way, Afton, I need to tell you something."

"Oh? What's up?"

"Something really great, actually! I—"

"Darling," Nayla says, "we must prepare our cleansing ritual before sundown. Otherwise, your soulmate will not rest well tonight."

I blink. I'm not sure which is more unbelievable, the princess cutting me off, or that she just called herself Afton's "soulmate." I'm irritated, but I have to know what she means, so I ask.

"A soulmate is your perfect self in another," Nayla answers. "You will find them only if you can recognize your spirit thriving within them. It is a very special meeting. They come just once in a lifetime." She lifts her shoulder with casual indifference. "Though, I once had two, but that was many rebirth cycles ago when I was an egret."

I have no idea how to respond to that.

The idea she speaks of is beautiful to consider. I'd like to think of Kayley as my soulmate, but I wouldn't even know how to recognize my perfect self. I'm not sure my perfect self exists. Though I think of Kayley as being perfect. Is that what Nayla means?

"Come, darling. It is getting late," Nayla says.

Every time she says "darling," I think of Kayley saying it to me. I'm not sure I can get used to it.

"Hey, thanks for meeting us at the park," Afton says with a hand on my arm. "I'll catch you later, okay?"

"Sure. Have fun," I say. "Remember, Grady goes to bed before midnight, so don't wake him up when you get in."

Afton just side-eyes me. Yes, that was a failure of a farewell. Besides, Afton knows. She's lived in the same house as him for the last two months.

As I sigh and mutter to myself what an awkward idiot I am, Nayla crosses by and turns her head to look at me.

"You are a good person, Rance, but I see bad omens in your future. May the Goddesses protect you." She touches my cheek—the hurt one—and continues on. Afton glances back, smiling with a joy that I've rarely seen on her.

I really hope this turns out well. I hope she's found someone to love and can be happy like Kayley and me. No one wants to see their buds heartbroken.

When they leave the park, I wave at them and then head home. But as I cross through the park gate, I stop and curse myself for being an idiot.

I forgot to tell her!

Chapter Four

"Rance, I can't believe you're here!"

Kayley's jaw had nearly hit the floor when I stepped into the little waiting room just outside the Chamberlin's main office.

"I was getting ready to call the Teddys and have them pick me up just as you called me," she says.

"At least your trip would have been nearly instantaneous. I had to isolate myself in the cabin of an Imperial cruiser for ten days while we crawled our way here."

"Well." Kayley steps up to me and reaches for my hand with a smile. "I'm happy you're here. By the way...what happened to your face?"

"Oh, nothing." I can't help but smile back. A smile from her makes everything better, which is good, because this closet space we're in is dreary—four flat gray walls and a single overdressed bench with gold trim. Any moment, someone will come in and kick us kids out of the museum for trespassing.

"So you really have an audience with the Emperor?" Kayley asks, eyebrows raised.

"The Chamberlin, not the Emperor."

"What's it about?"

"The Chamberlin's aide said she didn't know."

"So"—Kayley chews on her lip—"you agreed to come all this way for no reason? Come on, darling, I know you'd never say yes to something so sketchy."

"Well, there were many incentives." I grin.

But before I can elaborate, a knock comes at the door, and it opens—it's Bailiff Daughtry. She glances at Kayley and me, and notices our hand-holding.

"The Chamberlin is ready to see you, but he will not be ready for public displays of affection. Please be considerate of His Lordship and make sure you observe all the correct pleasantries, and that you remember to address him as 'Your Lordship' or 'Yes, Lord Chamberlin.' Use anything else and I will be there to promptly correct you."

"Of course. We'll do all that."

"You forget, Mr. He', how familiar I am with you." Bailiff Daughtry opens the door all the way and announces us as "Mr. and Mrs. Ransom Quigley He'," to which Kayley shoots her a confused look.

We step in and become enveloped by a world that is clearly not our own. The room is drowned in sensuous curvy lines, asymmetrical flourishes, soft pastel colors, gilded scrolls and shells, and a wallpaper that I can only describe as overdone. Five chests of drawers are lined up against the wall behind a large marble desk that's centered in the room. There's so much ridiculous decoration on them, I can't see where they would open. Then there's the ornate woodwork on the chair behind the desk. No one could possibly be comfortable sitting in that torture device for long.

Which is likely why the Lord Chamberlin is standing, rather than sitting, behind his desk.

"You may be seated," the Chamberlin says and motions to a pair of only slightly less dangerous-looking chairs in front of the desk. I'll have to remember not to lean back if I want to keep any holes from being made in my head.

As we sit, I'm greeted by a large oval painting that covers the front of the desk. It's an image of a throne room—the Emperor's, perhaps—with the ruler perched on a golden throne and surrounded by hundreds of attendants, petitioners, and aristocrats. Beams of light shoot out from behind the throne in some kind of attempt to deify the man who sits there. I always had my opinions of the court, but now I see they were far too conservative. These people are loony.

"The Empire is life," the Chamberlin begins, his voice resonant. "Life is civilization. Civilization is our citizens. Our citizens are the foundation, and the foundation is life."

"Wait, I just thought you said the Empire was life."

I feel a poke on my shoulder. It's Bailiff Daughtry, glaring down at me.

"Your Lordship," she hisses.

"Yeah, what she said."

"Rance!" Kayley hisses and elbows me.

The Chamberlin does not wait for my pleasantries. I'm not even sure he heard me speak. Perhaps he is immune to the sounds of someone who doesn't have an aristocratic title. He picks up a tablet and hands it to his aide, who then passes it on to Kayley, even though I reach out for it.

"Nothing can break the foundation, yet some persist. The foundation must not tarnish, and we all must do our utmost for the preservation of His Majesty's rule. For without it, there can be no civilization and, therefore, no life."

On the tablet's screen is an image of someone royal. She wears a sparkling black robe and a large turban with a silver bust of a long-horned bovine on the front. A confusion of opulent jewelry cascades over her arms and hands, and that's not even the most unusual thing about her. That would be her gaze, which is not that of someone who you would call sane.

"Queen Hathor de Avila, ruler of Canis Ludis," Ms. Daughtry explains. "Senior member of the Council of the Central Planets and owner of the only known yttrium deposit in the entire Empire."

"Okay," I say, because I have no idea where she's going with this. Does she want us to rescue her?

"We use yttrium in the engines of all of our space-going vessels."

I knew that, but I'm still waiting for the punch line.

"The queen also holds a very influential position in the Council, but she often takes her own stance, that is, shall we say, contrary to the Lord Chamberlin's wishes. It would be to His Lordship's advantage if we understood her motivations better. Disputes between her house and the Emperor's are problematic."

"His Majesty's advantage is the Empire's advantage. Advantage means power," the Chamberlin adds. "If our office holds knowledge, it is to our advantage."

"Therefore," Bailiff Daughtry continues, "we need to find out her intentions."

"Why not call her and have a chat, then?" I ask. Ms. Daughtry sneers at my question, but it's the Chamberlin that answers.

"Because she is quite mad." For the first time, the Chamberlin makes eye contact with me, and I see he is serious about his assessment of Queen de Avila. I can also see that he sweats a lot.

"She halted the off-planet yttrium exports two weeks ago," the bailiff adds. "We cannot be without that supply for much longer. If we can't get her to end the embargo, we will have to find other means. A use of force is not out of the question."

"Rance, what did you get yourself into?" Kayley whispers.

I'm wondering about that myself. I only thought I was coming here to listen to Mr. Puzzles pontificate for a while. Instead, we get this secret mission sort of thing. I'm fairly sure they're expecting us to go investigate this crazy queen. Maybe convince her to start up the deliveries again. For a million jorin and a clean slate, I think that's doable.

"The other Imperial agents that we've sent to Canis Ludis to investigate her have either not returned or returned with their heads removed." Bailiff Daughtry comes around to stand before us with her arms folded. "Queen de Avila is a stone that we have not yet been able to crack."

"Rance!" Kayley says in the loudest whisper she can manage. Then she blinks at the bailiff. "What did you mean by *other* Imperial agents?"

"As representatives of this office, you are Imperial agents."

Now here I thought that this would be some walk in the park, but...beheaded? I wonder if we can politely decline. Also, I'm not so excited about the whole *you belong to the Emperor now* thing.

"No..." Kayley says in a low voice. "We're not agents."

"Yes, you are," Bailiff Daughtry responds.

"No. I didn't agree to any such thing."

"Yes, you did, when you agreed to come here."

"No. I came here to speak with Parliament!"

"Oh? How did that go?"

Kayley clenches her teeth and keeps quiet. When I called, she told me she was still waiting for her audience with some top committee and was about to give up. I have a feeling I wasn't the only one that was tricked into coming here. While I'm embarrassed for being so hopeful, I feel horrible for Kayley because she really thought her words were going to reach those who could do something to support our planet.

"Agents you are, and agents you are not," the Chamberlin says, carrying on with his cryptic talk. I get more direct meaning from the Teddys. Of course, now that I'm connected to Teddynet, everything is both clearer and more confusing when I speak with them.

"As babes bearing gifts," he continues, "Her Highness will suspect nothing and appreciate everything. She will expect much, but also give. This is how we gain advantage."

"Doesn't that saying mean the queen wouldn't trust us?" Kayley asks.

"No, it does not," Bailiff Daughtry replies.

"Pretty sure it does," Kayley mumbles, then squeaks as she gets poked by Bailiff Daughtry.

"You are incorrect."

Kayley's face scrunches up, but again she holds her tongue, a bit too wise to get involved in another back and forth with the bailiff. She turns to me with an intensity in her eyes that I understand without words. We're getting out of here at the next available moment.

"Your Highness." I stand.

"Your *Lordship*," Bailiff Daughtry corrects.

"Yeah, what she said...ouch!"

"Where do you think you are going?"

"We're done here," Kayley replies, also standing. "I see no reason to do any of this."

She flips her hair and then fixes it. That's not one I've seen before, but I think I like it. My girlfriend is definitely irate, and I'd like to see Ms. Daughtry go up against a Kayleynado.

"I think not," the bailiff says.

"Who cares what you think." She must have learned that from Afton.

"You do not have permission to leave until the Lord Chamberlin dismisses you."

Kayley eyes him expectantly. To His Lordship's credit, he gives her the attention she deserves. He lifts his girth to his full potential height—which is taller than either Kayley or me—and regards her with curiosity.

"Well?" Kayley folds her arms.

"Only if I say yes, and not no."

Kayley frowns at that one and glances at me. I give her a shrug, as I also have no idea what that means, though I suspect we aren't just going to walk out of here.

"So then, Your High...Your Lordship, we'll be seeing you, yeah?" I ask.

To which he sighs and turns to his bailiff. "Are you sure these are the ones I requested?"

"Absolutely, Your Lordship." The bailiff bows with an arm across her chest. "We watched them for three months before verifying your request. Please understand they are from a minor colony and can barely speak proper Empire Common."

"What the hell are you talking about?" Kayley glares at her.

"My case in point, Your Lordship."

"Are they capable?" The Chamberlin turns to examine us once again. "We cannot delay any longer. Delay is not to our advantage. Only expedience completes the mission."

"Yes, Lord Chamberlin. We believe them to be capable."

"Then I do not say yes."

"Are you sure about that? Ow!" Kayley rubs her arm where the bailiff pinched her. "Are you sure about that, Your Lordship?"

"Surety comes with my position. As with all things, as the Emperor may wish, so shall I do. There is no doubt and, therefore, no concern."

"Well, that's all great, but we're leaving," I say and grab Kayley's hand. I hear a sharp inhale from the Chamberlin as we turn and jog to the door. Now I'd love to know what his face looks like at the moment, but leaving is more important.

"Guards," the bailiff calls, her tone almost sounding disinterested. The guards, all ten of them, surround us in an instant, the mean end of their rifles pointed at our heads.

"You can't do this! We have rights!" Kayley shouts.

"Not in the Emperor's domain, you don't," the bailiff replies.

"Fine, then let me speak to him!"

I hear the shuffle of padded feet making their way around the guards. The Chamberlin comes into view, his demeanor unchanged from the moment we walked into the room. He plays with his jowls as he circles around to face us. Kayley squeezes my hand, and I feel a shudder run through her.

I have to remind myself that this is not like any sort of stand-off we've encountered before. We're not talking to government lackeys here. This is the top of the top. Sure, the Chamberlin and his bailiff want something from us, but we're nothing but pets to them. They would as soon put us outside to play as they would have us spy on Queen de Avila. They might just as easily dispose of us, given we're not Imperial citizens.

"His Majesty is generous," the Chamberlin says with an uplifted face and gentle motion of his hand. "His generosity knows no bounds. He blesses his subjects with benevolence, and with benevolence does he listen."

"*You* are *not* subjects of His Majesty," Bailiff Daughtry adds.

That means no audience with the Emperor. No chance of getting out of this. No escape. We're going to have to go through with this.

"Now, be seated. Or be shot."

Chapter Five

"Shoot!"

"What is it?" Kayley asks me as she sits down on the bed, resigned to wait in this not unimpressive chamber. It's bigger than any single room in either of our houses, and every piece of furniture looks handmade, from the dark-stained wood desk with brass trim to the four-poster bed. The bed linens alone look more expensive than my house.

"We missed Afton's big party!"

"Oh, hell." Kayley reaches for her Sergo, then growls, realizing that they took it away from her. They took mine too. Not because they think we're going to call for help. That would be too easy for them to track. They just wanted to make us feel insignificant.

"Wait." Kayley's eyebrows knit together. "*That's* what you're concerned about? How about the fact that we're the Chamberlin's prisoners?"

"We're not prisoners. I didn't even hear the door lock." I walk to the door and grab the handle. "See? It's unlocked."

A guard stands outside, rifle in hand. He's facing us with a gruff sneer on his face.

"What do you want?" he says with the standard unfriendly guard's voice. I wonder if he speaks to everyone that way.

"Just saying hello." I smile and wave, then close the door and turn to Kayley. She frowns and folds her arms.

"Did you try Teddynet?" she asks.

"No, but only because you don't like me using it too much."

"That's because you get all spacey after. But this time, you have my permission. We have to get out of here."

I give her a thumbs-up and take a breath, accessing that now-familiar part of my brain that leads into a universe of all things Teddy. Anything a single Teddy knows, they all know, and now that includes me. I can upload stuff, too, but I haven't quite gotten the hang of that. Hence Kayley's "spacey" comment. She's not wrong.

Despite that little hiccup, it's quite handy. But today, it's not working at all. I reach out and get nothing back. It's blank. Dark. Empty. Maybe we're just too far away from a Teddy. It shouldn't make a difference, but what do I know about alien technologies? I shrug at Kayley, who rolls her eyes. So much for the easy exit.

"So, speaking of Afton, did you meet her?" Kayley asks.

"Of course. We saw a few movies together. None of them good, so don't be jealous." It's a little lie. I loved that one with the space battle!

"Not her, silly. Afton's girlfriend!"

"Oh, so she told you about that?" I pace the room, my hand sliding across the intricately carved wall molding.

"She's not a *that*, Rance. She's a *she*."

"Yeah, I know. I met her."

"You did?" Kayley jumps up. "What's she like?"

"Didn't Afton send you a picture?"

"Yes, but you can't tell what someone's really like from a picture."

I stop at a section of wall in the far corner of the room because I notice a crack in between two pieces of molding. It's dark over here, so my eyes could be playing tricks on me, but I think it stretches all the way to the floor.

"So?"

"So what?"

"Tell me about her!"

"So, yeah, the princess."

"Princess?"

"Princess Nayla de Avila. She's...unique. Right up Afton's alley, I guess."

"Did you just say Princess de Avila?"

"Yes, I did, why?" I turn away from my examination of the wall to look at Kayley. Her eyes are wide, and her mouth hangs open. She shakes both her hands at me with more vigor than I've seen from her all day. I shake my head and turn back to look at the wall again. I'm not sure why, but there's something about this crack that makes me think it's not accidental.

"Rance! Where's your brain? Princess de Avila means she's the daughter of Queen de Avila! The woman we're going to be investigating for the Chamberlin! Why isn't that registering with you? Are you even listening to me at all?"

"Sure, I am."

"Rance, what are you doing over there?" Kayley's footsteps come up behind me as I trace my finger along the crack. It goes up almost to where I can't reach any further. Then it feels like it might continue left, but I'm having a hard time feeling for it.

"Rance. Stop being a space cadet and talk." Kayley puts a hand on my shoulder. "Do you want me to start being a naggy girlfriend?"

"Not especially."

"I will, and I promise you, I can be pretty good at it."

"No need to threaten, KayKay. We've had enough of that today, don't you think?"

"More than enough," Kayley grumbles. "So. What. Are. You. Doing?"

"There's this strange crack in the wall. It seems strange to me because this room is so swank."

"Oh, well, that's not a crack. That's a servant's door."

I spin on her, searching her face. Kayley blinks at my sudden turn, but then I see her face change as the realization of what she just said hits her.

Kayley grabs my arm and tugs me out of the way. She places both hands flat along the wall and begins feeling around. For what, I'm not exactly sure, but I think she's trying to find the other edge of the door. I return to where I was searching and find the crack again, trying to meet up with her somewhere in the middle.

"Rance."

"What, you found something?"

"No. I'm just worried about Afton."

"Why? She can take care of herself."

"Not like that. I mean, what if Queen de Avila found out that the Chamberlin was trying to recruit us and sent her daughter to Afton as a spy? Or even to hire us as double agents?"

"Seems far-fetched, KayKay."

"Yeah, but"—Kayley bends down, following her side down to the floor—"when's the last time royalty came to Angelcanis? Can you remember there *ever* being a time?"

"True." I complete the top of the door and start looking for a handle. "We haven't ever had a visit from anyone higher than a parliamentary member. Do you really think this princess came to hire us? But we're not even there."

"Well." Kayley puts a finger on her lips, then watches the movement of my hands. "No, darling, that can't be it. There's no way this door swings open."

I stop and step back to examine the door in full. No hinges—sure, that would make sense. Which means...

I place my hands flat on the wall and push. The door slides back into the wall, and I can feel it lean to the right. That's how it works. It makes sense. Much quieter that way.

"Wait," Kayley says, touching my arm. "Let me lock the other door first."

She glides over to the door, arms outstretched as if she's trying to keep her balance, and reaches it without making any sound louder than her breath. A second later, she taps the lock and glides back over.

"How'd you do that?" I ask, amazed at her fluid motions.

"Do what?"

"Float across the room."

"Oh. You mean this?" Kayley lifts her heels off the floor and stretches her arms out again, then she performs her move again. If I wasn't watching her feet this time, I would believe that she was floating for sure. "Beryozka."

"Berry what?"

"It's a dance that I learned a long time ago."

"Why haven't I ever seen it before?"

"Because you never came to see me dance." Kayley pushes me forward, and we slide the door open the rest of the way. The corridor we enter is dimly lit, but there's enough light to see where we're going. It goes straight from the door and also breaks right into a bit of shadow. There's another light a little farther down, so that direction goes for a long way.

"Are we really going to do this?" I ask.

"You want your head chopped off?"

"Not especially."

"Then, let's go." Kayley takes hold of my arms and pivots me right. She gives me a gentle push, and we head down the long way. As we move, I get this sense that everything is pressing down against us, and then I realize that what I'm feeling is sound. A low rumble pervades the corridor, vibrating the air around our ears, but also covering up the beat of our steps. It gives me confidence until I realize we won't be able to hear anyone coming, either.

"You know, I figured it out," I whisper in Kayley's ear.

"Figured out what?

"How she does it...the princess, I mean. She floats, too."

Kayley looks at me as if I just rattled off a list of my favorite stones in my mom's garden.

"You still haven't told me what you think of her," she says.

"Yes, I did. I said she's perfect for Afton."

A shadow of human form slides across an intersection, and we push ourselves into the dark. It's gone as quickly as it came, and the two of us exhale in relief. We remain in as much cover as possible and continue down the passage, hoping for a hint of a way out.

"What did you think of her when you first saw her?" Kayley asks.

"Will you hit me if I'm honest with you?"

"Can't guarantee that, but if you tell the truth, then I'll be lenient."

I catch Kayley's eyes, and I see she's being honest with me. She always has been. At least as far as I know. I can't say the same for myself, and I've regretted it any time I have. But I'm determined to be a better boyfriend so that I don't have to regret even one second when I'm with her.

"The first time I laid eyes on her..."

"Yes?"

"It was like seeing a Goddess. Seriously. Her presence was like no one else I've ever met."

There's a junction up ahead. We pause to choose a direction, then move left.

"Is she pretty?" Kayley asks.

"Beautiful...ow!" I glance at her, feeling wounded. She shakes her head. I guess pinching me is *her* honesty in action. Kayley nods to herself after that. Not sure what she's approving of, but I can guess it's not me finding Afton's new girlfriend attractive.

"Still, I'm worried," she says as we creep towards a door. A real door. Something that seems like it could be an exit. I inhale and put my hands on it. "I don't want Afton getting heartbroken."

"Afton? No way. She's tougher than all of us combined."

"She's not, Rance. You only know one side of her. She can be more sensitive than you about certain things, and she doesn't have a lot of dating experience."

"None of us have a lot of dating experience, KayKay."

"Okay, true, but I know her other side. She's delicate where you'd expect her to be solid. Let's make sure she doesn't get hurt, okay?"

"She won't...ow!" I give Kayley another hurt look. "What was that for?"

"Promise."

"Promise what?"

"That you'll protect her from getting hurt."

"As if that's even a question."

"Good. Now, can we get out of here?"

"Absolutely."

I press the door, and a latch releases, and the door slides back. There's light—sunlight—coming through, and a green pasture greets our excited view. With elation welling up inside of me, I burst through the exit with Kayley, both of us smiling. This was almost too easy.

It *was* too easy.

We stop short as a group of guards rush out from behind a wall and surround us, weapons drawn. Kayley presses against me as I carefully raise my hands. These aren't conscripted farmers or daytime security agents. These are the Emperor's own elite, and I have no doubt they would mow us down if we made one wrong move.

"Did you really think to break your agreement?" Bailiff Daughtry steps in front of the line of guards. "Where would you go? Home? There is absolutely nowhere in our great Emperor's domain that you could go that I would not find you. Lucky for you, we still have need of you."

"We just felt like some fresh air," I try. "We weren't breaking our agreement."

"Wonderful. Now that you have had it, you'll be returning to restricted confinement."

Kayley and I share a look. We're not going to die—at least not yet. But we're also not free, and that's a real problem.

Chapter Six

We're thrown into a room much less comfy than the luxury suite we just tried to escape from. There are just four walls, one bed, and nothing else. The walls are solid graphcrete, and a solitary semi-globe of light hangs from the center of the room, throwing moody shadows in all directions.

Kayley sighs and drops herself onto the bed, which squeaks and squeals as the mattress gets compressed. Kayley doesn't weigh much, so that's a serious negative on our only place for rest. I'll sleep on the ground if I have to, though I'm hoping I won't.

"I'm glad you're here, KayKay," I say in an attempt to make her feel better.

"Yeah? I'm not."

That was expected, of course, but if I have to be in a situation that is completely screwed, there's no one else I'd want by my side. We may not be the strongest of our little gang, but between the two of us, I feel like we can accomplish anything.

The lock on the door creaks, and I tense, getting ready for anything. I know we're not going to die, at least not at the hands of the Chamberlin. Once we're on Canis Ludis, though, it's a different story.

The door swings in with a squeak, and two people get thrown into the room. It's Parrish and Grady! The door slams shut behind them without a word from our captors.

"Hey, you guys alright?" I ask as Kayley and I go to help them up. Neither is moving very fast, so I wonder what the Chamberlin's guards did to them. I don't see any cuts or bruises, which is good. Physical violence isn't the only way to hurt someone, however.

"Hey," Parrish says as he groans. "Didn't expect to see you here."

"Yeah, well. This isn't exactly what we thought we'd be doing here, either."

All eyes go to Grady as he stumbles over to the bed and drops himself down on it. He folds his arms over his chest and closes his eyes. Kayley and I share a glance. Then she goes to him, putting her hand over his.

"It's okay if you rest, Grady. Just let us know you're okay, yeah?"

Grady sticks a thumb up, and the three of us exhale. Our bud has seen enough trouble for a lifetime. This current situation isn't anything that he needs to experience in his life. He's here now, though, so we'll have to help him through it as best we can.

"What are you guys doing here?" I ask Parrish.

"Well, it's not like we had much of a choice. This woman—"

"Bailiff Daughtry, you mean."

"Yeah, her...I was over at Grady's place when she showed up at the front door, insisting that we come with her."

"Did she offer you money?"

"No." Parrish frowns at me. "Why?"

"Never mind. Just curious...it's not important."

"I have a question," Grady mumbles. "How are we getting out of here?"

Parrish, Kayley, and I look at each other, and it's obvious that the three of us have no idea. I'm not even sure we have the courage to try. Bailiff Daughtry is certainly someone who will do what she promises. I don't want her to promise to put a hole in our heads.

"Got nothing?" Grady asks, then sighs and sits up. "Okay. I guess I'll have to do it."

"Do what?" I ask.

"Find a way out of here."

"Yeah, I'm not sure that's a good idea, dude."

"Why don't we start with why we're in here?" Parrish suggests. "I would definitely like to know that before we decide to do something stupid."

"What makes you think we're going to do something stupid, Parry?" Kayley looks at him, her eyebrows coming together.

Parrish just looks back at her.

I tell them the entire story up to now, mentioning the offer to clear our records, but leaving out the part about the money. It's not all that certain that we're going to get any pay now. Then again, it's not all that certain we're going to get our records clear, either.

Parrish and Grady's faces become more and more rigid as I explain. They're well familiar with this kind of situation, as we've been in deep like this many times before. The crucial difference here is the level of our adversary. Though, I'm not sure exactly who to call our adversary, as it could be the Chamberlin, Bailiff Daughtry, or the queen of Canis Ludis. All three are equally dangerous in their potential to do us harm, and all three likely couldn't care less if we were dead or alive. The queen might be off her rocker, but the way the Chamberlin was speaking makes me think he's not all there, either.

"Dude, what are you doing?" I break from my pondering to watch Grady attempting to lift himself onto the metal tubing of the bed's headboard.

"Looking for a way out," he says as he stretches his hand out, trying to reach the air vent.

"Yeah, well, let me tell you, dude, trying that is only going to end in you getting hurt. Why don't you come down?"

"Come up with an idea, and I will."

I turn to Kayley and Parrish for help, but both of them shrug and continue to watch Grady balance precariously on the rusty bar of the bed frame. I really want him to stop, because I know what will happen when he fails.

But then I realize the reason I want him to get down may be that I want to go through with this mission after all. I came here because I wanted to help my buds have a future. Of course, the million jorin on top didn't hurt, either.

I catch Kayley noticing my face going through what must be a thousand different transformations as I consider what my actual position is.

"Alright, let's get on the same page," she says. "Grady, get down, and let's talk. We're only going to get through this if we work together, so we have to decide *what* we're going to do together."

"What are our options?" Parrish asks. "I mean, what are we thinking we can do or should do?"

"Well," I say, "we're here because of the Chamberlin's offer, however sketchy that seems, but if we don't want to do that, we can either plead to go home or try to escape."

"We tried to escape already," Kayley adds. "Obviously, it didn't work."

"So it's beg or go through with it?" Parrish asks, but then he gets distracted by the noise Grady is making as he scratches on the vent.

"Grady," Kayley warns.

"In a minute."

"Listen." I turn to Parrish and Kayley. "This might sound completely nuts, but we've got a lot to gain by taking and, of course, completing this mission. We have a lot more capability than we're giving ourselves credit for! This could just be a walk in the park for us."

"Or you could get shot, beaten up, jailed for life...oh yeah, and beheaded, darling," Kayley replies. "Hasn't your body taken enough punishment over the last year?"

"But it could totally be worth the risk! Just think, KayKay, you could get to actually address Parliament the next time you're here. Or Parrish, you could have a great job at a top school on one of the Central Planets!"

"Didn't you want us all to stick together?" Parrish asks, folding his arms.

He's right, of course. I don't want my buds to leave and have a life away from me. It's selfish, I know, but that was also before I really had a clear picture of what I wanted to do with my life. Sure, I had big hopes that I could get my father to come back to me. That's over now, so whatever he and I had planned, I'm going to do without him. He may just be a part of the problem, anyway. Kayley will be around, so she'll help me fight for the people of Angelcanis. Not that I wouldn't miss Parrish, or Grady, or Afton.

Speaking of Afton...why isn't she here? Is her new romantic partner able to pull some strings for her, or is Bailiff Daughtry worried about upsetting the queen because she took away her daughter's new girl toy?

A yelp from Grady stops my thought process. He's clutching the edge of the vent, his eyes wide. I swallow, hoping an accident was just averted.

"Grady!" Kayley shouts. "Down! Now!"

Grady sighs, then turns to jump off the bed frame. An itch runs down my back as I recognize the danger that he's just put himself in. Grady's not heavy, but that bed isn't going to support his gymnastics.

"No, dude!" I cry.

But it's too late. The moment Grady hits the bed, there's a sharp crack, and the bed snaps in half on one side, dropping him to the floor. He hits the ground with a shout, and Kayley goes to help him. All I can manage is to give him an "I told you so."

The door squeaks open, and one guard enters. We freeze, praying that we're not in any more trouble. He scans the room until his eyes land on Grady. He just stares for a moment, then pulls back through the door and locks it.

"Dude," I hiss. "Mass times acceleration? And did you forget that Albion's gravity is stronger than ours?"

"Anyway." Kayley takes a breath as she helps Grady up and dusts him off. "Let's decide."

"I'm not much for pleading," Parrish says, "and they'd likely just make us do it, anyway."

"After we made complete fools of ourselves," I add.

Parrish nods agreement. "I say let's go for it."

"Parry!" Kayley's mouth is half-open as she stares at him in surprise. I guess that means Kayley is leaning towards appealing to the Chamberlin's generous nature. The only problem I see with that is I doubt the Chamberlin has any idea what generous really means.

"Nope, nope, and nope," Grady says. "We need to be finding a way out of here. Now."

"That's not even one of the choices, dude."

"Well, I'm making it my choice."

"Well, I'm siding with Parrish on this one," I say. "No guarantee that crawling on our knees in front of the Chamberlin would get us anywhere, and even though there's lots of potential risk, there's also lots of potential reward."

We turn to Kayley, the final and potentially deciding vote. She stares back at me, her eyes narrowed just slightly. This isn't going to be easy for her, and I know I haven't helped her by choosing the way I did. There's a bit of disappointment in her face, too. For my choice, or something else, I'm not sure. Still, I think I've got some pleading to do right at this very moment if I want to get her to agree.

"KayKay," I say, taking her hands. "I know you still have nightmares about Cecelia's men capturing us, and I know you don't want to see any of us hurt ever again."

"That's true," Kayley says, her voice flat.

"But consider the other side of it for a moment. What we can achieve, not only for us. For Grady, and Parrish, and Afton, too. When I first accepted the invitation, I wasn't thinking about me."

Her eyes narrow a little more.

"Okay, I was thinking about me a tiny bit, but what really got me excited was the thought that everyone could be free from all the nonsense that they've put us through. We could live normal lives again."

"Is that what you want? To be normal? To be a citizen?" Her eyes do not waver even a nanometer from mine. The weight of her questioning presses down on me. When I said *normal*, I had meant not being on the run from muscle-bound individuals or attempting to break into a high-security prison. As long as Kayley and I can be together, I think the rest will work itself out.

"I just want to be with you, KayKay."

Kayley snorts. "Nice try, but that's not going to work, darling."

"Then let's do it for the others, if not for ourselves."

That hits the right button, and Kayley's entire expression softens. When it comes to helping others, she's like me, always putting her friends—and me—first. It's just one of the million reasons I love her like I do.

"Okay," she says, the edges of her lips curving up just a little. "Let's do it for our friends."

"Hey," Parrish says. "You guys don't need to talk about us like we're not here."

"But"—Kayley grabs me and stops me from turning around towards Parrish—"if this gets bad, we're running. As far away as will make us safe. I don't care if that means we live with the Teddys for a while. I'm not losing you, or anybody, over this."

I nod. We're in total agreement there.

Chapter Seven

We're jammed into the Chamberlin's waiting room again, only this time it's four of us rather than two. Plus, Parrish's muscular build means he takes up the space of almost two people. It's a good thing we're all friends. I wish we'd had a chance to shower, though.

I'm guessing the reason the Chamberlin wants to see us again is to make sure we're going to do what we've agreed to. I'm sure he's expecting to hear a positive confirmation come out of our mouths when he asks.

The doors open, and once again, it's the bailiff. She's not happy to see us, either, but there's a bit of weariness about her that makes me suspect we're not the only ones her boss is imposing on. He gets what he wants because of who he is. Even if that means stepping on everyone below him to do it.

"Enter," Bailiff Daughtry says, her voice dark and rumbly. "Stand there, in front of the desk."

Grady and Parrish take their time moving to the spot, their eyes lost somewhere in the ceiling. Neither one of them cares much for opulence, but there's something about the grandiose décor here that catches the eye. I guess when you're second only to the Emperor, you can hire the absolute best interior decorators in the entire Empire.

Bailiff Daughtry comes before us, her hands behind her back. She glares, making sure to catch all our gazes so we know she's serious. I never doubted it for a moment, but her attempt to intimidate is not having the effect on us she seems to want.

"I shouldn't have to, but I'm going to remind you that you are in an audience with His Lordship, and I expect you to address him properly." The bailiff examines Parrish and Grady for a moment, then turns to me. "That means the only acceptable response for you is 'Yes, Your Lordship' or 'Yes, Lord Chamberlin.' I don't think I need to remind you of what happened last time."

"What happened last time?" Grady asks. The bailiff's response is to pinch the skin of his arm and twist. Grady yelps, his hand flying over to cover the spot where she grabbed him. The look Bailiff Daughtry gives him stops him from saying anything else.

"I believe we have properly prepared them for you, Lord Chamberlin." Bailiff Daughtry takes a spot behind the four of us. She's leaning closer to me, but I have a feeling she's keeping her eyes on Grady.

"Time is of the essence," the Chamberlin says as he walks from the back of the room. "The lifeblood of the Empire must flow. Trade must commence. Profit must be acquired. If we cannot ensure the proper flow of materials, then our essence will cease to be."

"So, does that mean that time stops?" Grady frowns, his eyes sliding up. I close mine and shake my head, because I know Bailiff Daughtry is going right for him. "Ow!"

"Speak only when addressed! And eyes front!" She grabs the back of his head and twists it forward when he tries to look back at her. Parrish is trying hard not to look, and even though he's way taller than the bailiff, I can see the whites of his eyes.

"Our Majesty is a gracious man," the Chamberlin continues. "He wishes all his citizens to prosper and thrive. We cannot flourish without our essence. Commerce is life. Life is the foundation of the Empire. Without life, we do not live. Without life, we do not thrive."

"His Lordship wishes you a safe journey and success in your mission," Bailiff Daughtry says, "and requests you complete it with all possible speed."

I raise my hand just above my shoulder and duck my head, preparing for the attack that will come because I've done something to insult the Chamberlin.

"What is it?" Bailiff Daughtry asks, coming around to face me. Oh, good...no pinch.

"Well, just what is the mission? I mean, we're happy to help, but what exactly do you want us to find out?"

"When you know, then you will know," the Chamberlin replies. I look at the bailiff for a translation.

"There is a meeting of the Council next month, three weeks from today. At that meeting, we suspect Her Highness will attempt to use the embargo to negotiate another seat on the Council that she can appoint. If she gets it, that will throw the balance of power on the Council towards her favor. We can't allow that."

"You said you suspect?" I ask. "So you don't know for sure that's what she's going to do?"

"We were about to find out, but then..." Bailiff Daughtry looks down.

"Beheaded," I say, and she nods.

"Time is the lifeblood we have in our hand," the Chamberlin says, strolling around to his bailiff's side. "But our essence is not everlasting. Time is of the essence. So, you must use that which is given to you."

"What...are we being given?" Kayley asks, then quickly adds, "Your Lordship."

"Time," Bailiff Daughtry replies. "You are to leave immediately for Canis Ludis and complete your mission before the day of the Council meeting."

"What if we can't?"

"Then we will notify Queen de Avila that she has spies in her court and use that method to get her to release the embargo."

Kayley blinks. Grady and Parrish do, too. And I just want to be sure I understand correctly what the bailiff just said. We become sacrifices if we don't complete our mission in time? Our lives have no real meaning to the Empire, other than as tools to achieve what they desire?

"So you have no intention of clearing our records or—"

"If you are successful." The Chamberlin brings his towering hulk of a body in front of me. "*If.* Then this chamber will be honorable. This chamber will do no more, nor no less, than what agreement it made. *If* you achieve what it has set forth."

"Satisfied?" the bailiff asks.

Is that really a question? They tricked us into coming, then pinched us, locked us up, and now are threatening our lives. That is, if we don't complete a mission we never agreed to. We were going to agree to do it, technically. Even so, how could anyone be satisfied with this?

Perhaps Bailiff Daughtry is asking for her own gratification. Maybe she wants to think of herself as tough but fair, just like my athletics teacher.

Except I'm not learning how to play ball. I'm about to get into a serious situation where death could be the result.

"Not really, no," I reply.

"What else do you wish?"

Now *that's* a good question. If we can get the money and get our records cleared, that's a lot already. In some ways, it's more than we could ever hope for. Still, this is the second most powerful man in the Empire! He could grant us almost anything we desire. That's part of the problem, of course. What do I want? What do *we* want?

"Another two million jorin would be helpful," I say, just to see what the response is.

Oops. I forgot to tell everyone about the money. That'd be why my buds are all staring at me.

"Impossible," Bailiff Daughtry replies. "Besides, you already agreed to one million."

"Well, I agreed to come here and listen to His Lordship for one million *and* our records cleared. We never agreed to do anything else...ow! Stop that! It's the truth! Ow!"

"Enough," the Chamberlin says, halting his bailiff with a hand on her shoulder. "What is done cannot be undone. The choice is made, and you are chosen. There is nothing more to say. You must complete the mission in three weeks, or *we* will complete it in four. To speak is to delay. To delay is to endanger the Empire, and the Empire must not be in danger. Therefore, acceptance is the only solution."

"Can't we at least go home first?" Parrish asks.

"No. There is no time," the bailiff replies. "You must go immediately."

"My mom," Parrish mouths to me, and my stomach twists something fierce. She's been bad lately. In and out of hospitals to treat something the doctors aren't even sure about. He's been taking her to her appointments while he goes for rehab on his knee. I wish I could help him, but I've got no idea how.

Then I think about my mom. She's okay, but I would at least want to hug her and thank her for everything she's done for me before my head gets put on the chopping block. Literally.

"So that's it, then?" Kayley asks. "We're not going to be given a choice at all? Just go to Canis Ludis and try not to die?"

"Your Lordship," I add. Bailiff Daughtry eyes me but leaves Kayley alone.

"We chose you based on your reputation," the bailiff explains. "If we did not think you capable of achieving the goal of the mission, we would not have chosen you."

"No good deed goes unpunished, I guess," I mumble, remembering something my father had said long ago about the dangers of being a fighter for justice.

"I can't believe Afton's missing all this," Grady murmurs. A shock goes through me. Afton! We're going to be investigating her new girlfriend's mom! She can't know, or it might slip to the princess what we're doing. Then she'll tell her mom, and…heads will roll. We've got to keep Afton and…what was her name? Oh yeah, Nayla. We've got to keep them as far away from this as possible.

"Okay, we'll go. We're ready."

"Rance, what are you doing?" Kayley hisses and pinches my arm. She loves me, so it's not as hard as the bailiff's pinch, but her attention-grabbing is effective. I give her my best "trust me" look, and she glares back at me.

"On one condition," I add. Bailiff Daughtry rolls her eyes and folds her arms.

"What?" Then she holds her hand up. "I warn you. You'll get worse than a pinch if you try something."

"No," I reply, "I'm not trying anything. I just want to ask a favor that will benefit the Lord Chamberlin and the mission."

"Fine. What is it?"

"Promise to keep Princess de Avila and our friend away from Canis Ludis while we're there. If either of them finds out what we're up to, that's going to cause problems."

Bailiff Daughtry purses her lips, then nods. Good. She gets it.

"I can't guarantee it, but we'll do our best."

"You're the bailiff of the second most powerful man in the Empire," I say with a grin. "I think your best will be more than good enough."

Bailiff Daughtry gives me a sly smile and motions for us to turn around. As we depart, I suck in a breath and reach for Kayley's hand, but she smacks mine away. Okay. She's not happy about this, but I don't think we had much of a choice. I have a feeling we were teetering on the edge of the

Chamberlin's patience, and if we went over, well, we might not have ever left Albion again.

If I'm between a black hole and a supernova, I think I'll take the black hole. There's still the possibility of coming out the other side alive.

Chapter Eight

It's dirtier here on Canis Ludis than I remember it. And it smells. Filth piles up right next to the shuttle exit ramp, and a black smog hangs in the sky around the spaceport. It's raining black tar, and ever since we arrived, there hasn't been a moment when I didn't want to vomit.

At least it's not cold.

The others are better off than I am, though no cheerier. We all could think of an infinite number of places we'd rather be. Even Exodus, the high-security prison, was cleaner than this.

"Are we supposed to wait for an official escort, or should we just find a taxi?" Parrish asks. Bailiff Daughtry had mentioned that Her Majesty needed to be informed we were coming. That didn't guarantee they'd receive us with open arms. The last group of representatives left such a terrible impression on the court, the queen threw them out. Minus their heads.

"I'd be happy to get out of this muck as soon as possible," Grady answers. "Let's hire a taxi."

"No," Kayley says, despite the fact that all of us are getting soaked through. "Let's wait a bit. We don't want to start this...mission...off at a disadvantage. Not when there's this much at stake. A little dirt won't hurt you, Grady."

"Well, we could at least get out of this rain." Grady holds out a hand and watches as a small pool of black forms in the cup of his palm. He retches and turns his hand over, dumping the water on the ground.

Kayley and I have first-hand experience with the muck on this planet. The last time we were here, we got covered in it trying to escape a hand-hunter. She had wanted to capture me so she could fulfill a contract with a long-term client. It may be a common practice around the Empire, but I still think it's a strange way to get a spouse. Just get out there and meet someone already.

"Looks like we won't have to wait at all," Parrish says, pointing to a row of vehicles pulling up just outside the port. They're decked out in silver and turquoise—the colors of the queen. And if that wasn't enough to tip us off, the bevy of bodyguards that pile out of the first two vehicles definitely are.

"Let's go," Kayley orders, turning on her growly mom voice. "And remember, be on your best behavior. I'm not getting executed out in this filth because one of you decided to be funny."

One guard spots us approaching and beckons us towards a larger vehicle in the back of the line while a few others come out with umbrellas to give us cover as we walk. Another, who I think must be in charge, opens the vehicle door and waits for us. As we approach, he squints, then opens his eyes wide as he cranes his neck to observe us.

"Scarlett Kayley," he says. "What a surprise. I had no idea that you would be a part of this delegation. Her Majesty will be excited to meet you. I'm sure you know she's a big fan."

Kayley's gruff attitude evaporates, and she beams at the chief bodyguard, who offers her his hand to help her into the vehicle. Kayley graciously accepts with a girlish giggle and steps inside. I'd shake my head if I didn't just promise to be a good representative of the Empire. I'm sure Parrish and Grady are holding it in until we get inside our ride.

The chief smiles back when I nod to him. Then I duck into the vehicle to get out of this black toxin that's falling from the sky. But as I jump in, I bump into Kayley, who's paused just inside. She collapses forward with a yelp, and I fall right on top of her.

"Well, aren't you two in a hurry?" someone says. Someone with a very familiar voice. "Were you guys stuck with Parrish and Grady for so long, you couldn't bear it once you were alone?"

"Afton?"

Afton smirks and points a finger at me. Sitting next to her is Princess Nayla, who's abandoned her gossamer clothing for something still regal, but more practical: boots, pants, and a military-style jacket. Afton is wearing a matching outfit, though hers is black while the princess' is silver and turquoise. The princess also wears a turban—smaller than the weighty one her mother wears, but the design is the same.

"Ah, the newlyweds," Princess Nayla says, sliding back to rest on Afton's shoulder. "My congratulations to you both. It is clear now that you are fated to be together."

"Fated?" Kayley asks, staring at the vision that is the princess. Then she recovers with a shake of her head. "No, wait. We're not married."

"But it is your destiny to be together," the princess replies, the deep tones of her voice resonating about the spacious vehicle. "My inner eye has seen it."

"What?"

"Hey, can we get in already?" Grady sticks his head in as Kayley and I attempt to untangle ourselves and get up on the bench that wraps around the interior.

"Hey, you," Afton says to Grady, who looks in her direction and blinks. Then he blinks again when he sees Nayla. Before he can get a word out, Parrish lifts him up and slides him inside the vehicle.

"Wow," Parrish says when he gets in. "Didn't expect to see you here."

"Wait, how did you know we were going to be here today?" I almost jump off the seat as a thousand different questions fly through my brain. Are we caught? Does this mean the queen knows why we're really here? Is our mission over? Are our heads about to be chopped off?

And what happened with Bailiff Daughtry promising to keep these two away from us?

"Oh, I asked the Teddys where you guys were," Afton replies. "I wanted to introduce...uh...my...I wanted to introduce Nayla to you."

"Enchanted," Nayla says. "I must read all of your palms later. But first." She knocks on the window behind her head. "Let us begin our journey."

"Where is Teddy?" I ask, wanting to give our little pink fuzzy friend a piece of my mind. Of course, I don't have to. I've got some minor control of Teddynet now, and I could just upload my displeasure instead.

"Teddy is not available," comes Original Teddy's voice from the dark corner nearest the princess.

"Teddy, get out here," Kayley says.

"That is not possible."

"Why?"

"Recommendation for another topic of discussion."

"He's fine," Afton says. "Just hungry."

"That is accurate."

"The question is, why are *you* guys here?" Afton asks, tilting her head and peering at us with one eye. "It's strangely convenient that you happen to be on Nayla's homeworld."

I freeze, and Kayley also goes stiff next to me. How are we going to explain this one in a way that makes any sort of sense and doesn't give away our mission for the Chamberlin? There's not much reason for us to be here, and I'm sure Afton remembers that none of us ever wanted to set foot back on this planet again. I'm not about to remind her and insult her girlfriend in the same sentence.

"Gee, well," Kayley says. "We wanted to go see how Danny and Freddie were doing."

"Uh, yeah," Parrish adds. "Road trip, you know?"

"Road trip? And you didn't think to invite me?"

"Well." I motion to Nayla with a gentle hand. "You seemed busy."

"Uh, hello? Did you lose your brain completely over the last week, dorkelhose? This is where Nayla *lives*!"

I glance at Kayley for support, and she just stares back, eyes wide, and gives me a minute shake of her head. I sigh—no help there. Then I look at Parrish and Grady, and they're focused on drying their Sergos. I'm on my own.

"Yeah, but the last time I saw you two, you threatened me with bodily harm if I didn't leave you alone."

"Well, that's true," Afton replies with a shrug.

"Violence is never the answer, Surela darling," Nayla says, and she plants a soft kiss on Afton's cheek. Afton smiles and turns bashful. I see her cheeks going rosy, even in the dimness of the vehicle's cabin.

"Surela?" Grady whispers, but I cut him off with a hand on his arm and a shake of my head. That's a canister of radioactive waste we do not want to open. I'm still jealous that Nayla gets to use Afton's first name when I can't even think it in my head.

Still, when I consider it, I realize it means that Afton is comfortable enough around her new friend to drop her defensiveness about it. It's no simple task to get Afton to lower her guard and be vulnerable with someone. She's always been Ms. Impenetrable Wall of Emotion. I suppose I should just be happy for her.

"You still haven't answered my question, idiots." Afton is also very good at taking any warm feelings and jamming them into a barrel of ice water. I don't want to lie to her, because that would do damage to our friendship if she found out. Irreparable damage.

The other option isn't better, however. At least I don't think it is. Nayla would likely drive us directly to her mother, but I've got a feeling she and her mother aren't that close. It's still extremely risky. We have absolutely no way to know which way the princess would go.

I think I need to speak to a higher power about this.

"KayKay," I whisper into her ear as everyone settles in for the ride. "What do you think? Should we tell her the truth? Maybe it wouldn't be as bad as we think it might."

Kayley spins on me and grabs my hands, squeezing hard. Our eyes connect, and I can tell right away she's terrified of that suggestion. Then she looks over at the new couple at the end of the bench. Afton and Nayla are certainly happy together. I can tell because Afton never smiles like that. It's refreshing to see.

And Nayla can't keep her eyes off Afton. She's like a lost puppy with the gaze she puts on her. It amazes me that someone with that much status and power could fall for a tough-talking tomboy like Afton. No. I shouldn't think of her that way. Afton's got a lot of amazing qualities that anyone, once they got through her façade, would instantly fall in love with.

"Hey, bumble-brain," Afton says to me. "Are you going to answer my question, or do I have to come over there and beat it out of you?"

It does take some time to get behind that façade.

I glance at Kayley again, and she's as conflicted about the situation as I am. I don't have any other made-up stories to tell Afton. She knows us too well. Any false word that comes out of my mouth, she'll know right away that I'm lying.

Maybe if I tell the truth, Afton could help us convince the princess not to tell her mom. I think Nayla would be willing to keep her mouth shut if I can explain it well. In fact, she might be willing to help us! Imagine that!

"KayKay," I whisper, "I'm going to tell her."

"Rance!" she hisses back, but then goes quiet. She's come to the same conclusion I just did. I think. With a bite of her lower lip, she nods once at me. I nod back and turn to Afton, sucking in a deep breath.

"Okay, Aft—"

Really? She's not paying even the slightest bit of attention to me. Afton only has eyes for the princess at the moment. Perhaps an actual higher power heard me. Maybe the Goddesses granted us mercy and made Afton forget everything she just said.

"Darling." Nayla folds her hands over Afton's shoulder and looks at her. "Your paramour needs nourishing for her body as well as her soul. Why don't we invite your friends to an evening dine...once they refresh their clothes, of course."

"Sure, why not?" Afton rubs a finger under Nayla's chin, and the princess coos in response. They spend a minute making googly eyes at each other while my blood pressure happily drops.

We'll have to explain ourselves eventually, but for now, the Goddess of mercy has granted us some extra time to figure it out.

Chapter Nine

I'm getting a little bored of opulence. It's so much effort for just a little aesthetic effect. We had it in abundant globs at the Chamberlin's offices and momentarily at the suite Kayley and I stayed in before we stupidly tried to escape. Then last night's dinner with Afton and Nayla was a hundred-plate feast of only the rarest delicacies of flora found anywhere in the Empire. At the end of that meal, all of us were so full, they could have rolled us back to our rooms.

Now we're just outside of Queen de Avila's throne room, awaiting our introduction. We slouch in chairs that are all form and no function, yet clearly expensive. Silver-coated bars form the frames, while clear crystal makes up the seats. All of it is trimmed with buttons of turquoise and hints of gold. The walls are upholstered with soft but elegant materials that add a little warmth, while long, semi-transparent fabrics drape from the ceiling. It's all very...useless. Give me my living room any day. At least that's comfortable.

"Her Royal Highness will see you now." A snooty man who calls himself the queen's High Wazir motions for us to stand. It's just the four of us, as Afton and Nayla have taken the day to go sightseeing, and Original Teddy elected to focus on his mission to observe humans other than us. The Teddys are amassing data on the Empire to upload to Teddynet so their entire species can better understand us, even if we don't understand ourselves. It's a good idea, at least in concept.

I groan as I stand. Last night's feast went late. Really late. And none of us, save Afton, are late sleepers. Add all the food we stuffed into our faces—to be fair, it was fantastic—and there was no way any of us was going to get a good night's sleep. I'm also a little nervous about meeting the queen. Even though the chief bodyguard said she's a fan of Kayley's, I wonder just what we're going to get.

The throne room is another study in wasteful spending. The queen's throne perches high up on a dais, which requires a plethora of stairs to reach. A long handmade rug runs the length of the room, starting from the entrance and rising to the throne, which is a sight in itself. Far from the torture devices of the Chamberlin's office, this throne is tall, sleek, and clean. It's made from what appears to be solid silver and inlaid with accents of gold and turquoise. I guess Canis Ludis has a lot of that particular mineral.

And in it, of course, sits the queen.

The relation to Nayla is obvious. Queen de Avila has the same oval face, and even though Her Majesty has seen more years, I can tell that she was quite the beauty queen in her younger days. But time hasn't been all that gentle to Her Majesty. Wrinkles crease her face, and her eyes droop, likely from years of political turmoil. Her nose, like her daughter's, is aquiline, but it ends in a beakish hook. The queen slouches forward in the throne, supporting herself with a bejeweled cane that peeks out from her black r obe.

"Your Majesty, may I introduce the representatives of his Imperial Majesty. These young people—"

"Behead them!" the queen shouts. "Remove their heads and return their bodies to the Emperor!"

The four of us gasp. We were expecting a challenge, but not this. We could have at least had a chance to try to complete our mission, but now we're done. Our young lives—

"No, no, Your Majesty," the High Wazir says. "You already dispatched those representatives. These are the new ones."

"New ones?" The queen squints and leans forwards. "How are they any different from the last ones?"

"Well, for one thing, Your Majesty, these still have their heads attached to their bodies."

"Hmm, yes, you're right. I see that." The queen thinks for a moment. "No, wait! They could be organizing a coup against me! Execute them at once!"

"There's no coup, Your Majesty. That was just a rumor. You've already beheaded the person who started it."

"Your Majesty." Kayley steps forward and curtsies in the way only someone who's done it a thousand times can do. It's as close to perfection as anyone could get. "The Lord Chamberlin sends you greetings and wishes that you are in good health."

"Bull feathers! Tyrwhitt only wishes to hurry me into my grave!"

"We have brought with us a selection of herbs and salves to elongate Your Majesty's life, as well as a significant tribute."

"Tribute?" The queen's eyes brighten. "Tell me more."

"I'm sorry, Your Majesty. I do not know the details of the tribute."

"I have already added it to Your Majesty's coffers," the High Wazir says, "and I am pleased to announce it is indeed a healthy sum."

The queen grins and rubs her fuzzy chin. So, the bribe worked. At least for now. I let out a barrel's worth of air from my lungs. We really dodged a comet there. Maybe she's not as nuts as the rumors make her out to be. Just insanely bloodthirsty.

"Excellent," Queen de Avila says. "Make sure there's no auto-return on the funds and execute this lot. Make sure you use the rusty guillotine!"

"Oh, not again," Parrish moans.

Now I understand the challenge that the Chamberlin has with her.

Kayley steps back into our row and slides closer towards me. I do the same. If we're really about to die, I want to be as close as possible to her when it happens. If we're going to meet the Goddesses, I hope we can do it together.

"But Your Majesty." The High Wazir intervenes on our behalf once again. "We can't kill them."

"What? Why not?"

"Because the Council would make a move to dismiss you. Perhaps permanently."

"Ha! I'd like to see them try."

The High Wazir gives us an apologetic look. He's well aware of his regent's shortcomings. Perhaps there's hope in that as well. If he knows how to manage her, we might just get out of this alive.

Not that I've ever wanted to rely on anyone other than my mom and my friends. Especially when it comes to the political spiderweb that is the

Empire. No one is to be trusted because everyone has their own agenda. That's why I fight for the regular people. They need protection from the self-absorbed aristocrats.

I'll do anything to protect my friends. Even sacrifice myself. Kayley might have something to say about that, and certainly I hope it hasn't come to that, but if it has, I'm ready.

"As your senior adviser, I recommend you reconsider, Your Majesty."

"Thank you. Your recommendation has been considered. Bring in the guillotine!"

The guards in the room drop their long spears at us, while a pair of them move to open a closet with doors that reach up to the ceiling. Not good. Either we're about to get kebob'd or chopped, and neither is a very happy ending for us.

The contraption is nearly as tall as the ceiling is high. From its top hangs a very large and, yes, rusty blade. Even in its dilapidated state, it still looks very capable of removing our heads from our bodies in one fell slice. That's the point of it, after all.

I'm considering falling down on my knees and begging for mercy. If it works, then I don't mind looking like a fool. The only other option would be to blackmail or threaten her, which, given our current circumstance, is a risky thing to do. That could backfire, and then I might get beheaded twice.

"KayKay," I whisper. "Any ideas here?"

"How about begging for mercy?"

"I was just thinking that."

"So, why aren't you on your knees? I promise, darling, I'd be right there with you."

"Why me first?"

"It's your idea."

They secure the guillotine in place and arm the trigger. Then the guards approach. I swallow hard, hoping they don't pick Kayley first. I grab her arm and pull her back behind me. Parrish does the same to Grady. I didn't expect any different from him. Just like me, he cares more for others than he does for himself. I don't want the guards to take him first, either. They shouldn't take any of my buds. I couldn't bear to watch that.

"Let's go! Bring the first one!"

The guards glance at me and Parrish, trying to decide which one would make the best victim of their death machine. If it were up to Parrish, he'd go first, but I just can't let that happen. Parrish is a better person than I am. If there's any chance of us living, he should be the one who's spared.

"Take me," I say, standing firm.

"No!" Kayley cries out, tugging on my arm. But I have to be brave. This is the best thing I can do for her.

The guards grab me by the arms. Kayley tries to fight them, but one of them shoves her back, and she falls. I harden my face and prepare to meet my doom. Perhaps if Kwanon, Durga, and Sophia welcome me to heaven, it won't be so bad. At least there won't be any more strife or danger. I'd just have to wait until Kayley joined me. After she lived a long, full life, of co urse.

Then Kayley does something unexpected. She rushes the dais, bounding up the stairs two at a time until she reaches the queen and drops herself down in front of her. The guards are so focused on me, they don't react before she makes it up there.

"Please! Your Majesty! Don't kill us! We are just simple people from Angelcanis! We know nothing about the Empire, and just want to live our lives in peace! Please, we mean you no harm!" Kayley sobs as she prostrates herself before the queen.

Queen de Avila raises a hand, halting her guards from dragging Kayley back down the stairs. She leans down, squinting to examine Kayley's fiery mane.

"Get up, girl," the queen says. Kayley raises herself into a kneeling position, trying to dry her eyes of tears.

The queen gapes and sits back.

"You...you're...Scarlett Kayley!"

If I could see Kayley's face, I bet she'd be blinking at the queen this very moment. It might be between tears, but she'd be as confused as I am. Does Queen de Avila have poor eyesight? She's supposed to be a big fan of Kayley's. How did she not recognize her?

Though, I'm happy that she did.

"What are you doing here, girl?"

"Well." Kayley wipes her nose with her forearm. "Just trying to make a living, Your Highness."

Queen de Avila sucks in a breath and places a hand over her chest. Then she tries to reach out to Kayley, but she completely misjudges the distance and winds up just pawing the air instead. I guess her eyesight really isn't all that great.

"So, you're not Tyrwhitt's pawn, then?"

"No, Your Highness." Kayley sniffles as she answers. "We just want to work."

I have to give it to my girlfriend. She's skillfully mixed her true feelings with some made-up ones to make her plight, and ours, all the more believable. Her tears are genuine, as are mine. I only realize I'm crying after I feel a tear run down my cheek. Parrish and Grady are teary-eyed too, but that's only going to help us.

"Oh, my dear," Queen de Avila says. "Of course you can. Release them!"

"Thank you, Your Majesty!" Kayley says, and she bows her head again to touch the queen's feet. Her Majesty's eyes might even be a little wet, too. The queen touches Kayley's head, then strokes it as if Kayley were her child.

"I can never be too careful with the Emperor. He and Tyrwhitt are always plotting against me. They may rule the Empire, but I rule this planet, and only *I* determine what happens here. Sure, they can try to manipulate me, but I know their tricks!"

I close my eyes and sigh. One more crisis averted. One more escape from death that we've pulled off. I'm as tired of this as I am of being manipulated by agents of the Imperial government. It has to stop.

"So, my dear," Queen de Avila says, smiling at Kayley, "you'll join me for lunch?"

Chapter Ten

WE'RE LOUNGING ABOUT IN Nayla's salon, which is just part of her corner of the palace that's got to be at least twice the size of my house. I'm no longer surprised about things like this, however. The only thing that still gets me is the fact that we're even welcome in a place like this.

Nayla's quarters differ somewhat from the standard royal configuration. She may have walls with figures finely carved into them, but she also has a ton of plants and not a few pets. This salon that we're in reminds me more of the Teddys' solarium than a palace. Plants grow everywhere, but at least they're managed and trimmed to accentuate the room. Her animals live placidly in this artificial jungle. If they're unhappy about that fact, they don't show it.

We told Afton and Nayla about our almost beheading, but neither of them seemed that concerned about it. I'm not surprised by Afton's response. I knew as long as we weren't dead, she'd be fine. But I am wondering why, as friends of her new love interest, Nayla isn't more concerned about our well-being. So, I ask her.

"Mother threatens to behead everyone. She loves that machine. I've tried to convince her of the dangers of desiring too much, but she has no ear for my advice. Our stars are in conflict."

If Nayla weren't a princess, her struggle with her mom would sound just like any other daughter's. Maybe that's why she and Afton connect so well. Neither of them get along with their mothers.

"So why did you have to have an audience with her, anyway?" Afton asks. "I mean, like, why are you guys here, exactly?"

"So you're not happy to see us?" Parrish asks, doing his best to fend off the inquiry.

"No! Don't jump to stupid conclusions."

We're right back to where we were yesterday. Afton's going to keep pushing until she gets an answer, and I'm not so sure that we're going to satisfy her with anything other than the truth. I catch Kayley's eye as she sits across from me, her legs folded under her. Her silent glance is enough for me to know she's working on it as fast as she can. I better get on it, too, since we didn't have a chance to come up with something yet. The dinner party went too late last night. We have mere seconds to answer.

Original Teddy is next to Kayley, but I don't need to share a look with him. Each of us already knows what the other is thinking. He might be able to help via Teddynet...or maybe he can just be a temporary diversion. Then we can have a few more moments to come up with a plan.

"Nutritional is recommended," Original Teddy says. It's enough. Afton blinks and looks at him with a frown.

"You just ate. We even found some live stuff for you to snack on."

"Abhorrent," Nayla says. "Have you never considered the souls you devour? They cannot complete their journey through the karmic wheel of fate if you abruptly end their lives."

"Teddy makes no termination. Anima is unblemished. Continuation of itinerary is possible."

The princess stares at Original Teddy, and Original Teddy stares back. She's trying to understand his statement. I'm happy to jump in and explain it to her, but I think I'll wait a few more seconds so that Kayley can have the time to plan.

"What Teddy is saying—" I say after a minute.

"Be quiet." Nayla throws a finger up at me. "I must meditate on this and conclude the answer on my own."

This time, I catch Afton's glance. She's as puzzled at Nayla's response as I am. Well, maybe not nearly as much. After a moment of watching Nayla sit with her eyes closed, Afton gets bored and shrugs it off.

Which means she's turned her attention back to us. Our time is up.

"Not really liking the way you guys are avoiding answering me. That's a good sign that you don't want to tell me something."

"No way," Grady says. "We're not keeping anything from you."

"You're a terrible liar, Grady."

"I am not lying!"

"Really? This is just like when you tried to tell me you didn't eat my hoppyberry jam, but there's no one else that could have done it."

"That's not true!"

"Grady, we're the only ones who live there!"

Grady sags, apologetic for his attempt to evade. Afton presses her lips together and sighs. I can tell she regrets yelling at him.

"Listen, dude," Afton says, her voice softer. "I don't care that you ate it, but just don't lie to me about it, okay? I'm not cool with liars, and neither is Nayla."

Oh, great. If we can't come up with an airlock-tight lie, we might as well tell the truth. At least there's a chance they won't even believe us. But Kayley hasn't come up with anything yet, and saying nothing is just as bad as lying.

"Kayley's pregnant!" The words just leave my mouth before I even consider what I am saying.

"Rance!" Kayley cries out, her mouth hanging open. Parrish smacks his palm on his head and shakes it. Grady stares at me like I just grew an entire tree from my head, and the one person I was targeting is completely unmoved.

"Hilarious," Afton says in a flat tone. "I don't think your girlfriend saw the humor in it, though."

"No, I did not!" Kayley shouts and glares at me.

"You will conceive a daughter and a son one day," Nayla says, her eyes still closed. "But today is not that day."

Afton gives me an *I told you so* smirk. She might have just won a point or two on me, but I'm not looking to win one game. I need to be champion of the entire tournament. Only then do we get away free and clear of damaging our relationship with her.

"I am glad you guys are here, though," Afton says, reaching out and taking Nayla's hand. "It's been great to spend time with you guys and Nayla."

"Afton, are you okay?" Parrish asks. That would be my question, too. She's not one for making mushy statements like that.

"I'm fine..." Afton shakes her head, then it hits her, and she rolls her eyes. "Give me a break, alright? Am I not allowed to be happy to have my buds and my...and Nayla all hanging out together? Come on. You guys know, this kind of thing *never* happens to me."

"Nor I, darling," Nayla adds and squeezes Afton's hand.

"I mean, this isn't the same as you"—Afton points at me—"and Kayley. All of us saw that coming a thousand light-years away. It was going to happen at some point. I mean, I helped it along a little, but there was no doubt in anybody's mind that it was meant to be. Just like me and Nayla. Except only Nayla knew it was going to happen. It's great, isn't it?"

Kayley sighs. Her shoulders slump, and she looks at me, her eyes heavy with regret. My arms begin to itch, and I'm not so sure I'm going to like what comes next.

"Afton, we have something to tell you," Kayley says, and the floor drops out from under me. No! she can't!

"Kayley, wait—"

But Afton's attention is already on her. She's smiling, oblivious to the fact that Kayley is about to crush her happy moment. I plead as hard as I can with my eyes, but she gives me that *trust me* look, and I feel like I really need to jump off the planet.

"We've been hiding the reason we came to Canis Ludis, because we were worried about how you would take it."

"What does that mean?" Afton shakes her head. "You can tell me any-thing. You know that."

"Well, it concerns Nayla...and her mother."

With that, Nayla's eyes snap open, and her head pivots like an artillery piece to pinpoint Kayley in her sights.

"What?" Afton's eyes are blank. She doesn't understand, but I think she fears the worst. So do I. Kayley's brought it out in the open, and there's no way to put this fire back in its lighter.

"Please understand, both of you. We had no choice. The Chamberlin—"

"What did you do?" Afton growls.

"Give her a chance, darling," Nayla says, but her gaze at Kayley is getting stony.

"We...we..." Kayley sighs. "We're here to spy on the queen. The Cham-berlin wants us to find out what she's planning for the next Council meeting and possibly convince her to end her embargo."

"You guys are spies for the Emperor?" Afton shoots up, a finger full of deadly accusation pointed right at us. "You accepted a mission like that when you knew how that could screw things up for me?"

"We didn't have a choice. They tricked us," I say.

"You can't tell the queen," Parrish implores. "She'll execute us."

"That much is obvious," Nayla says, "but you have betrayed our trust."

"And don't you think we feel horrible about that?" Grady asks. Afton turns to him, her breath getting faster.

"You could have let me know before you got here," Afton says. "And then you tried to avoid telling me the truth. That hurts, you know."

Despite the disappointment that I know Afton is feeling, this could be going a lot worse. I don't think there was any way to avoid hurting Afton, especially after we lied. We'll have to try to mend our relationship with her, but the immediate problem is Nayla. If she tells her mom, it's all over. No High Wazir is going to help us get out of that.

"I know, Afton," Kayley says, "and I'm sorry. We're sorry. We would never do anything to hurt you. I hope you can believe me. I know this must be an awkward time for you, but always know you are one of us. That will never change."

"Yeah? Well, it certainly feels like things have changed!" Afton stands up and paces around the daybed that she had been sitting on with Nayla. "Are you guys that jealous of my...of my girlfriend that you have to split us apart?"

"Whoa, whoa," Parrish says. "You're jumping to conclusions."

"Am I?" Afton's eyes get wet. Now we're in uncharted territory. I've never seen Afton cry before. To be fair, I was never dumb enough to do anything to make her cry. That would just end badly for both of us. She'd be upset, and I'd have a black eye.

"So, that's what that meant," Nayla says.

"What meant?" I ask.

"As I told you before, Ransom Quigley He', there are bad omens in your future. I have foreseen it."

"Does that mean you're going to tell your mom why we're here?"

"It does not. But Surela and I will not associate with you until your strife completes its cycle." Nayla stands. "I will not put my soulmate through that. It is her time to find her joy."

Nayla reaches out for Afton, who's wearing more of her heart on the outside than she ever has before. She goes to Nayla, taking her hand like a little girl would take the hand of a parent.

"Afton," Kayley says in a whimper. "Please, forgive us. Don't leave. We need you."

Afton turns to her, a tear falling down her cheek, despite the fact that her face is as hard as it always is when she's angry.

"No," Afton answers. "No. All I wanted was for you guys to accept Nayla, but you couldn't even do that right, could you? Why is it so hard for you to let me be happy?"

"Afton, no! That's not it at all," I say, standing. "We like Nayla! But the Chamberlin has us under his control! We had to agree to do this."

"And *you* especially," Afton replies. "After everything I've done for you. You screwed this one up, buddy. Don't expect me to forgive you."

All the drive I had to solve this disappears. The energy inside of me is gone, replaced with infinite despair. I suppose there wasn't any good way out of this. We hoped Afton would understand. Now we may have lost a friend, and we still have to make good on our mission. I don't see how we come back from this one with everything as it was before.

"You may show yourselves out," Nayla says. "From now on, I expect you to keep your distance from us."

And with that, they walk away.

Chapter Eleven

WE WALK ALONG THE avenue that leads from the palace to our quarters. The place we're staying is in no way connected to where Afton is staying, and that isn't lost on any of us. Every step we take away from our friend is a reminder of how painful that separation is. I only hope Afton understands that, too.

As usual, it's raining. The darkness of the evening sky does nothing to improve our mood, nor does the murky rain that falls down on us. It's as if the planet knows we screwed up and is making sure we don't forget it. Not for a moment.

At some point, Kayley just gives up and sits down in the middle of the road. No vehicles are coming, but it's still troubling. She's our de facto leader, and if she quits, where does that leave the rest of us? I ask her what's wrong, but she just waves me off.

"I'm fine," she says. "I just need a break."

"KayKay." I squat down next to her. "It's raining, and we've got no rain gear. You getting soaked isn't going to help anything."

"Just give me a moment," she responds, biting her lower lip and hugging her knees to her chest. "Just a moment, then we can go."

I look to Parrish and Grady for help, but they're just as lost as I am. I've no idea if this is the end of our friendship with Afton, and I don't want to even consider that possibility. We've been friends for eight years. Add a few more years and that's nearly half my life. The hardest part of my life, too, and Afton was there for all of it. Losing her now would be like removing half my organs and trying to live as if I was unaffected.

As we have no care that black rain is soaking us to the bone, it's obvious that nothing is normal at all. Even Original Teddy, who should have come with us, hung back in the palace. I don't get the impression from Teddynet that anything is wrong, but it still makes everything feel totally broken.

"It's not going to help us complete the mission if we get sick," Grady says, hugging his arms about himself.

"True," Parrish says. "We've got to get the information the Chamberlin wants, then we can try to fix things with Afton. She's not going to just walk away from us after one little misunderstanding."

"Dude, are you kidding?" I wrap my own arms about myself. There is a chill in the air. "We can't just let this situation slide. The longer we wait, the farther she's going to get from us."

"No way," Parrish responds. "Not Afton. She may be angry now, but just wait until tomorrow. She'll be back to the same Afton she always was."

"Didn't you see her face?" Kayley asks with a sniffle. "Afton was crying! She never does that! We hurt her badly, Parry, at a time when she was already vulnerable, trying to form a relationship with Nayla. Imagine meeting the love of your life and wanting nothing more than your friends to accept that person. Then imagine those friends not doing what you really hoped they would. Don't you think that's going to hurt?"

"Why did you tell her, KayKay?" I ask. "She was already in a good mood, and we could have just let her question slide."

"When has Afton ever let something slide when she asked a second time? No, we had to tell her."

"No, we didn't," Grady says. "We could have come up with anything that was better than the truth. Afton wouldn't have cared if we were here to stand around and pick our noses. She just wanted us to accept her and Nayla as a couple."

"We did that," Parrish says. "When did we make Nayla feel like an outsider? If she felt that way, that's on her."

"She felt like an outsider the moment we told her we were spying on her mom," I say. "Before that, she was no different than any of us."

"Well, she is a *little* different," Grady corrects.

"So, what do we do now?" Parrish asks. "I still think the mission is a bigger priority. If we can stay alive for the next three weeks, and do what the Chamberlin wants, then we'll have the rest of our lives to get Afton back. If we make Afton the priority, we won't be alive long enough to enjoy our effort. Besides, guys, my mom isn't getting any better. She's going to need me to care for her around the clock soon enough."

"Don't say that," Kayley says. "Think positive, Parry. No one can determine her exact future."

Kayley shivers, and I wrap my arms around her. It's not just about sharing warmth, though. Both problems have shaken us hard, and we all need a little emotional support. Perhaps that's why Parrish and Grady move close to us, too. The rain is only getting harder.

I don't know what's best at this moment. It should be obvious, but it's not. Afton, walking away like she did, was a surprise. She'd usually just punch me in the chest, and that would be the end of it. But Afton's never been in love before. At least I don't think she has. Not like this. It's all happened so fast, but maybe that's because she was ready for it to happen. Only time will tell if the two of them will stay together. I'd be happy if they did, because that's what I want for all of my buds. To be as happy as Kayley and I are together.

"This is mostly my fault," I say as my head drops. "I should never have believed that woman would give us what I asked for."

"What did you ask for...exactly?" Parrish asks.

"Well, she offered it, technically. To clear our records of any criminal mischief or complaints."

"Oh."

"That, and a million jorin."

"Did you think we'd actually get that much?" Parrish asks, the tone of his voice making me feel as if I'm a child getting yelled at by my father. I've had enough of that for a lifetime. No one gets to tell me what to do. "And by the way, you never mentioned that to us."

"*Yes.* Actually, I did," I growl. "They needed us more than we needed them, and what they were offering seemed way worth whatever risk we had to take. And sorry for not telling you. I had a lot on my mind, okay?'

"And that didn't tell you something? Didn't you get clued into the fact that they were just trying to trick you?"

"And what about me, Parry?" Kayley asks, her eyes narrowing. "I had an *official invitation* from Parliament! Do you think I was stupid or naïve to accept that?"

Parrish opens his mouth, then closes it. He knows not to challenge Kayley about that. She never said much about the situation, but I know getting tricked like that must have had crushed her. And Bailiff Daughtry rubbing it in didn't help, either.

"This is stupid," Grady says, wiping the wet mop of hair from his face. He turns and paces, shaking his head. "We're out here in this nasty rain, getting who knows what kind of contamination into our systems, worrying about things we're never going to solve. This is such a waste of time."

"So then go to the hotel, if you think there's no point in trying," Parrish says, his face hard.

Grady stops his pacing to give Parrish a grimace that lingers. Maybe, at one time, before his parents' trial, Grady would have broken down. But not anymore.

"Oh, let's just go to bed, and everything will be fine in the morning? Are we even on the same planet right now?"

"Don't you see me getting wet, just like everyone else?"

"I see you, but I can't believe what is coming out of your mouth. You were barely there while my parents were on trial. Now you expect to just fix all our issues by saying 'don't worry about it'? Forget it, dude, you're not even in the same galaxy as we are!"

"Hey, do you think you're the only one that's had trouble with their parents?"

"Enough!" Kayley shouts. "You want to compare who's got the worst problems? Why don't you think about Afton, then? Her best friends just destroyed any possibility her girlfriend would fit in with them! Don't you think that's what she really wanted? Acceptance from us? And what did we do?"

Kayley trembles against me. She's angrier than I thought, but after what she just said, I'm struggling to be sympathetic.

"You mean, what did *you* do, KayKay?" I say. She turns to me with a smoldering glare.

"I did what I thought was right. Did you just want to keep lying to her? Yes, she's hurt, but we would have shattered her if we kept up our deception."

"Yeah, but now she thinks we don't care about Nayla. If we had the chance to show her we were willing to welcome her into our group, maybe she wouldn't have taken it so hard. Especially after we finished the mission."

I can see in Kayley's eyes that she hadn't considered that angle. But there's still conflict there. She doesn't agree with me. Not fully. I never claimed I had all the answers. I just don't understand why she thought telling Afton the truth was the right thing to do at that moment.

"You think you know best? Fine." Kayley stands. "I already told you, Rance. You don't know Afton as well as you think you do."

"I don't? She's been a..." I let my words drop off.

"Been a what?" Kayley folds her arms. "A better friend to you than I have? Yeah, go on, say it. That's what you want to say, isn't it?"

"KayKay, no." I sigh, my shoulders slumping. "That's not what I want to say."

"Then what?"

I drop my gaze. Kayley may be on the offensive, but I hurt her with my statement of the facts. Now my attempt to explain has turned into a global catastrophe. Nobody is happy with the situation we're facing. There is no way to avoid the torrent falling down around us. We'll have to just get through it, using whatever strength and courage we can scavenge. What happens after that is anyone's guess.

I look up at her, to let her see inside my mind. The moment our eyes connect, so do our psyches, and Kayley softens. She inhales, tightening her jaw to hold back tears that are ready to overflow. It's not me that's making her feel that way. It's the situation—one we've never been in before. We may die, or we may lose our friend forever.

"Guys." I motion to Grady and Parrish to join us. Both of them have distanced themselves from each other, not wanting to argue any more, but not willing to concede, either. "Let's not do this. Please? We need each other to get through this, and we're already down one man."

"Woman," Kayley corrects. I acknowledge this with a nod.

"We're missing a serious chunk of our team, and if we're fighting now, we won't survive this. So could we, please, for our sakes and Afton's, get this mission out of the way so we can focus on what's really important?"

"Getting Afton back," Kayley says.

"Getting Afton back," Grady echoes.

We turn to Parrish, the one member of our team who's been in denial about what we need to do, if only because he's got someone at home to worry about. His mom is his only family, and if he loses her, he'll have nobody. His father has been long gone from his life, and he's got no brothers or sisters, or any other family that he knows about. Perhaps that's why he prefers team sports over individual competitions. He just wants to feel connected to something.

"Alright," he says, pounding his fist into his open hand as I've seen him do during games. "Let's get this done so we can get our priorities in place."

"Great," Grady says, his teeth chattering. "Can we go inside now? I'm soaked."

Chapter Twelve

The next morning, we have a small bit of luck. A taxi is willing to take us all the way to the industrial quarter of Os, the second-largest and most dangerous city on Canis Ludis. Our destination is the ill-reputed Sin & Bone, a bar and nightclub that is notorious in our minds. We've come here to hopefully find a few familiar faces and start our investigation of Queen de Avila.

The nightclub we're about to infiltrate is the home base for all the hand-hunters in the Empire. They come here to find new jobs, wind down after a difficult hunt, or just trade war stories with their fellow hunters. It's a trade-only bar, so unless you're a hand-hunter or a prospective client, you can't get in.

To get around that minor issue last time, we played the part of marriage hopefuls. It worked, but this time we need to find an instant connection to the members inside the club. They'd let us in if we told them we're looking to hire someone, but the hand-hunters wouldn't speak to us about anything other than a hunt.

This time we're going undercover. We're going in as hand-hunters.

From my very distinct memory of my first encounter with Danny Lecker, one such infamous hand-hunter, I put together an outfit I thought would make me look the part. Grady went to a theatrical supply shop and found himself a cool overcoat and top hat, while Parrish just ripped the sleeves off his shirt and left it unbuttoned.

But out of all of us, Kayley is the one really killing it. In her high-heeled boots, PVC pants, and high ponytail she really looked the part. The military jacket we scrounged from a surplus store was just the perfect final addition. As long as she puts her acting skills to good use, no one will question her legitimacy at all.

"Hey, welcome!" the doorman says as we approach. "Haven't seen you four here before. Where are you from?"

Kayley drops her sunglasses down to stare at him, transmitting as much annoyance at being stopped as she can. The attitude is part of our deception. We don't want him recognizing us from last time. It was also night when we were here. Now the sun is just breaking over the industrial towers and kilometers of conduit that surround the area.

"Nowhere you've heard of," she says, pouring on the hand-hunter charm. "Any work inside?"

"Not this early in the morning, but take a load off and relax. The hopefuls will be here soon enough."

We were hoping to avoid the hopefuls, actually. Once they show up, the hand-hunters won't want to talk shop anymore. They'll be vying to catch a man for the next determined bride who walks in. It's been the tradition for hand-hunters to catch grooms, but I've heard they've been diversifying lately and will accept almost any job, save for hunting female brides for men. Most hunters are female, so I guess they object to that kind of thing. So do I. Those guys should just put in the time and find a bride on their own. After all, that's how it was before that princess hired the very first hand-hunter and snagged the man she'd been after.

"Who should we talk to first?" Grady asks as he peers around at the handful of patrons. The space hasn't changed, from the questionable stains on the floor to the burn marks on the wall. It's still dank, dark, and smelly. From the looks of it, they recycled everything in here by stealing it out of the trash.

"How about her?" I nod at a tall blond nursing a stiff drink at the bar.

Kayley doesn't wait for anyone to respond. She saunters right up to the woman and gives her a friendly greeting. We take up a position close by so we can hear their discussion.

"So how's biz?" Kayley asks.

"Never better," the blond woman replies. Her flat tone makes it obvious that the opposite is true.

"That bad, hunh? It's because of the queen, isn't it?"

The glare that flashes is a clear sign she asked the wrong question. The blond3274 puts her drink down on the bar and faces Kayley.

"What are you, new here?"

"Kinda," Kayley replies, losing her smile. "Is that not it, then? Because I heard—"

Kayley yelps as the woman grabs her by the collar of her jacket and lifts her up. Parrish jerks into action, but I throw my arm out and stop him from causing a scene. We're here to get information, not to destroy the place. We almost did that last time.

"Listen here, sister. Queen de Avila is the best thing that's happened to us, so get any thought out of your little head that she's the problem."

"Okay," Kayley squeaks.

"What's your name?"

"Kayley?"

"Cute name. You just starting out?"

"Uh, yeah."

The blond stares at her for a moment, then puts her down. She straightens Kayley's jacket and brushes her hair back into place. Kayley stays frozen the entire time. Then she pats my girlfriend on the cheek, grabs her drink, and walks away.

"Good luck, then," she calls over her shoulder. "Might want to get a bit more meat on those bones, though."

Kayley turns to us, still petrified from her encounter. I slide over to her, trying to balance my concern for her well-being with my feeble attempt to look as cool as the real pros here. When my hand touches her arm, she grabs it and squeezes.

"Okay, I totally misjudged that one," Kayley says with a slow sigh.

"Yeah, but consider it a successful test of your disguise," Grady replies.

Parrish glances around the room, spots something that catches his eye, and pushes himself off the bar.

"Hey," I hiss. "Where are you going?"

"Let me try this guy over here." Parrish saunters to a darkened corner. There's a guy there, dressed somewhat similarly to Parrish but with a military-style utility vest. He stands as Parrish approaches, an amiable smile coming to his face.

We wait in anticipation as they talk, hoping that Parrish doesn't get nervous like Kayley did. I don't blame her, though. This is really new territory for us, and there's a lot riding on our success, namely our lives, if we don't get what the Chamberlin wants. We're way more uptight than we usually are.

It doesn't take long for the conversation to finish up. The man laughs and pats Parrish on the shoulder as he shakes his head. He laughs again and returns to his seat. Parrish returns to us, defeated.

"What happened, Parry?" Kayley asks.

"Sorry, guys. I tried a different tack by asking if Princess Nayla was hiring. You saw the result of that."

"Okay, my turn," I say, focusing my attention on an older woman quietly minding her own business in a booth. She's got her knitting needles out and is quickly forming what I guess could be a sweater. She's probably making something for a grandchild, and anyone who is thinking kindly about another person has got to talk to me. Yes. I've got a good feeling about her.

"Not a chance, kid," she says as I approach. "Just turn around and walk away. I'm busy."

"I just wanted to ask you about what you're knitting."

"It's a sweater. For my grandson. If you want to ask questions, my rifle would be more than happy to talk to you for a few rounds."

Well, there goes that. We've apparently got a lot to learn about hand-hunters. Here I thought we were already experts, given our madcap exposure to one Danny Lecker.

As I turn to head back to my buds, I fail to see someone approaching and bump them head-on.

"Watch it, buddy! You want—"

I take a step back, cringing. I've got my hands up in a half-apologetic, half-defensive posture.

"Well, well, hello there, precious. Didn't expect to see you ever again. You married yet?"

It's Ms. Cool, aka Billie Morgan. We met her last time we were here, when we needed to get a security code that would get us onto Exodus, the prison station.

"Uh, not exactly," I reply with not a bit of hesitancy. I don't want a repeat of our last meeting. She tried to snag me for one of her clients and zapped me so hard with her stunner that I nearly vomited. She let me go when I told her Kayley and I were getting married, then gave us the code as a wedding present. I hope she won't be too disappointed that the wedding hasn't happened yet.

"Billie!" Kayley says as she comes over with Grady and Parrish, hopefully interrupting any thoughts Ms. Cool might be having about zapping me again.

"Well, hello." Billie gives her a once-over, nodding with approval. "Lookin' good, honey. Joining up, are we?"

"Not exactly," Kayley replies with an apologetic smile. Billie just chuckles.

"That's what your husband-to-be said. Do the two of you really need any more reason?" Then she narrows her eyes and pulls out her stun gun. "Or can I consider you two on the open market?"

"No! No! We've got plans!"

Billie wrinkles her nose, and her gaze lingers on me a second more before she moves on to Grady and Parrish, looking at them as if they're a lesser option. But Parrish catches her eye, and she pivots to face him.

"You married, Tall, Dark, and Handsome?"

"No," Parrish says, a small grin coming to his face. Maybe Billie isn't the only one who sees something they like.

"He's not for sale!" Kayley says and pushes Parrish back before the conversation can continue.

"So then, what *are* you kids doing here besides irritating my colleagues? And this better be good."

"We're here spying on the queen," I say to the horror of my buds.

"Oh? Do tell." Ms. Cool's response is way more relaxed than I would have expected. It's as if she's intrigued by the idea more than anything. Kayley picks up on it right away and leans in to whisper to Billie.

"Do you not like Queen de Avila?" she asks.

"I've nothing against her personally." Billie shrugs. "I've hung out with her daughter a few times. Goddesses, what a party girl she is."

"Wait, you know Nayla?"

"I do, and why are you saying her name like you're her best friend?"

"Our friend, Afton? You met her last time. Uh, she's kinda dating her."

"Look at that girly go! Good for her." Billie shrugs, but smiles. "Good for the both of them. Now wait—if you know the princess, why are you down *here* scrounging for information?"

"We couldn't exactly tell her we were spying on her mom," I explain.

"So that part is true? You kids are really doing something as dumb as that?"

"We kind of got tricked into it," Kayley mutters. "Now it's get the info or lose your life."

"Yeah, I've been there before." Billie puts her hands on her hips and glances around at the four of us. I can't tell if it's with pity, disbelief, or mild disgust. Perhaps it's all three. "What do you need to find out?"

We go over to her regular booth and explain the situation. Billie nods, slowly making circles around her chin with a finger while she listens. Kayley, perhaps needing to let some emotion out, tells her all the background behind it, too. How we took down Cecelia Nilsson-Lim, a parliamentary member, and the head of the Anti-Sedition Ministry, catching the Chamberlin's attention.

"Mighty impressive, kiddies. You sure you don't want to join us? We could protect you."

"Thanks, but after spending all that time with Danny, I think we're good," I reply.

"I thought I told you never to say that name in here again."

"Yeah, I forgot."

"Nobody forgets Danny Lecker, precious. I'm going to tell her you said that."

"Please don't."

"Fine, I won't, but I will do this for you. I might have a connection at the palace that could get you into the stuff you need. It'd be risky, of course, but you already guessed that. Give me some time to make the connection, and I'll get you hooked up...for a fee, of course."

"How much time? In three weeks, we're going to get our heads chopped off," Grady says.

"Don't worry, Gadget Man, Billie Morgan is very good at what she does."

Chapter Thirteen

"KayKay, are you sure you want to just ask anyone like that again?"

Kayley glances at me, but continues her confident stride into the market. Since we were way off the mark about the willingness of the citizens here to talk about their queen, we've come here to get a better feel for what people think of her.

The market is enormous, spanning an area that would cover all the houses in my neighborhood. That's like two hundred homes, plus their property! I think it must be possible to buy anything you could dream of here. Well, maybe not people. That's punishable by death anywhere in the Empire. Even on the colony planets.

The municipal division of the queen's court subdivides the market into seven sections, each with its own arrangement. Some are on a straight grid, like the produce market and the, yuck, meat market. Others are a bit more...organic, but also more interesting. From one section comes aromas of all kinds of spices from around the Empire, harmonious sounds from exotic musical instruments, and colorful textiles from every culture to delight the eye. Of course, we head there first, as far away from dead animal as we can get.

Our agreement was only to do some light shopping, meandering from stall to stall while we eavesdrop on the conversations around us. But in the last few minutes, Kayley's taken it on herself to rectify her impulsive mistake at the Sin & Bone.

I'm worried.

"Don't worry," Kayley says. "These are just normal people not trained in fighting, and I know better than to be direct like that again."

"I'm not worried," I say with a shrug.

"Yes, you are. I know that look, Rance. You can't lie to me."

"I'm not lying!"

Kayley just eyes me and continues walking down a row of stalls stuffed with piles of handmade carpets. She's pretending to admire all of their intricate designs when she comes across an old man sipping on tea from a dented metal cup.

"Welcome to Os!" he says and chuckles. I think I can guess why. Few tourists here. They usually keep to the capital or head south down to the islands and warmer weather.

"This one is nice...how much?" Kayley asks, rubbing her fingers across the fabric. The old man squints, then stands up to get a better look at the item in question.

"Ah, that one. Nice choice. From the Cilveki peoples of Pruinonis. The fibers come from tree bark. Very resilient. Two thousand five hundred jorin for that one."

Parrish gasps, and Kayley throws him a glare. He gets his negotiation mistake instantly and excuses himself by pointing at another stall across the way. Grady follows. It's probably better for us to split up, anyway. All we're doing is passive investigation, so we won't be getting into any dangerous situations. I hope.

"Hmm." Kayley looks at the rug again. "Any taxes?"

"Nope, all the stuff in the market is sales-tax-free, thanks to Her Majesty."

"Wow, your monarch is a generous woman."

"Indeed. I tell you what, just for that, I'll knock off two fifty for you."

Well, this guy won't be slandering his queen. Discounting his price just for complimenting her? He is without question a loyal subject. We should get moving on to the next merchant. Any more time spent with him is going to waste. I nudge Kayley in the small of her back to get her away.

"Is she really that generous, though?" Kayley asks, kind of like a journalist interviewing a local politician, trying to get the inside scoop.

"What do you mean?" The old man scowls, looking suspicious of her intentions.

"Well, it's just that off-world, there's a rumor that she's psychotic. That it's really the High Wazir that runs the planet."

He snorts and waves a dismissive hand at her.

"There's nothing insane about our queen, young lady. Except that she's not willing to just kiss the feet of the Emperor every time he says 'bow.' I'd be careful with that kind of talk around here. Some of us Osers are not all that patient with insults to Her Highness. Now, are you buying or what?"

I poke Kayley again, but she swats my hand away from her back. She's determined to get this old guy to say something he won't, and I have no idea why. Is she being hard on herself because she made a mistake?

"How about I tell *you* what?" she replies, and I scan around for Parrish and Grady, just in case we need to make a quick exit. After just our first conversation, too. "I'll pay you three thousand jorin for the rug, and for the truth about how you really feel about the queen."

The old man pulls away from her, the shock of her offer clear on his face. He stares at her, open-mouthed, as if Kayley had just stolen his money. His arm goes up, and he gags.

"Okay, maybe this isn't the rug you were looking for, honey," I say and make a nervous chuckle. "Let's go look at a few other stalls, hunh?"

My arm goes around Kayley's waist, and I pull her away from the old man as fast as her feet will allow me to.

"Now you wait just a minute!" he shouts at our backs. I look back to see him slam his teacup on the ground and point a shaky finger at us. At least now I know why his cup is dented. "You off-worlders are all the same! You think you can just come here and lay judgment down on our queen...our beautiful queen, because you heard some rumor?"

"No, of course not!" I reply with a smile, attempting to deescalate the situation. "Forgive her. She must just be hungry."

"Hey Alec, everything alright?" Another merchant comes around the corner. He's younger than the previously named Alec, and he looks even less inclined to accept insults about Queen de Avila.

"Hell no, everything's not alright. Those damn tourists just insulted the queen!"

"Rance, let's go," Kayley whispers, a tremor coming to her voice. I quickly nod in agreement.

We turn to head down a side row, but there's a woman there blocking the way. She mashes her lips together as she folds her arms. Great, another one who's coming to Alec's defense.

There's only one way left for us to leave from, and there's already two men walking down that path in our direction. They're not aware of the situation, but in just a few seconds, they will be. Parrish and Grady have disappeared, and now it's just the two of us against five angry locals. They may just be merchants, but we're not about to take them on except with a few choice words like "I'm sorry" and "We're leaving the planet right now and never coming back."

If only Afton were here, we'd be in a much less precarious situation.

Kayley grabs my hand and takes off, heading straight for the approaching men. I stumble but keep my balance and follow. Not that I have a choice. She'd likely drag me away from here if she had to.

"Hey, stop those two!" Alec shouts after us as we race away. The two men stop, staring at us to assess what danger we represent. Then Alec shouts, "They said they hate the queen!"

"We said no such thing!" Kayley shouts back as we fly past the two men.

"Then stop!" one of them says.

"Nope!"

One of them curses, and I glance back. Yep, they're giving chase, alright. Why does this keep happening to us?

I spy a row with lots of tall woven baskets and tug Kayley that way. Maybe we can hide behind a stack until they pass by. Or even hide in one of them. No. That's a bad idea. We have no idea where one of those might end up. Behind will do.

"We're losing them," Kayley says, breathless.

And that's when I feel something wet hit my back. It wasn't hard, so it's not a bullet or a dart, thank the Goddesses. But whatever it is, it's dripping down my back.

Kayley yelps and jerks forward. She's hit, too.

"Get 'em again, Sam! Get 'em again!" the woman shouts. I turn back to see three men aiming slingshots at us. They release, and before I can dodge it, a round white rock splats on my head.

No, not a rock.

"Rance!" Kayley cries. "Are you hurt? What is that?"

Then she squeaks as one hits her shoulder, breaks, and releases its gooey yellow contents all over her hair and face.

"Eggs. Bird eggs."

"Oh, yuck! Disgusting!"

We get pelted a few more times before we skid around a corner and find an empty stall to duck down in. I pull Kayley under the counter, and we squeeze into the small space, pressed together. Arms, legs, bodies...and eggs.

Kayley stares at me, breathing hard. I look back, wanting to clean the yolk splatter from her face, but also not wanting to touch anything that belongs to the embryo of an animal. It's not supposed to be there, on her face like that. It should be whole, in a nest, growing baby birds inside of it.

"That...that was so inhuman of them. How could they do that?" Kayley breathes rapidly, on the verge of tears. Not for the fear of our safety, but for the wanton destruction of life evidenced all over us.

"Well, I think it's because you pushed too hard, KayKay. We've got to let these people talk to us on their own terms. We can't force them to tell us what we want."

"I know, I know...I was stupid." Kayley looks down. "This whole thing with Afton's really got me off my good senses."

"Me, too."

Kayley meets my eyes. "We really got to get her back, Rance. Afton's never been in a serious relationship before. She needs our support."

There are shouts from somewhere nearby. I put my hand up to signal quiet as footsteps pound past our stall. They pause and come back, stopping somewhere nearby. Shoot. They know we're around here. All they have to do is peek into the stall to find us.

"You find them?" a man says.

"No, but we got them good, didn't we?" another replies.

"We sure did." The first man laughs. "They won't show their faces around here again."

"Serves them right! Come on, let's go tell Alec we avenged our queen!"

Their footsteps race off, and Kayley and I share a sigh, and then a hug, even though we're basically embracing already, squashed as we are in this tiny space. At least those merchants weren't looking to do us any more harm than some minor humiliation. It's not like they knew we were vegetarians.

Goddesses, I'm going to have nightmares about this.

Chapter Fourteen

WE'RE ABLE TO CONTACT Parrish and Grady via Sergo, but they aren't able to figure out where we are, and we can't find them, either. So we decide just to meet back at our hotel. Kayley and I need to change, anyway. Walking around soaked in bird embryo is not fun.

Kayley tries her best to be upbeat with me, but her mind is on Afton just like mine is. We've only begun looking for information, but keeping our heads in place is only part of our challenge. Without Afton in our lives, having heads doesn't seem all that exciting.

"Good afternoon, sir. Lady." A young woman clasps her hands together and smiles sweetly at the two of us as we pass by her booth. She's about our age, so I'm curious as to why she's addressing us with honorifics. "What brings you by today?"

"Uh, we're just passing by," Kayley replies, the sizzle in her voice hinting at her lack of patience for talking to anybody at the moment.

"Oh? Where you headed in such a hurry?"

"Back to our hotel."

"Where are you staying?"

"The Capitol District," I answer, as Kayley wasn't about to bother. She's already turning to walk away.

"Well. That's quite a ways away." Her eyes drop to examine my clothes, then dart over to Kayley's. She must spot something about us, because her mood changes, and her sweet smile transforms into an edgy grin for just a split second.

"What?" I step in between her and Kayley, going on the defensive.

"I see you've upset some royalists. Let me guess, you asked one of them if our queen is crazy. Am I right?"

"How'd you know that?" Kayley spins around.

"You're not the first tourists to make that mistake." Her grin gets a little wider. "Sorry about that, but some of the old-timers are a little sensitive when it comes to Her Majesty. She's been queen for most of their adult lives."

She just apologized for what the other merchants did. That must mean she's either not a royalist, or—and this would be absolute luck on our part—she doesn't like the queen at all. I can't be certain, but a few more questions should be able to uncover that.

"Thank you!" Kayley must've come to the same conclusion I did because she gets in front of me and beams at the woman. "I'm Kayley."

"Nice to meet you, Kayley. I'm Sara."

"What do you think of the queen?"

Oh, no. When Kayley said her sense was off, she must have meant it's gone to another dimension. Why, after all we just went through, would she try the direct tactic for a *third time*? I cringe and prepare to snatch Kayley's wrist and drag her to safety. We're going to have a long talk after this.

"You guys must really be uncomfortable in those clothes," Sara says. "Why don't you come into the shop? I can recommend some nice local outfits for you that I think you'll like..."

Kayley raises her hand and gets ready to decline. Good. She's not lost all of her brain cells yet.

"And we can talk inside, too. I've tea on," Sara adds after a slight pause. I get it. There's privacy inside, which means we can talk without worrying about egg projectiles.

I go to put Kayley's hand down, but she's already done it. More reasonable action from my girlfriend when just a moment ago she might have put us in jeopardy again. I'm okay with giving her a little leniency to decide what to do. Just as long as we don't have to go running for our lives again.

"Sure," Kayley says, back to her chipper mood. I'm sure both of us would be glad to get this slop off our backs. Besides being nasty, it's drawing attention to us. Unfriendly attention. We might have just gotten humiliated, but I'd hate to learn what the locals do to people that really make them angry.

"Wonderful!" Sara claps her hands together and does a little hop. "Business hasn't been all that great lately, to be honest."

We follow her inside, and she immediately begins shuffling through a rack of women's clothes. Most are similar to what she's wearing—a long tunic with a matching pair of loose pants that look a bit short. Sara glances back at Kayley and chews on her lip, then moves to another rack and rifles through that.

Kayley is intrigued. It's not something she'd wear normally, but my girlfriend could look good wearing an old towel. I think she's just happy to get her mind back to something more normal than trying to stay alive. I'm certainly welcoming the diversion.

"So, I would have thought most people here would be loyal to the queen," Kayley says, using more tact than she's done all day.

"Oh, most are," Sara replies, pulling an outfit from the rack and putting it up against Kayley. She nods and hangs that on a side rack, then grabs another and repeats her motions.

"Are you one of those? Or are you—"

"Why don't you try those two on?" Sara motions to a small dressing space just behind the racks. "I think those would match your skin tone nicely, don't you think?"

"Uh." Kayley has to look them over again, but smiles once she does. "Yeah, I do."

"Great, then why don't you do that while I try to find something for your...husband?"

"Oh, we're not married," I say, feeling like I've had to refute that too often recently. Kayley and I have been discussing it, and she's not bothered by it, so maybe it's just the overabundance of questioning that has been irritating me.

"Really?" Sara asks with eyebrows lifted. I think it's more of a surprised comment than a hopeful question. Whatever. I'm already taken, but if we could have used that to our advantage, I'd bet Kayley would be more than willing to let a few flirtatious comments slide by. Just as long as I didn't get too into it.

"So Sara, you said before that business wasn't good for you. How come?" I ask as I look around the booth. "It seems like you've got a wide selection here."

"Sure I do." Sara shrugs. "But ever since our taxes increased, people don't have as much to spend anymore."

Whoa, that's interesting. So people are unhappy because the queen is taking a bigger bite from their paychecks? That could be an angle we could use to get past that solid wall of royalist denial. People might not be willing to criticize the queen directly, but they might criticize her policies if pressed a little.

I wonder if Kayley heard that. She comes out of the dressing nook and catches my eye. She's come to the same conclusion. A second later, Kayley switches gears, and an excited smile comes to her face.

"So, what do you think?"

"Looks great!" I don't even have to pretend. If it weren't for her scarlet hair, Kayley could fit in well as a local. Sara's got fair skin like she does, so I think it wouldn't take much to disguise her as one.

"I'm going to try the other one!" Kayley says, but she stops before she heads back into the nook and turns to Sara. "So sorry to hear things are tough for you."

"Yeah, thanks," Sara replies. She runs her hands through her hair and sighs.

"Why did the taxes go up, by the way? Isn't the economy good, especially with all the exports off-planet?"

"Well, the rumor was that Her Majesty purposely cut back, just so we weren't reliant on the Imperial military for much of our income. I'm sure there's more to it, but I don't know. I just sell clothes."

So the embargo is affecting the locals, too. I wonder if they realize they're victims of a political play. Someone at court will know more, but we'll have to tread lightly there. Our one in evaporated overnight, and the princess won't come back around so easily. She's got plenty of reason to dislike us. We have to get back and strategize with Parrish and Grady. Maybe they found something out, too.

"Here," Sara says and presses a pair of pants and a matching shirt with fabric buttons on me. "I think this would look good on you."

Her eyes have a new level of intensity about them, and I wonder if we're walking into a trap. Is she really a royalist and about to turn us over to her friends for a week's worth of humiliation? Does that mean what she just told us isn't true?

"The other one is better," Kayley says as she comes from the changing area. Her eyes fall on the garments I have in my hands and appraises them.

With a nod, she puts a hand on my shoulder and moves me towards the nook.

The changing area isn't much more than a curtain that blocks off a closet space with no door. And the curtain doesn't close all the way. Kayley and I have changed in front of each other before, so I'm not bashful about that. It wouldn't bother me to change in front of Sara, either, but it might bother Sara, and we don't want to upset her.

As I take off my dirty clothes, the sound of scraping composites makes me jump. Then I realize it's just Kayley browsing the racks of clothes. I bet she's just trying to keep Sara focused on trying to sell us stuff while she grills her for information.

"You know, it's funny you should mention that your queen wants her people to be less reliant on military exports to the Empire. I heard a rumor that she was about to pull out an ultimatum at the next council meeting. I wonder if that's what it is."

"Oh? Where'd you hear that?" Sara tries to keep her voice from rising, but a few words get away before she brings it back down to its normal pitch.

"Oh, I know someone in the Chamberlin's office," Kayley replies, her tone casual. I can't help but smile. Kayley's lifetime of being onstage started when she was only four. She had a tiny part in a local play, but supposedly she stole the show. Of course, I don't remember it, but I have one of the promotional photos of the cast with her front and center in the image. No way this clothes merchant is going to beat her in a game of "let's pretend."

"Wow, you guys must be aristocracy, then."

"No way." Kayley chuckles. "But my parents have some connections. Have you heard anything like that's going to happen?"

I draw back the curtain and exit the nook. Both ladies turn to look, their eyes lighting up. I guess I don't look like a complete fool, then.

"Not too tight?" Sara asks, avoiding Kayley's question.

"No, not at all." I pretend to pull at the fabric, but I'm focused on determining if Sara is being honest with us. If she isn't, we'd better change back and get out as fast as possible. We don't want to be running away from a horde of merchants who just might turn to the authorities and say we stole what we were wearing. That'd be a good way to humiliate us, for sure, and potentially sabotage our mission.

"Come on, Sara," Kayley says, buddying up to her. "It's just us three in here, and we won't say anything. Do you really think the queen is mentally stable?"

"So, if you want to take both that outfit and the other," Sara says, pointing to me, then to Kayley, "they're usually two hundred fifty jorin each for the set, but I'll take four seventy-five, since you guys seem nice."

Sara folds her arms and deadpans a look at the two of us. Kayley freezes, and I do the same. This young woman is more crafty than we realized. I'll chalk that up to a lifetime of working in the market, which seems likely.

"Uh. How about four fifty?" I guess we have to play this game with her.

"No, sorry, four seventy-five is firm." Sara's mouth curves up. "You guys wouldn't want to travel all the way back to the Capitol District in those dirty clothes, would you? Besides, consider your purchase payment for the information I just told you. I mean, that's what you really wanted, isn't it?"

My mouth drops open as I turn to Kayley, who's smarter than me and doesn't let her reaction show. She smirks at Sara, finally understanding the game she's playing with us.

"What will you tell me if I add those slippers over there?" she asks, pointing to a pair on the shelf near Sara's head. Sara looks at them, then shrugs.

"I could give you a name. Maybe they know something I don't, or not."

"Okay then." Kayley's huntress eyes return to normal, and she's once again her calm and approachable self. "We'll take everything."

"Thanks so much!" Sara says, swiping her Sergo across Kayley's. "I really do appreciate the business. Things have been tough. That's not a lie."

"Wait, have you been lying to us?" I ask.

"Not at all." Sara beams. "I think the queen is nuts."

Chapter Fifteen

"Okay, now that you've had your chance to make fun of our outfits, can we tell you what Rance and I found out?" Kayley asks, hands on hips.

We've gathered in Kayley's room—they booked us singles—to share with Parrish and Grady what Sara told us. It's become clear to me that citizens of Canis Ludis don't openly admit they think their queen is crazy. If they do, then they're saying they trust you.

"We're not," Parrish says as he attempts to keep from breaking into a smile. I have to give the guy credit. Even when he wants to burst into laughter, he's still thinking about others.

"No, your outfits do that all by themselves!" Grady howls, rolling onto his back on Kayley's bed. "I mean, really? Where did you find those?"

"Dude, be careful," I warn. "She may just give you a very close look at her shirt with all the egg embryo on it."

Grady waves his hands at her in a weak attempt to avoid punishment, but he's still laughing. Kayley's not Afton, but I know my girlfriend. You don't want to push her too hard.

"So, you guys said you had something to tell us? Something you learned?" Parrish asks.

"Yeah, we got a little local insight into the rivalry between the Chamberlin and the queen," Kayley replies.

"We got a name," I add.

"And some slippers." Grady cackles, then ducks as Kayley throws one of the aforementioned pieces of footwear at him.

"Grady, I'm so glad you feel the need to fill the void left by Afton, but this really isn't the time," Kayley growls. The mention of Afton's name sobers the mood. Grady nods and moves himself to the edge of the bed to stare at the floor.

It takes a moment more for us to regain our motivation and continue this meeting. Until we get her to forgive us, at least one of us will be thinking about Afton every second of the day. We're not a team without her.

But it will be hard to get her to forgive us if we're all dead, so on with the mission.

"So, Queen de Avila doesn't want to be tied up with the Chamberlin...economically speaking," Parrish says, after Kayley shares our encounter with the wily Sara.

"When I was on Albion, I overheard something like that," Kayley says. "I think she's losing her leverage over the Council. One of the other councilors may try to challenge her and break her clout there."

"That would make sense," Grady comments, then nods as he rubs his chin. "She's got control over some serious military resources and a very influential seat on the Council. If she had the manufacturing power of somewhere like Magnaraprax, she could even challenge the Emperor for his throne."

"Do you really think that's what she wants?" I ask, finding myself short of breath.

"It doesn't matter," Kayley responds, "and it's not our problem. We're only here to do one thing, and that's find out what she has planned for the upcoming Council meeting."

"Yeah, but if we knew her motivation, wouldn't we be able to figure it out from that?" I ask.

"Yes, but we don't have time for an investigation of that scope. We'd need to go talk to people on the other Central Planets that we have no connection to, without creating suspicion. And don't forget, we have no way of getting off-planet. We're stuck here until the Imperial cruiser returns."

"That's not true. We've got the Teddys' ship."

"We don't have the Teddys' ship," Grady murmurs. "We don't even have the Teddys."

"We don't need *any* ship right now," Kayley corrects. "All we need to do is get into the palace and talk to the High Wazir."

Grady, Parrish, and I refute that suggestion with rude noises.

"KayKay, there's no way we're going to get in to talk to him, and even if we did, he's never going to betray his queen!" I move next to her and touch her arm. Kayley wants to take the direct route because she believes it will be our surest and quickest chance at survival. I'm certainly agreeable to the concept, except for the minor issue that it will exponentially increase our chances of losing our heads.

"Darling, listen," she says in a soft voice, "we've done this sort of thing before. You have been in tougher places than this. We can figure out a way to do this. Sure, we can get a lower-ranking official more easily, but eventually we're going to have to talk to the High Wazir. He's the only one that knows the queen's true motivations."

"Um," I say, "could we not do the 'darling' thing anymore? Every time I hear that word, I think of Nayla saying it to Afton."

Kayley opens and shuts her mouth, then nods, sulking a little. I comfort her by touching my head to hers, and she returns the motion. Now that I've brought that up, she'll think of it every time either of us says it, too, and that will just take all the endearment out of it. Better we just give it a rest for a while.

"How about 'honey'?" Parrish suggests.

"How about we get back to the plan?" Grady adds.

"Sorry." I raise an apologetic hand to my buds. Parrish just shrugs it off. He understands, but Grady rolls his eyes, still initiated into the world of dating. I wonder if he's ever had an eye for someone.

"Alright." Kayley claps her hands together, attempting to bring energy back into the conversation. "High Wazir. How do we get to him, and what questions do we ask him?"

"Well, we need a valid reason to be in the palace," I say.

"That's not so tough," Parrish says. "We're representatives of the Chamberlin. All we have to do is request an audience with the queen. Doesn't really matter what it's about. We just need to get inside."

"Okay." Kayley nods. "Good. So how do we get the High Wazir to talk to us outside of the court? He won't want to leave the queen. Especially when we're in there."

"We can tell him we've learned of a plot to assassinate her!" I suggest, but Kayley gives me a face of disapproval.

"No, darli—no, he'll never believe that."

"That we're willing to sell secrets from the Chamberlin?" Parrish asks.

"No...and suggesting we're willing to betray our employer might just be cause for the queen to chop off—"

"Don't say it," I say. "I think we're all well aware of Queen de Avila's preferred method of execution."

"Fine, but stop telling me what I can say and what I can't." I know Kayley's only mildly annoyed. She feels the frustration of the situation, just as we all do. She's not taking it out on me, not really, but her emotion has to come out, and if I'm her punching bag, that's okay. I can handle it. I can handle a lot more than that for her.

"Teddy," I say, our pink fuzzy friend popping into my head suddenly. Maybe he's trying to reach out to me via Teddynet. I'm not sure, because it's been hard to connect to him ever since we arrived on the planet. Still, if he's still inside the palace, he may be able to help us. "We popsicle the Wazir and bring him somewhere safe and isolated. If we can convince him we're not really agents of the Chamberlin, he might talk to us."

"I have a better idea," Grady says with a grin. Once he's got the three of us staring at him, he says it. "Truth serum. He'll have to tell us what we want to know."

"Oh, great," Parrish says. "So we kidnap and poison the High Wazir, and we expect to just get away with that?"

"Not poison. It's a drug."

"A drug *is* poison. That's why your body has to detoxify itself to get rid of it."

"He'll be fine."

"But will we?"

"We won't be if we don't figure this out," Kayley says. "Parry, honestly, it's the best idea I've heard so far. I'm not crazy about drugging someone, but our lives are on the line, if you remember."

Parrish sighs. I don't think any of us want to cause harm to someone else, not even if they deserve it. The High Wazir doesn't. At least not from us.

"Will the truth serum harm him in any way?" I ask.

"Not sure." Grady shrugs. "I haven't made it yet."

A collective groan comes from the rest of us. I shake my head. Kayley's disappointed, and Parrish...

"Dude," Parrish says. "You're talking about using an imaginary substance on the High Wazir? This plan already has too many issues. When did you think you were going to get that made?"

"After we get Teddy," Grady says, a self-confident smug look on his face. He has a point. Original Teddy, and possibly a few blue buddies, figure as important in this scheme. Without his popsicle ability, we can't get our hands on the High Wazir. It'll be tricky enough, but if we can find a place to talk to him, this might work.

"Oh, and we'll need the doc," Grady adds.

"Why? Isn't she in serious memory therapy right now?" I ask.

"She is," Kayley replies, "but we'll need her to administer the truth serum."

"Why?"

"So we don't kill the High Wazir. It's not exactly just some pill you can pop. Too much of the stuff is dangerous." Grady folds his legs under him and readjusts. His face looks a little pale. I think he's realizing the seriousness of what he's suggested.

"You want the Teddys to prototype the serum for you?" I ask.

"That's the idea."

I reach out into Teddynet and Teddy comm, trying to reach Original Teddy at the same time. We'll not only need him and the doc, but we'll need the prototyping abilities that are on the Teddy ship.

All seems quiet out in the Teddyverse. If there was some emergency, I'd know it, but nothing concerning is there. Original Teddy doesn't answer me, either. I still feel he's connected, just on "do not disturb" or something like that. I had no idea that was even possible. Then again, I am still very new at this, and it's not like I had any training on how to use it.

I reach out to Captain Teddy and his ship to see if I can at least get them. They're there, but I get a bit of a rude reply telling me to speak to Original Teddy for anything. This is certainly unusual. I know they've been busy with their human studies, but I don't think I broke any sort of Teddy communication protocol. Maybe I did.

"Rance!"

I blink as Kayley smacks my face. Not too hard, but just enough to snap me out of Teddy mode. She's seen it enough times now to know what needs to be done to get me back to reality. Personally, I think she might enjoy smacking my face just a little too much.

"Okay, I'm here. We need to go get Teddy. Then we can put our plan into action."

"Great." Parrish slaps a hand on his leg. "Now we've just got to break into the palace twice."

Chapter Sixteen

"Are you sure he's going to be there?" Parrish asks for at least the fourth time.

We're standing just outside the entrance to Princess Nayla's quarters. It's a miracle that we've gotten this far just on the Imperial credentials given to us by Bailiff Daughtry. They allow us access to anywhere that isn't part of a private residence or classified area.

It's good to be inside a warm, dry hall of the palace, with its tapestried walls and polycarbon-carpeted floors. Heat radiates from underneath our boots, soothing our aching feet. The Empire didn't design their uniforms for comfort. It's a good thing we only have to wear them while we're at the palace.

"Forget him. What if Nayla and Afton are there?" Grady says. "They see us, we're done."

"Easy, boys," Kayley says. "Rance said he's there, and Teddy knows we're coming for him."

"If he knows that, why doesn't he just come and meet us here?" Parrish eyes the guards at the ivory double doors just down the hall from where we're pretending to enjoy a moment of respite away from the strict manners of the court. The guards, who stand motionless, seem to understand. I'm sure they can't wait to take a break, too.

"Because, just like we can't walk in without permission, Teddy can't get out of there without the same," I explain. At least, that's the gist of what I got from his brief Teddy comm message. "He'd have to ask Nayla, and if he did that, we might as well just Sergo Afton and ask her to come out and play."

"Too bad we can't," Parrish comments. It's enough said.

"It's okay," Grady says, his tone not as somber as I'd expect it to be. "I've got another solution. Kayley, could you be a dear and go distract those guards for a moment?"

"Why me?" Kayley's eyebrows crunch together, and her eyes narrow at him.

"They're male. You're female. Do I need to explain further?"

"No, but that's a big assumption on your part. And you especially should know better." But a moment later, her face transforms into a bright and cordial expression. She's the best actor ever. I swear it. And I've seen a lot of cine.

Kayley saunters over to the two guards, twinkling her fingers. She catches their attention immediately. I've no idea what she's going to do to keep it while Grady does whatever he's got planned. If anyone can improvise a moment, at least out of the four of us, it's Kayley. That's what I'm hoping, anyway.

"If you put her at risk, I'm going to bash you, dude," I say, glaring at my bud.

"Easy," Parrish says. "He'd never do that."

"Exactly." Grady grins as he pulls a long tube and something that looks like a handle out of his jacket. I blink in disbelief, as I recognize it immediately. It's his tranquilizer gun the Teddys prototyped to help us get onto the SIR *Mursilis*. I thought that thing was long gone.

"Dude! How the hell did you get through security with that?" I ask.

"Simple. It's made from materials that don't show up on a scan. I considered that when we were planning our infiltration."

This is another kind of escapade altogether. We're not just looking for some vids. We're here to rescue a friend, and hope another friend doesn't find out. I'm not happy about the latter aspect. We've already betrayed Afton's trust once. If she finds out we did it again, we may never get her back. I can only hope she understands we're doing this to get ourselves out of trouble so we can focus on what we hold equally important: getting her back.

Grady hands the gun to Parrish, who's likely the best shot out of all of us. We're far enough away from the guards so they won't take notice of what we're about to do. So when Parrish raises the gun and takes aim, he hits them both with a single shot each. We make a quick job of hiding their sleeping bodies behind one of the larger tapestries. We'll retrieve them once we get Teddy.

"Do you think there's a vid in this hallway?" I ask Grady.

"Forget the vid, we have a bigger problem," Kayley says. "I found out from the guards that Nayla and Afton are in there."

"Maybe just two of us go in," Parrish suggests. "Less chance of getting spotted."

"Good idea," I say.

"You and Kayley go, then. Grady and I will watch the door."

"No," Kayley says. "I'm too obvious. Parry, you go with Rance. Grady and I will wait here and make sure no one goes in. We'll change into the guards' uniforms."

I sigh, then nod to Parrish for us to enter. Once again, our magnificent leader is right. Parrish is the best choice for this, and not all of us need to go. I worry about her being out here, but it might be just as bad inside. We've no idea who we'll run into. Servants? Likely. Guards? Possibly. Afton and Nayla? I'm praying hard to the Goddesses we absolutely don't come within a kilometer of either of them.

Parrish squeezes my shoulder, and we enter, closing the door behind us as silently as possible. The interior corridor is dim, appropriate for the time of day—not bedtime yet, but definitely at the point where someone might be winding down their day by reading or watching a vid or two.

The two of us take the left corridor, as Teddy directed, staying light on our feet in case we need to make a quick retreat. I'm bummed that Kayley's not here with me, but if there's anyone I'd trust without question to take her place, it's Parrish.

We come to a junction and make a right, but as we do, a servant crosses our path, too fast for us to do anything about it. We freeze, but the maid doesn't react to our presence. There's no doubt she saw us, so either Nayla has guests on a regular basis, or she's about to go alert her mistress that two interlopers are in her quarters. We'd better find out.

"Excuse me," I say to the maid, who pauses and pivots to face us with a bow. "The princess invited us to her evening seance. Where might we find Her Royal Highness?"

"My lords," the maid says and bows again, "the princess is in her bedchambers. There is no seance tonight."

Oops. I guessed wrong. Now this could be tricky, but I think, given the maid's acceptance of our presence, we might just get away without any trouble.

"Ah," I say, attempting to sound as disappointed as possible. "We were mistaken, then. Please do not disturb Her Highness on our behalf. We'll show ourselves out."

"As you wish, my lord. Pleasant evening to you." The maid bows and continues on her way without even a glance back.

Parrish nods approval at my quick thinking, and we continue on our way. One more turn, then we're at Teddy's room. At least, that's what I'm interpreting that Teddynet is saying. I've learned a lot about it in a short time, but it's still an alien technology based on non-human thought processes. I'm like a horse on ice skates. I might figure it out, but it's nowhere near my natural state.

"Well done," Original Teddy says as we open the door to his room. "Evacuation is recommended."

"No kidding," I say. "We should be free and clear all the way back. Kayley and Grady are guarding the door for us."

"Tell me something I don't know," Original Teddy says, and I blink. It's a word-for-word quote from Afton. A chill runs through me as our fuzzy friend's uncanny imitation hits me like a brick wall. A quick look at Parrish tells me it's unnerved him, too. I don't think Teddy meant it that way, but my sudden unintended broadcast over Teddynet clues him in.

"An unfortunate coincidence," Original Teddy says. "Acceptance of apologies is recommended."

"Don't worry about it," Parrish replies. "We all feel the same way. Let's get out of here while we can."

Teddy doesn't waste another moment. He springs up from his spot on the floor, and a microsecond later, he's with us, heading down the hallway we arrived from. Parrish sprints ahead and checks the corners as we make our way to the entrance and to safety.

Another turn. The coast is clear. No maids, no guards. We're almost home free. I didn't think this was going to be that challenging, given that we could get halfway into the palace without a problem. I've been dreading with my life that we'd run into Nayla and Afton. I wouldn't even know where to begin my explanation. Kayley's the master of words, not me. I'd just fall on my knees and beg for Afton to forgive us.

"Ransom Quigley He'."

No! Nayla! I'd recognize that deep, resonant voice anywhere. We skid to a stop and become icicles—frozen and hanging from a precarious edge. This is exactly what we *didn't* want to happen. How did she find us? I thought she was in her bedroom. Is Afton with her? I'm terrified to find out.

"Turn around," Nayla orders, and we obey, if with a little hesitance.

The princess is indeed ready for bed, dressed in a silken nightgown and silver robe with turquoise slippers to match. She has a mug in her hand and an annoyed look on her face.

And all glory and honor to the three Goddesses, Afton isn't with her, but what happens from here still could destroy any connection we've ever had with her, and that is terrifying.

"Princess, please forgive us!" I fall on my knees and prostrate myself before her. I don't know what else to do. "Teddy just wanted to get some air."

The thump on the floor next to me lets me know Parrish is following suit. I guess he's got no better ideas, either.

"How did you get in here?" the princess asks in a low voice.

"We, uh, entered through the main doors?"

"I am surprised that I did not foresee this." Nayla takes a slow breath. "It is of minor importance, however."

I risk a peek up at her. Her eyes still bear as much ill will for me as they did before, and I double down on my humility. It's only Nayla here, and while she's not calling for our heads to be removed from our bodies at this instant, the look in her eyes tells me we've done more damage to our relationship with her.

"Princess," I say, my face buried into the rug, "may I inquire how Afton is doing?"

"You may," Nayla replies. "She is fine. Comfortable and satisfied with all the luxuries the palace can provide. Happy to be my partner. Content to spend the rest of her life with me. Do you need to hear more?"

I get the tone in her question. It's more of a statement, really. The princess means to say, "She doesn't need you in her life," and I should be glad that I'm so close to the ground. That way, my heart doesn't have far to fall from my chest. I feel my eyes water up, and I close them. I can't even consider that we'll never see Afton again. It's not something that makes any sense to me.

"What do you plan to do?" I ask, my voice cracking.

"To you, Ransom Quigley He'? Nothing. As I've told you, darkness already clouds your future. I need not add to that, as my karma must remain in the light. Be thankful that Surela will not suffer your fates."

"Fates?" Parrish asks.

"Yes. I've read all of your palms, and there is no light there."

Okay, so Nayla won't turn us in, but her reason for not doing so is ominous. It's not at all comforting, but I think it might be a good idea to take this one moment at a time. Otherwise, I may just break down.

"Could you tell Afton that we wanted to see her?"

"I will not," Nayla replies, and takes a sip from her mug. "If you truly wish for her happiness, you will not seek her out, nor will you do anything to put her well-being in jeopardy. I would prefer if you do not contact her ever again. Otherwise, I will consider it an act of selfishness and use my position to counter it."

"Do you really care for Afton that much?" Parrish asks.

"Of course. One does not meet their soulmate every day."

I want to believe Nayla's words, but I also want to fight for my friend. No one who loves Afton that much would want to keep her from her friends. I think, anyway. I need to discuss it with Kayley. She'll know how much truth is in the princess' words.

"Now go, before I change my mind," Nayla says.

"Thank you, Princess!" I press myself to the ground as far as I can go. Parrish does the same. There's nothing we can do but retreat, and retreat we will. At least that gives us a chance to try again another time.

Chapter Seventeen

I DON'T KNOW HOW many minutes it's been since Kayley and I started staring at each other, with sullen faces and folded arms. We're waiting for the others to pick up Doc Elizabeth from the spaceport and return so we can figure out exactly what we're going to do.

Our mood is gloomy because I told Kayley what Nayla said to us. Kayley wasn't there, so I think how she imagines what went down is far worse than I remember it. Maybe I'm just in denial, but I think Nayla spoke out of anger and didn't really mean what she said. I'd like to think the princess truly cares for Afton and is just trying to protect her from getting hurt. When we solve our own problems, we'll be able to show her we won't be a danger to either of them.

"I don't know, Rance," Kayley says and sighs. "I just have this awful premonition that it's going to be a very long time before Afton forgives us."

"Yeah, but all we have to do is show them both that we had no choice. We could even play double agents and tell the queen what the Chamberlin is up to. That'd get Nayla—"

"No. No way. We can't trust the queen to do anything but execute us." Kayley begins her pacing routine around the modest hotel room. It's at least twice as large as our private berth on the Teddy ship, but that still doesn't give her much room. She chews up the floor space in a matter of seconds, fretting over our trouble.

"I think Afton might be able to help us convince Nayla and her mom!"

"Afton would likely knock you out before you said one word to her. Isn't that why you hoped to avoid her when getting Teddy?"

"You hoped we'd avoid her, too. Isn't that why you didn't want to go into Nayla's quarters?"

"No, it's not!" Kayley stops and turns towards me, flames rising from behind her eyes. She digs her hands into her scarlet mane and grabs handfuls to shake at me. "Did you forget what color hair I have?"

I roll my eyes, but she's got a point. She had said the same thing when we were there. That doesn't mean she wasn't worried about an unexpected face-to-face with her best friend. Out of all of us, only Kayley could know the full extent of how much hurt we had done to her. She's the only person Afton has fully opened up to. With the rest of us, she's always had an emotional wall that she could raise or lower, depending on what she wanted us to know. It's been a very effective means of halting anyone from prying deeper into her feelings.

"Of course not." I back up and drop on the bed, avoiding Kayley's continued stomp about the room. "How could I ever forget that?"

"It almost sounds like you want to." She gives me a small pout, but it's not serious. I understand the apology that's underneath her words, but my question wasn't exactly a cream-filled sweet cake, either. It had more of an edge to it than I intended.

"Never, KayKay," I say, remembering to soften my voice. She can handle it, but there's no reason for me to take out my frustration on her. There's never a reason for that.

She brushes her fingers across my shoulder as she passes by. I reach up and take her hand, but Kayley continues her march. I hold on for as long as I can, but I have to let go as she turns away from me, making a few laps in silence before she speaks again.

"Asking Afton for help got us into this position," Kayley says. "If things were normal, we'd have a solid plan, but..."

"Things are hardly normal," I finish. "And Afton adds more to our team than just her fair share."

"Meaning we're trying to accomplish an already dangerous mission with a big hole in us."

Kayley means more than just the loss of our team member. Afton's departure has left all of us feeling empty. She wasn't just our physical strength; she looked after each of us in her own way. We tried to do the same for her, but only Kayley could ever manage it. Still, all of us had a connection to her, and now that she's pushed us away—for an understandable reason—we've lost it.

I don't see how we'll succeed without her help. Afton is key to our success, and potentially our continuing to live. She could make this mission a breeze, if she'd be willing to talk to us. If I have to beg and plead for her to do it, then I will. I'll do whatever she asks of me. It's making that conversation happen that's the difficulty. Sneaking in to get Teddy lost us our one chance. Now Nayla will be on guard for us attempting to do it again.

"Do you think we could follow the two of them and then try to ask them at an opportune moment?"

"What makes you think we're going to get within a hundred kilometers of either of them ever again? After what Nayla said, she'll have given her guards orders to shoot us on sight." Kayley shakes her head. "No, Rance, we're going to have to do this on our own."

"She wouldn't do that! She's just angry with us. Give her some time to cool off, and we can try then."

"We don't *have* time!" Intensity comes back to Kayley's voice. "We've got less than two and a half weeks now, and we don't know Nayla that well. Other than the fact that she communes with the trees and claims to see the future, we don't know her at all! Which means we can't trust her, and as long as Afton chooses to be with her, I'm not sure we can trust *her*, either."

"Not trust Afton? Come on, KayKay. I mean, sure, she plays some dumb jokes—"

"That's not what I mean, and you know it."

Kayley is staring at me now, and I can tell that her patience with me is getting down to its bare bones. It's worn down from everything piling up on us, and I can't blame her if she loses her cool. What I'm worried about is what happens if both of us break at the same time.

"Yeah, I know that, but shouldn't we at least try? Give it a week?"

"Rance, we don't have time to play around here. If we waste a week trying to make them talk to us, we won't get that time back!"

"Yeah, I get that. But so what? We already know that."

"So what? Why are you being so dense?"

"I'm not being dense, KayKay. I just want you to be honest with me."

Kayley stomps up to me and takes me by the shoulders. She peers into my eyes as if she's searching for something, but then shakes her head.

"When have I not been honest with you?"

"Never! It's just that—"

"Just what?"

I snap my mouth shut, as I'm afraid of what might come out of it. That's the third time in this conversation she's cut me off from talking. I let a slow breath out through my nose, feeling the heat come to my face. I might have infinite patience with her at any other moment of any other day, but this whole situation has left me raw.

Perhaps because Kayley realizes that we're both about to go at it, or perhaps just seeing the fire in my eyes, she snaps her hands from me, keeping them up and patting the air in a calming motion. I know she didn't mean it, but it's hard for either of us to have a rational discussion right now. She turns away and resumes her pacing, except now it's at a fraction of the speed it was before. Kayley's contemplating our situation, and that means I should, too.

"Do you really think Afton's not an option?" I ask.

"Of course! I—" Kayley takes a breath. "I wish it was different, Rance, but the next time we approach her, we can't have our potential deaths to worry about. We have to be free of any trouble so we can just sit and listen to her. Hear her out so that we really know how to make things right with her and Nayla."

"Is that ever going to be possible?"

"I don't know."

Chapter Eighteen

It took a long time, but once the others returned, we talked out our issues, cried a bit, hugged, and then came up with the best, most foolproof plan we could to get the High Wazir and make him talk. If we were going to succeed at this, we'd only have one chance to get it right.

But then when morning came, we received a sudden request from the queen to meet with her, so we didn't get the chance to prepare at all.

"Hurry!" Kayley hisses as we race down the hallway, struggling to button cuffs and straighten jackets on our way to the courtroom's antechamber where we first waited to meet the queen. I have no idea why we're bothering. Grady's hair is a mess. My eyes have huge bags underneath them, and Kayley had to throw her hair up in a bun rather than wear it down like she normally does. We look like a bunch of bedraggled college students.

"Grady, push that thing down in your jacket!" I poke the tranquilizer gun sticking out from in between his lapels. It might not show up on scanners, but all the guards would need to do is look at him to see it.

"Breathe, all of you," Doc Elizabeth says. "Panic won't solve your problems, and if you go in there like that, you're bound to—"

"Don't say it," Grady growls, and gets a flick on his ear for his trouble. He flinches and rubs his ear, pouting like an elementary school kid who was just told to go sit in the corner.

This could be our one chance—after we risk our lives meeting with the queen, that is. We've no idea why she called for us. The plan was to request an audience with her, not the other way around. That would have taken a day or two to get approved and scheduled, giving us enough time to prepare for this moment. Instead, we're being thrust into the core of the sun and expected to stay cool.

"Parry," Kayley says. "Why are you so calm?"

"I just figure this is how we always do things, so why would today be any worse?" Parrish shrugs. He's got a point, but he also might be a bit cynical. After our botched attempt to break into Exodus, Parrish was seriously wounded to the point that he wasn't sure if he would ever play sports again. He's better now, but I know he gets knee aches from time to time. He walks okay, but I don't know if he'll ever be the same again.

Our target, the High Wazir, strolls through a back door and approaches us, coming to a halt a fair distance away. He appraises us with a hesitant gaze, his hands coming together so that the whites of his knuckles are as discernable as bean curd in that delicious brown sauce my mom makes. Gosh, that makes me hungry.

"I realize this was a last-minute request, but do get yourselves together," the High Wazir says. "You are as unkempt as a pack of beggars."

"Apologies, High Wazir," Kayley says and bows to him. "We were up all night on...Imperial business."

He rolls his eyes and pretends to be sympathetic.

"No rest for the wicked, I suppose." The High Wazir catches sight of Doc Elizabeth. "Who is this, then? Another representative? I don't recall there ever being five of you."

"This is Doctor Elizabeth Chapman," Kayley replies. At least that was one part of our plan we didn't need to prepare for. "She is the Chamberlin's official physician, and His Lordship has sent her to tend to the queen's ailments."

"Mmm, well, I doubt she will let you within arm's reach, but I will announce you."

Doc Elizabeth smiles and gives an awkward bow.

We're announced, and we make our way into the queen's throne room. Her Majesty squints at us as we enter, leaning forward as far as her armrests and cane will allow her to go. We line up, attempt to relax, and await her words.

"Do you know why I summoned you?"

"No, Your Majesty," Kayley replies, placing a hand over her heart and bowing her head. "But I am delighted to let you know the Lord Chamberlin has sent his topmost physician to examine your eyesight."

"Never mind all that. I don't want any quack doctors from that man. He's defied my rule for the last time. I am lodging a formal complaint to the Emperor!"

"But, Your Majesty, we cannot—"

"I know that, you strawberry tart! I'm not asking you to do anything. I'm telling you because I like you, and for no other reason. If I didn't like you, I'd chop your heads off and make myself a knit hat from that juicy mane of yours. Now you may go!"

"That's it?" I ask, realizing too late my voice was louder than I wanted it to be.

"What else you want, boy? My daughter's hand in marriage? Well, let me tell you, she doesn't like—"

"Ah, thank you so much, Your Majesty!" The High Wazir laughs, louder than he needs to, but it achieves his goal of silencing the queen. She wrinkles her nose at him, shaking her head. "I will see them out."

That could have gone much worse, but perhaps luck is on our side. We're about to get to the part in our plan where we'll lure the High Wazir to the back room, popsicle him, and then give him a jab of the truth serum Doc Elizabeth cooked up. The one minor issue is that Original Teddy isn't here. He was supposed to meet us, but he's still up on the Teddy ship. That's why Grady brought the tranquilizer gun.

But on our way to the palace, Elizabeth realized the compounds in the tranquilizer might interfere with the truth serum, so now we're not even sure if we can go through with this. But this might be the only chance we get. Next time we're here, we might leave without our heads.

"Ready?" Grady says, reaching into his jacket for his gun. All of my alarms fire off at once, and I lunge for him.

"No!" I smack at his hand, and he yelps, turning all heads in the vicinity in our direction.

"Is everything alright?" the High Wazir asks as he stares pointedly at the two of us.

"Uh, yeah, he just caught his finger on his Imperial standard." I point to the pin on Grady's lapel. Grady takes the hint and jams his pointer finger into his mouth, nodding in agreement. The High Wazir examines us for a few seconds more, then pivots and continues his escort.

"Dude, it's now or never!" Grady's voice is low, but full of intensity.

"We can't!" I shoot back.

"We can," Kayley whispers, coming up on my other side. "There's a side utility corridor coming up on the left. We charge him right before he gets there."

"What about guards?" Parrish asks.

"No guards in that area. We'll be fine, just be ready."

"KayKay, I don't like this..."

Kayley strokes the back of my neck, but her face is firm. We're going through with this. She's just priming me to be a contributing member of this half-stupid operation. I really hope this doesn't get us executed.

But likely, it will.

The side corridor comes up faster than expected. Kayley doesn't have the chance to get us into place and ready. So instead, she just yells, "Get him!" Everyone freezes in surprise but Parrish, who makes a dive for the High Wazir.

But he misses. The man somehow knew to dodge the attack. He spins and flies down the corridor, the five of us hot on his trail.

"Dammit, he heard us!" I cry.

We pound after him, hoping that his stately robes will slow him down. The High Wazir knows these corridors, though. He ducks down a side passage and rips open an access door. We follow, but the moment we enter the space, we realize he could easily lose us in here.

"Utility room," Grady gasps, breathing hard.

"Split up," Kayley says. "Elizabeth, guard the door."

"And what, exactly, do you expect me to do if he charges me?"

The utility area is of a decent size, as you'd expect in a palace. Even four of us spread out cannot cover every section. Our only hope is that we drive the High Wazir into a corner and trap him there. Before we can do that, we first need to find him.

The noise of the climate control system and the wisps of steam from the boilers deaden our senses. I can't hear my own footsteps, much less someone else's. If he were to jump out from behind some compressor or vent, I might not notice until he was already past me.

Then I hear a bang on something metal. It's not mechanical, and it's nearby. That's it. That's got to be him. I duck, keeping my head below the ductwork around me. I peer through an opening as I move, trying to spot him sneaking past me.

Suddenly the High Wazir leaps over me, coming from above, not below. I spring up, catching his foot, and we both tumble. He lands hard on the stairs, face forward. But my head cracks against the lowest step, and for a moment, I'm blinded.

"He's here!" I shout, scrambling to get up. I reach out for a handhold and grab a hot conduit instead. My fingers scream with fire, and I snatch my hand back, nursing it as the heat runs through it.

"He's coming to you!" Parrish shouts, presumably at the doc. My sight is coming back, but slowly.

"Oh, heavens!" Doc Elizabeth wails.

"Wait, High Wazir! We don't want to hurt you! We just want information!" Kayley attempts to stop him with reason. Maybe we should have tried that first.

"You have a strange way of showing it!"

Doc Elizabeth screams. I catch the moment she drops to avoid being run over. The High Wazir vaults a set of stairs to another exit, but turns around.

"I'm calling the guard!" the High Wazir says. "You have fifteen seconds to leave if you want to keep your heads."

Then he's out the door. Parrish comes over to help me up, and we gather at the exit. My hand still burns, and I'm momentarily distracted as I try to take care of it. I wonder why the High Wazir warned us like that. Did he believe Kayley's words?

Kayley frowns at us as we stare at her.

"What are you waiting for? You heard him! Let's get out of here!"

Chapter Nineteen

W E R O C K E T O U T O F the palace as fast as we can go and sprint through the royal grounds towards the gate. It's not far, but it's far enough to make us worry. If the High Wazir warned the guards at the gate, we're trapped.

The crack of a weapon resounds behind us, and a tree explodes next to me. Slivers of bark fly in all directions, pelting us. Another shot quickly follows. It comes so close, it buzzes my ear like an angry hornet.

"The guards! Take cover!" Kayley grabs my hand and yanks me towards some bushes.

We bury ourselves in the brush behind a large oak. It's wide enough to provide plenty of protection against the guards shooting at us from the palace. But that's just one side.

"Parrish, anyone coming from the gate?" Kayley hisses.

"No. Nobody."

"Keep checking."

Kayley motions to me to check the opposite direction while she and Grady take the sides. I think I should be able to stay close to the roots of the big tree and still get a good view. I crawl to the edge of its trunk and carefully stick my head out until I get a good glimpse of the palace.

Two gunshots in succession impact the ground before me, spraying dirt on my face. I wince and jerk back just before a third strikes a root right where my head was.

"Shoot, that was close," I say as I stare at the spot.

"By chance," Doc Elizabeth asks from her position huddled in between the four of us, "did you hear anyone say something like 'stop' or 'halt' or 'don't move'? Anything like that? Anyone?"

"No, why?"

"Guards usually say things like that, do they not? And don't they try to capture first, before shooting to kill?"

The four of us turn to stare at the doc as we realize something much worse than an arrest is happening.

"Do...do you think the guards are trying to kill us?" Grady asks, his voice barely a whisper.

Before anyone can answer, the ping of something metal smacks the tree and lands on the ground with a thud. That wasn't a bullet. I've heard that sound before, though, and I remember—

A sharp boom resounds on the other side of the tree, knocking our senses from us. I don't know how long I sit, dumbfounded, staring at the leaves in front of my face. Something tells me to move, but my body won't listen.

Then comes Kayley's hand across my face. I blink to see her wide eyes begging me to move. A second later, I'm up and moving.

We keep the trees between us and the palace. Whoever wants to kill us is in that direction. At least they were.

"It's got to be the guards, right?" Parrish asks.

"Then where are they?" I reply.

"Does it really matter?" Doc Elizabeth adds, running a hand through her hair. She's seen the results of all of our confrontations with danger, but has never experienced it first-hand. Until now.

"Which way out?" Kayley asks Grady. He takes a breath and looks down at the ground to consider, then points hesitantly back towards the gate we meant to leave from.

"You sure?"

"Yes. No..." Grady squeezes his hands together. "Wait, I think there's a maintenance exit this way. There'll be a guard, but we should be able to leave."

"How do you know that?" Doc Elizabeth asks.

"I memorized the maps we have."

A volley of gunshots blares out, ripping through the surrounding bushes. Grady and the doc cry out, jerking as if someone just pushed them. Both crash to the ground, and we dive after, seeking cover. Another volley flies over our heads, but we're already down.

"Grady!" My hands race across him, searching for the bullet hole. As I roll him, he screams, and my finger touches on a wet part of his jacket.

There's another spot on his back—the bullet went through him. I don't know if that's good or not, but I know my friend is going to bleed out if I can't get him out of here immediately.

I reach out into Teddynet and upload our situation, then await a reply.

"How is he?" Doc Elizabeth asks with a groan.

"Not good. You?"

"Just a graze, fortunately," she replies, holding a hand over her shoulder. "It hurts like hell, but I will manage."

I wonder why our assailants haven't overrun us yet. If they're guards, they should have us surrounded by now. Instead, whoever this is seems content to pick us off from a distance. Perhaps they're avoiding the guards, too. Which means this isn't the queen or the High Wazir trying to off us.

"Let's get ready to move," Kayley says. "Flat out run with everything you've got."

"Wait," I say. "Grady can't run. I don't even know if he can walk."

"I'll carry him on my back," Parrish says.

Doc Elizabeth slides over to him and does a brief examination. The grimace on her face is telling, and my insides start twisting.

"Take his jacket off and put pressure on those wounds." She tightens her jaw. "I hope we can get him help fast enough."

I do as ordered, trying my best not to think about what Doc Elizabeth just said. Grady cries out. I try to be more careful, but there's no easy way.

"Sorry, buddy, this will just take a moment."

"Don't call me buddy," Grady says through gritted teeth. "Afton calls me that."

The air goes out of me, and I try to finish up while taking the double jab of knowing I just hurt my friend—both mentally and physically. I was trying to help him, but did just the opposite.

"Ready?" Kayley asks, then takes a peek over the shrub—no shots. The rest of us tense our muscles, already sore from diving into the brush too many times. "Rance, you lead. Parrish, you're next."

I nod and take a breath. With as much force as I can manage, I launch off the ground and rocket towards the palace wall. I've no idea where the door might be, but if I get to the wall and just follow it, I'll have to find something eventually.

All the while making myself a highly visible target.

"Stop, you!" someone shouts. It's got to be a guard. I almost feel relief knowing it's them and not our would-be assassin. I'm still not going to stop.

There's a deep pop like someone opening a large canister. Then a shout, but I don't understand the words. I keep running, hoping the others aren't far behind.

But then the grenade explodes, throwing me into the wall. My shoulder takes the brunt of the impact. I crumple to the ground, my ears ringing.

"Fan out!" a guard yells. "Find them!"

Something inside me forces me to get up. My head is spinning, and I can't focus. I don't even know if I'm headed in the right direction, but I keep moving. Even if the exit isn't here, to stick around would be suicide.

Automatic weapons fire and plasma weapons erupt from somewhere behind me. I flinch, ready for the hit, but nothing comes. They're shooting in the other direction. Towards our attacker.

Another explosion rocks the ground, and I stumble. Then there's a hand under my shoulder, keeping me steady—it's Kayley! She does her best to pull me along, but she's struggling, too. Neither of us can keep this up much longer.

"You two! Stop, or I'll shoot!" a guard yells from behind us. We're already at full throttle. There's no way we can stop without falling on our faces. It's easier to keep running if we can manage it. Our tanks are getting close to empty.

"Stop now, or else!"

Kayley lets out a terrified wail. She's gasping for air, and I'm right there with her. I try to catch her gaze, but a too-quick turn of my head makes my eyes roll back in my head. I don't know how I manage to stay on my feet. I won't try that again.

If we stop, we become even easier targets for the assassin. If we keep running, the guard behind us will shoot. Neither is good, but I'll take my chances with the guard. He doesn't kill people for a living.

A shot rings out, and the guard screams. There's a thump and then nothing else. I was right to fear the assassin more. Still, why did our attacker kill the guard? Are we next?

The answer comes when bits of brick burst from the wall, spraying us with sharp pellets. I suppose our assassin wanted the pleasure of killing us themselves. Really, it's no comfort to know that.

The guards fire back, releasing volley after volley as they seek revenge for their fallen comrade. The sound is thunderous, filling my ears with a cacophony of blasts until I can barely hear anything else. Their guns blow off so many rounds, I think they're just trying to take out anything, including the trees.

"Guys, come on!" It's Parrish, waving us on from a gate just up ahead. A bullet strikes the wall near him, and he hits the ground next to where Doc Elizabeth is with Grady. A guard is there, but she keeps spinning her head between us, them, and whatever enemy we all currently face. She grips her rifle, knuckles white, but doesn't know where to aim it.

Kayley stumbles and knocks into me, forcing me forward. We both go down, face-first. Soil fills my mouth and nose, and I cough, trying to expel the dirt. My nose throbs, and I feel it's about to drip blood. I reach for Kayley, and she grabs me back. Together we pull each other up and lumber towards Parrish.

"Let us out! Please!" Kayley cries at the guard who's huddled down next to us.

"I can't! I supposed to be arresting you!" She ducks as another bullet pelts the wall above our heads.

"For what? We're the ones getting shot at!"

The guard glances out, then grabs her radio and tries to call her captain. No answer. She tries again. Still nothing. A sharp breath, then she looks at us, then back out into the grounds. She lifts her rifle up to her shoulder and sights down it, searching for...what?

It doesn't matter. A second later, her body convulses, and she collapses. We duck, but no more bullets come. No more are needed. The one that struck her in the head did the job.

Doc Elizabeth breaks our stunned silence. "I hate to say this, but if we don't move Grady soon..."

"We know," Kayley replies, trying to hold back the emotion in her voice. She looks down at the deceased guard and says a quick prayer. Then her eyes turn to me, and she speaks one word: "Keys."

I feel sick rummaging through this poor guard's pockets, but if we stay here, we'll suffer the same fate. Kayley goes to the other side of her and helps. I say my own prayer for her as we search.

"Guards coming our way," Parrish warns.

"Shuttle is available." Original Teddy's voice pops into my head via Teddy comm. I let out a happy moan, and Kayley's eyes dart over to examine my face. I must be smiling.

Kayley holds up a single large key and smiles back, then her face stiffens, and she turns towards the gate.

"Keep down," she says. "We're not dying today."

With a glance at the approaching guards, I help Parrish load Grady onto his back, and we fly out the gate.

Chapter Twenty

"Down the avenue and left!" I say, directing everyone towards the Teddy shuttle. We've got a ways to go before we reach the landing pad and safety, but now that we're out of the kill box, I think we can relax.

We're pretty ragged after that hellride. Parrish, as athletic as he is, is slowing with Grady's weight on his back. He's limping, too, which means his knee is hurting. Kayley's got one arm locked with Doc Elizabeth to make sure she stays on her feet, but Kayley's likely leaning on the Doc for support too.

"Let me take him for a bit," I say. Parrish hesitates, but then nods and dips so I can take Grady onto my back. I loop my arms around his legs and lean forward. Grady moans, but he wraps his arms around my neck, and I take off.

"Just a bit farther, dude." I don't want to consider what happens if we don't get there. We have to. For Grady's sake. For all our sakes.

As I turn the corner, a figure in black steps from the shadows to confront us. It's a woman, I think. The short cape around their shoulders covers the shape of the body, and the full face mask hides the face completely.

But I'm more concerned with the two long blades in their hands.

"Oh, hell," Parrish says, stepping in front of Grady and me. I don't know what he thinks he can do while he's weaponless. He's tough, but he's not experienced in fighting arts like Afton is. Man, what a time to be without her.

The dark figure steps closer, slicing their weapons through the air. If their intentions weren't already apparent, they are now.

"Guys, run. I'll—"

"You'll what?" Kayley asks. "Parry, you run, too!"

"Teddy, we would appreciate some help!" I call over Teddy comm as I back away from the approaching human chopping machine. They could be the one who tried to shoot us at the palace, or they could be part of a team trying to kill us. Not that I'm overly particular about the details.

Parrish grabs a pair of covers off the nearest trash bins. That doesn't slow down the death dealer in black at all. If anything, Parrish may just have invigorated their desire to slice us to bits.

"Assistance in transit," Original Teddy replies. But how do we hold our killer off before he gets here?

"Get out of here!" Parrish shouts.

I've no choice. I can't fight or defend myself with Grady on my back, so I find the nearest alley and burn down it.

"Over there!" Kayley shouts behind me. They're going a different way, I think. Good. We should split up. Maybe.

Teddy can keep track of me, and I him, but the others don't have Teddy comms with them. No matter how many times I tell them, they always forget. To be fair, I've got mine inside me, via nanobots. They've got to remember to bring the earpiece.

I find an alcove and duck down inside, sliding Grady off me to rest against the door. His face squeezes into agony, then relaxes again. He's got to be barely conscious, and with every moment, my bud is slipping away a little more.

I glance both ways down the alley. Maybe I can find an exit and either meet up with Teddy or get Grady straight to a hospital. Whatever it is, I need to do it now.

The clang of metal echoes down the alley. Parrish yells, then there's another crash. He's trying to save us, but no way is he a match for a trained killer.

"Parrish, run!" I shout down the alley, hoping he hears me and takes my advice. I shout again, but there's no reply. All becomes quiet, and the blood drains from my body. I don't want to even think that the black demon might have just ended my friend's life.

There's no time to wonder. I turn back to Grady, trying to make a quick decision about what to do. Nothing comes, so with a struggle, I get my bud onto my back and take off again, trying to get to safety as fast as I can.

But the black assassin is there, blocking our escape. I cry out in surprise and back away, but there's just so much backing up I can do. This alley is short, and it's only got one way out. The only way to go is through this silent killer.

"Listen," I say, stalling for time. "Let my friend go, and you can have me. Okay? He's already wounded. No fun in killing him, right?"

Nothing, just a step forward. Closer to us. Closer to ending our lives.

"Hey, come on." I take another step back. "Are you really going to make this so easy on yourself? I mean, don't you just get bored sometimes? Crave a little challenge now and then?"

The figure in black stops. Maybe they're considering. Or maybe they're about to pull out a gun and just shoot us. But then they flip the blade in their left hand around and toss it at me. It lands at my feet, the blade pointing back at them. I stare down at it, well aware of what it means. My words worked, and now I have to fight this killer with a weapon they're a master at.

I won't last a minute, but it'll be even less if I don't pick it up.

"Sorry, dude," I whisper to Grady. "I was really trying to save you, but it looks like you and I are about to meet the Goddesses together. Don't worry, I'll be up there, waiting for you."

The assassin scratches the ground with the tip of their blade, motioning me to get on with it. I sigh and move towards the wall so I can put Grady down again. He'll be out of the way. Not that it matters. This will probably be over in a few seconds.

"I hope you're going to give me at least some kind of fighting chance," I say, picking the blade up. It's lighter than I expected, but well balanced, and it certainly seems laser-sharp. I grip it with both hands, the way I've seen actors do. Perhaps it's correct, perhaps it's not. It won't matter for long.

The figure in black moves into a stance, swinging the blade over their head horizontally. I just keep mine out in front of me, hoping that I can at least block an attack or two.

Then the assassin strikes.

The attack comes quick. Faster than I expect. My blade comes up. It's a successful block. But their blade comes across and slices me on the shoulder. I yell in pain and back away. The cut isn't deep, but it stings enough.

The assassin moves back into position, readying another strike. I put my blade out again. I was lucky that time. This time may be it for me.

The killer spins, sliding the blade through the air at my head. I move to stop it, but they evade, dropping to slice at my leg. The blade connects with my thigh and draws a line across it. Fire burns into my muscle, and I drop.

I'm not done yet. I lunge, the tip of my weapon aimed for the killer's head. It's unexpected, and they're forced to an awkward position to parry. The killer knocks away my blade and thrusts forward, punching me in the chest.

I stumble back, falling onto my butt. I'm totally open, yet the figure in black pauses. It's an opportunity, and I take it. I shove myself forward, charging at the assassin with the edge of my blade. They block it, but the weight of my motion continues. I knock the killer onto their back, and I fall on top of them.

My hand lands on—oh! Yes, this assassin is definitely a woman. Her yelp of surprise confirms that. My moment of embarrassment loses me the initiative. The killer puts her boot into my stomach and throws me back. I fly through the air and land hard, dropping my blade as my head connects with the ground.

Not a second later, she's over me, her blade pointed at my throat. This is it—I'm done for. Well, I tried. My mom's really going to be upset. Kayley, too. Heck, everyone will be. Except for whoever put this black-caped woman in their employ.

"Why...why are you doing this? Who put you up to it?" I say in between hard breaths. "What did we do to deserve this?"

"Deserve's got nothing to do with it." She flicks her blade, catching me on the cheek. "That's for being a pervert."

"Really? You're trying to kill me, and that's what you're upset about?"

"A lady's got to have her standards."

I cry out as the tip of her blade digs into my shoulder. I throw my hands up in surrender. There's no way I'm getting out of this, but I can at least beg for Grady to be saved.

"Please, let my friend go. He'll never seek revenge or try to hurt anyone. He just wants to design stuff. I don't even know if he'll make it, but if you've got any molecule of decency in you, you'll—"

I scream as she drives her blade deeper into my shoulder, twisting it as she presses. My eyes fill with tears until I can no longer see.

"I don't get paid to let people go," she growls.

"Okay, okay...please just stop!"

"Huh, you're not the problem they said you'd be. More of a weakling, I'd say. No challenge at all."

I blink, trying to clear my eyes. Her comment strikes me. Even if I don't live, I need to know who it is that wants us dead. Sure, we've been a headache for the conspirators that are trying to overthrow the Emperor, but enough for them to want to murder us? Have we caused them that much trouble?

"Who said? Who hired you?"

"Ha! Not falling for that one." She pulls her blade from my shoulder and raises over her head, ready to end my life. "I'm done playing with you. Time to say goodbye so I can go find your friends. Especially that pretty redhead."

"No!" I scream.

But the blade never drops. The assassin stands frozen, until something tips her off-balance and she comes crashing down on me, stiff as a plank of wood.

Or a popsicle.

"Rance!" Kayley cries as she rushes to my side. There's a cut on her face, but she's otherwise unharmed. Original Teddy and the blue buddies are there, too. So is Parrish. He's a bit bloodied but in no way dead, thank the Goddesses.

I roll the assassin off me, inhaling a very welcome breath of alleyway air. I feel the adrenaline drain from my body, and suddenly I feel like I could lie here forever. But my exhaustion only lasts for three seconds.

"Forget me. Grady! We've got to save Grady." I fly up to find where I left him. Doc Elizabeth is already there, tending to him with some device I can only guess the Teddys brought her.

"Relax," she says. "I've stabilized him. Once we get him up to the ship, we can do more. For the rest of you as well. And me."

"Exodus is recommended," Original Teddy says.

"Yeah...yeah, let's get the hell off this planet."

Though, in the back of my mind, I know we'll be returning. We're not leaving Afton here. No way.

Chapter Twenty-One

It was exactly thirty-two seconds before Kayley kicked me and Parrish out of Doc Elizabeth's room.

I know that for certain because I was counting every precious second. From the moment we brought Grady in and laid him down on the exam chair, the doc and Kayley were already cutting his shirt off to get at the bullet holes. I stood there, covered in blood—some of it mine, some of it Grady's—and just watched, frozen in fear for my friend's life. Two times Kayley asked me to get out of her way. There wasn't a third.

On the shuttle ride up, Doc Elizabeth had taken a brief look at my shoulder, then shoved a few bandages and some pain-blockers in my hand and told me I'd be fine. I was only concerned with Grady, so I didn't think much of it.

Grady wasn't conscious when we took him to the shuttle, running as fast as we could. I had fallen twice, and then the blue buddies had taken over for Parrish and me. It was for the best. Parrish had cuts all over him from the assassin's blades. Doc Elizabeth put *his* bandages on for him.

"Do you think..." Parrish doesn't want to say it—we might lose Grady forever. It's bad enough that we've lost Afton. To lose another friend is not something any of us want to think about.

"I don't know. I don't know," I whisper back.

I put my back against the corridor wall and slide down. My head is throbbing from blood loss, and I'm too tired to stand. Parrish joins me, his arm rubbing against my good shoulder. The connection is welcome. It reminds me I'm not alone in my feeling of helplessness. Inside the room across the hall, our friend is dying, and there's no way to know if he'll survive.

"What did we do to deserve assassination?" Parrish asks the air.

"Deserve's got nothing to do with it," I reply.

"Huh?"

"That's what that killer answered when I asked the same thing."

"You talked to them?"

"It wasn't much of a conversation. She was too busy stabbing me to say anything of real importance."

I rub my eyes. They're strained from staring at the blank door that leads into the doc's room. I'm trying to imagine what's going on inside, but I don't really want to. I'd rather be in there seeing what is happening.

"So it was a woman."

"Does it matter?"

"No, but...I guess I'm just surprised."

"Danny Lecker has a power suit and heavy weapons. Why should *this* surprise you?"

"You're right. It doesn't matter. There's only one thing that does right now."

"He'll make it." I attempt to sound confident, but my voice goes flat. It's not convincing at all. "But it's not the only thing we've got to worry about."

"You mean"—Parrish shifts, angling himself in my direction—"you're worried about Afton?"

"Is that a loaded question?"

"No. Just looking for the truth."

"Aren't we all?" But before Parrish can reply to my rhetorical question, I add, "No. I mean, of course, I'm worried about Afton, but don't forget, we're not out of the woods yet. That assassin was just the tip of our problems. We've got a little more than two weeks to complete our mission, otherwise some woman in black won't be the only one trying to kill us."

Parrish exhales slowly but raggedly for someone who's trained most of their life to run long distances. Everything is weighing on him just as much as it is any of us. Plus, he's got his mom to worry about. I don't even really know what's going on with her other than she's been sick. Now I feel horrible for not being a better friend and visiting her, or offering Parrish help for whatever he needed to take care of her and himself. I guess it's no use feeling sorry for myself. I deserve any blame that comes my way, but

Parrish will just pile all the responsibility and emotion onto himself until he can't take it anymore, and I don't want to see that happen to him.

"So what are our choices?" Parrish asks.

"Nothing you're going to like."

"Tell me."

There he goes again, trying to shoulder the burden for everyone. He doesn't even realize that he's in the same exact situation as all of us.

"We run, or we find a way to do the impossible," I say.

"We've done the impossible before," Parrish replies with all the confidence of a tournament-winning coach. I wish I could be more like him.

"True, but one of these days, dude…"

"One of these days, what?"

"Our luck is going to run out."

"Yes, but"—Parrish lowers his head towards me—"why does that have to be today? Or tomorrow?"

Parrish brings up a good point, but until something happens, it's all philosophical nonsense. Of course, I really shouldn't be saying that. What he's trying to tell me is a principal idea in the faith that I follow. The Three Goddesses tell us not to get caught up in what happened yesterday or what might happen tomorrow. Today is your focus, and you should make it the best day that you can.

Only, I'm not feeling very faithful today.

Today isn't a day I want to focus on. Yesterday, either. Who knows what tomorrow will bring, but it's my only hope. I can only pray that Grady survives to see tomorrow, or that when I wake up, I've solved our problems. Or even that tomorrow, we're somewhere safe.

"It doesn't," I reply. "But there's only so much that we can control."

"No doubt, but we can't worry about the stuff we can't control."

"No, we should absolutely worry about the stuff we can't control, dude. Those are the things that are going to kill us."

"We're all going to die one day. That doesn't worry me. What I'm concerned about is whether or not I've lived a good life. Then, if I die, I do so with no regrets."

"Figures you'd say something like that," I mutter.

"Huh?"

"Never mind." I sigh. "I mean, you're right. You're never not right. You've always got it figured out…and I wish I could be more like you."

"Dude." Parrish levels a look on me only a schoolteacher would use. Especially when they're about to download some important data into a student's brain. "Don't get down on yourself. You've done so many amazing things. Especially when it comes to the people you care about."

"Thanks, dude, but I can't seem to remember any of those."

"That's because you don't think of your actions as important, or even special."

"They're not." I shrug. "I'm just doing what you'd do. Only you wouldn't think twice about it."

Parrish stares at me for a long moment. He's not angry.

"Do you remember when you put yourself in danger so that we could get the data off the *Mursilis* safely?"

"No, I didn't."

"Do you remember going to your father and asking him to help you, even though just the sight of him caused you grief?"

"How you do you know that? You weren't around for that."

"Kayley told me."

"Oh."

"And do you remember, even though you were hurt, putting on Danny Lecker's power suit and then running to find Afton, because we all feared she was injured?"

I just shrug. Parrish was on Teddy comm, so he knows everything that went down. I just think he sees it differently than I do. If he were there, wearing that armored suit, he would have done the same thing. What I did isn't special. It's what anyone would have done.

"What's your point, dude?"

"You're more like me than you think, Rance. You're always praising me for stuff that I see you do on a regular basis. I don't know why you think I'm so great."

"Are you kidding? Parrish, you're amazing! You think I put myself in danger? What about you, running into Exodus so that we could free Freddie? You almost ended your athletic career!"

"Not almost," Parrish says, his voice low. "I can run, but not at the level the professionals can. Not anymore. Why do you think I'm considering a coaching career now?"

"No!" I shake my head, not wanting to believe his words. He doesn't deserve to lose his dream because of one situation that wasn't even his fault. "Dude, no! You can! I know you can!"

Parrish just smiles, a wistful look in his eyes. My heart sinks even further than before. Not him! He doesn't deserve it. Parrish is the most honorable, most considerate human that I know. It's not right that he gets punished for trying to help us. It's not right at all.

"We all make sacrifices, Rance. I don't regret my choices. Sure, I'm a little bummed that I can't compete on a pro level, but I found something else that I can do that I know will fulfill my soul just as much."

I squeeze my eyes shut. I know he's content to follow this alternative path, but I can't help but feel he's given something up because he had no other choice. And I can't do anything about it.

I've failed all my friends, and I'm helpless to make it right. Despite all that we've accomplished, I've always known it was them, and not me, that achieved our goals. Now Grady dangles over the edge of death, Parrish's injury has forced him to give up on his dream, and Afton...

Afton has lost all her friends because we were stupid and selfish. Now she's gone, and there's no simple way to get her back. We've invited more trouble onto ourselves, and for the first time, I think maybe she's better off without us. She's safe from harm, she has someone who cares about her, and she will never want for any material thing ever again.

"You alright, Rance?"

"Fine," I reply with a sniffle. It's a complete lie, and I can't hide the fact that it is. Parrish knows me too well, anyway. Even if I was trying, I couldn't deceive him.

"I know what you're thinking," Parrish says. "I know, because I feel the same way."

"Yeah? How am I feeling?"

"Like you seriously messed up. That everything's your fault, and you've got no way to fix what's wrong."

"Got it in one. One million points for you, dude."

I rub my forearm across my nose. It's not pretty, but neither is junk dripping out of it as I tear up. I'm about to become a sniveling mess, and I don't really care. The Teddys might understand what I'm going through, but they don't feel regret the way humans do. Parrish is the only other one here, and he's right there with me.

"Can I say something?" Parrish asks.

"Of course."

"Afton is missing us, just as much as we are her."

"How can you be so sure?"

"Come on, Rance. If she truly met the love of her life, don't you think she'd want to be sharing every happy moment with us? She may put on a big show of being tough, but you've got to know she's got the same hang-ups, the same fears, the same hopes as we do."

"Afton *is* that tough."

Parrish laughs.

"Kayley is tough, too. So is Grady, in his own way. And just because someone is tough doesn't mean they're not sensitive," he says.

"Kayley was trying to tell me something like that about Afton, too."

"Because it's true, dude. No one wants to be that much of an individual. That's why we all connect, and it's also why we're all still hanging out with each other. We make a great team, Rance."

I know there's truth to Parrish's words. I might not be able to accept them fully at the moment, but somewhere down inside of me, I know he's right. Parrish is always right, and if he's right, that means we need to do whatever we can to stay together.

Which means we've got to do whatever it takes to get Afton back.

"Okay," I say.

"Okay, what?"

"Afton. We don't leave until she's with us."

"Was that even a question?"

I frown at him, wondering just exactly what we've been discussing if not that. Then I feel my mouth curving upwards. Yep—Parrish does it again.

The door dissolves before us, and Kayley rushes out, desperately searching for us. A second later, she catches Parrish and me on the floor, staring up at her, hopeful.

"He's going to make it," she says, breathing hard. Kayley wipes a sleeve across her eyes and blinks. "Come in and see him. Get yourselves checked out, too."

Then she returns to the room, ready for the next challenge.

Chapter Twenty-Two

THE NEXT EVENING, WE find ourselves back on Canis Ludis, putting ourselves at risk to meet with Billie Morgan, who I still think of as Ms. Cool. She said she had something to tell us.

I wouldn't have expected to meet her here, in the waiting room of the rail station, where we're forced to endure the cries of babies and the smell of travelers who haven't had a chance to get clean. I'd suspect most hand-hunters would have their own means of transportation around the planet, just so they could avoid this infestation of humans.

"Well, hello, precious. Fancy meeting you and the gang here," Ms. Cool says.

"You called us here," Kayley points out.

The Royal de Avila Station reminds me of the woman it was named after—completely nuts. It is nearly impossible to navigate through this place without some kind of guidance. I'm glad we're not trying to get on a train. Just to reach one, we'd have to wind our way through a labyrinth of corridors and cross-corridors, stairs, and elevators, and then choose the right gate for the specific door on the train we'd need to get on at. I don't understand how anyone does this on a regular basis.

"Hey, Billie," Parrish says with a smile...a big smile.

"Hey yourself, handsome." Billie reaches out and touches Parrish's chin with a wink, then turns to me. "I've got some bad news, precious. We can talk, but someplace more secure."

"Then why did you suggest we meet here?" Kayley asks.

"Because, girly, they've got single-use toilets here. Come with me, I'll tell you what I know." Billie grabs Kayley's wrist and tugs her away.

"Wait," I say. "What about us? Can't we hear, too?"

Billie looks me up and down.

"You two are really attached at the hip, aren't you? I'm so surprised you're not married yet. Alright, fine. Let's go. You, too, handsome."

Parrish and I follow Billie and Kayley to the toilets. It's not a bad idea, actually. For one, they're likely cleaner than the seats in the waiting area, and for another, each toilet is its own room. We may get a few curious looks going in and out, but it's better than someone overhearing us.

"So?" I ask once we're all jammed into the stall. It's only designed for one person to occupy, so it's fairly cozy. Good thing we all know each other.

"No dirt on the queen, unfortunately," Billie says, and the three of us let out an exasperated sigh.

"Why'd you drag us in here, then?" Kayley asks, with a bit of an edge to her words.

I was getting my hopes up, too. Even if we were getting thrown off Canis Ludis, at least we could return to the Chamberlin with the mission completed. Then we could return our focus back to our troubles with Afton. Instead, we're headed to purgatory on the Teddy ship.

"Because I have something that relates to the queen...and your friend, the one who's dating the princess."

"Afton? What about her? Is she being held against her will?" Parrish asks.

"No. Not that I've heard, anyway."

"So, what then?"

"There's talk that Her Royal Highness is attempting to push her mother off the throne."

Silence hangs in the room for a long moment. Parrish, Kayley, and I share an anxious look. If Nayla really wants to dethrone her mother, Afton could be caught up in the middle of the struggle...and if the princess fails, they'll execute Afton right along with her.

"How real is this talk?" Kayley asks.

"It's very real. My sources are legit." Billie chuckles. "I hunted each one of them for their spouses. Now they're happily married into three of the most important families on Canis Ludis. Lucky guys. They were running for their lives when I went after them. Now they realize just how big a favor I did them. They owe me on a permanent basis."

"You should start charging them, too, for your services," Parrish comments. Billie turns to him, considering. Then her eyes light up, and she smiles and nods at him.

"Just for that, I'd give you a freebie," Billie says. "I could hook you up with a lovely noble lady...or guy. Whatever you want. Or maybe...I could just keep you for myself."

Parrish seems cautiously enthusiastic about that idea. But Kayley is edging in between him and Billie, clearly annoyed.

"Can we get back to the important news, please?" Kayley says through gritted teeth.

"Sure, Red. What else you want to know?"

"How about when? Who else is involved? And why?"

"The why is easy. Hathor de Avila is nuts, and her daughter is tired of her mom's nonsense."

"Is that whole..." I wave my hands around in imitation of Nayla. "Is that for real?"

"Your guess is as good as mine, precious. As for who else is in on it, probably some of the high-ranking officials. Maybe someone Imperial, as well."

I shiver at that thought, even though it's not all that surprising. We've been dealing with Imperial messes for the better part of a year. As unstable as the queen seems, she's done well to fend off the claws of the Emperor. He and his ministers would like nothing more than to rule this planet and its highly sought-after resources. So Billie is right. Support for Nayla likely comes right from the top.

"The Chamberlin?" I ask.

"Not directly," Billie replies. "If they found him out, all the Central Planets would do some of their own overthrowing."

"How do you know so much about this stuff?"

"Well, I go where my job takes me, and that's usually right into the thick of these plots and coups and stuff. After you get to experience it for a while, it all seems like the same thing, just with different people."

I'm impressed. I always knew Danny Lecker was a clever lady, but I guess you'd have to be for the hand-hunting gig. It makes sense then that Billie is also sharp. To capture an elite, I guess you've really got to be on top of your game. I'm glad she's on our side now. I wouldn't want to face her in a dark alley. Again.

"Well, boys and girl. That's what I've got. It's been a moment hanging with you in this cushy little spot, but I've got to get back to work." Billie waves two fingers and turns to go.

"Billie?" I say. "Can I ask you a question?"

"Sure thing, precious. Shoot."

"Why do you do it? I mean, why are you a hand-hunter?"

Billie looks at me as she opens the door. Her smile is warm and sweet, like feeling the first rays of the sun on a cool morning. It's brief, but I'm touched by its sincerity, and by the vulnerability that she allows me to see. A few seconds later, it disappears into a grin.

"Because I'm a hopeless romantic. Catch you later, kids."

She blows Parrish a kiss and slips out. Parrish blushes but watches her go. I wonder if he's considering dating Billie for real. She's probably a few years younger than Danny Lecker, but that still puts her almost ten years older than Parrish. Well, I guess love knows no age limits. If it worked out, I'd be happy for him.

"Now what?" I ask.

"Now we get out of the toilet, maybe?" Parrish suggests.

"Not yet," Kayley responds. "We need to figure out what to do with this information."

It's a good point. We need to plan carefully here. I wouldn't want Afton, or even Nayla, to get into trouble they couldn't get out of. They'd never be forgiven if they attempted to take Queen de Avila from the throne by force. Not when that woman would like nothing better than to make use of her favorite head-chopper.

Maybe Nayla wouldn't get the guillotine since she's the crown princess. But that wouldn't get Afton out of trouble. Even if she didn't lose her head, she could still get thrown in jail for the rest of her life, just for falling in love.

We could tell Afton, hoping she believes us, and then get her off this nutty planet. I'm not so sure about that, however. I don't think I could do it if I had to choose between leaving Kayley and saving my own life. What kind of life would I have without the best thing that's ever happened to me?

"Guys, I think we know what we'd do if Nayla didn't take the throne, but what if she was successful? Afton would be dating a monarch, then, wouldn't she? How awesome would that be? Maybe we don't need to do anything but wait." I smile at Kayley and Parrish, despite their frowning faces.

"Well, yeah, but that's still a colossal risk to take with Afton's life," Kayley responds. "I think it would be better to get her out of there, and then whatever happens, happens without her in the middle of it."

"She'd be totally heartbroken," Parrish adds, "but at least she'd still be alive."

"We'd have to tell her the truth to get her to come with us," I say. "And she might not. Afton's not thrilled with us at the moment. We might not get her back that way."

Kayley presses her lips together. I can almost see her shaking her head.

"If Afton won't listen to reason," I continue, "we're going to have to take her by force."

"Oh, yeah," Parrish says, "because Afton wouldn't knock you across the park if you challenged her."

"Yes, Rance," Kayley adds, "none of us are a match for her. I mean, I doubt she'd hit me, but you? Definitely."

Then it hits me. Not unlike how Afton might, should I tell her that her girlfriend is a terrible person. We don't need to overcome Afton's muscle. W e *will* have to get close enough to her to make it work, and we're going to need a few hands, and possibly a few tentacles.

I reach out and upload my message. I won't know when it will get received, but I'm confident it will. Then we just have to wait.

I smile. Afton will be safe. We're going to save her.

"Rance." Kayley narrows her eyes at me. "What are you up to?"

"Nothing."

"Liar. I know that look. What did you just do?"

I grin at both of them. It should have been this simple from the start. Afton will be raging mad once she realizes what we did, but at least she'll be safe. I might even be willing to take a punch or two if I know she's clear of the guillotine. It'll be totally worth it.

"I just called the Teddys," I say.

Chapter Twenty-Three

We were completely ready to spend the next few days preparing for our plan while we looked after Grady. None of us had given up on the idea that we could still achieve the Chamberlin's mission—and get Afton back. We were hoping to have a new plan of action ready to go ASAP.

Then, as we were leaving the station, we received a communication from the High Wazir requesting we return to our Imperial quarters at the hotel. The message didn't give a reason, but the tone of it was fairly insistent. We don't want to irritate him any more than we already have, so Kayley, Parrish, and I are going to see what all the fuss is about.

"He won't throw us in jail, right?" Parrish asks as we make our way from the spaceport to our on-planet accommodations.

"Don't you think he would have done that already?" I reply. "He's the least of our worries right now."

"How so?"

"Grady might be out of danger, but he's still got a long recovery ahead of him. Which reminds me..." I turn to Kayley. "You never explained how you saved his life."

"Nano-reconstructive procedure," Kayley replies, not looking at me. She's got her leader's face on, and her gaze is focused somewhere far ahead of us. If the High Wazir were in sight, she'd be staring him down as she stomps towards him.

"Wait, nanos?" I say in disbelief. "I thought you didn't want Doc Elizabeth to use them on us after she put them into me."

"This was different. These nanos disintegrate once they complete the procedure."

"What? So I don't have nanos in me anymore?"

Kayley stops, forcing Parrish and me to do the same. A quarter turn and she's facing me, still in boss mode.

"Your nanos are permanent. The Teddys refined them after what they learned from putting them into you and developed these. There was more, but Elizabeth wasn't really clear about the rest. Can we get this over with so we can go get Afton, please?"

I blink, and in that microsecond, Kayley pivots back and continues her advance towards the taxi stand. A full three seconds later, it hits me that I was the test subject for an unproven Teddy technology.

"But why are you mad at me?" I ask as we slide into the taxi. "I didn't know they were going to make me a lab animal."

"I'm not mad at you."

"But you *are* angry."

Kayley blasts lightning from her eyes and inhales sharply—that's my answer. If I had to guess, which is much wiser than asking her outright again, I'd suspect she's upset about the nanos and worried about me, while being annoyed at the High Wazir and worried about Grady, while also being worried about saving Afton. That would be enough to put a nuclear furnace behind anyone's eyes.

"Maybe I should do the talking once we get to the hotel," Parrish suggests.

When we arrive, our taxi has trouble finding a place to park. There's a load of baggage filling up the driveway. To make matters worse, it looks like the porters are bringing more out rather than in. As we get out of the taxi and walk past it, I glimpse a bag that seems familiar.

"Hey," I say, heading over to it, "isn't that—"

"You three." A man in the silver-and-turquoise uniform of the Queen's Guard beckons us. "Come with me."

I glance at Kayley, and she jerks her head at the man. So we obey her orders and follow him up to our quarters and into Kayley's room.

Or should I say, former room. They've emptied it of everything except the furniture, and even that has no blankets, sheets, covers, or other upholstery on it. Someone took out all the drawers from the dressers, and all the lights have had their shades removed.

The High Wazir's back is turned to us, but the moment the guard announces us, he spins around.

"What is going on here?" Kayley demands.

"You are being moved out. That is what," the High Wazir replies.

"To new quarters?" Parrish asks.

"No. You are being moved off-planet. By order of Her Majesty, Queen Hathor de Avila, you are dismissed as representatives of the Imperial government and must return to Albion, or wherever else you came from. Her Majesty has other more pressing issues to deal with, and candidly, you are taking up too much of my time."

"What pressing issues?"

"That is a matter for the court. Her Majesty's court. Not the Emperor's. That is why you must leave. Immediately."

This is problematic, to say the least. Even if it means we aren't being given up as spies, we're not going to get to complete our mission and get our reward. I'm glad the queen won't turn us into headless dolls because we tried to get the High Wazir to talk—or for any other reason—but we still need to save Afton!

"Whoa, whoa, whoa," I say, holding my hands up. "Our orders come from the Emperor. You can't just kick us out."

The High Wazir raises his chin and stares down his nose at me. He holds that gaze for a long moment, then folds his arms.

"Under penalty of death—by beheading—you are hereby forbidden to return to Canis Ludis for a period of no less than one thousand years."

"Why go through the trouble to put a time limit on it?"

Before the High Wazir can reply in what I expect will be a very irritated tone, Kayley grabs the back of my shirt with an "excuse us" and drags Parrish and me out into the hallway. She pushes us outside of the royal guard's hearing and presses us up against the wall.

"What?" I say to Kayley's laser-beam stare.

"You realize what this means?" she hisses, her lungs ripping through all the oxygen in the air at a fast clip.

"Can the queen really do that?" Parrish asks. It's a rhetorical question. I think he wants to know if our order from the Emperor overrides the queen's.

"Do you really want to stick around and find out?" Kayley responds.

"Yeah, but KayKay," I say, "there's got to be some kind of diplomatic protocol for something like this, right? I mean, wouldn't the queen have to file some form or make an official complaint or something?"

"Or just chop our heads off like she's done with the last group of agents?"

"Well, that's a good point, but couldn't we at least try to make an official protest with him and see what happens?"

"If you didn't notice from earlier, I'm kind of done with experimentation."

"Yeah, but if we just give up without trying, we lose, KayKay. Plus, we'd lose any access to Afton if we're not here. We'd have to wait until they're both off-planet and then try to approach them with that bizarre entourage the princess brings around. And as you might remember, I haven't had the best track record with that. I say we give it a chance. We've got nothing to lose if we try, and everything to lose if we don't."

Kayley throws a look at Parrish and waits. She wants his opinion, too. Seeing as how it would be his neck on the line as much as it would be ours, I'd say that's mighty considerate of her.

"I agree," Parrish says. "We've got to try. It's not an experiment. We've got an outcome we already need to get."

"Fine, but I'll be the one to talk. You," Kayley says and points at me, "will just mess it up."

I shrug. I've no issues with that. Kayley's boss, so if she wants the responsibility on her shoulders, she can have it. I'll just be the one to massage it out of them later.

The High Wazir watches Kayley put on her show of Imperial outrage against this kind of treatment with a mild level of amusement mixed with a bit of irritation. She's doing a great job and, just as I expected, stops short of making any threats. I likely wouldn't have had the self-control to do that, so I'm glad it's not me.

"You are welcome to lodge any level of protest you wish...with the Chamberlin. The Council will debate the outcome of that. But my orders are explicit. You are to be off-planet by midnight tonight, or you are to be arrested and tried for assault on a member of the court."

"We weren't trying to hurt you!" I cry. "We just want to ask you some questions!"

"Rance!" Kayley breathes fire at me for my sudden outburst. Oops. I didn't mean it. It just came out. Still, if we get out of this alive, it's going to be death by Kayley.

My words have a curious effect on the High Wazir, however. His brow softens, and he unfolds his arms and clasps them behind his back. He turns away from us and pads around the room, following a similar path to the one Kayley took just two days ago.

"Yes. About that. Just what were you trying to do?"

Kayley gives me the *don't say a word or else* stare. I press my lips together and look down, bowing out of the conversation as best as I can. I don't know what she's going to tell him. The truth? Maybe, but I doubt it. Lying won't get us anywhere, though.

"Well, you see…" Kayley chews on her lip in a convincing display of hesitation. "Well, you might find this a bit…unusual, but Princess de Avila's current…partner is a very close friend of ours. We haven't been able to see her since we've arrived on-planet, and we are honestly worried about her."

"So you tried to kidnap me?"

"No! No, not at all. We just wanted to find a quiet place to ask you some questions and maybe see if you could get us in to see her."

"You're right." The High Wazir stops his stroll and faces Kayley. "All of this is highly peculiar. Can you provide any proof that you have a connection to this woman? If, in fact, Her Royal Highness is seeing someone at the moment, that is."

Kayley pulls her Sergo from her pocket and flips through image after image of Afton, together with any assortment of the rest of us. There's even one image I remember taking, just before last summer. Kayley and Afton have their arms wrapped about each other and are pressing their cheeks together as they radiate enormous smiles at the camera. My chest gets tight just seeing it, remembering a time when it was just the five of us with no worries about anything other than when we would hang out next.

The High Wazir examines each image with interest. I even see a smile come to his face at a few of the more ridiculous poses we performed for some of them. But once Kayley is done, he clears his throat, and his pompous demeanor returns.

I wasn't expecting Kayley to go with that angle. It doesn't get us the information we wanted out of him, but that plan was dust the moment he escaped our grasp.

I'm also wondering why he's taken a sudden interest in us at all. Does he really believe we weren't trying to harm him? If so, why not speak to the queen on our behalf and let her know it was just a big mistake? Of course, it wasn't. We *were* trying to get him, and the queen might just decide to execute us for the sheer enjoyment of it.

"You are to remain here until I return, after which I will escort you directly to your shuttle and off-planet. Do not leave this room, and do not contact anyone."

He steps out the door, but then he turns around.

"Trust me when I say this is for your own good. It is not safe for you here any longer."

As the guard closes the door behind the High Wazir, I turn to Kayley and Parrish with a raised eyebrow.

"What just happened?" I ask.

"He might not admit it, but I think the High Wazir is trying to help us," Parrish replies.

"Help us? We tried to kidnap him."

"True," Kayley says, coming over to me, "but I think he sees an opportunity that he can't pass up."

"Which is what?"

"We have no way of knowing for sure. Perhaps we should just do as he advises and trust him. It's the only option we have that doesn't risk our lives, and honestly, guys, I'm really done with that."

I can't argue with that, so I sit down on the floor, because the bed is now just a frame, and the chairs are gone. This empty room is kind of like our current outlook.

Bleak.

Chapter Twenty-Four

Several hours pass before the High Wazir returns. By now, the three of us are going a bit crazy, and our stomachs are growling something fierce. We're ready to complain to him about our treatment. We aren't his prisoners. He has no right to hold us like this. But none of that matters when he opens the door...

And Nayla and Afton slide through after him.

The princess pauses just inside and scans the room as if searching for some hidden source of spiritual energy. When her eyes come to Kayley, Parrish, and me, they look right through us. She acknowledges our presence, but it's as if we're as important to her as a single speck of dust might be to a room cleaner.

Afton tries to hide her emotions as best as she can. I can tell she's surprised but happy to see us. Her face betrays a bit of confusion when they land on the cuts on my face and Parrish's. But what really shakes her is when she notices one of us is missing.

Grady.

"What's the meaning of this?" the princess asks, moving further into the room until she can pivot around in a complete turn.

"As I mentioned, Your Highness, these are the Imperial representatives who claim acquaintance of your betrothed." The High Wazir ducks his head and motions towards us.

"I am well aware of who they are. What has happened to this room?"

"We have searched it for any illegal data equipment, Your Highness."

"I don't care about that. This arrangement is completely wrong for the energy lines that pass under this hotel. The bed must face north, not west, and this dresser here..." The princess moves to the drawerless box and raps her knuckles on it. "It should be jade, not blue. This brings bad fortune to anyone who sleeps here."

"Well, that explains it," Kayley mutters.

"Are all the rooms like this?"

"Searched or arranged, Your Highness?"

"Arranged, of course! Get me the plans for the interior design of every room in this building. The karmic flow of each must be corrected."

"Yes, of course, Your Highness." I get the feeling he wants to roll his eyes as he bows. "But what about the Imperial agents?"

"What about them?"

"They are being dismissed from the planet. Queen de Avila no longer desires their presence."

Nayla's gaze darts towards us, and for the first time since she entered, the princess takes a long examination of our condition. Then she turns back to the High Wazir as she waves a hand in our direction.

"What happened to them?"

"Someone tried to assassinate us!" I answer with such force, Nayla takes a step back. I realize my mistake, so I quickly bow and add, "Your Highness."

As I return upright, I notice Afton's face has gotten paler, and her eyes are bigger than usual. I know she wants to ask, but she stays quiet. It's not just Afton who's worried about us. I'm concerned about her, too. What's happened to our brash bud, who would have made fun of us at least twice before finding out if we were truly okay? Something's going on.

"Ransom Quigley He', did I not warn you?" Nayla says, her finger making some sort of circle in the air before me. "Did I not read your stars correctly? I told you this would happen, yet you remained, despite my premonition."

Afton shifts on her feet, tugging at her loose tunic and pants, then looks away, trying to distract herself with something interesting in the room. Only there isn't anything. So, the kettle is bubbling and ready to boil over. Afton wants to know what happened to us. Maybe telling her would knock her out of whatever forced reserve she's in. I wonder if I told her about Grady, if she'd even come with us back to the Teddy ship to see him.

Maybe once we were there, we could get her to stay.

"Answer me, Ransom of Angelcanis." Nayla's tone darkens.

"I stayed because Afton is more important than any trouble I might get in," I answer.

"More important than your own life?"

"Absolutely."

Afton moves again, this time folding her arms in front of her. She's pretending disinterest, but her lower lip is quivering. I'm glad my words are effective, though I'd prefer not to make her upset. We've already done that plenty of times this trip. If we want to convince her to come back with us, getting her mad isn't the way to do that.

"Then you are a fool, Ransom Quigley He'," Nayla says, looking down her nose at me. "I do not hope for your death, but it seems inevitable. If you choose to ignore the signs, then you have already written your fate."

Nayla turns and offers her hand out to Afton, who looks at it with hesitation. She glances back up at us, then at the princess. I don't know what she's thinking, but I understand Afton is not ready to leave yet.

"Come, darling," Nayla says. "Let us purify ourselves with crystals. There are many negative wavelengths in this building."

"Afton," Kayley calls, her voice wavering. She reaches a hand out, and Afton's eyes drop to it, staring.

I should say something before they leave and we lose the chance to talk to her. Possibly forever. As much as I try to find the right words, my mind stays blank. It shouldn't be this difficult, but I'm afraid of saying the wrong thing. One wrong word or phrase, and our friend walks out that door and disappears from our life. I turn to Kayley, but she's as helpless as I am.

Nayla reaches out and takes Afton's hand in both of hers. The princess caresses it and smiles at her, but Afton only returns a hesitant smile to her. That doesn't stop Nayla from wrapping an arm about Afton's waist and leading her to the door. Afton looks back, her mouth open as if she's about to say something, yet she stays quiet.

Until they reach the door.

"Wait, wait," Afton says, untangling herself from Nayla's embrace. "Where's Grady?"

"Darling, don't—" Nayla starts, but Afton cuts her off.

"I'm sorry. I need to know." Afton's eyes plead with the princess, until Nayla sighs and releases her. Afton gives her a small smile in thanks, then turns to Kayley. "He's alright, isn't he?"

Kayley drops her gaze and takes a moment before answering. An inhale comes from Afton, and her brow wrinkles.

"No," Kayley says, her voice almost inaudible. "He's not."

That's all Afton needs to break away from Nayla and confront Kayley. "What happened?"

"Darling," Nayla calls. "Come, we must go."

"The assassin shot him," Kayley explains. "We had to take him up to the Teddy ship. There was a lot of damage, and he almost bled to death."

"No!" Afton cries. "He's going to be okay, right?"

Kayley just gives Afton a wistful smile, and it deflates her. If Afton was concerned before, I can only imagine what she's feeling now. We've all taken our turns to look after Grady, especially when his parents' trial was happening. But ever since Afton moved in with him, she's assigned herself to be his official bodyguard.

"Darling," Nayla says again, this time with more force in her voice. "Your fate must remain separate from theirs. They are on a path of ruin, and you should not follow. Let us leave them to solve their own challenges."

Conflict is written all over Afton's face, and as much as I dislike thinking this way, I really want to take advantage of her distress. Kayley's already doing it. I'm trying to catch her eye, but Afton's blocking my view, and Nayla's got her eyes locked on me. One wrong move, and the princess will use it against me. She might be a little odd, but she's observant and very much not stupid.

"You know, you could come with us," I say, reaching out to Afton. "I can't guarantee he'll be conscious, but if he is, I bet he'd be thrilled to see you."

"You think?" Afton asks, her tone hopeful. "He's not dying, right?"

"Enough, darling." Nayla comes up behind her and takes her by the arms. "That would only upset you more. Sorrow does nothing for your complexion but create fault lines. I don't want you to do that to your beautiful face."

Nayla reaches up and strokes Afton's cheek with the back of her finger. The caress breaks Afton from her struggle, and she turns to the princess, who continues to soothe her. A soft hush from Nayla's lips, and all the tension releases from Afton's shoulders.

Not good. We're losing her. I mean, I don't want Afton to be sad, but if she's not, then she won't come with us. I finally connect with Kayley's eyes and motion with my head for her to try something. Kayley shrugs and shakes her head.

I guess this is up to me.

"Afton, just come see him for an hour," I try. "So you can see him for yourself. Then you can do your purification thing. We won't bother you after that."

Nayla pulls Afton into an embrace, then steps around her to confront me.

"Ransom Quigley He'—"

"You know, Rance is just fine. Everyone else calls me that."

"I will not," Nayla counters. "It is a corruption of your true self."

"Have it your way."

Princess Nayla inhales deeply through her nose and momentarily closes her eyes. Her hands rise, palms upright, then turn over as she presses her anger down. I think it's anger, anyway. It's hard to tell, as her voice never comes above a tight clip.

"Ransom Quigley He', are you truly that selfish?"

"Selfish about what?"

"You said before that your friends are more important than your own life, yet you still try to drag Surela down with you into your darkness. Do you not care for her? Do you not wish her happiness?"

Oh, that's just mean to use my words against me like that.

"Of course I do! I love Afton! We all do!"

"Then, like a bird from a cage, set free the things you love. You need not worry about Surela any longer. She is in my keeping, and I will care for her with every cell in my body. Let her go and be on your way."

I feel my jaw go slack. Her words have stunned me into silence. Am I being selfish? Should we let Afton go so she can be happy? With the princess, she could have everything she needs. With us…what could we offer her other than more problems, more pain, and possibly an untimely death?

Wait, no. Afton is in danger if she stays here!

"Come now, darling." Nayla leans up and pecks Afton on the lips. "It's time to let go of people who do nothing but cause you harm."

"But, wait. No. I want—" Afton protests, but Nayla spins on her and presses a finger to her lips, and Afton goes quiet.

"Remember, they came here as spies. Not to wish you well."

Afton's eyes lift to look at me, then Kayley, and then Parrish. My body sags. I don't know how to combat that statement. We can't deny our reason for being here, and we have no excuse for our choices. I guess you can try to care for someone so much, you wind up ruining things for them because you were too overbearing. My intentions were good, but I needed more than that to do right by my buds.

Afton's jaw tightens, and I'm sure she's remembering just how much we messed up on her. Grady's condition broke her out of that fury, but only for a moment. Now her mask descends on her face, and any distress she was showing a second ago dissolves.

"I hope Grady's better soon," Afton says and turns. She wraps an arm around Nayla, and they walk out.

Chapter Twenty-Five

THE SPACEPORT IS NOT where I was hoping to be right now. Well, it kind of is, but not in this manner. If Afton were here, ready to blast off-planet with us, we'd be all set. But she's not. Her replacement is the High Wazir and five royal guards. He's about as excited as we are to be here like this.

At least this place is nicer than the train station. A vast dome, supported by four large arcs, covers over all the ticket counters, luggage drop-offs, and gate ramps. The denizens of this place, as unwashed as the rail passengers, move with purpose and speed. There isn't a lot of waiting around here. Thousands of ships take off and land here every day. No one has time for a nap or an overpriced meal.

Except for us. All we can do is wait. The Teddys should be here any moment to pick us up, and then we're expelled with severe prejudice from this planet. Then we've truly lost Afton. We can't come back here unless we are looking to separate our heads from our bodies.

"I will watch after your friend," the High Wazir says as he approaches. "Palace politics can become challenging, and I am sure you would not want her to get caught up in them."

I raise an eyebrow at him. Maybe I'm wrong, but it almost sounds like he knows something is about to go down. Which means whatever words he just used to calm our concerns about Afton just got smashed under my fear that she's going to get hurt.

"Thank you," Kayley says. She's hiding her own worry well. Either that, or she has some plan to get us out of here before we're gone for good.

I wait until the High Wazir walks away, then slide close to her. I'll bring Parrish in after. The three of us chatting might appear suspicious.

Kayley gives me a sad smile when I take her hand, pretending to comfort her. I am, of course. But it's a good enough ruse to be whispering in her ear without attracting too much attention from the guards.

"You okay?" she asks, looking into my eyes.

"KayKay, we're giving our escort the slip. No way are we leaving Afton on this planet."

Kayley jerks back, throwing a fast look at the guards, then rips me forward into an embrace, her mouth getting close to my ear.

"No, we are not putting ourselves or Afton at any more risk!" Kayley hisses. "We will wait until we can find a safe way to contact her, and then we will reach out. Until then—"

"You want to lose her forever?"

Her embrace gets tighter, and that's all the answer I need. We're all conflicted over Afton. But I'm not willing to just wait around until it's convenient for us to reach out to her. Nayla will have Afton so fully brainwashed by then that she might forget us completely.

"What did you have in mind?" Kayley asks.

"Give me a moment."

Kayley folds her arms and watches me. I won't impress her with what I have in mind. I just hope it works, despite the lack of sophisticated tactics.

I check the location of the guards—four of them huddle around the High Wazir, while the fifth stands at the ready. He's focused on the passing travelers rather than us. Good. We'll surprise them when we move.

"What's up?" Parrish whispers as I motion him over.

"Get ready," I say. "Follow me on three."

"Rance," Kayley warns, "we are not going to run."

"We're going to make a break for it?" Parrish asks, his face brightening.

"No," she replies. "We're not doing anything that stupid."

"One," I say, checking the guards again. Parrish tenses, ready to launch from his seat.

"Rance." Kayley grabs my arm. "We are staying put. Running only gets us executed."

"Two...leaving gets Afton executed." I take hold of her hand and squeeze. "They won't shoot us. I know it."

Kayley narrows her eyes at me, then sucks in a breath. Her gaze goes to the High Wazir and his men. She might be calculating our chances, which may be worse than I'm making them out to be. We better move before she thinks through it.

The corridor is just on the opposite side of the main thoroughfare. We'll have to get through the mass of people walking by, but once we're on the other side, we're covered. The guards won't shoot through the crowd to get to us. At least I think not.

Here goes nothing.

"Three...go!"

I jump up, tugging Kayley with me. She starts out resistant, then her muscles fly into action. Parrish is already three steps deep into the mass of travelers, dodging through them like he's playing his favorite sport. The startled pedestrians halt, fearful of a painful impact. It leaves a path for Kayley and me to follow.

"High Wazir!" a guard shouts. But we're already through. Safe from shooting. They'll have to chase us down. With the lead we've got, we'll be free in no time.

We're at the corridor entrance two seconds later, bursting through the swinging door with a boom. Parrish hesitates and looks back, checking to make sure we're with him. I wave him on, and he takes off again.

I grin as my feet pound on the floor. They thought we were just going to sit there and take it? No way. We've got a friend to rescue. No royal fuddy-duddy is going to stop us. We'll leave this crazy court coup behind and make our way home. Too bad we won't get our records erased, but there's still time for that. Now is all about the exit.

Or the lack of one.

"Whoa!" Parrish skids to a halt at the end of the corridor. The literal end of the corridor. As in, there's nowhere to go from here. We've just cornered ourselves.

"No! There's got to be an emergency exit or something!" I shout. I was sure of it. Well, Original Teddy was sure of it. He's the one who uploaded a map into Teddynet for me to examine—part of their study of the planet and its architecture. I didn't get an image of a door, exactly. I just knew this was the way out.

Boots pound behind us. Kayley gasps and spins, only to get a spotlight in her face. I raise a hand to block the beam, but it's so strong that I still have to squint.

"I don't know what you were thinking," the High Wazir says from somewhere behind the wall of light. "If you thought you would somehow evade the guards, know that there's a lot more of them than just the five I have with me. I would have brought more if I had suspected this foolishness."

Great. I should have thought this through. Not even better, just at all. Teddynet is still a mystery to me. If I want to master it, I need more practice. I'll likely have time for that. Now we're leaving Canis Ludis for sure. I just hope it's in the Teddy shuttle and not in a coffin.

"Hands on your head!" a guard shouts. "Now, turn around and walk backwards towards us."

"Okay," Kayley says, "we're doing it. Don't shoot, please?"

We've no choice but to comply. I messed this one up, alright. Kayley's ready to smack me, or hit me, or express her frustration on me in some other unpleasant way. I'll take it if it means she gets us out of here safely.

We progress slowly, careful of each step. It's awkward to walk this way, and I don't want a stumble to get mistaken for an attempt to resist. The High Wazir might not want us dead, but these royal guards might be as unstable as the queen they protect. I'm not giving them a reason to make me target practice.

I wince as something heavy hits the floor, vibrating the entire corridor. A second later, I realize it was only a spotlight because it's now illuminating the wall to my left. Whoa. That freaked me out something serious. That was way louder than I would have expected one of those things to be when they drop.

Wait...*all* the spotlights are shining in weird places. Only one of them is still on us. It's quiet behind us, too, save for some strange breathing.

That's when I get the tickle of Teddynet in my brain, and I grin.

"Teddy!" I shout and turn. He's there along with a pair of the blue buddies. "What happened to the exit?"

"Exit is available," Original Teddy says.

The five guards and the High Wazir are frozen in their popsicled positions. I should feel bad for them, but I'm so excited for freedom that I just don't have time to feel sympathy. They'll be fine, other than the extreme anger they'll experience because we got away.

"Holy Sophia!" Parrish shouts, and he leans over, hands on his knees. "I thought they really had us."

"Yeah," Kayley says. She shivers. "Teddy, which way out?"

"Teddy says follow the leader." Original Teddy is really taking this study of human culture to another level. I think he might know more about us than we do now.

We run, heading back the way we came. Teddy leads us down a side corridor and down a set of stairs. There's an emergency exit at the bottom.

"No, wait!" Kayley cries. "There's an alarm on that door! They'll know where we are!"

But I'm already in motion. My hands reach out and slam the latch bar, sending the door flying open.

"No, there isn't," I say when nothing happens.

"Dude," Parrish says. "Even I know alarms like that are silent."

And of course, they're right. No sooner are we down the path than the lights of a security vehicle flash, illuminating us in a spectrum of red and blue. We duck behind a hedge, peering through to observe them. They're headed in our direction, but whether they've found us is unclear.

But the squad of royal soldiers, headed towards us in a full sprint, seem like they are perfectly zeroed in on us.

"Yeah, we should get moving," Parrish says, spying the soldiers at the same time as I do.

"Shake a leg," Original Teddy says and darts across a field, moving perpendicular to the guards. The blue buddies chase right after him, and the rest of us follow, trying to keep up with the Teddys' significant ground speed.

We duck behind a building, looking for some kind of hiding spot. There's a basement stairwell, but it's shallow—no luck there. Then a row of maintenance vehicles. Forget it. One of them's a tanker truck. If that gets hit, everything in the surrounding area will go up.

"Here! Here!" Kayley cries and points to a large metal container. The Teddys hop in without hesitation, but as I get close, a rancid smell hits my nose, and I break.

"No way, that's a trash container!" I yell. Kayley grabs me by the arms and shakes me.

"You got us into this mess, so deal with it! Get in!" She spins me around and shoves hard. I go head forward into a stinky stew of refuse.

I'm baptized by slop, and I raise my head out of the putrid liquid, gasping for air. A second later, Kayley's entrance into the smelly hell knocks me back under. I rise again, seeking oxygen, but the foul taste in my mouth makes me think I might have just swallowed something nasty.

"Goddesses, Kayley, I've been poisoned."

"Yeah? That's still better than a bullet in the head. Keep your voice down."

"Are we all here?" I say, following her order.

"Yeah, I think so," Parrish replies. "I doubt they're going to look in here."

"You bet your life on it?"

"I think I already did."

"Teddy is available...and floating," Original Teddy adds.

Well, that's at least one positive. Nobody hurt, only seriously nauseous. I pat my body, hoping for no cuts or scrapes. That's when I realize my Sergo is in my pants pocket. It's fairly waterproof, but whatever this muck is, it's only partially made of water. At least the boxes and containers I'm bumping into tell me this isn't a sewage container. That'd be completely horrible, though this is just one small degree above that.

"Parrish, have a listen and let us know if you hear anyone coming," Kayley says and exhales. "I'm glad I wore something old and comfortable today."

"Don't worry, KayKay," I say. "We'll be out of here and into something clean soon enough."

"Yeah? And where exactly are we going to get something clean? Our luggage is on the shuttle by now. Not to mention, we still have nowhere to go or stay."

"Maybe Sara can sell us some new outfits."

"And take all of our money in the process."

"Do we have a choice?" Parrish asks, then suddenly shushes us. "Someone's coming."

A second later, there are voices outside. They're close, but the echo inside the container makes it seem like they're far away. I feel Kayley latch on to me and move me back against the wall. She presses against me, her hands along my shoulders.

"Check in there!" a voice says.

"In there? Nobody'd be dumb enough to go in there, Sarge," comes the reply.

"Check it, anyway!"

Parrish pulls back as a light flashes down the entrance to the container, lighting up the trash soup that we're floating in. It passes across rusty water, torn-up cardboard, and a sea of decaying food scraps. When I realize that there might be bits of dead animal in here, too, I get a shiver down my back.

Parrish inhales when the light crosses over his hand. It pauses there, and his eyes widen. Did they get us? But then it continues on into the darkness of the space. Then, to our relief, the light shuts off.

"Stupid," the voice says, resonating around us. "There's no one down there." They move away from our container.

We all sigh, and I feel Kayley touch her forehead to my shoulder.

"Why, Rance? Why did you ever think staying on the planet was a good idea?" she asks.

Why, indeed? There's got to be something I'm forgetting. Some detail that should smack me in the face with its glaring certainty, but is instead eluding me. Do we have some special contact we can make use of? No. A safe location to hide in? Nope, I would have figured that out, too. Maybe it's something about what we need to do. Something about saving Afton...

"Wait, what day's tomorrow?"

"Thursday," she answers.

"That's it," I say, the understanding of my decision coming clear in my head. "Tomorrow's Thursday, that's why."

"What's the day of the week have to do with anything?" Kayley moans.

"Afton goes running on Thursday mornings," Parrish answers, then sucks in a breath. "Yeah! She'll be out of the palace, and we can get to her."

"You'd better hope you're right. Afton hasn't exactly been herself lately."

"No," Parrish replies. "No matter what, Afton would never give up running. She told me. It's the one time she feels completely free."

"Alright." Kayley pokes me in the chest. "Let's go find some clean clothes...and a new place to stay."

Chapter Twenty-Six

WE DIDN'T FIND A place to stay, but we found a round-the-clock gym to clean ourselves up in. Their little shop even had exercise outfits we could buy. They were even more expensive than the duds we bought from Sara, but the disguise is nearly perfect. No one will suspect we're doing anything other than going for a morning run.

Of course, we're dead tired from getting no sleep, so we won't be doing much running.

The Teddys have lost none of their usual chipper attitude, however. Original Teddy says they're not tired because the clock on the ship is equivalent to around thirty-eight Empire hours. They'll rest when we've got Afton, but until then, they're our power packs.

There was a good deal of speculation on where Afton might go for a run, but when we called up a map, Parrish picked the location right away—a park right near the palace. There's a path there that follows a small stream, then bends towards a hilly area to return near the palace gates. If Afton was going anywhere this morning, it'd be there.

"You look good, KayKay," I say as we stroll down the soft paved path just as the morning mist is clearing. I would never normally be up this early, but since we didn't sleep, it was easy. We had to get here before Afton started her run to spot the location where we'd confront her. The Teddys are standing by to popsicle her in case things get rough. I really hope they don't have to.

"Really?" Kayley yawns and glances down at herself. She's wearing a pair of pink shorts with a white liner, and a white sport shirt. It's a bit more fashion-forward than she likes to dress for her workouts. Usually an old T-shirt and her favorite cozy pair of sweatpants will do. Her hair is also in a ponytail, as opposed to the tight dancer's bun she normally wears.

"Really. You should try doing that kind of style more often."

"Nope, too complicated." Kayley adjusts the band holding her hair up. "I don't care what I wear when I exercise. The point isn't to look good, it's being healthy. And Rance..."

"What is it?"

"I really wish you'd get into the habit. I don't want to see you get sick when you're thirty."

Exercise is a good idea, but it's been difficult to start any kind of good habits since we've been neck-deep in danger for the past year. Kayley and I could exercise together. I wouldn't mind one bit going for a run with her. It wouldn't feel like exercising at all, then.

We find a spot and position ourselves in the brush. Afton, if she is out this morning, should come our way in just a few minutes. At least that's what Parrish thinks.

I sit down, leaning my back against a tree and stretching my legs out. Kayley sits next to me and leans her head against my shoulder. Parrish is just across from us, mimicking our slouch. We're all exhausted. Yesterday wasn't the dull day we thought it was going to be. We should have just been taking a quick ride up to the Teddy ship. But no. I had to believe that we could reach Afton here.

I yawn and close my eyes. Just for a minute. Kayley or Parrish will let me know when Afton's about to show up.

I remember a situation with Afton not unlike this. We were much younger, but we had already laid the foundations of who we are today. Afton, Grady, and I were hanging out at the time, and she wanted ice cream, but Grady and I had totally stuffed ourselves at lunch, so we weren't hungry at all. Afton took off on her own, and we had to spend the rest of the day trying to locate her. When we did, she just dismissed our complaints as not important. Afton wanted to do what she wanted to do, and if our desires or interests didn't jibe with hers, then she'd do it by herself. I always thought that strange. If she wanted to have friends and hang out, then she couldn't be so unwilling to compromise sometimes.

I smile to myself as these memories cross past my eyes. Afton was even more of a delinquent back then than she is now. I guess time has softened her rage while giving her wisdom at the same time.

"Rance!" I feel someone grab me by the shoulders. "Rance, wake up!"

Wake up? Oh, shoot!

My eyes fly open, and I stare into Parrish's excited face. He points to the path and attempts to explain something to me I am totally not getting. I blink a few times, and he shakes me again, then he gives up on me and grabs Kayley to shake her.

As the fog clears from my brain, realization hits me like a cargo ship overshooting its dock connection. But it's more serious than that.

"No!" I push myself up. "Did we fall asleep? Does that mean we missed Afton? What about the Teddys? Shoot!"

"What?" Kayley pushes up with a jolt. She looks around blinking for a moment, then her eyes go wide. "Wait! Did we just sleep?"

"Yeah," Parrish answers. "We all did."

"No!" Kayley pounds the ground. "Did we miss her? Where's Teddy?"

"Not here." Parrish peers up into the trees, where Original Teddy and his blue buddies were supposed to be. He turns to me. "Rance, can you find them?"

"Hold on."

I shake the remaining sleep from my brain and try to get something from Teddynet. There's nothing there, so I try Teddy comm.

"On reconnoiter," Original Teddy replies. "Determination of alternative direction in progress."

I share that with Parrish and Kayley. Kayley shakes her head, clearly angry with herself. I'm upset, too. How did I let myself slip like that? Sure, I'm tired, but this is my bud. I can't let her down, and here I am, doing exactly that!

"Teddy, give me your position. We're coming to you."

The moment I'm clear where they are, I motion to Parrish and Kayley and take off. Sleep is still muddling my brain, but the disappointment in myself is forcing my adrenaline to kick in. A minute after we take off running, I feel a boost of energy, and I use it to get to the Teddys as quickly as my legs can move.

"They're trying to find a spot to cut Afton off!" I shout as we force our way through the brush. Branches and vines resist my advance, attacking my arms and smacking my face. I don't care. We screwed up...again. If we don't save this situation, I'm going to hate myself for a long time.

"Rance," Kayley says, breathless. "This is stupid. We're sleep-deprived, and there's no way we're going to convince Afton to do anything. Not like this."

"No! We don't have time!" But as I say it, I realize that she's right. This is a half-assed attempt to save Afton now. We can barely think straight, and we're running through the forest with no actual sense of direction. Sure, I know where the Teddys are, but I don't know how to get there.

Still, I press on.

Our course leads us uphill. That's got to be the right direction. I don't know if this bandage on our failed plan will even work, and I have no way to calculate how fast Afton is running or how far she has to travel to get to where we're going.

My heart beats hard, and I find myself constantly catching my breath. But the thought of losing Afton keeps my feet moving as fast as they can. I can only hope the Teddys can locate an interception point and our lapse in vigilance won't be the end of this attempt.

"Rance," Kayley gasps, stomping through the underbrush. "How are you going to talk to her if you can't even breathe? Let's admit defeat and make a better plan."

"No, Kayley," I reply. "She's so close! We may never get another chance like this!"

"We could have one next Thursday," Parrish corrects.

"It might be too late by then," I shoot back, "for her and us."

The closer we get to the Teddys, the clearer their location becomes to me. I press harder, hoping we can meet up with them in the next minute.

"Teddy, where's Afton now?"

"Approaching contact point."

"Will we make it?"

"Unknown."

That's not the answer I want to hear. I gather whatever strength I have left and break into a sprint. The branches of the undergrowth scrape and slice my legs, but I ignore the pain. It's trivial compared to intercepting Afton. Kayley calls after me—I can already hear I've put distance between her and me. That's not ideal. Kayley needs to be the one to do all the talking. Maybe I can hold Afton until she gets there. I've got no idea how to do that, but I'll have to try something.

I break out of the forest and onto the path, swinging my head both ways, hoping to catch sight of her.

"Teddy, where is she?"

"Unknown."

"No! Find her!"

"Attempt not possible."

I consider rushing off in either direction, but I realize it's useless. Sure, I've got half a chance, but if I run into her, then what? I'm the one that Afton is angry at the most. She might listen to Kayley, but me? If Afton were herself, she'd slug me a good one, and that'd be that. My jaw would hurt for a week, but we'd have her back.

No, Afton is under some kind of spell. Nayla's got her under her full control, and unless we break that bond, we're never going to save her.

I just wish I would have figured that out yesterday.

Kayley and Parrish bust through and halt next to me, their chests heaving. I close my eyes and hang my head. Our fuel tanks were already empty when we started this mission. We never had a real chance to prepare for the battle we'll have to fight to bring Afton home. Of course, that's only if she wants to come home.

"Where is she?" Parrish asks.

"Gone," Kayley replies, sounding as if she doesn't believe her own answer. "She's gone."

Chapter Twenty-Seven

I LIE DOWN AND shut my eyes, only to open them again a second later. At least that's what it feels like. In reality, I'm sure a great deal more time has passed. Hours. Days, maybe, but I hope not. We don't have that kind of luxury. Still, we had to rest. There was just no more energy left for us to s
pend.

The hotel room we found is small, but that's the least of our concerns. It's discreet, and away from any sort of major thoroughfare where the queen's guards might search for us.

Kayley is beside me, so bereft of strength she didn't even curl up to me the way she normally does when we're together. Maybe Parrish—sleeping on a cot not far away—and the Teddys being in the same room put a halt to her thoughts of coziness. Whatever. We're not here to be romantic, anyway.

My Sergo buzzes, and without thinking much about it, I pick it up and answer the call. It could be my mom, or Doc Elizabeth, and those would both be important calls.

But it's not.

"Where are you?" Bailiff Daughtry's irritated voice asks. Oh, great. After the queen, she's the last person I want to talk to.

"I'm sleeping. That's where I am. What do you want?"

"To talk to you."

"You're talking."

"In person. This isn't a conversation for a Sergo transmission. We need to meet."

I sigh. This is like having a scrape and rubbing sandpaper on it. But I know she won't leave us alone. And the fact that she's got my Sergo ID means she'd be able to track us down even if I didn't tell her where we are. Then she'd be apt to give us a few sharp pinches for being deceptive.

"Fine, I'll send you the location."

"Standing by."

"Can you wait an hour? Also, could you bring us a change of clothes?"

There's silence on the other end.

"We will retrieve your luggage from the shuttle and bring it to you. How's that?"

"Well, fine, but maybe just one bag each. There's not a lot of space here."

Bailiff Daughtry and her minions are early by a few minutes. I don't know the exact number of minutes because I wasn't watching the time. Once I disconnected with the bailiff, I set an alarm for fifty-five minutes and went back to sleep. She beat even that.

Parrish stumbles to the door as the Teddys make themselves scarce. It's well known that we're connected to the Teddys, but I still think it would disturb the Chamberlin something terrible if he knew we had an alien race involved in Council business. Of course, there is the Teddy ship in orbit overhead. Maybe they just don't want to know.

"Why are you here?" Bailiff Daughtry asks as she strides into our single bed with the convertible sofa room. "The Imperial quarters are much more...spacious than this. As representatives of his Lord Chamberlin—"

"Yeah, well, we were kinda kicked out of there," I reply. The bailiff turns on me faster than a tornado tears through a prairie.

"What? Explain!"

So, as I hand Kayley her bag, I tell the bailiff how we tried to get the High Wazir to answer some questions for us, and how we had failed severely. I also told her about the assassin, but didn't let her know about Grady. That would call attention to the ship that should remain unnoticed.

"Disastrous." Bailiff Daughtry exhales through her nose and shakes her head. "How could you have fouled this mission up so badly?"

"Oh, how could *you*!" Kayley proclaims, interrupting my attempt to respond. That's fine. If she wants to take charge of this conversation, she's welcome to. I'm only going to mess it up, anyway.

All eyes turn to her exasperated face. She reaches into her bag and pulls out what looks like a shiny bolt of material and shakes it at Bailiff Daughtry, who shifts her weight to her other foot and crosses her arms. Even through the bailiff looks upset, her shoulders relax a little, and that just confuses me.

"What is it?" she asks, her voice calm.

"You got the wrong bag!" Kayley whines. "This is my dance costume stuff!"

"And why exactly did you bring costumes with you on this mission?"

"I didn't bring them on the mission! I took them with me to Albion because I wanted to take a few classes at the Vazhiny School. I had some free time while I was waiting for my meetings, and that was something I always wanted to do since I was little!"

"Did you take a class?" I ask.

"Well, I was about to, but…" Kayley's eyes dart towards the bailiff.

Bailiff Daughtry huffs and rolls her eyes. She won't take any blame for ruining Kayley's chance of a lifetime, nor will she accept any responsibility for the situation we're in.

"You are not here to prance around on your tiptoes! This is a serious matter! You are here to find out the information as requested by His Lordship, and then you are to convey that information to the Lord Chamberlin or to me!"

"Yeah, well, that's not going to happen," Kayley shoots back. "The High Wazir threatened execution if we're found anywhere on Canis Ludis, so that puts a big damper on our moving about. Find someone else to do your spying."

If it were cold enough in our room—and it nearly is—I'd be watching steam burst from the bailiff's ears. Just in case she goes ballistic, I step between her and Kayley. That way, I get pinched first. Bailiff Daughtry certainly seems pissed off enough to clamp down on any part of Kayley she can get in between her fingertips.

As the stalemate continues, I wonder just what she's going to do. If Bailiff Daughtry accepts we're of no more use to her, she could let us go, or she could tell her minions to shoot us down so she doesn't have to worry about us talking. I don't think she'll kill us, but we've been through so much terror lately that I'm a bit numb to the prospect of dying. Still, I could also be doing something to avoid it.

"I don't think so," Bailiff Daughtry says, a wicked smile lighting up her face. "You are to follow the Lord Chamberlin's command to the letter, and then, and only then, will he consider getting you off this Goddess-forsaken planet."

"And how do you expect us to do that?" Parrish asks, sounding irritated himself. "We can't move around, we can't get noticed. Heck, we can't even talk to anyone that might know something!"

"That's your problem. You can complain about it as much as you like, but remember that if you don't come through, we'll have to take matters into our own hands and cut you loose."

"What does that matter?" Kayley asks. "We're already in danger of getting executed. What's the difference if we've got one more death threat?"

"The difference is that I will tell Her Majesty where and how to find you."

"You wouldn't!"

"The business of the Empire supersedes any right you think you're entitled to. Do I need to remind you of your lack of citizenship?"

She had to go there. It's not really membership to the Empire that we want, it's the benefits that it could bring to us. The clearing of our records. The new start to our lives. Those things mean more to us than any sense of belonging to something like the Empire. What do I need to belong to other than the group of buds I've already got?

"You have five days to get the Lord Chamberlin what he requests. After that, you are no longer of use to us."

"Hold on!" Kayley's shout stops the bailiff from walking out. She looks back at Kayley with mild contempt. "We may have burned some time, but we've got at least another ten days."

"Not anymore, you don't. Your poor handling of this mission has forced me to call in additional resources. The Chamberlin is unhappy with my performance, so I must be prepared to accept responsibility to complete this myself, and I will not short-change my chance at success just so you can have the luxury of a few more days. No. Get the information in five days, or our arrangement is done."

As Parrish, Kayley, and I stare wide-eyed at each other, the bailiff strides out, slamming the door behind her.

"Harsh," Original Teddy says, popping out from wherever he was hiding.

"Couldn't agree more," Kayley snarls, then sticks her lower lip out.

"So does that mean we're still going to do this stupid mission, after all?" I ask.

"Do we have a choice?" Parrish says.

It's a fair question. I'm not sure we do. I'm all for grabbing Afton and getting as far away from this planet as possible, but there's a bit more involved in making that happen than I want to admit. We haven't had much luck trying to get our bud, and to make it successful, that's going to be a full-time job. I don't know how we're going to tackle both.

"Well," I say, "for now, let's at least pretend that we're following orders. Then, the first chance we get to grab Afton and get out of here, we take it."

"Sounds good."

"Ow!" I rub my arm where Kayley just slapped it. It's deserved. I've got to let her lead.

"You're doing it again," she says and glares at me. "But I agree. The first opportunity to get Afton, we take it...and go."

Chapter Twenty-Eight

BILLIE MORGAN, WHO IS quickly becoming one of my favorite people in the entire Empire, sent us a tip she learned while on a hunt. Nayla and Afton are having lunch in the fashion district of the capital today. We got in a taxi the moment we found out, despite our concern about getting spotted. Afton is worth every risk we have to take to get her back. Besides, we have some experience with sneaking around. They won't find us so easily.

"KayKay," I say and turn around to her again, "are those shoes really the only ones you have? Is there no way to make them quieter?"

"They're tap shoes, and no, I can't make them quieter."

"Well, take them off, then."

"And walk barefoot on the sidewalk? No thanks."

"But everyone is staring at us."

"That's just your imagination."

"That flashy costume doesn't help, either."

Kayley's face gets red, and her eyes narrow at me. I'm just stating the obvious. We asked Bailiff Daughtry to get the rest of Kayley's luggage, but she refused, saying that she wasn't a concierge service. We couldn't get it ourselves, as there are likely guards posted around the shuttle. That's also going to make getting off-planet difficult, but we'll figure that one out when we're ready to.

The costume, despite being very attention-grabbing, is quite stylish. A halter top with lapels, like a suit jacket, folds neatly into a pair of very shiny high-waisted white pants. The legs of the pants are wide, and her top has gold sequins all over it. If she were up onstage, she'd be the star of the show, but down here on the street, she's just a curiosity.

"Well, at least I don't look like a beggar," Kayley says about my choice of casual outfit. I chose it for comfort, as I expected to be crawling around dark and dingy locations in search of a place to observe our target for today.

"I like the little hat," Parrish says to her, trying to be supportive. Kayley just glares at him.

We reach the corner where we plan to set up our spying routine and cut into an alleyway. Across the street, diagonal to our location, is the garden café where Nayla and Afton will spend their afternoon, along with a few of Nayla's friends. Among them is the woman who hired Billie to hunt down her potential spouse. If it weren't for her, we'd never know about this luncheon. I say a little prayer to the Goddesses that Billie is soon successful.

"What time are they supposed to arrive?" Parrish asks.

"Noon, but don't expect them to be on time," Kayley replies. "An entourage the size of Nayla's takes time to coordinate."

"KayKay, are you cold?" I ask, trying to make up for my stupid comments from earlier.

"No. If I was expecting to be cold, I would have brought the cape."

"Because that wouldn't have drawn any more attention."

She doesn't get the chance to skewer me with a long and drawn-out lecture on how she chose the best outfit she could for our little surveillance mission. It's true that the leotards and tights she had as other options not only would have drawn attention, they might have gotten her arrested for indecency. It doesn't matter, because here comes Afton, Nayla, and her entourage of bodyguards and flower girls. Anyone who was staring at Kayley before is now captivated by the parade headed to the garden café.

"Okay." Kayley glances around, then looks up and points to an emergency escape just above our heads. "Let's get positioned up there."

"Teddy," I call over Teddy comm. "Are you in place?"

"Sitting by," Original Teddy replies. They're monitoring the entourage for us from the park just down the block. As would-be tourists, they catch a little attention, but as I suspected, no one has been brave enough to strike up a conversation with them.

We climb up the ladder and get in place just as Afton and Nayla sit down with their guests. We should be well hidden up here, as there's laundry and a few old towels hanging from the railing. I've also got an electronic spotting scope that we found at a second-hand store.

I make use of it and zero in on our targets. First, Nayla. She's in her usual lounging pose with one leg up on her seat and an arm draped across Afton's shoulders. It makes my teeth grind. It's like the princess is letting everyone know our bud belongs to her.

When I turn the scope on Afton, I get a bit of a surprise. Other than when she was angry with us, Afton has been exuding deep contentment and occasionally a little girlish excitement when she's with Nayla. Today, though, she seems distracted. As Nayla's friends chat animatedly, Afton stares at her water glass or at the passersby. Her mouth never opens, even when someone addresses her directly. When Nayla caresses her cheek, she has no reaction.

"Something's up," I say. "Afton's upset."

"Let me see." Kayley snatches the scope from me and peers through it. She spends the next few minutes observing the lunch party, as quiet as the warm breeze that moves down the alleyway.

"Well?" I've run out of patience waiting for her diagnosis of the situation.

"Maybe. She could just be bored," Kayley replies. "She usually fidgets more when she's upset."

"Are you kidding? She was totally fidgeting! Let Parrish look. He'll know for sure."

"Even though I'm her best friend?" But Kayley still hands the scope to Parrish, who takes a moment to figure out how to use the thing.

"We should get closer," I say.

"Rance, no. We move now, and Afton will spot us."

"Behind all these people? No, she won't. Parrish, what do you think?"

"She does look a little unhappy," Parrish replies, peering through the scope.

"Don't use him to get your way!" Kayley pokes me.

"KayKay, I'm telling you, something's bothering her."

"Maybe you're just imagining things."

"What do you mean by that?"

Kayley puts her hands on my shoulders so she can look me in the eye. I catch my breath, because I can see just how serious she is.

"Did you ever consider that Afton's exactly where she wants to be? That we're the bad friends in this because we're messing things up for her?"

I stare at her, open-mouthed. Did Kayley just suggest that we should walk away from Afton like Nayla told us to? That she's better off without us and our meddling?

But we're not meddling. We're trying to save her from execution. I don't want to split her and Nayla up. That's something that Nayla is making us do! Her desire to become queen is putting our friend at risk!

"No." I shake my head. "No way. That doesn't matter. Afton's in danger, and we need to help her. I'm getting closer, and if I have a chance, I'm going to talk to her and tell her what's going on." I turn to leave.

"Don't you dare! Rance! Get back here!" Kayley curses more in five seconds than I've heard her do in an entire year. "Parry, get him!"

I hop down off the landing and hit the ground running. If Parrish is going to come after me, let him. But I think he's on my side about this. If it comes down to it, he'll support whatever I do.

I hate going against Kayley like this, and I don't want to fight with her, but if I get it right, she'll understand and help. I don't see how I could be wrong here. If any of us were in trouble, no one would question what we should do. We'd take care of it for them. Now we throw another person into the equation and suddenly it doesn't add up anymore? That makes no sense to me.

As I dash across the street, I signal the Teddys to close in, then make my way towards the café. We might need some popsicle power if things get hairy. I'm not planning to do anything stupid...well, anything *too* stupid.

"Dude." Parrish puts a hand on my shoulder as he catches up with me. I spin on him, but he raises his hands. "Hey, I'm on your side on this one, but you can't just cut her authority off like that. You know what that does to her."

"Yeah, but"—I turn back around and keep going—"she'll see. Kayley will see we're right, and then she'll accept what we have to do."

"*If* you're right. Kayley also has a really good point, Rance. As much as it may hurt us to do it, if Afton wants us to leave her alone, we've got to respect that. At least for now."

I turn to look back at Parrish to show him I'm not agreeable to doing that. Parrish may have jogged with her every morning, and Kayley may be her close confidant, but neither of them were there at the beginning. I know when Afton wants to be left alone, and I know when she's silently asking for help. Grady knows, too, and if he were here, he'd agree with me. Afton staring off into space means there's something seriously wrong.

Which is what she's doing right now. Staring right in our direction.

"Oh, shoot!" I duck and shove Parrish through the nearest door. He yelps, his hands flying over his head. I'm just glad he's got amazing balance. Otherwise, I'd be falling right on top of him.

"What the hell are you doing?" Parrish drops firm hands on my shoulders and plants his feet.

"Afton," I whisper. "I think she saw us."

Parrish's face goes gray. He glances out to the street, then slides me into an aisle of the store I flung us into.

"Are you sure?"

"She was looking right at us. I'm sure of it."

"Shoot. We've got to tell Kayley."

"Yeah, but we've got to make sure we're clear first."

I call Original Teddy up again, asking for any update about Afton's position.

"Negative," Original Teddy replies. "Currently at nutritional...but does not partake."

"See?" I say to Parrish after I relay Teddy's message to him. "When have you ever seen her not eat? She's upset for sure."

"Okay, but did she see us or not?"

"Well, if she's not moving, maybe not. We should check."

I lead Parrish out of the store, and we tiptoe—at least until two kids laugh and point at us—to the edge of the building. I sign to Parrish that I plan to peek around the edge.

"Go ahead, but Rance..."

"What?"

"She can't hear us. You don't need to use sign language."

The side of the building adjoins the café's perimeter hedge. It's nice and thick, and about chest height. I rise from a squat until I can see just over it. It takes only a second to spot their table, but even less to notice something's going on. Afton is standing, her arms folded. Her face reminds me of a child that was just told they couldn't have ice cream because they didn't finish their dinner.

Nayla is gazing up at her, still in a semi-lounging position, but now her hands are in her lap. Then she pats her cheeks and says something to Afton. I can't read lips, so I've got no idea what, but I can tell it's not a compliment about how Afton looks today.

This isn't good. I think they're fighting, but I can't tell for sure. I should tell Parrish to get Kayley down from the escape landing and bring her here. She might be able to tell what's going on.

"Idiot!"

My arm gets yanked, and I lose my balance, landing on my side next to Parrish...and a pair of tap shoes.

"Oh, hey, KayKay. I was just about to come get you. You might want to get out of sight. Afton was just looking this way."

"Well, she's not going to see me, jerk. They just left."

"Left?" I roll back up and look over at their table. Sure enough, Afton, Nayla, and the entourage are heading towards the park.

"Get up," Kayley says. "We're going after them."

Chapter Twenty-Nine

"One of us should go ask their companions what that was all about," I suggest as we rush towards the park.

"Good idea," Kayley replies. "Parry, go find out what happened."

"Why me?"

"Because you're gorgeous and single. They'll be falling over each other to talk to you."

Parrish shrugs, then pats me on the shoulder and jogs over to the café. Two women from Nayla's entourage who didn't leave with the rest are sitting at a table, leaning their heads together in what I can only imagine is speculative gossip about what just happened. He approaches them with a big, friendly smile on his face. The women take notice and sit up straight.

"I could have done that," I say, trying to catch up with Kayley's power stride, her shoes beating out a fast tempo as she clip-clops down the sidewalk.

"No, you have to come with me."

"Why?"

"Because you and I need to talk, that's why."

I blink at her, unsure of what we might need to discuss. We're about to go spy on Afton, so that's not it. Grady? Maybe. I'm sure she's as worried about him as I am. What else could it be?

"Uh, sure...right now?"

"Yes, right now." Then Kayley pauses and scans inside the park. "Actually, let's get into position first. Let's try over there, behind the slide."

"Where are they?"

"By the swings. Come on." Kayley grabs my hand, and we dash down a wooded path that leads around the playground. It's just secluded enough that neither Nayla nor Afton should recognize us. And even if they did, Kayley's stage costume makes her look like anyone but Kayley. Another bonus—the path is soft dirt and leaves, neutralizing any percussive noise from Kayley's shoes.

As we get in close, just on the opposite side of a big oak tree from where the swings are, I spot Afton and Nayla. Her entourage is giving them some space. Nayla is sitting on a swing while Afton paces in front of her, arms folded. She's shaking her head and staring at the ground in front of her feet.

"Rance," Kayley whispers.

Nayla's head follows Afton as she walks back and forth. She's telling Afton something, but we're just a little too far away to hear her words clearly. I lean forward, turning my ear towards them and cupping it. It works a little, but mostly to capture the sound of birds and the rustling of the leaves.

"Rance!" Kayley hisses, poking me on the back.

"What?"

"Let's talk."

"But," I say and point back towards the swing set. "Afton and Nayla."

"They can wait."

"Can they?" I look behind me. Afton is still pacing, but now her arm is waving about with intensity.

Kayley sighs and settles against the trunk of a tree opposite me. She bends her leg up towards her and wraps an arm round it, pulling it close. I can tell she's struggling to find the right words to say, and it makes me tense.

"Rance, darling..." Kayley shakes her head. "Sorry. I didn't—"

"It's fine, KayKay. Just tell me." I know the "darling" just came out of habit, because she wants to let me know she's sincere in what she's about to say.

She delays her words for a moment more, finding interest in a twig lying on the ground next to her. She picks it up and scratches lines into the soil. I try to be patient for her, but I feel this urgent need to turn around and find out what's happening with Afton. I'll have a talk with my girlfriend any time she asks for one. However, she could have picked a slightly better time than this.

"Rance, you and I have been friends for a long time, so I know you. I know that when you do things on impulse, it's because you recognize the need to solve the problem immediately. Honestly, it's one of the things that I love about you. That you care so much for others that you don't even stop to consider the consequences of what might happen to you if you get involved."

I give her a nod and press my lips together, preparing for the "but" part of her statement. I know it's coming. She's not the only one who knows her partner well.

"But—" And there it is. "When you guys decided that I'd be the one to run this team, you gave me the authority to make choices as to what is best for the group and what's not."

"And I totally support you on that, KayKay. There's no one better to lead than you."

Sustained screams come from the playground, making both of us scamper to the edges of the oak tree. Afton is shouting at the top of her lungs, her face to the sky. Her arms are pressed back, and she balls her hands up into fists. Nayla just watches as she moves the swing back and forth in minute movements.

Kayley and I share a wide-eyed look, both of us breathing heavy. I've never heard Afton cry out like that before. Her voice breaks, and I cringe at the pure sound of pain that explodes from her. Kayley's right. I'm dying to rush out there and save Afton from whatever is torturing her.

"I'm going out there!"

"No!" Kayley dives on me before I can get up. We fall, and I land hard on my back. Kayley smashes against me, her face pressing against my chest as she fumbles to grab my arms and pin me down. Her surprise action knocks any quick response out of me, so I let her hold me down.

"Rance, you. Can. Not. Do. That." Kayley's breathing hard. "That's what I'm trying to tell you if you'd just listen to me for once!"

Afton's screaming stops, and I stare up at the leaf canopy above me, considering Kayley's words. I don't think she's trying to stop me from helping Afton. I'm sure she'd do anything to help her best friend. So would I, and when I hear Afton crying out in pain, I'm there. No questions asked. Somewhere between those two things is the point Kayley is trying to make.

"I do listen to you." I inhale deeply, feeling the warmth of Kayley on top of me. She relaxes her grip and shifts to get more comfortable. That's fine with me, but I wonder what'd happen if anyone found the two of us like this.

"Rance, please. Please consider what your actions do to others. Especially when what your heart is screaming at you to do puts someone in danger. I learned that lesson the hard way, and now Parrish's dream of being a top star in some sport is over. I don't want you to make the same mistake I did."

"So this isn't about stealing your authority?"

"It's about that, too, but this is more important. Consider that your actions could hurt any one of us. Grady, Parrish, Afton...and me."

My arms wrap around Kayley, holding her against me. That I'd do something that hurts any of them is bad enough. If it hurt Kayley, I would never forgive myself. But we *have* to help Afton. The sound of her desperation still rattles in my bones, even minutes after she released her agony to the world. I'm not sure how to balance this. So I ask the only person I know who can give me the right answer. Kayley.

"So what do we do?"

"We be patient and listen." Kayley pushes herself up and turns her head towards the playground. "Hearing her scream like that freaks me out, too, but she's not hurt. No one is attacking her. We need to understand what's really happening before we can act. Get it?"

I look up at her as her silky hair hangs down over me. I could never get bored with this view. Never.

"I love you, KayKay," I say. She blushes and playfully smacks a hand on my chest.

"And you, idiot." She grins. "Never forget that I love you, too. And I only want the best for you. For all of us."

"Okay." I smile at her. "But if we want to listen, shouldn't we get a little closer?"

Kayley turns her head towards the playground, considering. A second later, she moves to a crouch, surveying our area. The moment she spots a location, she points and motions for me to follow.

The spot Kayley's found is just around a small bend in the path, where it dips in closer to the swings. There's another big oak here, and a thick amount of undergrowth surrounds the tree. We can plant ourselves behind it and eavesdrop to our pleasure.

Afton is done expressing her pain, but not done moving. Nayla's up and walking with her, too, a hand on Afton's shoulder. Afton doesn't seem to acknowledge it. I wonder if that means she's mad at Nayla. It's a bit early in their relationship for a serious fight, but this is not a normal situation.

"Darling," Nayla says in her usual resonant tone. "You need to accept the present and forget the past. What's done is done. No one can take back the hurt that buries itself deep inside you. You must find a way forward."

"I know that," Afton replies. "But it still isn't right. No one tells me what I can do."

"Of course, but there are some situations that you put yourself into that will only end in suffering. I can't allow you to go down that path."

"You can't me keep from that stuff, Nayla, no matter what your intentions are."

"I can, and I will. But it's only because I love you."

I try to catch Kayley's response, but she's focused on Afton and Nayla. If she's having any thoughts about what we just heard, she's not reacting. Me? I'm totally reacting. I get what's going on here. Nayla is keeping Afton from us, and I can't allow that. But I did just promise Kayley I wouldn't do anything on my own.

"Please, Nayla. Just let me be free to do what I want. To go where I want."

"No, Surela. I cannot. I know it's difficult to see the things that are causing you pain when you are inside of them, but I see them, and I care for you too much to see you hurt again. You may be upset about it, but in the future, you will see it was better for you this way."

That's definitely it. Afton is Nayla's prisoner. There's no doubt about it. We've got to break her free. Free like she was before she met this spacey daughter of an insane monarch. Afton might be mad at me for doing it, but once she's free, she'll see what Nayla was doing to her.

"Kayley, I'm grabbing Afton, and then we run. Okay?"

Kayley turns and frowns at me, then raises an eyebrow. So she's not getting it. Maybe I've just got to explain it better.

"Rance, I don't know what you think you just heard, but even if it means Afton is in trouble, we can't just go rushing in there and grab her. Nayla's bodyguards would be on us in a second, plus they'd inform the queen that we're still on-planet."

"Yeah, but…" I check Afton to see if there's any change, but there's not. "Afton needs us, and this is the best opportunity we have! We've got to do this now!"

Kayley stares at me as I feel panic creeping up my back. We're running out of time. A few seconds more and they might decide to leave. Then we'll have lost our opportunity to save our bud. There may not be another chance like this.

"We're leaving," Kayley says, her tone as firm as ever.

"What? No! We've got to—"

But before I can finish my complaint, she shoves me back, stands up, grabs my arm, and yanks me along. I rush to get to my feet just as we get to the path, before I become a human sled.

"Hey! What are you doing?"

"We'll get her back. Don't worry. This just isn't the time or place. We slip up here, and we could lose her forever. Is that what you want?"

"No."

"Then," she says and presses a hand to my cheek, "trust me, okay? I miss her, too. A lot."

I nod. I can't stand suffering. Especially if it's my buds. But I've got to trust Kayley. I've got to believe what we're doing is right, and that at the end of our efforts, we'll be back to being the same gang we've always been. I won't consider any other outcome.

Chapter Thirty

On our way back to meet with Parrish and the Teddys, a large convoy of military vehicles passed by and gave Kayley and me a serious fright. Were they looking for us, or did this have something to do with the alleged coup? With no option for now but to get off the streets, we return to our tiny hotel room and decide to talk things through—together.

Parrish had no luck—unless you count the ten offers of marriage and eleven Sergo IDs—getting information from the café patrons. The only thing that Nayla's friends wanted to discuss with him was when they'd be seeing him again. He had no choice, so he made lunch dates with both of them, neither of which he'll be able to keep. Kayley nixed the idea the moment she heard it. Even if he could get some inside gossip on Queen de Avila's court, the risk of Nayla and/or Afton seeing him is too great.

And now that we're about to make our grand plan for Operation: Snag Afton, we can't have any distractions like that.

"Well, hello." Doc Elizabeth waves to us from inside the portable globe that the Teddys brought with them. "Are you all well? You seem distressed, and Kayley, love, you've got some dark circles under your eyes. Not sleeping well?"

"Well..." Kayley ducks her head away from the spherical screen to touch her face just below her eyes. "Things have been a little rough down here."

"Reconnoiter was unsuccessful," Original Teddy says. "But ParryParry totally scored."

"Oh? Do tell."

"No, no." Kayley waves a dismissive hand at her. "We didn't call for that. How's Grady?"

"Hmm." The doc presses her lips together. "How, indeed."

"Don't you know?" I shout. "He's under your care!"

Doc Elizabeth's eyes narrow at me, and she gets closer to the camera.

"Of course I know, Mr. He', no need to get snappy. He's undergoing a new procedure, and since he's not right here with me, I don't have an up-to-the-moment status update. He's doing fine, but we've had to rebuild some of his organs."

"Rebuild?"

"She means the nano-reconstructive procedure that I told you about," Kayley explains.

"Grady's not going to like that you put nanos in him." As much of a tech-wizard as Grady is, he's also highly phobic of having tech inside his body. It's a strange contradiction, but my bud is, for lack of a better word, peculiar sometimes.

"Not to worry. Once he wakes up, he'll never even know they were there," Doc Elizabeth replies, her face brightening.

"Just how often does that happen when you care for us?" Parrish asks.

"Experimental is imperative," Original Teddy answers. "Concern is extraneous."

I flash a frown over to our fuzzy buddy. But he's correct in his statement, of course. When it comes to humans and Teddys, we're integrating all sorts of things these days. Healthcare is just one of those, though due to the quirks of the human body, Teddys haven't been able to come up with a perfect system. Yet.

"Trust me," she says, "this is exciting new tech. It's worth a chat, as there's more connected to it than just healing. It's not news for now, but when you can, I'd really like to share our findings with you."

"Of course," I reply. "The moment we can grab Afton and get off this Goddess-cursed toxic waste dump of a planet."

"It's not that bad," Parrish comments. "I kind of like the parks they have here. There's—"

Parrish's embarrassment sensor must have gotten the message I was transmitting. After he stops talking, he motions for us to continue, then looks away.

"Looks like we're down Grady," I say. "That's going to be a problem. We need situational awareness."

"Then we should hold off until he's up and ready," Kayley says.

"We don't have any time to wait!" I try to keep from raising my voice, but it goes up in pitch rather than volume. I sound like a rat that's had its tail stepped on. "In five days, we're done, or Afton's done, or who knows? Maybe all of us are burned offerings by then!"

"Easy," she says, touching my arm. "Five days is more time than you think it is, and we'll figure something out about Grady's position."

My smile to her is as weak as it gets. I'd like to believe her, but her attempt to calm me is as effective as putting fossil fuel in a fusion reactor. The sentiment is there, but good intention won't make the engine roar. I was really counting on Grady being back in action, as his bird's-eye view was going to be critical to the success of the mission. Now I've got no idea what we're going to be able to pull off.

I'd rather not sit here and pine over the loss of two of our team members. Important team members. Well, all of us are important. That we've been having failure after failure is proof that we can't win a race with a metaphorical vehicle that's missing two of its wheels.

"Hey." Kayley puts her hand under my chin and lifts my head to catch her eyes. "We're going to get Afton. I promise."

"Then what do we do? With no Grady, we're completely blind."

"Recommendation is available," Original Teddy says.

"Thanks, Teddy, but hold that thought for a moment. This is really important for us to figure out."

"Can we even pull anything off?" Parrish asks. "I mean, we're really short-handed. A mission may not be the best idea."

"What are you saying?"

"Well, rather than us going in there to get her, we could have someone do it for us."

I tilt my head at Parrish, waiting for his explanation. Whatever it is. I want to give him a fair chance, as he often has excellent suggestions, but I can't quite imagine what he's talking about. We've burned most of our connections related to this situation already, and the Chamberlin isn't going to give us an extension. Not when he's mostly given up on us ever getting the info he needs.

"The High Wazir," Parrish says. "He might not like us, but I get the feeling he's sympathetic to our situation. I mean, look, even though he had to kick us off the planet, he still got Nayla and Afton to show up so we could see them before we left."

"It's a good observation, Parry," Kayley says. "But the one minor detail you're forgetting is he expected us to leave the planet, and we didn't. His own neck would be at risk now if he lent us a hand."

"No way to get yourselves up here, huh?" Doc Elizabeth asks. "You'd have an army at your disposal if you could come here and get your plan into action."

"We don't need to go anywhere to connect with the Teddys," I say, tapping my head. The doc turns her gaze on me, but it's more neutral than I would expect. So I elaborate. "Teddynet! Remember?"

"Oh, yes, of course!" Her eyes open up wider, and a little blush comes to her cheeks. "Of course. Yes, I remember. How about Captain Cortell, then?"

"*Lieutenant Colonel* Cortell," Kayley corrects, then pulls back when she glances at me. "What? We're linked over social feed, so I get notification of his promotions."

I could be jealous that my girlfriend has been secretly talking to another guy, who is well secure in his career and not half-bad to look at, but I don't have the time. Besides, Kayley's just not the unfaithful type. Still, I can't help but feel a little miffed.

"Uh, how about we get back to your little dilemma?" Doc Elizabeth suggests. "Do you really not think you can do this without Grady?"

"We're not sure. Grady adds a vital advantage to our capabilities. So far, we haven't thought of any workaround."

"Recommendation is still available," Original Teddy says.

"Okay, what is it?"

"Teddy will reconnoiter."

I stare at him for a few seconds until it hits me. The equipment that Grady uses to provide surveillance was all created by the Teddys. Sure, they designed its interface for humans, but they should know how to use it. Once I dig into Teddynet, I *know* they know how to use it.

But the operation of the equipment isn't the problem.

"Teddy," Kayley says, hopping on the issue before I can bring it up. "That's great, but we need to be able to communicate clearly with whoever is providing coverage for us."

She smiles at Original Teddy, the apology clear on her face. There's no easy way to turn down his offer of help. Especially when Teddys would just help without being asked. It's not because they like us or anything like that. In their society, when there's a problem, everyone just gets together to solve it until it's fixed. Needless to say, they don't have a lot of strife or conflict in their communities.

Parrish goes glum. Elizabeth does, too. And I'm a bit surprised Kayley would turn them down so quickly. We were almost there, too. Original Teddy's mastery of Empire Common is getting better and better every day. We've been around him long enough to get anything he says, even if his choice of vocabulary is sometimes a bit odd. Teddys have a spoken language, but they don't use it as much as they used to. Teddynet—

Wait...that's it!

"Teddy, could you upload surveillance images into Teddynet?"

"What?" Kayley turns to me. "What are you onto?"

"That is accurate, of course," Original Teddy replies. "Don't be a dumbass."

I think Teddy is taking this colloquialism study a bit too seriously. It's getting out of hand.

"So, Teddy can read the maps and transmit them to you?" Kayley asks.

"Not exactly. Teddynet isn't a point-to-point communication system," I explain. "That's Teddy comm, but Teddy comm can only transmit audio. Teddynet is more like a gigantic shared database. I'd need to dig in and find what Teddy was sharing, but once I found it, we'd know exactly where to go, and how to avoid people we don't want to bump into." Parrish and Doc Elizabeth nod their heads, but I'm not sure they get it. That's okay. Kayley's the one I've got to convince, and as I wait for her to consider, I'm praying to the Goddesses that she'll be okay with it.

"Alright," Kayley says after a moment. "We'll go with that, but we have to test it first. If you get dizzy on me, Rance, then I'm pulling the plug."

"Don't worry," I say with a smile. "I won't."

"Mmm-hmm. It's not like I haven't heard you promise that before."

Chapter Thirty-One

Because we're so good at this, and because we desperately want Afton out of danger, we put together a solid plan in an hour. It's not our best record, unless we're judging the other plans by their levels of potential success. The Teddys have their end figured out, and we are just waiting for the last wire that will complete our mission circuit. It's likely the most critical of all the parts.

Where's Afton going to be?

"Anyone have any ideas?" Kayley asks, as we pack our bags and hand them over to the blue buddies to ferry back to the shuttle. I'm too preoccupied with our Afton plan to worry about exactly how they plan to do that. If Original Teddy says they can, then I'll just have to trust them.

"Do you think she'll go for a run in the morning?" I ask Parrish.

"Maybe. She did nearly every morning when we were back home, but we stopped running together after she moved to Grady's. It's too far to meet up from my place."

"We can't rely on a maybe," Kayley says. "We need something more concrete. It's the weekend. Perhaps they're going out tonight? Somewhere social? Where does Afton like to go?"

I stare at Kayley, as I think she just stated she has no idea what her best friend likes to do in the evenings. She catches my look and raises an eyebrow.

"What?"

"KayKay, tell me you never hung out with Afton on a Saturday night."

"I..." Kayley shuts her mouth, then opens it again, incensed. "Well, I've been hanging out with *you* for the last few months, so how would I know?"

"How about before that?"

Her eyes drift up to the edge of the ceiling, and she pokes her jaw with a finger. I'm a bit disappointed. Sure, it's been a few months since they've really hung out—and granted, that's my fault—but they've had years of BFF time.

"I think that's the wrong question," Parrish says. "It's not what she enjoyed doing, it's what she's always dreamed of doing."

"What do you mean?" Kayley asks.

"I mean, Afton is dating a *princess*!" Parrish flings his hands up. "A wealthy one at that. And one who considers Afton to be her soulmate. I don't know about you guys, but I got the sense that Nayla would do absolutely anything for Afton. So, if there's something that Afton's always dreamed of doing on a Saturday night, that's where I think they'll be tonight."

I nod at Parrish's assessment. He's spot-on, and if we can think of what might be in Afton's dreams, we might just figure out where she'll be tonight.

But just when that last piece of the puzzle is about to be dropped into place, I get the feeling that something's not quite right. Doubt is seeping into my brain, and I'm not sure why. This is the purest mission we could ever be executing. Our friend is in trouble, and if we don't do something, she could die. Why should I hesitate to take action?

"I can't think of anything," I say. "Maybe we should wait."

I feel two pairs of human eyes and one pair of Teddy disks swivel to gawk at my downcast gaze. I don't want to meet their confused faces because I don't have an answer why I feel this way. I know they're going to ask, and I don't know what to tell them.

"Rance, why are you saying that? You're the one that's been pushing for us to get her. What's going on?"

And there it is. I shouldn't be happy that Kayley was the first one to put the question to me, but I am. Confirmation that someone cares is always a nice thing.

"I don't know, KayKay. My chest just got tight after Parrish came up with his idea."

"Hey, don't blame me for coming up with it. I just thought I was stating the obvious."

"Rancid contains sensitivity to malfeasance," Original Teddy says, and I blink at him. I know what he said. I just don't understand why he said it. Me? Feeling guilty? Over what?

"What do you mean, Teddy?"

"Conditions are apparent."

I slump, looking to Kayley for clarity on that reply. She shakes her head, uncertain as I am about what's in my head. Only Teddy would have an equal chance of figuring it out. Especially if I had uploaded something. I'm not sure if I did that, but I'm no expert user of Teddynet.

"Never mind I said it, let's just get back to it."

Kayley rubs my arm and gives me a supportive smile. This isn't easy for any of us, and we've all displayed our share of quirks over the last two weeks. There is no us without Afton, and even trying to consider it has done some damage to our psyches. I can only hope that it hasn't done so much damage that we can no longer function properly.

"So, are there any suggestions?" Kayley waits for a reply before continuing. "Actually, I have one. Afton used to tell me she always wanted to see me onstage. Of course, she has, but just in the little recitals that we did at school. I think she meant that she hoped to see me on a big stage one day."

"Yeah, but that's Afton's dream for you, not her own," I say. I chuckle as I remember how she tore up the dance floor at the mayor's fundraiser. "Afton was a great dancer, and she loves music, but she never wanted to dance like you did. I remember how she always praised your dancing skills, KayKay."

"Yeah," Parrish says. "And I know she always wanted to see a big performance."

I grab my Sergo and start running through the performance listings for tonight. There's quite a few—nearly every genre at any size venue. I filter out all the small stuff, as Nayla would never be caught dead at a tiny venue unless it had some unique aura. Afton's not one for intellectual music. Musicals aren't really her thing, either.

Then I come across a few big shows. That's something Afton could dream of. There's no massive, 300,000-seat venue in our town. There's not one of those anywhere closer than Bradbury, but Yeomanry's got three. I could totally picture Afton and Nayla in the royal suite, high above the body-crushed masses. Afton would lose herself in the music, while Nayla likely would be running through the next day's astrological chart.

"Hey," I say, seeing a familiar group's name come across the listings, "have you guys ever heard of The Chosen Three?"

"Sure, they're huge," Parrish replies. "Multi-planet tours, millions of fans. I think I've even heard that they've won every top award on the Central Planets."

"Goddesses!" Kayley gasps. "Afton loves them!"

"Really?" I say. "I would think she's more into alternative mash than mainstream stuff."

"Are you kidding?" Kayley smacks my arm. "And you're supposed to be her friend? How could you not know? She's got an enormous poster on her wall at home."

"When have I ever been in Afton's room?"

That silences Kayley until something exciting occurs to her. Her eyes light up, and she pumps her fist.

"That's it. That's got to be it," Kayley says.

"How can you be so sure?"

"When has a touring act like that ever come to Angelcanis?" Kayley raises her hand at us. "Let me save you the effort of answering. That's right. Never. We're just too far out of the way for them. Plus, they probably can't. Outside of their contractual space, since we're just a colony."

"Okay." I shrug. "I guess we're going to a concert tonight."

"That's cute, Rance, but we're never getting in there."

"Why not?"

"Because." Kayley points at the listing on my Sergo screen. "It's been sold out for months."

"So we sneak in?"

"And risk getting caught trying to break into a massive concert like that? With all the extra soldiers we've seen around lately? No, we've got too much attention on us. We need to slip in and out unnoticed, and the only way we're going to do that is to pretend we're fans."

"Which means we need tickets," Parrish says. "Can we forge a few?"

"Maybe, but that won't get us up into the luxury suite level. We'd need to be aristocrats, or wealthy business owners, or something."

My shoulders drop. We'd need more than fancy costumes and fake passes to get in and around, not to mention into the royal suite, or anywhere near it. All the elite know each other. They may not like each other, but if one of them looks at us sideways, we're in trouble. The only way we might make it work is if we were with someone. I don't know any elites...

But Parrish does.

"Maybe we just need to get friendly with a few aristocrats," I say with a grin at Parrish.

"Huh?" Parrish tilts his head at me, but Kayley gets it right away.

"Yes!" She claps her hands together, and Original Teddy sticks his tentacles into his ears. "Yes, Parry, dear. Don't you remember you have two dates for tomorrow?"

"So, what's that—" Parrish inhales, then turns red. "Oh! I do. Wait. No. No, I can't ask them!"

"Why not?"

"Because that's not nice. I shouldn't lead them on like that. I wasn't even going to go."

"Parry, that's our connection to the inner circle, and it's all we've got." Kayley presses her hands together and puts on her best *pretty please* face. "Come on. Do it for Afton."

"Ugh. Alright." Parrish flips open his Sergo and thumbs through his ID listings until he finds the codes and makes the call.

"Put it on speaker," I say.

"Hell no."

I grin again. I was just needling him, because there aren't many opportunities to poke at such an honorable guy. There's very little he does wrong. Even what he says on the call is what every father dreams of when someone rings up their daughter.

Parrish hangs up. "Okay. We're on for tonight."

"Oh, Parry, thank you!" Kayley rushes over to him and squeezes him tightly.

"Maybe you shouldn't thank me so quickly. I had to agree to bring dates for their friends."

Chapter Thirty-Two

We arrive at the side entrance of the stadium, which is reserved for celebrities and royalty. Lower-level aristocrats can also get in this way, so we await our dates just outside the door. I'm not exactly jumping up and down to meet any self-important, spoiled brat children of the queen's court. It's exactly these kinds of people that get me riled up about how unfair the Empire is when it comes to wealth distribution.

And I definitely don't need a date. Kayley is and always has been the one for me. I'm sure she feels the same way, and I bet she's also dreading meeting whatever slimy guy she's got to entertain for the evening. Let's hope we can get away from them in record time.

"Okay, I think they're here," Parrish says, nodding to a limo that's just pulling up.

"Teddy in place?" Kayley whispers into my ear.

"Yep, he's already on suite level, and his two blue buddies are standing by at the shuttle, ready to popsicle any guards and come get us."

"How did he get up there so fast?"

"Well, he's a Teddy."

The limo stops right in front of us, and two security guards pop out to open the rear doors of the vehicle. The moment that happens, Parrish's two admirers fly out and nearly knock them over with their zeal. A young man and a young woman follow them out, scanning the area. They're about our age, the woman perhaps a little older and the guy a little younger. Both are wearing what must be the height of rich-kid fashion, which is just overpriced versions of normal people's clothes. Still, they look elegant compared to me in my slightly wrinkled shirt and pants, and Kayley in the only stage costume she has that could pass as a ball gown, minus all the fancy trimmings.

"Oh, my Goddesses!" The woman gasps as she lays eyes on Kayley. "You guys got Scarlett Kayley to come? How'd you manage that?"

"Well, Yaz." One of Parrish's dates—I think he said her name was Isabella—turns to her, a smug look on her face. "My father *is* the minister of finance, you remember?"

"It's so nice to meet you! I'm Yazmeen." She curtsies, then squeals, her fists shaking as if she just won the grand prize in the lottery. "I can't believe I've got a date with Scarlett Kayley tonight!"

"Wait." Kayley lifts a finger, glancing between her and the young man. "*You're* my date tonight?"

"Hey, I'm Fenric," the young man says as he approaches me, a slight blush coming to his cheeks, "but all my friends call me Fen. You can call me Fen, too."

My jaw goes slack as I trade glances with Kayley. To be fair, we were only told that we were here as dates for their friends. No one ever said who'd they'd be, and they're way more smitten with us than I would have expected. This is going to be a challenging evening to get through.

"Ransom. But call me Rance." I offer Fen a shy smile, already thinking of ways to knock his level of interest in me down. Telling him I'm with Kayley would be the obvious solution, but then Fen and Yaz might balk, and then we'd have no escorts up to the suites.

If Afton knew what we were doing just for her, she'd be on the floor, howling with laughter.

"You're going to love the show! The Chosen Three are the best!" Yaz wraps her arm about Kayley and leads her to the entrance, just behind Isabella and Sukayna, who are on each one of Parrish's arms.

Fen glances at them, then turns to me, an expectant look on his face. I shrug and offer him my arm. I guess that's what he was expecting, since he takes it and settles close to me. He's taller than me, but his touch is as gentle as Kayley's, so it's easy for me to imagine it's her rather than him. I still feel like I'm cheating on her somehow.

The suite is, as expected, overstuffed with luxury to the point it's making me physically ill. Gold mirror lines all the walls in some attempt to look artistic, but it fails miserably. The eight lounge chairs are made from—yuck—animal skins, and they're decorated with gold studs in the shape of crescent moons and covered with geometric shapes and stars on the back. There's a bar, and a table with some snacks on it, and a drop-down vid screen with camera controls to zoom in on the action onstage.

"Ooh, herbals!" Yaz says and detaches herself from Kayley to go examine the bar. Kayley exhales and leans on the back of one chair. That is, until she realizes what it's made from. She yelps and hops back.

Meanwhile, Yaz is busy digging through the selection of bottles on the bar. She grabs a glass and begins mixing a few of them together like a mad chemist. I've never liked the taste of them, but they're not created for flavor. The herbs that are in them are for stimulating various parts of the brain to produce some mood enhancement, whatever that may be. The effect is mild, so it would require a ton of them to overexcite the hormone production centers of the body. I tried having that much once, and I passed out. The way Yaz is going at it, she could get there within a few drinks.

Which gives me an idea.

"Fancy a drink?" I ask Fen, who's still locked on my arm.

"Who, me? No, thank you. I don't like herbals, they taste horrible."

"But that's why you mix them with fruit juices."

"Well, I don't know..."

"Come on. I'll fix you a light one. You'll never be able to taste the stuff. Promise." I move to the bar, tugging Fen with me.

I watch Yaz run through her construction of another concoction, presumably for Kayley. Kayley won't, though. She's never had even a sip. And since we're on a mission, there's no way that she'd want to lose focus. Especially one this important.

"Hey, what's that one?" I ask, pointing to the bottle in Yaz's hand.

"This one gets you in the mood," Yaz replies with a grin and waggle of her eyebrows, "if you know what I mean...wanna try?"

"Uh, maybe a little early for that one."

"Aww, aren't you guys cute being all shy together? Okay, it's a first date, I get it." Yaz's eyes dart around the bar. Then she snatches a curvy bottle full of blue liquid from the back and hands it to me. "Here. Perfect for you two. Just a mild relaxer."

"Does it go well with melon juice?" Fen asks.

"Absolutely! Enjoy, boys!" Yaz takes a big gulp from her glass, then grabs the other glass and turns towards Kayley.

"Uh, she's not going to drink that," I say, pointing at the glass. "She hates herbals."

"No?" Yaz frowns. "What do you suggest, then?"

"Just compliment her a lot. She likes that."

Yaz shrugs, then gulps down the remainder of her drink and hands me her glass as if I'm her servant. I hand it to Fen, who puts it on the bar for me.

"Thanks for the tip," Yaz says.

I smirk as she makes a direct line back to Kayley and reaches out to touch the skirt of her costume, rubbing it between her fingers. I think Kayley's going to have an easy time getting rid of Yaz. She's doing all the work for Kayley already.

Which brings me back to my date. I give him a smile and proceed to find the best balance between juice and herbal, hoping to distract him long enough so I can slip one of the other, more potent concoctions into his glass. I don't really know what I'm looking at, so I pretend to search for a bottle of tea while I examine the other herbals, hoping their shape will give me a hint as to their contents.

The lights in the stadium go dark, and a cheer erupts from the stadium floor far below us. Yaz joins in with the cacophony and drags Kayley to the edge of the balcony, where Parrish and his dual dates are already.

"The show's starting," Fen says, anxiously rubbing a finger on my arm. "We should get over there."

"You go first. I'll bring the drinks over."

Fen beams and leans towards me but hesitates. Then, with the quickness of an apprehensive schoolgirl, he pecks my cheek and darts away. I can't help but chuckle. He is cute. I'm going to feel bad when I knock him out with an excess of herbals.

The concert kicks into high gear the moment the band takes the stage. I join the others and hand Fen his drink, clinking glasses with him. He seems to be sincerely happy to be sharing the moment with me, which doesn't help my guilt. I'll have to rush him to drink as much as possible so that we can get this over with soon. Poor guy, he deserves someone better than me to share this night with.

It's not long before all of us are in the throes of concert euphoria. In the middle of a slow, cushy number, my mind turns to Afton. I wonder just how much she's enjoying herself. She's got someone she's happy to be sharing this night with, but does that mean she's forgotten about us? I hope not, because it'll be a huge surprise for her when we bust through the door of the royal suite.

"Come on, just one kiss?" I turn my head to see Yaz with her face nearly buried in Kayley's. Kayley's doing her best to fend off Yaz's lips without being mean about it, but Yaz is so herbed up, I'm not even sure getting smacked in the face with one of the lounge chairs would stop her.

I try to get Parrish's attention, but he's so enthralled with the show and his two lovely ladies, he'll never notice my plea for help. Shoot. I've no idea how I'm going to do this. I've got to monitor Fen's drink level while trying to pry the romantically charged Yaz away from Kayley. I don't know how much time is left in the concert, but I've a feeling that the band is on the bottom half of their set. Maybe they'll do a bunch of encores and give us some extra time.

"Has anyone told you that you are the most beautiful girl in the entire universe? I want to dance with you," Yaz says, slurring a word or two. I think I may have used that line on Kayley once or twice, which must be why her smile at the compliment is only half-hearted. I can't blame Yaz for being attracted to my girlfriend. She's certainly not the only one here who i s.

Yaz wraps one arm around Kayley's back and pulls her close. Kayley tries to gently protest, but Yaz is stronger than she looks. She gulps down the rest of her drink and tosses the glass into the back of the room. Her other hand slides down to Kayley's waist and strokes her hip. Kayley squirms and slaps Yaz's hand, but it does nothing to stop the frisky attack.

Heat is building inside of me, sending off every single "protect Kayley" alarm in my body. I tighten my fists, fighting myself from socking Yaz a solid one across her jaw. I can't ruin the plan. We're doing this for Afton. I just have to be patient.

"Having a good time?" Fen asks, hopeful. I turn back to him, trying to smile, but he sees through my poor attempt and frowns. I sigh, my shoulders slumping. It's over. I can't trick him any longer. Not while I'm in a panic about my girlfriend's honor.

I don't want to let anyone down that's been nice to me. If there was some way for me to make it up to him, I would. Like...oh...I don't know. What could I do for a nice guy like Fen?

"Stop! I'm not that kind of girl!" Kayley shouts, and that's all I can stand. I look into Fen's eyes, then channel my inner Afton and kiss him hard.

"Sorry, Fen. You're sweet, and you deserve better. I'm going."

Fen's drink slips out of his hand, and he stares at me, stunned. I give him an apologetic smile and turn towards Yaz and the struggling Kayley. Yaz's got her tongue out and is trying to stick it down Kayley's throat while Kayley's trying to shove her face away. In one breath, I jump and tackle Yaz to the ground. We land with me cradling the back of her head to stop it from a nasty bump. But how we land—me on top of her, with my hand behind her head and our faces close together—makes Yaz think something completely different is going on.

"Hey! I'm not into guys!" Yaz shouts, trying to push me away.

"Me neither," I reply, getting up. "Sorry, Kayley's with me."

I grab Kayley's hand and rush towards the door, only briefly wondering what kind of chaos I just created. We've got to focus on getting Afton now and hope that goes better than our blind date.

Chapter Thirty-Three

"WE'RE ON OUR WAY, Teddy," I say as Kayley and I scamper down the hall towards the royal suite, hand in hand. The guards take notice of our flight but leave us alone. I guess this might be normal behavior up here. It's to our advantage, but I don't want to press our luck.

"Rance, slow down!" Kayley says, dragging me down to a walk. "We're clear."

"You okay?"

"Yeah." She takes a deep breath and puts her hands on her hips. "Wow, she was strong."

"Sorry I didn't stop her sooner. I hoped that the drink I gave Fen—"

"It's fine. I just didn't expect her to drink so much." Kayley looks at me. "You didn't have any of that stuff, did you?"

"Me?" I wave my hands. "No way."

"Because I thought I saw you kiss—"

"Nothing happened!"

"Oh, okay. Not that I would care, you know. You would have done it for the mission, so it's not like it would have meant anything." Kayley grins. "Fen was kind of cute. If the situation was different, I could be jealous."

"Yeah, he was nice, but I didn't even hold his hand. I felt bad for deceiving him like that, though."

Kayley raises an eyebrow and opens her mouth to say something, but then Parrish arrives, pounding to a stop just behind us.

"Hey, why did you guys run out of there so fast? I thought the plan was to slip out one by one." He bends down to press his hands against his knees and catches his breath. "I had to make some excuse for you and told Izzy and Suki that I'd be back."

"Yazmeen had a little too much herbal," I explain. "And her hands were getting a little roam-aroundy with Kayley's body. No way I could let that happen."

"Oh, okay." Parrish nods. "But what about Fen, then? He looked disappointed when you ran out...mentioning something about you giving him the best kiss he's—"

"Oh! Well!" My voice gets loud, blocking out the rest of Parrish's words. "You know, he had a lot to drink, so he must have imagined it."

Parrish just looks at me.

"Parry, you'd better get back," Kayley says. "Just tell them I was feeling sick or something and Rance took me to the toilet. Keep your Teddy comm handy for when we get Afton, and then we can rendezvous with you."

"Got it." Parrish salutes. "Good luck. I'll be waiting for your call."

"Yeah, and don't have too much fun while you're waiting," I say with a grin. Parrish's face goes red, and he lets out an embarrassed laugh.

Kayley watches Parrish go, then holds her hand out to me. I take it, and we stroll down the corridor to the royal suite. We pass by it, pretending to be going elsewhere.

"What was it like?" Kayley asks.

"What was what like?"

"Kissing Fen."

"I didn't kiss him!"

"Then why are you blushing?" Kayley smiles. "Don't worry," she says. "I know I'm the only one for you."

"Yeah, let's just go with that, okay?"

I catch about five royal guards outside the suite as we pass by. Kayley makes me stop just down the corridor from the suite's entrance so we can get a better glimpse of our challenge. She leans against the wall and pulls me towards her.

"Kiss me so it looks like we're just here making out," Kayley says, putting her arms around my neck.

"We *would* just be making out," I reply.

"No, silly, I'm going to count the guards again."

"So you're going to do it with your eyes open?"

"Just kiss me already."

I press my lips to hers, and the warmth of excitement and familiarity courses through me, head to feet. Kayley returns the kiss with an equally strong passion, sighing softly as she presses into me. The intensity is a little surprising. Maybe she had some of those herbals, after all. I'm not complaining.

We hold the kiss for what could have easily been eternity, but also feels way too short. As we separate, our eyes connect, and I'm filled with a happiness that could never be duplicated by looking at anyone or anything else.

And then I remember we're on a mission.

"How many?"

"Huh?"

"How many guards?"

"Oh!" Kayley blinks. "I forgot to count."

That deserves an eye roll, and I execute one flawlessly. Still, there is one benefit to her forgetting—I get to kiss her again.

This kiss is even better than the last, and I'm hoping that this is some kind of karmic reward for doing the right thing, whatever the right thing was. An image appears inside of my closed eyelids. It's Kayley, surrounded by layers of shiny white fabric floating in the air about her. She smiles at me and reaches out a bejeweled hand.

"Oops," Kayley says again softly, the edges of her mouth turning upward. "I forgot again."

"KayKay, what's gotten into—" I can't finish my sentence before our lips connect, but that's okay. I could do this all day long.

Kayley murmurs something into my mouth, and my eyes pop open.

"What?"

"Seven. There's seven of them," Kayley says, wrinkling her nose. "How many could Teddy zap at once?"

"Not seven. Plus, he's got to be close enough to get any of them."

"Let's ask him."

I comm Original Teddy and explain the situation to him, glancing over to the mass of heavily armed men and women and uploading those images to Teddynet. He mulls them over for a moment, then comes back with a reply.

"Three is best," he says over Teddy comm.

"Hmm...that means you and I need to get rid of four. No way we can do that. Not with them loaded down with artillery and armor the way they are. They're like walking tanks."

"But that means they're not going to be able to run too fast, right? Maybe we can use that."

Yet I can't think of how. They've got guns, so they could just shoot us if we tried to get them to chase us. Though they might not. There's lots of people around. A lot of important people's kids. If one of them got shot, that'd be the end of that guard's career, and it might make them a candidate for the queen's guillotine.

"You there! Imperial agents!"

"Uh-oh," Kayley mumbles.

Kayley and I look towards the sound of the voice, and sure enough, one of the royal guards is pointing at us. He gets the attention of the others, and three of them follow him towards us, weapons rising. So much for keeping the rich brats safe.

"You two stay where you are! You're under arrest!"

"Well, isn't this convenient," Kayley says.

"I wouldn't call it that, exactly...up for a run?"

"Not really."

"Teddy, you've got your chance at three once we pull the others away."

"Supermurgitroid," Original Teddy says.

"And where are we taking them, exactly?" Kayley asks, pinching the folds of my sleeve and tugging on it as she swivels away from the approaching guards.

"Doesn't matter, go!" I grab Kayley's arm, and we bolt down the corridor.

"Halt, or we fire!"

"No! Don't shoot, you idiot!" another guard shouts. "You could hit someone on this floor! You want to lose your job? Get after them!"

Thank the Goddesses for intelligent guards. I guess this is why they're on the elite team.

Kayley and I pump our legs, trying to put distance between us and them. But not too much. They have to have some hope of keeping up with us. I glance back, but we've already cleared the bend in the corridor. That gives us a moment to figure out where to go next. I grab Kayley's arm and bring her to a stop to think.

The corridor continues to bend ahead of us, and there's an elevator not far away. That means there's a stairwell nearby too. That won't work. The guards could just call down and trap us inside.

A sizzle like an electrical short circuit whizzes by our heads—great, they're already here. We've no choice but to sprint down the corridor again. I hope we can figure something out, but there are few ways off of this floor.

"What are they shooting at us?" Kayley shouts.

"Stun needles!" I reply after a swarm of them pass by, slamming into the outside wall. The guards adjust their aim and get closer. I switch spots with Kayley and press her towards the inside of the curve. It'll be harder for them to hit us that way.

But we get too close. A door swings open, right in our faces. We dodge to the side just in time to avoid a girl coming out of the suite. The girl lets out a squeak as we rocket by. Then she screams and drops to the floor, convulsing.

A guard curses and orders another to stop and check on her. That guard protests, but he obeys the command.

"Don't worry, we've got them running in a circle!" his commander replies.

"Circle?" Kayley asks.

Oh, what idiots we are. Of course the stadium's circular. Or oval-shaped, anyway. And we're headed right back to the royal suite. Which means...

"Keep running! Back to the suite!" I grin at her, and Kayley's eyes light up.

They think they've got us in a trap, but they're the ones that'll be shocked. Literally.

"Teddy, coming back your way," I say as quietly as my breathless voice can manage. We've still got to get there without the guards zapping us, and both Kayley and I are losing steam fast. I'm already gulping air as quickly as I can, and I feel the sweat dripping into my eyes. As long as no one else comes out of a suite to surprise us, all I have to do is keep running along this slight left bend.

The entrance to the royal suite comes into view, and Original Teddy is there, just sliding his last victim into a utility space.

"Felicitations," he says as he waves a tentacle at us. "Position of known defenders?"

"Right behind us! Get ready!"

Original Teddy bounces over to the side wall and pulls himself up while Kayley and I head towards the door. Just behind it is Afton, our reason for once again making a mess of the system. I don't care. She's totally worth it.

"Freeze!"

"Exactly!" Kayley shouts as both of us spin to face our three pursuers.

"What?" The lead guard's brow wrinkles as he approaches us, suspicious.

"Sergeant, where's B team?" another guard asks. That stops him, and he looks around.

"Anytime now, Teddy," I say. "Please?"

"Hold your horses," Original Teddy replies, causing the guards to spin to see who's behind them. They don't get the chance. Teddy popsicles them in their half turn, and the three of them topple.

"Thanks, Teddy," I say.

"Gratitude testimonial is unnecessary. You are Teddy."

"Yeah, I keep forgetting that. Maybe one day we'll be able to return the favor."

"Benevolence has been achieved, Rancid. That is why you are Teddy."

Chapter Thirty-Four

KAYLEY AND I TAKE a deep breath and step into the royal suite, leaving Teddy to clean up and guard our backs. It's dark, save for a pair of lamps over the bar. There's enough light to discern the furniture and the lack of people, save for two occupied lounges at the far end, near the balcony.

I thank the Goddesses for Nayla's presumed insistence on privacy inside the suite. Still, confronting her is going to be much harder than getting around a team of elite guards. Though, to give those guys credit, they would have had us if we didn't surprise them with Teddy.

"Who's there? Why are you disturbing us?" Nayla rises from her chair and turns. "Who are you? Why did my guards allow you inside?"

"Don't blame them. They had little choice," I reply, approaching her, taking one slow step at a time. Kayley stays next to me and matches my pace.

"Ransom Quigley He'," Nayla says and claps her hands. The lights come up to a comfortable level, and the princess goes from a backlit silhouette to a fully illuminated figure. She's stunning in a silver-and-turquoise gown that hugs her waist and then blooms into a long skirt.

At the mention of my name, Afton jumps up, flipping around in her seat to stare at us. Her eyes are wide, and her mouth hangs in suspense. I think she's happy to see us, but there's definitely some level of reserve that holds her back from tackling Kayley and me with a huge embrace.

"Odd that I did not foresee this," Nayla says, coming closer. "Are you sure you gave me the correct time of your birth?"

"Of course. One thirty-two in the morning."

"I will have to recalculate, then." She comes face-to-face with Kayley and me, glancing between the two of us. "You've gone through the trouble to neutralize my guards, so whatever it is you are here for, you deemed it important enough to risk your lives."

"Afton is very important to us," Kayley says. "And we would do anything for her."

"Except go away, apparently."

"That we can't do."

"And I cannot allow you to speak with her. Surela is on a long road to recovery, and for you to interfere now would do her untold harm. No. It is not possible. You have wasted your time coming here, and put yourselves at serious risk. My mother will gladly take your heads if they put you before her."

I wonder just how much of what Nayla says is real, given that she's preparing to overthrow her mother. I wonder if Afton even knows that. Has she noticed the extra security around the palace that we saw on our way here? Or the intensity in the High Wazir's eyes lately? If she did, then she must know the danger she's in. Given that, why does she choose to stay with Nayla? Does Afton feel so remote from us she considers the princess to be her only refuge? I have a hard time believing that, but the battle for Afton is just beginning, and I think we've got plenty of ammunition to win the fight.

My eyes turn to Afton, who watches us, silent. Something is seriously different about her, and I can't tell if that is a good or a bad thing. I get the sense that she's more open but more vulnerable. That defensive wall that's been her mask for ages has come down, and that both gives her happiness and a great deal of fear. I can certainly understand. I was once in the same place.

"You can't keep Afton from us. She's not your prisoner, and she's well capable of speaking for herself. You think you know her? Well, I've been her friend for eight years. I know all the struggles she's been through, because I was there when they happened. You don't know what's best for her."

"Ransom Quigley He', you have no idea of the true thoughts inside her head. You have no means to discover her true suffering, even if she were to tell you, which I assure you, she has not."

"And what about me?" Kayley says. "I'm her best friend. Afton tells me everything! I know what bothers her."

"Best friend?" Nayla snorts and takes a step closer to her. "That you care for her, I have no doubt, but you are no more equipped than your husband here to do anything to heal Surela's pain."

"For the last time, we are not married!"

"My dear, you have already accepted him as your life-partner. Stop continuing to deny your truth. Just as Surela and I are fated to be together, so are you and he."

Kayley huffs and crosses her arms. I know what's in Kayley's mind, so I don't refute Nayla's words. They're true. Kayley knows they're true. She just doesn't want to admit that Nayla might be right about something. Though, Nayla has been right about a good many things ever since we met her. Whether it's been through some kind of spiritual vision she's had, or the efforts of a very talented contingent of spies and hackers, I'm not sure.

I get the itch down my back, and I know we're just wasting time debating with Nayla. She won't let Afton go. Not that I blame her. Afton is an amazing person, and nobody who falls in love with her would want to let her go. If they got Afton to fall in love with them back, I can only imagine what kind of special relationship that'd be. Afton would be a generous, caring, and protective partner. She'd make anyone feel special. She's not the kind to buy flowers every day, but I'd bet there would be no shortage of moments that would send anyone into their own blissful heaven.

All that means is that I've got to be careful about how I handle Nayla. If I hurt the one Afton cares about, she'd never forgive me. It's bad enough I'm on her trash list as it is. Even if we get her back, there's going to be a very long process of rebuilding her trust in us.

But that's for another time. Right now, we've got to get Afton free of the danger she doesn't even know she's in.

"I don't want to hurt you, Princess," I say. "We're not here to take Afton by force."

"That is appreciated. I am allergic to violence."

"But Afton needs to know the truth and make her own decision."

"And what truth is that?" Despite Nayla's strong posturing, she steps back and places a hand on her hip. This must be something else that she didn't foresee.

"That you intend to overthrow your mother and claim the throne for yourself," Kayley says. "Is that why you really want Afton? Do you need a queen by your side so you can feel protected while you rule over a planet that you stole?"

"What?" It's the first word from Afton since we entered. I'm jumping for joy that Nayla hasn't been able to silence her completely.

"Nothing, darling," Nayla says, but her eyes say something different. There's fear there. "They're lying. It is a desperate attempt to steal you away from me."

"No, we're not, and you know it! You're putting her in severe danger, and we're here to save her." I turn to Afton and give her my most earnest look. "Afton, if we weren't absolutely sure about this, we wouldn't be here. You're in real danger, and Kayley and I won't just stand back and watch you be executed."

Nayla sighs and glances back at Afton, whose worried look tells me we've scored some points and made a heavy dent in the absolute trust that our bud seems to have in her girlfriend. What bothers me, though, is that we've uncovered the truth for her, yet she still looks to Nayla for answers. Afton's not coming with us yet.

"If the coup is already in motion, then let us take Afton," Kayley pleads. "We can keep her safe. And if things go your way, we'll bring her back."

"No. Surela is in no danger."

"How could you say that?" Kayley steps forward. "When you know that if you fail, your mother will execute Afton right next to you? Do you actually care for her? Because someone who loves her that much would never treat her life like it was nothing!"

Nayla's hand comes faster than I would ever expect, striking Kayley across the face before I can even move. Kayley cries out and twists from the power of the slap. Her hand presses down on her quickly reddening cheek as her eyes get watery.

"Nobody hits Kayley!" I shout, raising my hand. Rage is burning through me, and I charge at Nayla. I don't know what I'm going to do when I reach her, but there's no logical thought running through my head. Nayla hurt Kayley, and she's got to pay for that.

"No!" Afton shouts, flying over her lounge chair towards me. "Rance, no!"

Her plea is enough to make hesitate. A second later, Afton reaches me and grabs my wrist. I don't resist. I just stare at her, shocked that she'd choose Nayla over Kayley. It just doesn't compute in my head. We've been telling the truth this entire time, risking our lives for her, and yet, when it comes down to it, we're not her first concern.

"Rance, please," Afton says, her voice softer now. I glare and yank my wrist out of her grasp, then turn my back on her to check on Kayley, who's holding back her tears.

Once I see she's okay, I confront Nayla again.

"You are a complete fraud," I say through gritted teeth. "You claim to care for Afton, and yet you keep information from her. Important information that could save her life. You say you abhor violence, and then you slap Kayley across the face."

"Forgive me," Nayla says, dropping her gaze. "I do not know what came over me. This is the first time I have been in love like this. I have tried to meditate, but my feelings for Surela affect me in ways I do not yet understand."

Her farce is so ridiculous. I almost feel like laughing, but it's like she believes her own nonsense. Nayla rubs her eye as she glances at Kayley and sniffles. It's a great act, and I've got no idea how to break Afton free of the play. All I can do is once again state the truth and hope she believes me.

"Afton, you know us," I begin.

"No," Nayla says, her voice breaking, "please don't destroy the healing I have begun in her. You have no idea what that would do to her."

"And you have no idea what you're doing to our friendship with her! So you can shut up for a minute and let me talk to my friend, who can make her own decisions."

"Okay," Afton says, standing up straight as if she's preparing for a flood to overtake her. "I'm here. Tell me what you came here to say. I'm listening."

"The first thing you should know is that we really miss you, and we're sorry if you feel we broke your trust. I know we've got a lot to make up to you, and whenever you're ready, we hope you'd give us the chance."

Afton shifts and rubs a hand across the other arm. She tries to maintain her gaze, but she fails, and it drops to the floor. That's not much of a surprise. At a moment when she was trying to build a bridge between her two worlds of romantic love and friendship, we smashed her hopes to the ground. I know she's badly hurt, and I'd give anything to fix it.

"The next is that, despite Nayla keeping you from us"—I catch Nayla's eye to show her I mean what I say— "and despite her hitting Kayley, we don't hate her. All of us were happy for you when we learned you had met someone. We want to like her, too, but this keeping you away from us is not something we can accept."

That brings Afton's eyes back up to lock with mine. She's showing me how much the rift between Nayla and us bothers her, and I have to agree. We never wanted this, but here we are.

"Finally, Afton, we are begging you, with all our hearts, to come with us. Despite how your princess is denying it, a coup is happening, and if it's not successful, your life will be over." When I think about never seeing her again, I wipe the edge of my eye. "I have to do everything I can to protect you. I have to, because I never want to lose you. *We* don't want to lose you, Afton. You mean too much to us."

I can tell my words have shaken Afton to her core. She is literally trembling as she considers my plea. Whatever Nayla has done to our friend, it's broken down any of the walls that Afton had built to protect herself. Now she's defenseless, and without some genuine care, Afton will become a fragment of herself.

Does that mean that Nayla really is doing what she claims to be doing for Afton? Has she stripped away her mask so that she can build a stronger, more mature persona? If so, does that mean we're interrupting that process? If we take Afton away from Nayla now, can we finish what she started? So many doubts hit my mind that I stagger from the weight of it all.

Afton turns to Nayla, who looks at her with the eyes of an innocent. She takes Nayla's hands and pulls her closer. As I watch, I go to Kayley and take her in my arms, needing her as much as she likely needs me in this delicate moment.

"Darling," Afton says in a soft voice. "Please tell me the truth. Is there a coup? Are you planning to overthrow your mother?"

"My love, I would never lie to you," Nayla replies. "There is not. I do not know why they believe there to be one."

Kayley protests with a noise from her throat. My expression of disbelief is more vocal.

"She's lying, Afton! I don't know why, but she is! You have to believe us! We're your friends. Nobody cares for you more than we do."

"Then why did you lie to me about why you came here?" Afton's fiery gaze meets mine, and I shrink as I see all the hurt come through at once. "Huh? You betrayed my trust when all I wanted from you guys was for you to be happy for me. But you couldn't even find it in you to do that, and you call yourselves my friends? No. No, I'm not going anywhere with you. The only person I can trust is here. I don't believe in you anymore."

Kayley whimpers and presses against me. I'm feeling no stronger, and if Kayley weren't helping to hold me up, I might just fall to the ground and not be able to get up.

"You need to go," Afton says. "All of you. You guys cause me too much pain. I'm sorry, but I can't see you again."

I back away, Kayley moving with me. My head is shaking from side to side. This is not a reality that I would have ever believed would happen. Not this. Not Afton.

Goddesses. We've just lost our best friend.

"Take care, Ransom Quigley He'," Nayla says in a small voice as we're walking out. "Your bad omens are not yet over."

Chapter Thirty-Five

I HAVE NO MEMORY of returning to our cramped hotel room, nor of climbing into the bed, my clothes still on, and falling asleep with Kayley in my arms. I *do* remember my dream—my bleak dream of nothingness, of emptiness, of this feeling that a part of my body was missing, but I couldn't tell what was gone. I wasn't even aware it was a dream until I felt the sun fall on my eyelids. I'm not yet ready to wake up, but I can't sleep anymore. It's like our friendship with Afton—locked in a state of limbo.

She dismissed us like we were some bad influence ruining her life. Maybe we are. Or were, now that she's kicked us out of it. My body aches to consider we were the ones hurting her all this time. I don't want to believe that, but Afton seemed so certain of it last night, and I can't help but feel some level of guilt for not respecting my friendship with her. She's right. We should have told her exactly what was going on the moment we met them here.

That thought keeps repeating in my head, over and over and over.

Until the door smashes open and a mob of royal soldiers burst through, grabbing and flipping us on our stomachs and binding our arms and legs.

"You shouldn't have tried to stay on-planet," the High Wazir says, strolling through the door. "Now you've put me in a most difficult position."

He waves his guards out and looks over our cramped quarters, distaste well apparent on his face.

"How did you find us?" I ask.

"You've made some friends in the aristocracy," he replies. "Friends whose parents have very important positions in the court. The moment the princess' guards put in their report, it did not take long to find out how you got in. By the way, all of them were very disappointed to find out your true intentions here. You'll not be spending time with them again."

Parrish bows his head. Even though we all knew it wasn't something that was going to last, I think he was truly enjoying himself in the company of Izzy and Suki, and they seemed like they genuinely liked him. Not that it's a hard thing to like Parrish. His noble outlook and honorable demeanor are his winning combo every time.

"But that's not why you're here," Kayley states. My brain is still fuzzy from the abrupt wake-up, but hers is razor-sharp. I wonder if she got any sleep last night.

"It's not, no." The High Wazir folds his arms and paces in the square meter of open space remaining on the floor. "As I told you last time, you are not safe here. What I didn't tell you then was that the danger was not only from arrest and execution. The court's intelligence ministry looked into your claim of an assassin, and after investigating, we determined you were telling the truth."

"Why would we lie about that?" I ask.

"And if you're just here to tell us about that, why bust the door down?" Parrish asks.

"Because you are under arrest," the High Wazir replies. "And by Her Majesty's explicit command, I am removing you from the planet. This time, however, I am personally escorting you to the hatch of your shuttle and making sure it launches before I walk away."

"Didn't the queen command you to execute us?"

"Not using those specific words, no. And I would truly like to avoid any more beheadings. You may have come here to spy on Her Majesty, but that isn't what's keeping you here. Your assault on Her Royal Highness' guards, as regrettable as that was, was also not because you wished to harm the princess or Her Majesty. I also thank you for not seriously injuring any of Her Royal Highness' guards. That aside, you are simply creating too much chaos on our planet, and I cannot allow you to stay one minute longer. Since you are already dressed, we will leave immediately."

My eyes swivel towards Kayley. I guess there are no real options here. Bound as we are, the High Wazir could just have his guards treat us like luggage and carry us all the way to the Teddy shuttle. We've lost Afton, perhaps forever, and until we right all the wrongs we have done to her, there's no way she'll see us again.

"Wait, you said you found out about the assassin?"

"Oh, yes. As it turns out, she is a well-known Hand of the Emperor."

"An Imperial assassin was trying to kill us?"

"If you say so, though I would be confused as to why that might be the case, since you were here on bequest of the Emperor himself."

Yes, why *would* the Emperor want to kill us? Wait—I know what the answer is, and the moment Kayley looks at me, I know she does, too. We know all about the arrangement Cecelia Nilsson-Lim and Jinse Shaloo had with the Emperor, and he doesn't trust us with that knowledge. The question is, can we trust the High Wazir with our knowledge? Whose side is he on, exactly?

Perhaps I should poke a little and find out, but to do that, I'm going to have to give him something.

"High Wazir, you know who we are, right?"

"I didn't until Her Majesty recognized you, but then I did my homework."

"Then you know what we've accomplished."

"Yes, and I see what you're getting at, but that still doesn't explain the Imperial assassin. Surely, there are others, equally accomplished, who could have done the job, and not—" The High Wazir purses his lips when he catches sight of our sour faces. "Apologies. I didn't mean to imply that I wanted you dead. As you remember, it was I who stopped Her Majesty from executing you on your first audience."

"Actually, that was me, begging for my life," Kayley corrects.

"Ah, yes, that is true. I stand corrected, but I hope it is clear that I have done whatever is in my power to ensure you did not end up in the guillotine."

Well, I can believe that. Which means he's not a member of the conspiracy. He could have just had his guards shoot us if he wanted us dead, so I guess that's another plus for him.

I catch Kayley's eye once more, and she nods.

"We understand, which is why we want to share something with you. We know why the Imperial assassin was after us and why she was from the Emperor's own people."

"Let me guess, you've made some powerful people very unhappy."

"Wow, that's totally it," Parrish says. He just gets a glance from the High Wazir.

"That's the gist of it, but it's a bit deeper than that," I say.

"You mean there's a conspiracy in the Empire?" The High Wazir folds his arms and points his smug face right in my direction.

I should have known. He does work for the monarch of a powerful planet, who also holds a senior position on the Emperor's council. Why wouldn't he be aware of these things?

"What do you know?" Kayley asks.

"What do *you* know?"

And just like that, we're back to stalemate. He's got to have information useful to us, and I'm sure the opposite is true. We still shouldn't trust him, because he's got his own motivations, but we can at least relax knowing it wasn't him or Queen de Avila that hired the assassin. I would still like to know who it was, however.

"If we tell you something important, something I'm sure you won't know, will you tell us everything you know about the assassin? You know, since you're looking out for us and all."

The High Wazir chuckles and smiles. I guess he wasn't expecting me to negotiate, and I scored some points with him. That's good. I hope it's enough for him to agree.

"Alright, I'll hear this all-important information that might be of value to me, and I'll tell you what we know about the assassin. But"—he raises a finger—"if I already know what you tell me, I won't promise to do anything but get you off this planet safely. Agreed?"

I nod—I can't do much more than that, cuffed hand and foot like I am.

"On Magnarapax," I say, "there's a Jinse Shaloo factory that contains rows and rows of quantum portals. Many of them are already in operation. Though, after we were there, likely a few less than before."

The High Wazir's eyes grow larger as he rubs a finger along his chin. I try to keep myself from grinning, but it's difficult. Not only will he now spill all the information he's got on the assassin, but we just learned that the portals weren't something the Council knew about, which means the Emperor didn't know, either. They definitely belong to the conspirators.

"High Wazir," a guard says as she rushes in, but he holds up a hand to silence her and turns back to me, a small upward curve to his lips. Here we go. Once we know who sent the assassin, we can get Lieutenant Colonel Cortell on it. He might not be able to stop her from attacking us again, but he can arrest whoever's responsible. Provided it isn't the Emperor, that is.

"High Wazir, forgive me, but this cannot wait. There's been an attempted coup at court."

That gets our attention. The High Wazir spins on the guard, aghast. If his eyes were big when I told him about the portals, they're moon-sized now. His mouth moves as he tries to form words, but he takes a few seconds. All I can think of is how Nayla deceived us with her spiritual aura nonsense. But that doesn't fill me with nearly as much anger as how she brainwashed Afton. Now Afton is likely to be executed right alongside the person she thought she could trust. Goddesses, I can only imagine what she's going through right now.

"The queen?" the High Wazir finally gets out of his mouth.

"Safe, sir. We have caught the ones responsible. Mostly."

"I can't believe she lied!" I blurt out in frustration. We're about to be shipped off-planet, and Afton needs us now more than ever.

"Rance!" Kayley cries. She'd clap a hand over my mouth if she could, but it's too late. The High Wazir and the guard turn on us.

"Who is *she*?" the High Wazir seethes. "What do you know about this?"

"You'll find out soon enough," Kayley mutters. "But we had nothing to do with this. In fact, we tried to stop it last night."

"Impossible!" he cries, realizing exactly what she means. "Princess Nayla would never!"

"But our friend Afton had nothing to do with it!" Kayley pleads. "Please, get her released."

The High Wazir's eyes shoot up to the corner of the room. He's trying to think this through as fast as he can. Now that he knows the queen is out of harm's way, his shoulders have settled a little, but this could be an ongoing situation, and he's here wasting time with us as insurgents are fleeing his grasp.

Once the uncertainty behind his eyes clears, he blinks and looks at Parrish, Kayley, and me.

"The three of you are coming with me. I can't spare guards to watch over you here."

"As if we had a choice," I mutter, but the High Wazir hears me.

"And you're going to tell me everything you know about this. Maybe then I will see fit to get you off the planet in one piece."

"What about Afton?"

"I cannot help her. Her fate lies with Princess de Avila now. Best pray to whatever deity you believe in to show mercy for your friend."

Chapter Thirty-Six

It's awkward to sit with my hands bound behind my back, but at least we're not flat on our bellies as we ride in the royal guards' vehicle, the three of us squashed together in the back seat. A pair of guards watch us from the reversed bench at the front of the cabin, weapons in their hands and scowls on their faces.

I can't blame them for being so tense. This is a tough situation for them. I'm sure many of them had a great adoration for Princess Nayla, and now they're likely struggling with the inevitable outcome of her failed coup. None of them wants to be the one to execute her.

"Maybe if Her Royal Highness begs forgiveness from her mother, she'd be willing to spare her life. Don't you think?" I say to the guards, trying to sound hopeful.

They just stare at me, until one leans forward and gets in my face. She's breathing hard through her nose, as if she's preparing to spit fire at me.

"You have no clue what you're talking about, so unless you want a plasma round in it, keep your mouth shut," she says, then sits back. There's no contentment on her face from rebuking me, so I wonder why she said it. I guess she was just trying to let off a little steam, and I was the fastest way to make that happen.

"We like her, too," Kayley says to the female guard. "We don't want to see her executed, either."

The other guard powers on his weapon and cocks the firing mechanism, and Kayley pushes behind me, taking cover as best she can. I move in front of her. I don't want him to fire, but if he's going to, then he can shoot me first.

Original Teddy disappeared before the High Wazir arrived, which was good. Having to answer questions about him would not be very helpful to our current situation. I think he's following us, but I can't tell exactly where he's at. The images he uploaded into Teddynet are not very clear. He must be moving at a fairly fast pace.

"Hey, eyes up, we're stopping," the driver calls back. "There's a vehicle blocking the road. Could be there are still some conspirators around."

"Got it." The female guard, clearly the more senior of the two, turns to her partner. "Let's go out and keep an eye on our flank."

"Are you sure that's wise?" I ask.

"I don't care what's wise. I care about protecting the High Wazir. You want to do to something wise? Get your asses down on the floor and keep them there until we come back."

Even with the extra space created by the guards getting out, it's awkward to follow their suggestion. Now Parrish's got his back against the seat, I've got my back against his knees, and Kayley's head is on my stomach. If doing this is going to save us from a seditionist's bullet, then I'm okay with it. Then again, I'm always down for a little cuddle with Kayley.

There's a pop, and bits of the armored plexiglass window spray into the cabin, covering us with bits of clarified metal. I squeeze my eyes shut, but way late. Luckily, none of it gets in my eyes.

"Sniper!" the female guard yells, and a sudden thunder erupts outside the vehicle. I push myself over Kayley, and Parrish swivels and lands on his side next to me. Projectile after projectile rips through the cabin. Their trajectory is getting lower, and at this rate, there's no way we'll avoid getting torn up by these armor-piercing rounds.

"We can't stay here!" Kayley cries, reaching her foot up to kick the door release. It slides open, and she rolls out, falling to the ground with a yelp. I worm my way into position and fall out after her, hitting the ground hard. The impact takes the breath out of me. I gasp for breath, desperately trying to put air back in my lungs.

Parrish lands on me. It hurts, but his shoulder in my gut gets me breathing again. He apologizes, but I'm quick to dismiss it. He may have just saved my life.

A guard goes down with a grunt, and the others rush for cover. Our two dart around to our side of the vehicle and hit the dirt. Then the female guard notices our unfortunate puppy pile and pulls Parrish off of me.

"Stay behind the wheels!" she warns.

"Uncuff us then!" Kayley shoots back.

"No, you're prisoners."

"We're going to get shot if we can't defend ourselves," I shout.

"Shh, keep your voice down."

It gets quiet, and I wonder if the guards were successful in their defense. The attackers could just be repositioning, but we don't want to try peeking.

"How many are there?"

"Don't know. Maybe two."

I'm surprised that only two insurgents ambushed the High Wazir and his elite guards. They could be royal guards themselves. If we're to survive this, we're going to need to run for some real cover, and possibly a lot farther than that. I have no intention of testing the quality of their weapons training.

A whistle screams through the air, and the other side of the vehicle explodes, lifting it off the ground. The vehicle groans and tilts towards us, threatening to crush us if it keeps falling. I start to scramble to get away, but the guard grabs me and drags me clear.

"Stay there, or I will sit on you! They want us to run so they can pick us off."

"Well, we can't stay here. We're going to be crushed if that happens again!"

"Relax, an aerial unit is on the way. We'll pinpoint them soon enough."

I feel stupid. She just schooled me hard on a bit of combat I thought I already knew. It makes me realize how amateur we really are. Sure, our team may have gone through a bit, but we're not soldiers. We don't know tactics, and we don't know how to win a war. I hope it never comes down to us having to figure it out, because that would mean the situation is beyond terrible.

Another missile hits the ground just behind the vehicle and sends a large amount of dirt into the air. We're pelted by it as we cover ourselves as best we can. The female guard covers Kayley's head, and I'm grateful, but it'd be nice if she'd unlock our handcuffs so Parrish and I could do the same to our own heads.

The sergeant from the lead vehicle lands next to us and gives us a once-over. Satisfied we're unharmed, he turns to his guard.

"The aerial unit is sixty seconds out. Keep your heads down and watch your tail. We don't want them coming around to flank us."

"What about us?" I ask.

"What about you?"

"Can we at least have our legs free in case we have to run?"

"And risk you doing something stupid? Forget it."

"Hey, we survived that assassin on the palace grounds."

That makes him frown hard. I guess he was there to experience that hellish moment.

"What do you know about that?"

"Only that she's an Imperial agent."

"Well, that Imperial agent is out there right now. That's why I'm not going to give you the chance to make yourselves targets. She will take you out the second she spots you."

The sergeant pats the female guard on the back and dashes back to the front of our convoy. A few rounds fly between the vehicles, just missing him. I don't know whether to feel relieved or even more freaked out that it's not a bunch of insurgents attacking. If that truly is the assassin out there, that means she's after us, not the High Wazir. And we never found out who hired her to kill us.

The aerial unit arrives just in time, buzzing over our heads, headed towards our attackers. The female guard pumps her fist and cocks the trigger unit on her weapon. She's ready to back up the aerial unit and ensure our assailant is down.

A screech comes from the aerial unit. A missile flies off its rails, headed outwards. A millisecond later, the muted thump of an explosion comes from a distance away. Our protector tightens her grip on her weapon and waits for the command to charge.

But it never comes.

A missile shoots out in reply, hitting the aerial unit head-on. It explodes into a million pieces as a massive fireball fills the sky.

As if we angered a sleeping dragon, a swarm of demon insects follows the first. Every missile targets our vehicles and blasts section after section away. Our cover tilts and shudders as if a giant hand keeps slapping it. We squeeze in tight to the truck, but there's so much debris in the air, there's no way to avoid it all.

The constant pounding of the explosions is taking a toll on my ears and my brain. Kayley and Parrish aren't faring any better. With no way to block the roar of sound to our ears, we're likely to be deafened in a matter of minutes.

"Release the Imperial agents to me, and I will spare your Wazir!" The assassin is appealing to their lack of loyalty to Parrish, Kayley, and me. It's a reasonable tactic, given they've got a more important issue to be dealing with. All the same, I hope they don't see the logic in turning us over.

"Okay!" the sergeant replies. "Give us a chance to get them ready!"

That was fast.

"You've got twenty seconds. After that, I'm turning everything over there into dust!"

Kayley's wide eyes look at me. She's wondering the same thing I am—are we going to get turned over? There's no way to know until it happens.

Multiple pairs of feet pound our way, and a moment later, the High Wazir, his sergeant, and another guard hit the ground around us. Here we go. I really hope that he's not about to turn us over.

"Do it," the High Wazir says, and I become frozen with fear. No—he couldn't. Could he?

I hear multiple clicks, and my arms and legs come free. It takes a few seconds for the blood to get flowing, but when it does, I flip over to come face-to-face with the High Wazir.

"What are you going to do?" I ask, my voice shaky.

"When we say, you're going to head to the tree line over there. Don't worry, my guards will keep the assassin's head down long enough for you to escape. But"—the High Wazir holds up a finger—"once you're clear, I want you to head to the palace entrance and wait for me there. If I have to chase you down, I will be very upset."

"Ten seconds!" the assassin shouts.

"How do we get there from here?" Kayley asks. "You took our Sergos!"

"Sergeant."

The sergeant takes a stack of units from a satchel he's brought with him and drops our Sergos into Kayley's hand.

"Five seconds!"

"Go, now!"

As we dash towards the trees, weapons of all kinds unleash a hailstorm of fire in the assassin's direction. I've no idea if they're trying to hit her or not, but I've got no time to care. I'm pushing my stiff legs as fast as they can go.

Despite the torrent of weaponry the royal guards are hurling at the assassin, she still directs a few shots at us. But the guards' covering fire have put her off her concentration, and the shots only impact the surrounding trees. It's a small blessing, but I'll take whatever the Goddesses want to send my way.

After a few minutes of killing our legs, Kayley lets out an elated gasp, and Parrish grunts in relief, slowing to rest on the branch of a pine tree. I stop as well. We've got to catch our breath and get our bearings. We've also got to decide if we're going to obey the High Wazir's command. I suspect we will, given Afton needs our help to escape the guillotine.

But first, we need to get ourselves out of the woods.

Chapter Thirty-Seven

"How far is the road from here?" I ask as we trudge through the forest, hoping Kayley's Sergo—the only one with battery life left—is steering us to safety.

"Not far, just over that hill," Kayley answers, pointing to the area ahead of us. I certainly hope she's right. We've been walking a good amount of time now, and the High Wazir might have already arrived at the palace. Which means he's wondering where we are. "Teddy on station?"

"Yep. I still don't know how they sneaked onto the shuttle, though. They never stop amazing me, even with Teddynet in my brain. We should take some tips from them on infiltration."

"You think?" Parrish keeps his head focused on the ground before him. I think his knee is hurting. It's not like we've been considerate of his injury. We haven't had that luxury. Maybe Doc Elizabeth's new microcellular repair technique will help.

The Teddys could come pick us up, but once they broke security at the spaceport, the only place we could go is up to the ship. But before we can do that, we've got to save Afton.

As we top the short hill, the road is there, right where it should be. It's a good thing, too. The sun is on its way down and will disappear below the horizon in less than an hour. None of us are the wilderness type, so if we get stuck out in the middle of nowhere in the dark, we'll be in big trouble.

"Hey, there's two vehicles coming!" Kayley calls, pointing once again. "We could be in luck. The decals look official."

Before I have a chance to even give her my opinion, she charges down the hill, arms flailing about. I call after her to wait, but she keeps going. I glance at Parrish, hoping he can handle a downhill run.

"Go, I'll catch up," Parrish says with a pained look on his face. When I hesitate, he gives me a gentle push on my shoulder. I nod, because that's all we need to communicate an entire conversation's worth of words, and make my way down after Kayley.

She's waiting at the side of the road for me, her head turning back to check the location of the vehicles more often than necessary. Two seconds before I reach her, she turns back to the road and begins jumping up and down, waving her hands over her head with as much vigor as she can muster. I do the same, mostly because I don't want to her to feel foolish if they pass us by.

They don't.

The vehicles slow and stop near us, their headlights aimed right in our faces. We raise our hands to block the glare, but the headlights remain on. I guess they didn't get the hint. There's an easy way to solve the issue, however.

"Come on, let's go see who it is."

"Wait, Rance," Kayley says, reaching out for me, all her excitement from before replaced with caution. I turn to her, wondering what's brought it on.

"Stay where you are!" a female voice thunders from a speaker mounted on the top of the vehicle. Even though the sound is distorted through the crappy horn of an address system, I still recognize the voice, and it makes me shudder.

"Oh, why her and why now?" Kayley says, shoulders slumping. I can't agree more. Bailiff Daughtry is definitely at the bottom of our "hope to see you soon" list.

Parrish catches up with us and takes a deep breath. "Is that who I think it is?"

We don't have long to find out. A woman, about the bailiff's height, steps out of the vehicle, followed by two others, likely Imperial escorts. I'd know for sure whether it's her if these lights weren't blowing my retinas up.

"Hey, guys, I'd say we should run, but I don't think I could manage it," Parrish says.

"Nobody's shooting at us, so we'd just be wasting our energy," Kayley replies, her voice low. "And as irritating as it might be to share a ride with her, we might not get another opportunity for a lift."

"What a surprise." Bailiff Daughtry—I'm sure it's her now that she's close enough to see her smirking face. "You do not look well at all. What happened to you?"

"Well, first it was the High Wazir busting into our room, then an Imperial assassin attacked us. Then—"

"You know what?" She holds up her hands. "I don't care. You're not dead, so clearly the assassin wasn't successful, and you're not under arrest, because the High Wazir doesn't have you. So all I need from you is what you owe me. Do you have the information?"

Kayley narrows her eyes at the bailiff. I think she's ready to murder the woman, which I wouldn't blame her for, but we were hoping for a ride, not to take our frustrations out on someone who *so* deserves to be used as our punching bag.

"Not with us," I say, placing my hand on Kayley's shoulder. "It's at the palace. That's where we're headed. If you give us a lift, then you'll have it sooner."

"Amusing," she says in a voice that's completely bereft of humor. "You could have just said you were still working on it, but I see now that you had absolutely no intention of holding up your end of our deal. Yes, I'll be giving you a ride, alright. Straight back to the Chamberlin, where you will answer for your failure and make clear to His Lordship that I had nothing to do with it."

There's a possibility I didn't consider. Not that I would have ever thought up a situation where we met the bailiff on a dark road in the middle of nowhere. Last time we talked to her, she was so adamant that we finish the job that I just assumed she would do anything for us to get it done. Then again, she's never really done anything *for* us.

And now she wants to put all the blame on our shoulders to get the Chamberlin off her back. That won't end well for us, so I'd say that's out as an option.

"We won't be going with you," Kayley says a low growl. "You gave us five days to finish the mission, and even though that's way fewer days than we made the deal for, we were going to finish it. Now, we've gotten a little sidetracked for personal reasons, but you will *not* end our deal before it's over."

"Is that so?" Bailiff Daughtry seems content to have a war of words with Kayley. That means she thinks she can win. I've no doubt that's true, but convincing Kayley to back down is going to be difficult.

"We have a *deal*!" Kayley says. "And unless you want to go tell His *Lordship* how you screwed the mission up because you were too hasty, you'll transport us to the palace and let us complete what we came here to do!"

"Who do you think you are, speaking to me like that? I am in charge of the affairs of the most powerful man in the Empire, and no one, especially a half-breed colonist whelp like you, is going to tell me what to do. Now either you get in that vehicle, or I will have you dragged into it!"

Most powerful man in the Empire? Did I hear that correctly? I thought that honor went to the Emperor, not his lackey. Sure, the Chamberlin does have a ton of power. More than anyone save for the Emperor and the Prime Minister.

Does that mean the Chamberlin is part of the conspiracy?

I look over at Parrish to see if he took notice of that little slip, but if he did, his face isn't telling. Maybe we should try to provoke her—while we're still standing—into giving away more.

"You think you can threaten us with violence?" I say, holding Kayley back from sending her fist into the bailiff's face. "You hired *us* to do something *you* couldn't do yourself. So unless you want us to walk away from you right now, you'd better step up and do the simple thing we're asking for. A ride. Or are you so self-important that you need help to lace your boots?"

"Oh, Mr. He', you really are clueless, aren't you?" Bailiff Daughtry crosses her arms and shakes her head. "It's amazing to me you escaped that assassin. With your level of ignorance, she should have made quick work of you three."

"She?" I go stiff, the realization hitting me that we're in a much worse situation than we thought. "I never said the assassin was a she. Not even when I first mentioned the attack."

"So?" Her face contorts, and she pulls back. "Of course she's a she. They all are."

The bailiff's guards get tense. One of them puts a hand on the strap of his rifle, looking ready to slide it off his shoulder and put not a few holes into us. If that's not proof that it's the bailiff who wants us dead, then whatever happens in the next few seconds will certainly provide it.

"Even if that's true," Kayley says, spreading her hands, "how would you know how good she is?"

"Yeah," Parrish adds. "And why do you, manager of the Chamberlin's affairs, need an assassin?"

"Because I do!" Bailiff Daughtry shouts. "Because stupid brats like you can't get simple things done! Now get in the vehicle, or we will strap you to the roof!"

If the bailiff ordered the assassin to kill us, that could only mean one thing. She's part of the conspiracy. Hell, she could be the head of it. And we were well on our way to figuring that out. Perhaps she knew the High Wazir would help us, too.

And why else would she be here, on this road, and at exactly the right time to find us?

I do a fast survey of the area, uploading as many images to Teddynet as I can. The Teddys should be able to figure out where we are from those. I just hope they can get here before we get shot, because I'm about to break the bailiff's anger wide open.

"You knew, didn't you? You knew we'd figure out your little scheme, and so you had to get rid of us before we could tell the Emperor what you were up to. Maybe that's why you even recommended us to the Chamberlin. So you'd have a convenient way to make it happen. Did you tell Princess de Avila you'd support her coup, too?"

"What the hell are you on about?"

"Minister Crowley, Deputy Brownrigg, Cecelia Nilsson-Lim...and you. Do you really think you can overthrow the Emperor?"

"You have no idea what you're talking about. But it doesn't matter. You are no longer useful to me." An evil grin comes to the bailiff's face. "Kill them."

Kayley moves first, kicking the bailiff hard in the shin. She cries out and drops, grabbing her ankle. Parrish and I are next, reaching the guards before they can get their weapons off their shoulders. Parrish slams his shoulder into a guard's gut, just like he's done a thousand times on the field. This is no game, but it's just as effective. The man collapses with a grunt.

I reach out and grab both ends of my opponent's rifle, shoving it hard into his face as it hangs off his arm. Then I try ripping it away from him, but he locks his arm around the strap. The rifle twists in my hands, and I spin it to butt the guard in the face with the stock. The strap makes it difficult, and it's only a glancing blow. But it's enough to put him off-balance, and I use that to throw him to the ground.

Shots ring out from the vehicles. Two more guards are there, taking aim. They're shooting high to avoid hitting the bailiff, but they're going to find their level in no time.

"To the trees!" I shout. Parrish grabs the rifle from the downed guard and hobbles off, Kayley and me right behind him.

But my opponent grabs my ankle, sending me to the ground. He climbs over me, trying to lock my arms behind my back. I spin to face him, and we wrestle for dominance. He pins one of my arms, but I poke him in the throat with my other.

"Rance!" Kayley cries as gunfire forces her down. Parrish fires back. I don't know if he's hit anything, but I'm a bit preoccupied. The guard's got his weight on me, and I can't shake him loose. He reaches down towards his belt. A knife!

Something lands next to my free hand with a clop. I don't know what it could be, but if it can stop a knife, I'm going to use it. My hand finds something tough and stringy, connected to something heavier. I hope it works.

As the guard's knife comes free from its sheath, I swing my hand at him with all my strength. A black-and-white something smashes him on the side of his head. He shouts and rolls off me, unconscious.

"Get lost, or we shoot the bailiff!" Parrish yells at the guards in the vehicle. He wouldn't, or at least I hope he wouldn't. But his warning is at least somewhat effective. They pull back, but they don't leave. Good enough.

"You little tart!" Bailiff Daughtry howls, clutching her ankle. "You broke my leg! What the hell do you have on your feet?"

"Nothing. I'm barefoot. You've just got weak ankles," Kayley replies, a load of sassy sweetness dripping off her words.

That's when I realize what the object is in my hand. It's one of Kayley's tap shoes. The metal plates aren't that heavy, but they certainly make for an ad hoc weapon. Still, I must have hit the guy pretty hard.

"Teddy," I say into the comm. "We need a ride home, please."

Now all we've got to do is figure out what to do with Bailiff Daughtry.

Chapter Thirty-Eight

I wanted to take the bailiff with us as our prisoner, but Kayley said no. Her guards would have done anything to get her free, and who knows how many Imperial ships are in orbit. Just to be safe, we sparkle-jumped to the next system so we wouldn't have to worry about some star cruiser lighting up our tailpipe. That didn't go so well for us the first time it happened. We don't want a next time.

We all need a moment to catch our collective breath, and I'm really dying to see how Grady's doing. I miss my bud, and the entire shuttle ride up to the ship, I prayed to the Goddesses for him to be well enough to talk to.

And now that we're standing before him as he lies on Doc Elizabeth's exam chair, my thoughts go from Grady to our other friend. There's no question in my mind that we're going back to get her, and I know everyone else feels the same way. All we need to figure out is how. The answer can wait until we're done talking to Grady, but it can't wait for much longer than that.

"Hey, dude," I say, touching his arm. "How are you feeling?"

"How do you think I feel?" Grady responds in a hoarse voice. "You've been shot before, too."

"Yeah, but that was by a plasma dart. You got hit with a high-velocity projectile."

"Then think of it like I got hit by a bit of space debris..." Grady coughs, but waves us away when we reach out to help him. "Just not as fast."

"Easy, Mr. Sugiyama," Doc Elizabeth says, putting a hand on his forehead and then readjusting the cap that's on his head. "You're not in danger of bleeding out again, but the new tissue needs time to strengthen and integrate into the rest of your body."

"New tissue?"

"Yes. Intestines and kidney, mostly, but the lowest ribs as well. All of it was a bit of a wreck." Doc Elizabeth chuckles and smiles to herself. "Sounds like a dinner my uncle used to enjoy."

I'm not sure if she meant to make that comment out loud, so I won't say anything about it. I don't even want to see it in my head. Still, there's something more important on my mind. Something I noticed a second ago that seemed wrong.

"Elizabeth, you remember your uncle," Kayley says. "That's great!"

That wasn't it, but it's still interesting.

"Sorry, what?" Doc Elizabeth blinks at her.

Then I remember. "Say, Doc." I reach for the cap on Grady's head and lift it up. "Why is Grady bald? Did you do brain surgery on him or something?"

"Er, no. That's an unfortunate side effect of the procedure and subsequent therapy. But don't worry, it'll grow back."

Grady makes a valiant effort to push my hand away, but he's still weak. I put the cap back for him and give a small supportive smile.

"My head looks like a rock," Grady mutters.

"Don't worry, dude, Afton's not here to laugh at you."

His face drops, and I realize my attempt to cheer him up was more like stepping on his bare toe. Immediately I feel like a complete jerk. My shoulders go up in an apologetic shrug, and I take a step back, hoping someone else will fill in the big hole I just left in his mood.

"When are you going to get her?" Grady asks, his eyes darting between Kayley, Parrish, and me. "That's why you're here, right? To plan and re-equip, and then you're going to save her."

No one wants to meet Grady's eyes after that. It's hard enough to see him like this, and even though we're all hopeful he'll make a full recovery, we don't want to then tell him he's in no shape to go. Not after all we've been through.

"What are you guys not telling me?"

"There's been a few developments since we brought you back up here," Kayley says, sitting down on the edge of the seat. "Grady, Bailiff Daughtry hired the assassin that shot you. And that assassin is still there, looking for us."

Kayley proceeds to tell him about how we think Bailiff Daughtry is a major part of the conspiracy to overthrow the Emperor. She mentions our last run-in with the assassin, and how we tried to stop Nayla's coup but failed.

As she speaks, Grady's chest rises and falls at a faster and faster rate until Doc Elizabeth drops a hand on Kayley's shoulder and tells her to stop. Grady's heard enough, and telling him more won't be helpful to his healing.

"What are we doing here, then?" Grady's voice breaks as he tries to shout. "We're wasting time! Come on! Let's get packed and get down there!"

Kayley pats his leg and looks away when Grady stares at her, expecting an answer. His eyes turn to me, Doc Elizabeth, and then Parrish. We don't want to cause him any more grief than he's been through already.

"Why won't you answer me? Are you not going to save Afton?"

"Oh, we're going," I reply, my voice soft but still full of conviction.

"Then let's go!"

"Why don't you get some rest?" Doc Elizabeth suggests. "Let them go eat, and then we can talk, alright?"

"No!" Grady forces himself to sit up. "I've been lying here for days, and I can't do it anymore! Afton's about to die down there on that hellhole of a planet, and all you guys are doing is hanging around here, looking at me like she's already dead!"

A grimace comes to his face, and he collapses back on the chair, his neck arching back. We're in shock and helpless, but Doc Elizabeth rushes to his side and helps him relax.

"Go, go, go," Doc Elizabeth says, prompting us out with a wave of her hand. "He's just overexerted himself. Goodness knows it's not the first time. He'll be fine. Go eat. I've got my hands full here. I don't want to have to treat any of you for malnutrition."

And so we go, unwillingly, down to the canteen, and try to put food into our tight stomachs. Original Teddy spots us and comes over with the captain. If he's concerned about us, it's difficult to tell. Teddys don't show emotions on their faces. That's what Teddynet is for. Then again, I haven't noticed many emotions even when I'm hooked up to it.

"Nutritional is recommended," Original Teddy says.

"Yeah, we know," I reply, "but we're not all that hungry. Too much on our minds that's bothering us."

"Distress after nutritional is superior to disquiet with deficiency in nutritional," Captain Teddy says. It takes a moment for me to figure it out, but the captain is right. No one wants to be hungry and upset at the same time. If nothing else, we should eat so we can feed our brains and figure out our Grady conundrum.

"We can't take him with us," Parrish says, kicking off the conversation. It was always going to come to this topic, so it's better that we just start off with it.

"True," Kayley says. "But he's going to hate us for a long time if we just tell him no."

"I can't handle any more people who I care about hating me." I drop my head on my arm and pull a piece of black celery from the stalk. It doesn't make it all the way to my mouth, though. I'd rather stare at it for a moment, wishing that I could wave it and magically make all of our problems disappear.

"Teddy will support," Captain Teddy says. "Teddy does not forget Teddy."

"Thank you, Captain," Kayley says with a smile. "We will certainly need your help when we return to Canis Ludis. The problem we're discussing is a little more personal."

"Description of complication is requested."

"We're trying to figure out how to break it to Grady that he's still too hurt to come with us," I say. "If we just tell him he has to just stay here and rest, he's going to be furious with us. I don't know what we can tell him. It doesn't seem like he'll accept anything other than 'Let's go.'"

"Gratin is also Teddy," Original Teddy says. "Presence on planet is possible."

"He's too weak to stand, Teddy," Kayley says. "We can't be worrying about him while we're saving Afton. Grady would be a liability in the field."

"What if we just let him do his usual?" Parrish suggests. "You know, let him run the surveillance again, but up here from the ship?"

"I'm concerned that he won't be able to keep up a level of concentration to do the job for us. Parry, we're dead if we lose our eyes and ears inside the palace."

I get an image in my head of Grady connected to a bunch of heavy cables as he lies on Doc's chair. His eyes are closed, and there's a mask over his nose and mouth. The image came from Original Teddy, I'm sure of it, but what he's trying to show me is confusing.

Then another image pops in. This one is totally abstract, but I get it. The Teddys can hook Grady up to what I'd describe as a temporary Teddynet and Teddy comm connection. His body would have to be sedated during the connection, but his brain would still be active. Then they'd disconnect him once the mission was over.

"Guys, I think the Teddys have a solution that will satisfy Grady." I explain it to them, and Kayley nods along in agreement, but Parrish shakes his head.

"No way Grady is going to let you connect his brain into Teddynet like that. He's so cyborg-phobic, it's not even funny. We won't even get a single wire near him. It's already amazing to me he lets Elizabeth touch him will all those sharp tools of hers."

"Well then, Parry," Kayley says and claps him on the shoulder, "you're going to be the one to convince him."

"Wait, what? Why me?"

"Because if he knows how skeptical you are about this, he'll listen to you."

Parrish sighs, looking defeated. Kayley's got a point, and I'm thinking that's the end of that argument. I'm also glad I'm not the one to talk Grady into it. Parrish has more patience than I'll ever have. If I had to do it, Grady and I would end up not talking to each other for a month.

And like I said, I'm done with my buds hating me. From now on, I'm going to give them as much love and understanding as they can handle. And if they end up getting angry with me for that, I'll just have to pour it on some more.

I really hope I never lose any of them, ever again.

Chapter Thirty-Nine

GRADY LOOKS LIKE A cyborg octopus that ate a man's head and remained there because the view was nice. Eight thick cables, connected to a box at the back of his neck, stream out from all angles. His body rests upon another container that the Teddys connected the cables to. I don't know what the cables are made of, but they seem organic. When I asked Original Teddy, all he did was upload an image to Teddynet, and when I saw it, I was even more confused.

"How do you feel, dude?" I ask Grady's immobile body through Teddy comm. They sedated him so he doesn't freak, and he nearly did several times in the process. At least now he's comfy. I hope.

"Totally spacey, dude." His synthesized voice rings in my ears. His mouth can't move, so Teddy comm is reading his brain signals and creating a fairly realistic version of what he sounds like. "It's not so bad, but once we're done with the mission, I want this thing destroyed. I'm never using it again. This is only for Afton's sake."

"Yeah, I know she's going to appreciate it, dude. As soon as she gets back on board, we'll bring her to see you."

"I think we're ready for a test," Doc Elizabeth says. "Teddy connected a carrier wave transceiver to the Canis Ludis main network."

"Great, I can watch a couple of vids. Maybe score you and Kayley a nice dinner reservation at some fancy bistro," Grady says. His sarcasm comes through with such clarity that we all have a little chuckle at his comment.

"So, what's on?" Parrish jokes. "Anything good?"

When Grady doesn't respond, we turn to the doc, who shrugs and turns to the blue buddy who's running the system. She also shrugs with arms and tentacles, then checks the equipment.

"Guys," Grady's voice comes across, sounding panicked. "It's all over the news! The execution is happening tomorrow morning. Nayla. Afton. Some general and a minister. And it's going to be broadcast to the Central Planets!"

"Tomorrow? Shoot!" Kayley pulls out her Sergo and taps away at it. "What time is it on Canis Ludis now?"

"Just about dinner time," Grady replies, beating all of us. "The broadcast has local palace time marked on it."

"We don't have much time left."

I sigh. I should have known that it would turn out like this. Who can complete a mission in hours that usually takes days to just plan? I want to be confident and say, "Us!" but, just like Kayley and Parrish, I'm worn out. We're three people—okay, maybe three and a half—trying to do the work of five.

"Wonderful!" Doc Elizabeth claps her hands together and smiles. She's not being sarcastic, so I swivel my head to look at her as I feel my forehead wrinkle. She catches me do it and waves a hand. "No, no, not about the execution. I meant we've had a successful test of the system. We'll need to test him with whatever systems you bring down with you, but mostly, I think it's working."

"Well, let's get on it then. Better to get prepped now, and maybe we can catch an hour or two of sleep before we go," I say.

"You're forgetting something," Kayley says.

"Right, sorry." I hold up my hands. "You're supposed to say that. I promise it won't happen again."

"I couldn't care less about that, Rance. There's still an assassin down on the planet that will kill us the moment she sees us. That's what I'm concerned about."

"How do you know she's still there? Maybe she left with Bailiff Daughtry. I wouldn't expect that woman to stay around after you busted her ankle."

"The bailiff's still there," Grady says. "She just gave a speech offering the full support of the Emperor to find any remaining insurgents against the queen."

"We can't fight an Imperial assassin." I pace back and forth. "We've no weapons. No training. It's just been pure luck that we've escaped her twice."

"Weapons wouldn't do us that much good against someone who can just pick us off at a distance, anyway. We'll never see her coming," Parrish says.

"Okay, how about we get the hand-hunters to help? They can track down the assassin, and then we can capture her."

"They won't help us. Not even Billie," Parrish says, perhaps with a little twinge of regret. "They may not like the Emperor or the aristocracy, but they're not going to go up against the system that gives them work."

I reach the end of the room, then trudge back in the opposite direction. This doesn't seem as hopeless as other situations we've been in. Perhaps it's because we've got more experience now. Or maybe we're just naïve as to the real danger.

When I consider the threats we've encountered on this mission, I realize that our scrape with the afterlife was much closer than it's ever been. Take Grady, for instance. We could have been just a few minutes from losing him.

And now Afton is facing the same situation. No—it's worse. The Teddys don't have the tech to put someone's head back on their body. Once the guillotine falls, that's the end of her. Even if we get her free, I've a feeling that she'll never be the same. Losing Nayla is going to hurt her badly. I don't know what it is about the princess that Afton fell in love with, but I can tell she fell deep.

"Rance, sit down," Kayley says in a soft voice. "Trust me, that doesn't help."

"Grady," I say, "since you're connected to a carrier wave, can you call the lieutenant colonel? Maybe he's got a suggestion."

"And what do you think he can do for us?" I get the sense that Grady is shaking his head. "He'll be there in a second if we have evidence that Bailiff Daughtry is part of the conspiracy, but until then, he's got to obey orders, just like everyone else. No, I think we're on our own with this one."

"Maybe you're not as alone as you think," Doc Elizabeth says.

"What do you mean?"

"Well, I...." The doc pauses and glances at me as I make my next lap. She's blinking as if she's lost her train of thought because of my constant stomping. Then Kayley grabs me and pulls me down to sit next to her. The doc smiles and nods to her, then continues.

"What I mean is that I'm sure you've heard the Teddys say how you are all one of them. You may understand the words, but I don't think any of you—even you, Rance—really grasp how deep that connection is for them. Since I've been on this ship a really long time, I've come to learn what that means, even without a Teddynet link."

"So, you mean the Teddys will help us, even if we don't ask?" I ask.

"That's a serious simplification of what I'm saying, but yes. Look around." Doc Elizabeth puts her hand on the blue buddy's shoulder and then motions to the equipment in the room. "None of this was my idea, nor my execution. I can't even fathom how they made this work, but they did. They understood your concern about Grady, and they solved it."

"Doc, I get it, but..." I shake my head. Maybe I don't get it. Sure, the Teddys have always been there for us, but I can't figure out how they could help, other than being the just-in-time transport they've always been. They can't fight, not really, anyway. And I don't want to risk any of them against the assassin. If that woman's got no care for human lives, what would she do with a Teddy?

"Rance." Kayley squeezes my shoulder. "You have a connection to them that none of the rest of us have. That's got to be a way to something, right?"

"Well, sure it is, KayKay, but all I can do is upload stuff to them, and something comes back. I've only ever sent data or images...never an abstract idea. I wouldn't even...know...how...to..."

"Rance? Are you okay?" Kayley tilts her head at me and looks at me with some concern. But I barely notice her movements. Image after image comes at me. They're suggestions. Concepts. Solutions. There are hundreds of them. Thousands, even. It's like I'm watching a river of ideas come flowing by me.

Then I spot one that's brighter than the rest. I reach for it, and it expands in my mind for me to read. Of course—it's so simple a plan, it has to work!

"Rance, talk to me. What's going on with you?" Kayley puts her hand on my cheek and turns my head to look at my face. I blink. She's there, but the river continues to flow by for a second more. Then it dissolves into the background, and reality comes back to me.

"Dude!" Grady says with gusto. "Nice one!"

Parrish and Doc Elizabeth come to kneel before me, the looks on their faces going from concerned to confused when a huge grin grows on my face.

"Why are you smiling like that?" Kayley asks, then frowns. "I thought you had this Teddynet thing under control."

"Well, I do, and I don't."

"Speak clearly," Parrish says. "We don't understand."

"Rance found an idea," Grady explains. He must have seen it, too. "In the river."

"An *idea*?" Kayley asks.

"An awesome idea," he says. "The Teddys came up with it."

"Well, stop keeping it a secret, then!"

"A distraction," I say. "A very, very *big* distraction."

I explain the vision I have in my head to the three of them. How we'd all move around, how we'd keep everyone safe from the assassin, and how we'd ultimately be able to rescue Afton and bring her home. It was a ton of information that hit me all at once, so I hope I'm telling it correctly. The Teddys will have their part down, but it'll be up to us to do the heavy lifting. I think it's possible, especially now that Grady can access the full plan any time he wants. We'll have to pray that the Goddesses are going to grant us f avor.

And if they don't, we'll just have to stumble through it like we always have before.

"Oh, dude," Grady says, "this is going to be so killer!"

"Grady," Kayley says in her mom tone. "Please don't use the word *killer* to describe our mission."

Chapter Forty

I WISH I COULD see the looks on the guards' faces when the first Teddy climbs the palace wall. It's not that tall, and a human could climb it with ease, but it would take a few minutes. A Teddy can scale it in about two seconds.

So when the next few, followed by the next few, and then the next few, fly over the wall, the guards go into a panic. I'm guessing they've never seen a Teddy in real life before. They have no idea what to do, and many just stand and watch while others radio their superiors, seeking advice.

A near thousand Teddys come over the walls like a tsunami, landing in the palace grounds and popsicling every overwhelmed guard they lay their enormous eyes on.

Getting them into the palace wasn't the hard part at all. It was the genius idea—developed via Teddynet—of hiding them all in plain sight that made the Teddy deluge possible. Once the flash mob assembled, there was no stopping them.

Kayley, Parrish, and I meld into the Teddy flood, wearing brightly colored jumpers. A few Teddys lift us over the wall and carry us with them as they spread across the palace grounds. A few seconds later, we're through the palace entrance and making our way through the halls.

Alarms ring through the palace. Screams and shouts echo around us. It's complete chaos, and any palace personnel that come across our massive wave of Teddys get carried along with us. The Teddys disarm the guards as they're passed down the line. I don't know what happens to them after that, but I get the feeling they're deposited somewhere safe.

"Grady! We're inside, approaching the throne room," Kayley shouts. "Which way do we turn once we're there?"

"Go right, then left at the end of that hallway. That'll take you into the barracks."

"Barracks? Do we really want to go that way?"

"Well, you should have taken a left the moment you got inside."

"Yeah, that wasn't going to happen," Parrish says.

We're not really in control of where we're going, and that's a bit of an issue. The Teddys are just steaming ahead, filling up any room or corridor that we pass. Only the throne room gets bypassed, as that would have definitely resulted in violence. Although the queen likely escaped the moment we flew over the wall.

With a bit of effort, we get the Teddys with us to head towards the barracks. I doubt there are any guards left there. They would have raced out to protect the palace, only to be overwhelmed by Teddys once they were outside.

There's Teddys all over. They swing from chandelier to tapestry and back again, chittering with excitement as if they've just been given a very large toy to play with. They're not wasting any moment to enjoy themselves. I'm just glad no one's hurt, which is a huge miracle.

"Teddy, be careful," I shout to Original Teddy. He's somewhere ahead of us, but I can't see him. Only the occasional Teddynet image gives me any idea that he's still with us.

I duck as a swinging Teddy nearly decapitates me just before we enter the barracks' foyer. I turn back, only to have another fly from the other direction. This is nuts. So much is happening at once. There's no way to monitor everything.

There's an enormous pair of double doors at the barracks entrance. They're shut, and likely locked, but that doesn't stop the Teddys from trying to open them. They climb all over them and try to use brute force to shove the doors open, but the heavy portal is sealed shut. It's not going to happen.

"Let's go back," I shout, trying to be heard over the cacophony of Teddy calls, "to the original route."

"Teddys are completely packing the hallway," Parrish says. "How are we going to get through?"

"Single file," Kayley says and spins me around. "Hurry. It won't take long for reinforcements to show up, and we're not here to defend the palace from an assault."

We do our best to push through, and the Teddys are trying to get out of our way, but it's a slow process. Even when a few climb the walls to make space, we have to go around them, too.

"I think we brought too many Teddys," I say.

"They're clearing out," Grady says, "but it's going to take a while. They designed the palace to be confusing to attackers."

"Yeah, well, it's doing its job."

"Here, let's go this way," Kayley says, opening a door. "This takes us through the banquet hall."

Banquet hall? I don't remember seeing one. Then again, the queen never invited me to a meal. Only Nayla was ever so gracious.

As we enter, I sense the vastness of the space. The queen could feed a thousand people in here. I search for another way out, but Kayley's already found it and is heading right for it. I follow, but pause. There's a group of humans huddled in the corner. Their anxious eyes stare out at the sea of Teddys flowing in.

A scent of something savory hits my nostrils, and I connect the people with the smell. It's breakfast time for them. I realize too late that it was a horrible idea to come this way. A warbling Teddy cry spreads through our fuzzy allies, and they swarm in to find the food. They press past me, and I grab the edge of a table to keep from getting knocked over. Pots and pans clatter to the ground, and a large bowl resounds with a clang as it bounces off the wall. Screams come from the humans as they try to flip a table and hide behind it. I try to go to help, but I can't get to them.

"Teddy, cool it! You're scaring them!" Kayley shouts, and instantly the Teddys part and flow around them. "Rance, come on!"

There's no way to fight the tide of Teddys, so I upload the thought of me going towards Kayley. A second later, I'm surfing over them, my body balanced on the tips of hundreds of tentacles, until I'm put down right in front of Parrish and Kayley. Kayley doesn't approve of my transport solution, but she turns and shoves the door open anyway.

The door opens into another mass of Teddys. They're just waiting to exit, but once they catch a whiff of breakfast in the kitchen, they turn and shoot into the hall. I raise my hands up to protect my face, but I should give them more credit. The Teddys won't hurt us. It's just that the sight of a thousand Teddys in one place is severely unsettling.

"This isn't working. We're wasting time!" Kayley growls with a curse. "Grady, where do we go?"

"Well, you've got two choices. Left will bring you to the back door of the prison vault, but that's the long way around. Right will get you to the stairs and the lower level's main entrance."

Kayley looks between the three of us and presses her lips together. It's hard to think with all this racket, but if anyone can do it, she can.

"Rance, you and Teddy take the front. Parrish and I will take the back."

"I've got to find him first!"

"Teddy is available," Original Teddy says, climbing over a few of his brethren to land before us.

I turn to go, but Kayley grabs my arm and pulls me back to connect eyes with me.

"I know you really want to save her, but don't be reckless," she says, her face firm. But then it gets softer, and I see fear there. "Please, Rance. No one else gets hurt."

I give her a reassuring smile and a quick kiss. We don't have time for more, and she'd likely push me away if I tried. It's not an "I might never see you again'" moment, so there's no need to draw it out. We know each other's thoughts, and that's enough.

With Original Teddy squawking commands and sounding like a broken radiator, we make our way to the stairs in record time. The Teddys parted for us like a fault line opening up. All we have to do is race down the middle of them.

Before we descend, I glance outside one last time. Many of the Teddys have either already left or are stationing themselves along the walls, watching for any signs of a counterattack. We're safe for the moment, but if Afton is still locked up down here, we'll need to find her quickly.

"Okay, let's go," I say and hit the stairs, taking two at a time. Original Teddy does his own version of that, but along the handrail, swinging himself from side to side.

We land in front of a door, and I snap the image and upload it to Grady. He knows what to do, and in a few seconds, the awesome computing power of Teddynet will have it unlocked for us. I drop to my knees and prepare to open it and slip in.

"Teddy," I whisper. "How many times can you popsicle?"

"Teddy is not a vending machine," he replies. I guess that's his way of saying he doesn't know, but I'm not so sure about this extra level of snark he's been pulling lately. He must miss Afton a lot, too.

"Well, save one for Afton, just in case. We may need to take her out of there without her permission."

"That is probable."

"Go on my count," Grady says.

"Any guards in there?" I ask.

"You bet. Ready?"

"No, wait! How many?"

"And in three...two...one..."

"Grady!"

"Go!"

The door unlocks with a click, and I've no choice. I slam it open and burst through, diving and rolling across the floor. A plasma dart blasts from the opposite corner and hits the wall behind me. Then another from behind a desk. They've got me in a crossfire!

I scramble behind a chair, but it's poor cover. Three shots burn right through the seat back, singeing my arm as I snatch it away. The guards realize I'm pinned down and increase their fire.

"Teddy!"

"Wear your shirt, Rancid!" Teddy replies and slingshots himself into the room. The guards try to track him, but he's just too fast. One guard drops in a second, but Teddy has to bounce off two walls to reach him.

I peek from behind the chair, now full of holes—it seems like we're clear. Or at least, we've scared off any other would-be attackers for the moment. I slide over to the nearest popsicled guard and grab his gun. Maybe it will come in handy, if I can figure out how to use it.

"Okay, we're in. KayKay, how about you?"

"Still making our way. We're free of Teddys, but Grady wasn't lying. This is all the way around to the other side of the palace."

"Understood. We're standing by."

"No, don't wait for us. We don't have time for that. If you find her, get her out as quickly as you can, and we'll meet you."

I sigh and look at Original Teddy, hoping the two of us will be enough to get Afton out. I don't know what awaits us in the prison labyrinth. All we have is Afton's cell number, and there are no maps down here. If any remaining guards were to trap us in, we're done for.

"Thanks for saving me, buddy, but can you still popsicle after that?" I ask him.

"That is not accurate. Invigorate is required."

"Teddy!" I stand up and peer down the hall to get our bearings. "I told you to save one for Afton. Now what do we do?"

"Teddy recommends sweet talk."

"Yeah? Great." I slide down the hall and drop my voice to a low hiss. "I don't think that's going to work...and by the way, Teddy, the saying is 'keep your shirt on.'"

"Teddy is corrected."

Chapter Forty-One

THIS IS IT. THE only thing that stands between Afton and safety is the door to her cell, and that will be open the moment Grady's got the code. Once we've got her, we'll meet up with Kayley and Parrish, and Canis Ludis will become just a terrible memory.

"Teddy, I'll go in and get her. Stay out here and keep an eye out for guards," I whisper. "I'll only be a few seconds."

"Eye, eye," Original Teddy replies, pointing to each of his large disks.

"Okay, keep both eyes out, then."

As we wait, Afton's dismissal comes back to me like a knife in my gut. *You guys cause me too much pain.* I don't know why she'd say something so hurtful like that. Before, if Afton was angry with me, I'd get my ears pulled, and she'd yell a few sharp words in my face. Then that'd be the end. Nayla changed her in a way that made Afton hate us. I'll never forgive the princess for that, but it won't matter for much longer. We may be saving Afton, but Princess Nayla de Avila is still fated to meet the guillotine.

There's the click. I grab the handle on the door and open it with as much calm as I can muster. No need to frighten Afton before we save her. I suspect she's in a delicate place, given that she must think everyone's betrayed her. But once she sees me here to rescue her, that'll change.

I step inside the cell and give my eyes a moment to adjust to the black hole inside. A small bit of light streams down from the status lamp of an emergency light, spraying an orange hue across the back wall. The cell is much larger than expected, with a shower and toilet off to my right and a bed to the left, several paces away.

That's where I catch Afton's backlit figure, sitting on the bed and facing the back wall. Her head hangs low, as if she's dozed off. She might well be asleep, since she hasn't even acknowledged that someone's entered the cell.

"Afton," I whisper, and I take a step in. "It's me."

I frown when she doesn't respond, so I approach her.

"Afton!"

"No," comes her sharp reply.

"Afton, I'm here to rescue you! We've got the Teddy shuttle waiting, and Parrish and Kayley are here, too."

"Go away."

I stand up straight, pausing just a step away from her. This isn't the situation I had imagined when I arrived. Sure, she might protest or be angry, but she'd still come with me. Why is she reacting like this?

"Afton, we have to get going! We can't hold the palace for long. Reinforcements are almost here, and the guards the Teddys popsicled will wake up soon, too!"

"Then go. You don't need to save me."

"Hey, I get you're upset with me. We can talk about it all you want, but we've got to go now!" I reach out to grab her arm, but she hears me, and her hand flies out, slapping my hand away.

"What don't you understand?" Afton spins to face me. "I don't want you here. Get out!"

Even in the dim light, Afton's face is full of outrage. I step back, shocked at the level of hostility. She's like a wolf protecting her den, only that den is a cage meant to keep her in, not make her safe. My chest tightens, and my hands clench. We don't have time for this.

Original Teddy's got no more popsicle power, and there's no way I'm going to match her in a hand-to-hand fight. She's taller, stronger, and well trained in fighting arts. If I tried to take her out of here by force, I'd just get beaten senseless for my efforts. I've got to talk her out.

"I can't leave without you, Afton. No matter what you think of me right now, you're my friend, and there's no way I will let them execute you."

"You don't care about me!" Afton spits. "You and everyone else just decided to do what was best for you. No one even thought for a minute how your actions would affect me!"

"That is so not true! I went to see the Chamberlin because they promised to clear your criminal record so you could be free to do what you wanted. You could go to Officer Candidate School. Isn't that what you always dreamed of?"

"I'm never joining the military. Violence only creates more violence!"

"Is that what Nayla tells you?"

Afton shoots up from the bed, her finger in my face. I take another step back, but resistance is building inside of me. I can't let her take over this conversation.

"You don't get to say her name!"

Fury brings heat to my face, and my hands turn into fists. Here I am trying to save her life, and she's treating me like I just caused the situation she's in.

"Don't you realize where you are? What's about to happen to you?" My hand fires up, and I point right back at her. "Nayla did this to you! Nayla lied to you!"

"No! She loves her mother! She'd never harm her!"

"Accept it! She's the one who betrayed you!"

"No!"

But something breaks in Afton's voice. Her second denial lacks the fire of the first. She knows there's truth to what I say, and as much as I hate to use that against her, if it saves her life, I will. She may hate me forever, but that won't be as hard to bear as watching her die. Not when I know I could have stopped it.

"We were there two nights ago to stop this from happening. Do you think someone who doesn't care about you would do that?"

Afton glares at me, her body shaking. If it's from anger or despair, I don't know, but I have to keep going. We're getting low on time.

"Now come with me and live your life. Just as *you* want to, not as some spacey girl tells you to. That's never been you."

I open up my hand to her. She glances at it, then looks me in the eye again. Time disappears, and I lose sense of the moment. It's both too long and too short. I've wasted so much time talking to her, but I feel cheated, too, for not saying enough. We should be out the door already, yet I could never leave until I knew for certain she would come with me.

"No." Afton looks down and shakes her head. "No, I don't want to."

"I'm not leaving without you." I shake my offered hand, motioning for her to take it.

"Rance, you don't understand. Nayla's going to die, and I..." Her voice cracks. "I don't know if I could live without her."

"You can, and you will!" I step towards her, reaching out to take her shoulders. "You think I don't know how you feel right now? I know how hard it is to love someone. It's like you can't even breathe if you're not with them. But Afton, I promise, you can get over her, and you'll find someone else. Maybe not for a long time, but you will, and I will be there every step of the way."

"I can't, Rance." Afton sniffles and wipes a tear from her eye. "I can't. Just leave me."

"Never."

"Please, Rance." Her voice turns pleading, weak.

"No." I grab her shoulders. "Now let's go!"

"I can't!" Afton shouts. Her hands shoot up and strike me hard in the chest. I fly back, crashing against the wall. Light flashes across my eyesight as my head impacts the hard surface. I lose my balance and collapse to the ground.

Once my sight comes back into focus, my eyes find Afton. She's on the floor, too, her face buried in the crook of her arm. Her body heaves as she sobs, grieving for a dream that's been smashed to pieces and ground down to fine dust under the boot of this political mess we call an Empire.

"Why won't you just let me die?" Afton whimpers.

I blink as my senses come back to me and my brain resumes normal function. I know she is in a terrible place right now. Death seems like the only option for a hopeless situation. But I also know that Afton is stronger than the despair she feels. I just have to give her some hope.

"I can't. That'd be like killing myself," I reply. "And I still want to live. I want you to live, Afton. You are a part of us, which means it's impossible for me to let you go."

"Rance..." Grady's voice comes over Teddy comm. I forgot he was there. He must have heard the entire conversation. "Please tell Afton I'm here and that I'm fine, and that I can't let her go, too."

I tell her.

"Grady's okay?" Afton asks as she looks up at me.

"He will be. And he didn't survive just to lose you now. None of us did. I hope you realize, Afton, that if you are that sure you want to die, all of us would just stay here with you. We may have totally screwed up on you, but we're determined to make it right. Even if it kills us."

Afton wipes a sleeve across her eyes, her frozen expression telling me there's a thousand thoughts going through her brain. Then, in the small sliver of light that catches her face, I see the edge of her mouth curl up. A wash of anticipation hits me. Hope. Afton feels hope.

There's a shuffle of feet behind me, and a pair of shadows fill in the light coming from the corridor. Kayley and Parrish. They take stock of the situation, then bolt into action. Parrish drops next to me and helps me sit up.

"What's going on? Why are you guys still here?" Kayley says, moving swiftly to Afton's side.

"Oh, you know, we're just taking a break."

That gets a snort from Afton, but Parrish and Kayley find no humor in it. Both of them are looking between Afton and me, their foreheads going tight.

Parrish lifts me to my feet, and Kayley does the same for Afton, helping her to stumble over towards me.

"Rance," Kayley says, fear creeping into her voice. "We've got to go."

"Tell Afton you love her first."

"What?" She blinks and glances at Afton, then back to me. "Of course I love her! She's my best friend."

"Don't tell me, tell her. You, too, Parrish."

"No question," he says, turning to Afton. "We'd do anything for you."

Kayley still doesn't get it, but she turns to Afton, anyway, taking her by the shoulders.

"Hey, I don't know what's going on, but if telling you that I love you gets you to move, then I love you more than the universe. Can we get out of here now?"

Afton locks eyes with Kayley, then leans down and kisses her on the cheek as she pulls her into a soft embrace. Kayley smiles, still confused, but hopeful.

"And what about you?" Afton asks, turning to me.

"If I haven't made myself clear how much you mean to me, Surela, saying a few more words won't fix it."

Then I catch sight of the look that makes my heart fly. That snide Afton-face that I didn't know how much I missed until she brought it back.

"Okay, fine. I'll let you guys save me," she says with a soft smile.

"Great! Teddy, get—"

Afton's hand clamps over my mouth, and I jump.

"But first, we save Nayla."

"Afton, no!" Kayley says. "We don't have time for that!"

"I'm not leaving without her. There's no way she's mixed up in a coup. Nayla doesn't have a mean bone in her body. We've got to save her. And if you're not willing to do it, then I'll go alone."

Afton's sudden ultimatum paralyzes Kayley, and she looks to me for an answer. I don't have one. Not yet, anyway. I should have known this was coming. And here I was patting myself on the back. Now Afton's used my own words against me, and I can't find an angle to combat that.

I get what Afton is saying about her, and it may even be true, but I don't trust Nayla. She's made every attempt to keep Afton away from us and could even be working with Bailiff Daughtry to remove us from Afton's life permanently. I want to believe that Nayla is as good and as kind as she seems to be, but I remember how difficult she was when I first met her. All I wanted was my seat, and she refused to give it to me. Sure, she was waiting for Afton. But she could have made that clear.

Saving Nayla would make Afton ecstatic. It'd prove to her we care for her as much as we say we do. Not just about her life, but her happiness. That'd go a long way to mending the rift that's come between us. We can't just stroll over to her prison cell and pop her out, though. There's bound to be at least five of each type of security personnel watching her. After all, she's the leader of the insurgency.

What do we do with her once we've rescued her? I can guarantee she's going to cause trouble for us. We were trying to get our lives back on track when all this began. That won't happen if we become willing members of a failed coup attempt. Unless...she didn't actually do it? Is that even possible?

No luxury of time to figure that out. Ah well. It's only our lives. We've risked them before.

"Oh, hell, Surela," I say with a sigh. "I think you're just taking pleasure in making life difficult for us. Fine. We'll save Nayla. But if she freaks the Teddys out, I'm blaming you."

Afton just smiles and nods towards the door.

Chapter Forty-Two

WE SIT INSIDE THE emergency stairwell that leads to the top of the tower where Nayla's being held. There's a small reception area just outside the elevator doors, and five guards cover the area, heavily armed and ready for action. Other than that, only a table acting as a proxy barricade blocks the armored door leading to her makeshift cell.

"Ready?" I whisper as I catch everyone's eyes. Parrish nods and tightens his jaw, Afton nods, Original Teddy gives me a tentacles-up, and Kayley...

Kayley wrinkles her nose and looks again at the guards. She's right to be wary of our chances. We've only got two pistols, and Original Teddy thinks he can popsicle one of them. That still leaves two.

"We shouldn't be doing this," Kayley says, with a quick glance at Afton, who's keeping her eyes on the guards. "We don't have any backup if something goes wrong."

"Yep," Afton says and flings the door open. Her gun points at the nearest guard and takes him out with a single shot.

The rest of us have little time to react. Parrish hits the next guard, and he goes down. Original Teddy flies up and over the remaining three. He whips his tentacles around one guard's legs and pulls them out from under him. He falls forward, but fires his weapon before his face meets the ground.

The remaining two back off, taking cover behind a table. Parrish and Afton pull back to the stairwell. Plasma bolts fly in all directions, burning holes in the floor and walls with a crisp sizzle. Smoke fills the air, and we're blinded. But so are the guards.

"Get to the door," Afton says. "We'll keep them pinned."

"Unless they call for backup," Kayley responds.

"Yeah, they already did. I heard it."

Kayley huffs and shakes her head.

"Come on," I say, taking her hand. "We don't have time, like you said."

We dash towards the door, keeping our heads low. But Kayley trips and falls with a yelp. I spin, reaching out to grab her.

A plasma gun screeches, and a millisecond later I'm on the floor, a numbness forming in my left arm. Shoot. They got me. I hope it's not too ba d.

Kayley knows better than to announce our location again, but the smoke is clearing, and soon enough we'll be exposed.

"Grady, get that door open!" I hiss, daring to speak only as loud as I need to so he can hear me.

"With pleasure," Grady responds. "You know, running things this way has actually been kinda fun...just don't expect me to do it again."

"Just get the door open!" Kayley shouts, forgetting our attempt to keep hidden.

The reception area fills with gunfire from both sides. Bright streams of white-hot fire flies just above our heads, threating to drill molten holes into our skulls. Kayley keeps on her hands and knees, dragging me to the door by my shirt. Pain hasn't yet reached my brain, but I know it's coming, so I do as much as I can to move myself along before I become more useless than I already am.

"It's just waiting for you to slide it open," Grady says. "Have at it."

We both grab the handle and rip the heavy door open. It crashes into its receptacle with a ground-shaking thud. Then we're through and slamming it shut again. We may be trapped, but at least we're safe from plasma fire.

A smoky haze covers the room. If Nayla's in here, she's not making herself known. There is light passing through some of the smoke from the back, so there's got to be another room behind this one.

"Rance," Kayley says, breathless and worried, as she does her best to check me over. "Where are you hit?"

"My arm, but it's not a big deal, KayKay. I'll be fine." I should know. I've been shot before, and that was way worse than this is.

"No, you won't. You might not be feeling pain right now, but the moment you do, you're going to go into shock, and then you'll need to be carried out of here. I'm calling the shuttle in. We'll find a window and get aboard from there."

Kayley gets on Teddy comm and calls for Doc Elizabeth. But I stop her before she can call for the shuttle. We're so close to rescuing Nayla, it'd be stupid to quit now. We made a deal with Afton, and we have to hold up our end, or she'll go right back to hating us. I didn't agree to do this so we'd be right back where we started. I wanted to show Afton that we really mean what we told her. Going back on our word just makes us a bunch of liars, and we've lied to her too much already.

"Kayley, we have to. We promised Afton."

"But that never included you getting hurt!"

"It's not like we didn't know the risks!"

Kayley mutters a curse under her breath. "Do you have a death wish or something?"

"No! Never!"

"Well, you're not headed in the right direction! And I'm really getting tired of seeing you hurt!"

I stare up at her, realizing how my reckless antics affect her. It's no different from how my actions affected Afton. My choices have consequences, and those repercussions can hurt the ones I care about. I can't just do whatever I want anymore.

"Who's there?" Nayla's voice calls out from the back room as the firefight dies down to the occasional blast outside the safety of the cell. If we're going to do this, now would be the time.

"Kayley, I'm sorry if I've worried you. I've only ever wanted to do the right thing, and if that means putting myself in harm's way from time to time, then I'm willing to do that. But I promise to consider your feelings before I do. Okay?"

Kayley raises an eyebrow, clearly not expecting that level of detail in my answer. She'll need to see action from me to really believe it, and I definitely plan to. However, we need to get Nayla and get out of here before we get surrounded.

I push myself up and take a few steps towards the back room. The wound on my arm hurts now, and I hope I've got enough stamina to stay on my feet as it gets worse.

"Princess, it's Rance! We're here to rescue you!"

Kayley sighs behind me, resigned to what's happening for the moment. I fully expect her to let me know when she has an objection again.

Nayla appears out of the smoke, her hands up, ready to protect herself or run. She tilts her head sideways as she peers through the haze at us. She seems different, but I'd expect that anyone facing execution might have a different outlook on life.

"What happened to your hair?" I ask, catching sight of her new short bob. It makes her seem younger...and more vulnerable than I've seen her before.

"Easier to aim the blade over my neck, apparently," Nayla answers, rubbing a hand through her hair to the back of her head. A frown comes over her face, and she looks up at us. "Why would you save me?"

"We don't really have time to discuss that, Princess. We've got to go." I hold my hand out to her, just like I did to Afton.

Nayla nods and runs towards us, her eyes expressing the hope and anxiety of the moment. Once the shuttle is here, we're home free.

"Not just yet," Kayley says, her gaze focused on Nayla. The princess slows, and she walks the last few steps with a serious wrinkle on her forehead.

I turn to Kayley, confused why she'd choose this moment to pause our rescue. Wasn't she the one who was just saying how we were out of time?

"Before we take you out of here, I need to know," she says, coming toe to toe with Nayla, "how you really feel about Afton."

Nayla shakes her head and stares at Kayley. Her mouth hangs slightly open, and I'm sure, just like me, she has no idea why Kayley is pressing her here and now. This is no time for a showdown between the two of them. If Kayley's got misgivings about Nayla's intentions, she could just as easily discuss them with the princess when we're flying out of here.

"KayKay, we don't have time for this," I say. The wound in my arm is jamming needles into me. For a moment, I get dizzy and have to place my hand on the wall.

"Yes, we do. In fact, there's no better time."

"We could get caught if we wait any longer!"

"Well, that's up to the princess, now isn't it?"

Kayley lifts herself to her full height, nearly eye to eye with Nayla in her slumped stance. I sense a level of humility in her I hadn't seen before. If I had to guess, I'd say her feelings for Afton are real, but Kayley won't accept my assessment. I could just grab Nayla and pull her out of here, but that won't keep the promise I just made to Kayley just a few minutes before. Only Nayla's words will free her—if Kayley believes them.

"You lied to her," Kayley says, "and it wasn't some small little lie. You put Afton in danger. They were going to execute her, thanks to you. I begged you to let her come with us, but you thought you knew her better than we did, didn't you? I should smack you just for that. But I'm giving you the chance to prove to me you're worth our effort."

"I don't know what you want to hear, but"—Nayla drops her head—"I hope you believe me when I tell you, I would never try to overthrow my mother. Yes, she can be a bit...excessive, but I have no wish to take her throne. I believe someone wishes to create an imbalance in my mother's rule."

"The bailiff," I say. I could bet on it.

"Fine," Kayley says, folding her arms, "but you've told me nothing about your feelings for Afton. That's what I care about. So say it...and trust me, I'll know if you're lying."

Nayla looks up, first into Kayley's eyes, then out to where she must imagine Afton to be. A tear slides down her cheek, yet she doesn't stop gazing outside the cell. It is almost as if she can't.

"I have never been in love before. Not like this. I thought I had everything under control, and I desperately want to help her heal those wounds inside her. But, I admit, seeing her here like this, I realize I was wrong about keeping her away from you, and I deeply regret every second I denied her access to her friends. All I want now is to be with her. Nothing else matters to me. Not even my standing as heir."

"Well, keeping your status as crown princess likely is out of the question. At least for now," I say. Nayla's response is to just curl the side of her mouth up at me. I guess that means, like she said, that she doesn't really care that much about becoming queen.

Kayley glares at the sullen Nayla. She's judging the truth of the princess' answer, and for all our sakes, I hope she decides quickly. I know I just said I'd consider Kayley's feelings before taking any action, but she's making it difficult to keep my promise. We really need to go.

"Guys," Grady says, "I've got some bad news. A battalion of soldiers just arrived at the gates. You've got to get out of there. Now or never."

"Okay," Kayley says, pointing a finger at the princess. "You can come with us. But if you *ever* hurt Afton again, I promise you, I will find the nearest airlock and push you out of it."

Nayla breathes a sigh of relief. We may all be getting out of here, but this is far from over. I can only hope that Nayla can prove the truth of her words to Kayley. Otherwise it's going to get seriously uncomfortable on the Teddy ship.

Chapter Forty-Three

WE TEAR DOWN THE stairs, hoping to reach the rendezvous point faster than the queen's army can get there. At least they don't know where we are, so that's a bonus. If it wasn't for Grady's all-seeing eye, we wouldn't know where they were, either. We've got the advantage for now.

Parrish and I are in the front, with Kayley and Nayla just behind. Afton covers our backs while making sure Nayla sticks close to her. They're holding hands so they won't separate. Maybe I should do the same with Kayley.

"Whoa!" Parrish shouts, and Original Teddy flies up to the ceiling.

Parrish comes to a skidding halt as a trio of bodies slide out from the darkness to block our way. It's the bailiff with one of her guards.

And the assassin.

Parrish raises his weapon, but the assassin is faster. She slices the barrel off with her blade, sending it ricocheting off a wall. In the same motion, she spins and throws a foot into Parrish's gut. He flies backward, landing hard on his back. His head crashes against the wall, knocking him out.

A plasma shot comes from Afton, just missing the guard. He goes to return fire, but another shot from her puts him down. The bailiff, just behind him, stumbles, trying to take cover. She falls into the dark and pulls herself clear.

Now we're only faced with the assassin. That's trouble enough. She won't stop until we are dead.

"Get back!" Afton shouts, rushing forward. She fires three shots in quick succession. The assassin anticipates her aim and is well clear of the volley before Afton even squeezes the trigger. Afton takes aim again, but misses. The assassin keeps in constant motion, frustrating Afton's attack.

I pull back, putting Kayley and Nayla behind me as they drag Parrish clear of the fight. I've got nothing but my body to protect them if the assassin gets past Afton, and the only other weapon in the area is out of reach in the guard's holster.

Afton fires again, but to no avail. She's not experienced with a firearm, and her opponent continues to easily evade every shot she gets off. At least the assassin doesn't have the chance to attack. Maybe I can get around them and snatch the guard's weapon. Then we'll have the advantage again.

But that'll leave Nayla and Kayley undefended. If I've got nothing to protect me, they've got even less. I can't let either of them get skewered at the end of the assassin's blade. I have to wait for my moment.

That moment comes when the two combatants pause, coming to a temporary stalemate. Afton seems to realize she can't shoot the assassin, and there's no opening for attack for the woman in black while she's avoiding plasma bolts. Afton keeps her pistol up, and the assassin stays in a low stance, ready to spring in any direction.

I upload an image of a frozen assassin, so that Original Teddy can see it through Teddynet. A second later Teddy uploads a blank image. There's nothing, just black. I get the sense that means he can't popsicle yet.

"You meddling kids aren't getting away this time!" Bailiff Daughtry shouts, coming out of the dark to sneer at us. She's hobbling along on one foot, which makes me think Kayley really broke her ankle. Good. She deserves it. "I'm putting an end to you and your making a mess of my plans!"

"So it was you!" Kayley says. "You're the one that created this coup and framed the princess."

"Not exactly me, but happy to take credit for it." The bailiff grins. "No offense, Your Royal Highness, but you were too easy to use as a scapegoat."

"How dare you try to create a rift between my mother and me!" Nayla cries out, eyes full of fury. "They will execute you for this!"

"Unlikely," the bailiff replies. "A legion of soldiers surrounds the palace right now, and they're not on your side."

"A bunch of auxiliary reinforcements won't scare us," I reply. "We've got quite a few tricks up our sleeves."

"Have all the tricks you want. You'll never get past her!" The bailiff flings a finger out to point at the assassin. "She's the best in the entire Empire!"

"She might be good, but she'll get tired eventually, and my weapon is faster," Afton growls.

That may be, but we don't have time to wait until the assassin gets fatigued. Soon enough we're going to be overrun by soldiers, and then it won't matter who's better at what.

"Why do you want us dead?" I ask, stalling for time so I can think of a plan. "What did we ever do to you?"

"Are you serious?" Bailiff Daughtry replies. "We would have already been in control if it weren't for you!"

"Good to know we're making such an impact," Kayley says. "And once you're done, your little coup will be over."

The bailiff bursts out laughing.

"You think this ends with me? Oh, now that's a good one. You'll never stop us with your little brat pack! There are thousands of us at all levels of power, and soon enough we'll be ruling the Empire."

The bailiff is defiant, but there's exhaustion behind her eyes. We really are messing up her plans, more than she's admitting. I'm sure Kayley realizes it, too. Which means we don't need to stop thousands of conspirators. We just need to stop the ones who are causing the actual problems.

"I'm tired of waiting. You want to dance with me for real, pretty?" The assassin offers Afton one of her blades. Afton's eyes dart down to it, but her pistol remains aimed at the woman.

"And give up my advantage? No thanks!" Afton's weapon discharges, catching the assassin on the arm as she moves to evade. That doesn't stop her from sliding past Afton and charging me, both blades raised.

I'm about to be sliced into bits. No way I can dodge this.

Original Teddy drops on her from the ceiling and pulls her away. The assassin yells out, her blades flying over her head, but Original Teddy is already gone, the only one who can move faster than the woman in black.

She slides on her knees towards Nayla and Kayley, her weapons sticking out like a pair of spears, ready to impale them. Without thinking, I dive and tackle the assassin, knocking her into the wall. She's slimmer than I remember, but there's plenty of muscle rippling beneath her dark cloak.

The woman snarls and brings an elbow up into my eye. Her swing continues, and her blade catches me across the chest. I jump back, fearing the worst. But that opens up Kayley and Nayla to attack. The assassin takes advantage of the moment and thrusts a blade out.

Nayla shoves Kayley away, and the assassin's blade slides through her thigh just as easily as a finger moves through water. Nayla screams and collapses, clutching her leg. I press my attack again, wrapping my arms around the assassin's body and throwing her as hard as I can. She flies into the corner of the room, but twists and lands on her feet.

Afton lets off a torrent of bolts, and again the assassin evades, rolling towards the bailiff, who pulls away in fear of getting shot. Afton's firing continues, but she's a millisecond behind.

Then the assassin strikes at her, slicing and stabbing at the same time. Afton spins out of the way, but just barely. She fires again at the woman, but the assassin is already under her shot, diving for Afton's legs.

Afton jumps over her, rolls into a somersault, then spins to fire, but she misses. I again become the target of the assassin's attack, and I do my best to avoid it, but I get a slice across my hand as I try to block the blade. I fall back, clutching my hand to my chest and sucking in a breath.

The assassin and Afton face off again, and I wonder just how many shots Afton's got left. If this keeps up, she'll run out, and it'll be the assassin's blades against Afton's hands. Afton may be skilled in fighting arts, but the assassin is an expert. With her weapons, it'll only be a matter of time before Afton succumbs to her attack. Then we're all done.

I've got to come up with something before then. I just don't know if I can. My wounds are not deep, but they sting something harsh. It's hard for me to maintain my thoughts, and I really need to stop my bleeding. Kayley's too busy taking care of Nayla, and Parrish is just waking up. It's just Afton and me protecting us, and we're quickly losing this battle of attrition.

"Give it up already," Bailiff Daughtry says. "You won't win. Not here. Not ever. You and your little friends are no match for us! We will be victorious in the end!"

Afton sighs and fires a shot at the bailiff. She goes down with a grunt, but she's not dead. I don't know where she got hit, but at least we don't have to hear her annoying babble any longer.

"I'd prefer not to say it, but thank you," the assassin says. "She was really getting annoying."

"So are you," Afton says and fires a shot at her. It's lazy, so the assassin dodges it with ease, but it gets the message across.

There's a distant but steady din echoing through the corridors. The soldiers are here, and we're out of time. The assassin could just stand back and wait, but I've got a feeling that's not her preference. She wants the satisfaction of ending all of us, and her only way to do that is to kill us all now. We've been complicating that as best as we can, yet there's only so much we can do. At some point, one side will falter and it'll be over. I just hope it's not us.

I'm trying to provide Afton as much support as I can, but my wounds are pulling me down. I can barely focus, which means I'm not going to be much help in a split-second situation.

But maybe Original Teddy could be.

"Last chance to have some fun," the assassin says, holding one of her blades out to Afton again. "If you say no again, I won't hold back anymore. A shame, really. You've got nice eyes."

"Sorry, I'm taken," Afton says and starts firing. I've got no time to think of an image to send to Original Teddy.

Everything happens in slow motion. The assassin slides under Afton's aim and thrusts towards her legs. Afton's wide open. She tries to pull back, but the assassin's momentum keeps her moving. Afton's body twists to avoid the points of the blades. It's not enough. In a second, she's going to get impaled.

"Teddy!" I cry, praying for him to do anything he can. Even a distraction would help. I try to push myself up, but pain shoots up my arm, and I fall back down. I can only watch as the inevitable happens before my eyes. Afton's eyes widen, and I know she realizes the same.

We've lost.

Then the strangest thing happens. The assassin's slide comes to a halt, and her arms freeze. She can still move her head and legs, but her attack is thwarted. She cries out in anger, her body stuck in its position.

I can't believe it. It has to be Teddy. He didn't have enough energy to popsicle the assassin entirely, so he focused only on her arms and torso.

Afton lifts a leg and kicks both her blades from her hands. The assassin falls back, but without the ability to move most of her body, her movement is awkward, and she lands on her butt.

"What have you done to me?" the assassin cries.

Afton grins and stands over her, gloating.

"We *beat* you, that's what we did," she says, and with a quick swing of her foot, she knocks the assassin out. Her unconscious body flops back and crumples to the ground.

As Afton rushes over to Nayla, I move to check on the bailiff—still alive, but we've no chance to take her with us and bring her to justice. If we're lucky, we might just slide through the massing soldiers. We can't afford to take anyone else with us.

I pull off the assassin's hood and inspect her face. She's not much older than we are. I wonder what would have to happen to someone to make them choose this as a job. If I were a ruthless person, I'd end her life now so that we'd never have to face her again, but I can't find it in me to do it. Maybe she's just as much a victim of her circumstances as we are. Still, if I never see her again, that'd be just fine with me.

I grab Parrish's hand and help him up. Then I upload an image of the shuttle to Teddynet. If we can evade detection, safety will be our next stop.

Time to get out of here.

Chapter Forty-Four

"KEEP GOING, IT'S NOT much further!" Kayley says, as breathless as any of us. We're all a mess, save for Original Teddy, who's taking point. He keeps forgetting to wait, but I hope that means it's clear all the way to the exit.

I've got my arm underneath Nayla's shoulder, and Afton takes the side with her wounded leg. Nayla whimpers like a child who's been given no supper, but I'm trying not to be cruel. We all thought the princess was lying to us and didn't genuinely try to hear her out. Now we know better.

Parrish leads the way, armed with Afton's gun. It's the only gun we've got, so we'd better not run into any soldiers. Just like Kayley, I'm done with violence. I don't want to see anyone hurt on either side. Let's just be away, and then I can close my eyes for a long, long time.

"Take the next right, and that'll bring you outside," Grady says. "Then you can meet the shuttle near the palace gardens."

"Almost there, darling. Hang in there," Afton whispers to Nayla. Ever since I asked Kayley to stop using it, the term of affection sticks out at me every time someone uses it. I miss hearing her say it to me. It's like using those three little words without using them. I still can't understand how Afton and Nayla got to that point so quickly when it took Kayley and me nineteen years to figure out our feelings for each other.

"Halt!" a voice shouts as at least two dozen soldiers swarm about us. I falter, going down on one knee while Afton struggles to hold Nayla up. This is what we wanted to avoid. There's no way we can fight all of them off. Not with one gun and two wounded.

"Hold your fire," a familiar voice says. A moment later, the High Wazir strides through the contingent of reinforcements. He stops just a few steps before us. His gaze floats from person to person, examining our wretched state. But it's only when it lands on Nayla that any actual reaction comes from him.

"Princess," he says, moving to her, "what happened to you? How are you wounded?"

"Do not pretend to be concerned for my health now that you've sentenced me to death."

"But I did not," the High Wazir replies. "I begged Her Majesty for leniency on your behalf, despite thinking you were a fool to have tried to push your mother from the throne."

"And you were the fool to believe I would ever attempt that. So now what?"

The High Wazir looks upon Princess Nayla for a long moment. Longer than expected. I would have thought it would be obvious to him what happens next. We get arrested, and everyone is right back where we started—facing a sharp blade slicing through our necks.

"High Wazir," Kayley says, keeping her voice gentle, "we are no threat to Her Majesty or this planet. We only want to go home. Her Royal Highness can come with us until she can prove her innocence."

"That is not something I can allow," the High Wazir says, his voice flat. "You are to accompany me to the infirmary so that we may treat Her Royal Highness' wound."

"What's the point of healing her wound if you're only going to execute her?" I cry.

"That is not for me to contemplate. The rest of you are now equally in contempt with this attempt to free her."

"Come on! This is ridiculous! Her Majesty doesn't really want to kill her daughter!"

The High Wazir scratches his chin and takes a long look at Nayla. I've got a feeling he doesn't want to return her to imprisonment, and he's already said to us he didn't want to see any more executions. I wonder if we can find a way to make it easy for him to let us go.

"Listen," I say, glancing around at the soldiers as they tense, waiting for my next words. I'd better choose them carefully. "Just give the princess a chance to explain and you'll see she's not guilty."

I wince as the slice across my chest reminds me it's there by firing off a stinging pain across my body. It's not the only hurt bothering me, but it's definitely the most severe. I suck a breath in through my teeth and bow my head.

Kayley comes to my aid, taking over as Nayla's crutch. She checks to make sure that the princess is comfortable and gets a nod and a smile as confirmation.

The High Wazir watches the entire process with interest. I think he's in no hurry to send us to our deaths. There's got to be an angle that gets him to let us go. I just don't know what it is yet.

We're certainly not going to fight our way out of this, so our best chance is to talk our way out. Kayley's our best option for that. I just need to tip her off on the idea.

My meandering mind recalls the bailiff. She's hurt and in need of medical assistance. If she died on Canis Ludis, it would be a political nightmare for Queen de Avila, and that might just be what Bailiff Daughtry wanted, minus her own death.

"So, what do you say?" Kayley asks. "Will you let her go?"

"Perhaps I would," the High Wazir says, responding to my proposition, "but that is not for me to decide. I do what Her Majesty commands. I can only make suggestions to the royal ear. If I had something suitable to mention, that is."

If I heard that correctly, he's offering me a way to get out of this. It's a subtle message, but I think I've got it.

"High Wazir, I apologize for forgetting this, but Bailiff Daughtry needs medical attention, close to here."

"What?" The High Wazir's eyes go wide. "What happened to her?"

I start to answer, but Kayley elbows me in the ribs, and I double over. That hurt, but I'm just glad she caught on as fast as she did.

"High Wazir," she says, "this may sound convenient coming from us, but we believe the bailiff was the true mastermind behind the coup."

"That *is* mighty convenient," the High Wazir replies, "and difficult to believe. Especially when we have Her Royal Highness' seal on correspondence about the attack, but...if you have proof of this, then I will accept it and bring it to Her Majesty, who, as you might suspect, would be glad to receive such evidence."

"We can provide a recording of her confession to exactly that," I say, remembering how useful Teddynet has been in situations like this.

"A recording?"

"Yes, vid and audio. There would be no refuting its source."

"Where is the bailiff? Her care is paramount. We'll deal with this recording later."

Kayley tells him the location, and the High Wazir immediately dispatches four of his soldiers. Then he turns to Nayla, examining her face. I suppose he's trying to figure out if we're lying to him or not, as it'd be on him if everything we just told him was a fabrication. That's fine with me. I respect him for being as cautious as he is intelligent.

"Royal Highness," the High Wazir says. "Is what they say true? Is Bailiff Daughtry behind this?"

Nayla's eyes drop to the ground, regret flooding her face. Afton senses something and moves closer to her, rubbing a comforting hand across her back.

"There is one thing that is true. I am a fool," Nayla says. "A fool to have believed that her admiration of my quarters was as innocent as she had pretended it to be. Now that I am aware of the conspiracy to dethrone the Emperor, I can see her offers of friendship were only a ruse to get access to my royal seal. My ignorance put my mother in danger, and that I regret."

I tell the High Wazir of our encounter with Bailiff Daughtry on the road, and how she hired the assassin. Then about the bailiff's confession as we freed Nayla. As he listens, his face remains passive.

"When may I view this vid?"

"As soon as we can download it for you," I say and tap my head. "It's in here."

He stares at me, and I feel my body shake, if not from the wounds inflicted on me, then from the desperate hope that he's about to do what I think he is, and let us go. Let us *all* go. Of course, he could just as easily order his guards to lock us all up, and I am really, really hoping he doesn't do that.

"What I am about to command is for the good of our planet, and for the benefit of Her Majesty, Queen Hathor de Avila." He connects eyes with every guard in the room. "You are to tell no one that you saw Her Royal Highness. She was not to be found anywhere in the palace, nor will you tell anyone about Bailiff Daughtry. This has now become a classified matter of state, and under penalty of death, you are not to tell anyone about what has just transpired. Have I made myself clear?"

"High Wazir," a woman says—it's the guard who tried to protect us from the assassin's attack. "I will personally ensure that this remains secret, and I will execute anyone who dares mention it to anyone."

The High Wazir nods at her, then turns back to us.

"I trust your shuttle is on the way to retrieve you?"

"Yes, it is," Kayley replies.

"Good. Then I will wait with you until it comes. I am still under command that you are to be removed from the planet."

"We understand, High Wazir. Thank you."

"Please look after her. Our princess is more precious to us than you know."

Chapter Forty-Five

"You kissed someone else? A boy? How does Kayley feel about that?" Afton says, staring at me from her spot in the grass next to Nayla.

"*Kayley* is fine with it," Kayley answers, glancing at me. "I was there when it happened."

I sigh. Nothing less than a major headache is what I should expect now that my momentary lapse in judgment is out in the open. At least the view we've got is nice. Afton wanted Nayla to get one last glimpse of her homeworld before she leaves it for a while, so we came up to the Teddy solarium garden and made ourselves comfortable on the new grass the Teddys put in. I think they stole it from my backyard.

Canis Ludis is beautiful from high orbit. The oceans shine in a soft blue, the mountains are a startling maroon, and both mix with the crisp white clouds that float everywhere but over the cities. A dark smog smothers those population centers.

"I don't really know why I did it," I reply and shrug at Afton. Whatever way this comes out of my mouth is going to be wrong. "I guess I was thinking about you when it happened."

"So"—Afton leans forwards, brow wrinkling—"you kissed him while you were thinking about me? That doesn't make it better, buddy."

A few throats get cleared, though Kayley just shakes her head. Nayla drops a light slap on Afton's arm and gives her a *tsk* for trying to make fun of me.

"Wait." I take a moment to collect my thoughts. "I mean I just didn't want to let someone down who'd been kind to me, and I was thinking back to the time when we were waiting in line for you guys to sign up as recruits, and Afton, you, well, I know you said that wasn't for me, but it kinda was, wasn't it? I was just trying to make Fen happy, even though I really couldn't."

"You're not making any sense, dude," Grady says. "And besides, we all saw Afton kiss you."

"You did?" Okay, panic is really setting in now.

"We did," Kayley replies, poking my shoulder. "And I was really jealous until I found out that Afton meant it for me. After that, I didn't mind so much."

"Really?" I can feel heat coming to my cheeks. They knew this whole time and said nothing? "So then you get why I did it, right? It was for Fen. To show him he was a good guy."

"That wasn't very nice, Rance, no matter what your justification," Doc Elizabeth chides. "I'm sure that boy came to that event hoping to meet someone. Not only did you lie to him, but then you contradicted yourself. If you wanted to apologize or comfort him, a hug might have been the better choice."

"I owe you all an apology as well," Nayla says. I'm glad for the change of topic. "If it wasn't for my foolishness, this situation would not have happened, and I am truly sorry for that. But I am very grateful to all of you for your rescue."

"We didn't mind," Grady replies. He's sitting in a floating chair that the Teddys made up for him so he could get around while his muscles heal. He still looks strange with a bald head, but the Teddys made him a few knit caps to wear. I wonder where they got the yarn.

"None of us wanted to see you executed, Princess," Kayley says.

"Please, call me Nayla. I no longer wish to be addressed as a royal. It is tiring."

"Sure," Kayley says with a smile, then swallows. "I just wanted to make sure you knew that, despite our differences over Afton, we all like you, and we are very glad that you and Afton met."

"I don't understand this *Afton*," Nayla says with a frown. "Why do you always refer to her by her middle name? Surela is her name, and you should be happy to speak it."

"You're kidding!" I stammer. "She never told you?"

"Told me what?" Nayla turns to Afton, looking for an answer. Afton gives her a shy smile and ducks her head.

"Surela is her mother's middle name," Kayley explains. "You can understand why she doesn't like it, and why she's only let her father call her that."

"Nonsense," Nayla says, gazing at Afton. She reaches out and runs her fingers through Afton's hair. "Surela is a beautiful name, and you need to get over its connection to your mother. Just because she has trapped you in a cage of guilt does not mean you need to deny yourself, darling. It's time to be free, yes?"

Afton's head bows even lower. She's trying to hide the hurt and shame that's covering her face. She leans into Nayla, who wraps her arms around her and pulls her close. It's still strange to me to see Afton so vulnerable, though I suppose it's what's always been inside of her. Maybe this is what Kayley meant when she said Afton was more sensitive than I understood.

"Is this what you've been doing with her?" I ask Nayla. "Helping her to get over her mother?"

She nods, the edge of her mouth turning upward in a way that looks wistful.

"We made some positive advances, before..." Nayla tilts her head and goes quiet. I don't blame her. It must have been difficult for her to be accused of overthrowing her mother. That's as much of a life-scarring event as my father walking out on me.

"Nayla, I know it's only been a few hours since we left," Kayley says, attempting to broach some delicate subject, "but have you given any thought to where you will go? I mean, you're welcome to stay with us for a while. Though..."

Afton lifts her head along with an eyebrow as her eyes land on Kayley. Then my shoulders get tight as I realize there's a great big disagreement bomb about to explode. Parrish sees it, too, and slides off the tree trunk he'd been resting on. This better not collapse into a vocal firefight.

"Though, what?" Afton challenges. "Nayla is staying with me."

"At my house?" Grady shoots back. "You were going to ask me first, right?"

"Of course I was, but it's not like you were going to mind, right?"

Grady frowns but keeps his mouth shut.

"Listen," Kayley says, raising her hands. "All I am saying is Nayla might not consider herself royalty anymore, but there's plenty of people, some of them bad, that still will. We don't have any way to protect her on Angelcanis, and I worry that we'd be inviting trouble."

"I can protect her," Afton states, sitting up straight.

"No fighting at my parents' house!" Grady barks. "It'll get messed up."

"What makes you think—" Afton huffs. "*Your* house will get messed up? Who do you think cleans up the place when you're glued to your computer for days?"

"My parents would never approve." Grady rolls his eyes and turns away.

If it wasn't for the serious conversation, I'd have a chuckle or two at them. They're like their own married couple, arguing like that. I'll bet Nayla sees the humor in it. Still, Kayley was right to bring this up. This could turn into a big problem if someone finds out where Nayla is living.

"KayKay, did you have any thoughts about it?" I ask.

"Yes, but I wanted to see what Nayla thinks first."

That kind of answer tells me she doesn't know what to do. She may have hoped the problem would take care of itself. It's not going to, which means things are going to get a little heated. I just hope they don't get so heated that we're back to the beginning. Our level of trust with Nayla and Afton is sketchy at best. Sure, we scored some points saving Nayla, but it won't take much to fracture it into splinters again.

"I did not consider Kayley's point," Nayla says, "and it is valid. I was hoping to stay with Surela. She still needs my help to overcome her struggles."

"Why don't we try to think of this practically?" Parrish suggests. "We already know the danger of Nayla staying on Angelcanis...with Afton and Grady. But what are the other options?"

"She could stay here," Doc Elizabeth suggests. "It's not a planet, but it would be hard for anyone to get to her here. I wouldn't mind having a little human company on a normal basis."

Nayla smiles and nods at her, but Afton wrinkles her nose. That's not promising. I get the feeling that this is only going to end one of two ways. Afton's way, or badly.

"No," Afton says. "The ship isn't always around, so we wouldn't get to see each other for long periods of time. You know how that feels, Rance. Would you want to do that to me, too?"

"Of course not—"

"I didn't get to see *him* for six months, either," Kayley says, irritation seeping into her voice. "And since you're asking, no, I wouldn't want that for you or Nayla."

I press my lips together. Ever since we snatched that vid from the *Mursilis*, things haven't been normal for us, and danger seems to find us with ease these days. Adding Nayla into the mix will most definitely pour a load of rocket fuel onto the fire.

I wonder if she really has anywhere else to go. Most of her friends must be on Canis Ludis, and her mother's enemies could be anywhere. Our enemies certainly are.

"Maybe we can just figure it out as we go along," Grady suggests, his eyes watching Afton. It's his attempt at keeping things cool between all of us. We've all had it rough for the last few weeks, and nobody really wants to aggravate our wounds by arguing.

Save maybe Afton.

"I keep telling all of you, there's nothing to figure out! She's staying with me, and that's all you need to know. It's not your business to decide where we go and where we don't."

"But your actions put us in danger, too," I say. "It's not just about you, Afton. That's why we're trying to figure this out. Together."

"Whatever you've got to figure out is your problem, not mine."

"Surela," Nayla says, trying to calm her. "We've discussed this. There's no need for you to project negative energy on those you care about. They're not the ones who want to do you harm. Remember our mantras."

"I don't need that right now! All I need is their answer." Afton shoves a finger at us and narrows her eyes. "Are we staying at Grady's, or are we leaving? You keep saying you want me around, but you're pushing Nayla away. Wherever Nayla goes is where I'm going. And if you don't like that, too bad."

The soft approach isn't working. And here I thought Nayla was helping her get in touch with her feelings. It seems Afton's feelings are exactly where they used to be, and I've had enough.

"Why can't you get it through your thick skull that we're trying to protect *both of you*, Surela? You think we're trying to split you apart? We could have done that by leaving her in her cell! But we were thinking of you, *our* friend! I certainly didn't need to risk my life for Nayla—"

Afton jumps up and shoves me hard, catching the long cut across my chest under both her palms. I cry out and land flat on my back. Parrish jumps up and grabs Afton before she can do more damage. A second later, Nayla and Kayley fly in between the two of us, their arms out.

I shut my eyes as fire stretches across my chest. I have had no time to heal, and I bet the assassin's cut just reopened. It'll have to wait. I push myself up on my elbows and catch Afton's stare.

"You didn't let me finish. I was about to say that I didn't need to risk my life to save Nayla, but I was glad to do it, because it was for you." I get up and stand in front of her. "You're one of us, Afton. We don't exist without you. If you're telling us you and Nayla are inseparable, then that just means she's one of us now."

"This changes things," Nayla says, eyes widening. "I will need to consult my oracles."

Afton steps up to me and takes me by the shoulders. We lock eyes so tightly, I almost miss the tear that slides down her cheek.

"Sorry." She sniffles. "I thought you were going to say something hurtful, and I freaked out. I shouldn't have doubted you. You guys saved Nayla, and you tried to fix your screw-up. That means a lot to me."

She brings me into a hug, and I wrap my arms around her. Not too tightly—I'm still in pain. It's a brief embrace, and when she pushes back, she catches my eyes again. Something is different about her. Afton seems lighter, less burdened. Perhaps the grin that spreads across her face is proof of that.

"So, Kayley doesn't mind you kissing others, huh?" she asks with a slow, sultry drawl in her tone.

"Yes, I do!" Kayley shouts, stepping closer. "He was just doing it so we could save you!"

But Afton isn't deterred, and by the evil look on her face, I know she's about to cause trouble.

"Surela...don't you dare!" I say, trying to push away from her.

"That last one *was* for her, but this one is for you." Afton pulls my face close to hers.

"Hands off my boyfriend!" Kayley tries to pry her arms between us to break us apart, but Afton is too strong. My efforts to get her off me are ineffective, and my hand slips off Afton's shoulder and gets tangled up with Kayley's arm.

"Ransom Quigley He', there are dark stars in your sky, still," Nayla says. "But this time, I will save you from them."

She reaches in between Afton and me, twisting Afton's head towards hers. Afton just blinks as Nayla plants a soft kiss on her lips.

"Darling, what did I say about being an agent of chaos?" Nayla asks, her fingers holding Afton's chin.

"That you loved that about me?" Afton beams at her.

Nayla smiles and kisses her again.

Kayley and I share a warm look. We're locked in a tangle of arms in a most awkward but beautiful moment. If there was ever a question about the risks we took to get Afton—and Nayla—back, here's the answer.

I will never turn my back on my friends, ever, because being with them is the one thing that makes life tolerable. Despite our problems and our regrets, we have each other, and keeping us all together is worth any risk I'll ever have to take.

Books by Marc B. DeGeorge

Origin Story Series

The Starship Sneak

The Reckless Rescue

The Traitors' Trial

The Conspiracy Clash

The Deadly Discord

Air Born Series

A Universe Upon Us

A Call to the Sky

A Challenge for the Sky

About the Author

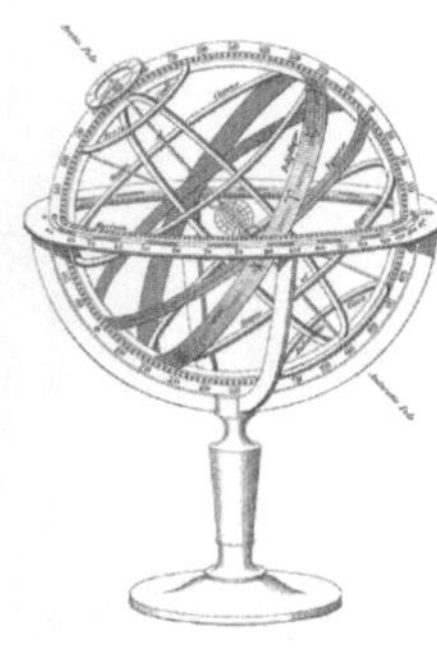

Marc B. DeGeorge has made every attempt in his adult life to maintain a balance between how much science and how much art he dabbles in. Sometimes, he's even successful. When he was young, he wanted to be an astronaut, and then an aeronautical engineer—he even went to Space Camp! But then he learned how to play guitar and his space dreams took a back seat. He spent a decade playing professionally in bands and studying music in college (university only took five years). These days, things have come round full circle, and Marc envisions the future by writing books that imagine what challenges humanity may face, and what we might accomplish together.

When Marc isn't writing, he performs traditional Japanese music on shamisen and writes, shoots, and edits performing arts photos and documentaries under the MuseMarc Studio name.

amazon.com/Marc-B-Degeorge/e/B09LDCNVHV/ref=aufs_dp_fta_dsk

facebook.com/MarcBDeGeorge

instagram.com/marcbdegeorgeauthor/

goodreads.com/author/show/22081012.Marc_B_DeGeorge